Catching Fire

CATCHING FIRE

Kay Nolte Smith

Coward, McCann & Geoghegan
New York

Library of Congress Cataloging in Publication Data

Smith, Kay Nolte.
  Catching fire.

  I. Title.
PS3569.M537554C3   1982   813'.54   81-22175
ISBN 0-698-11134-6   AACR2

The text of this book has been set in Electra.

The author gratefully acknowledges the following for granting permission to quote
from copyrighted material:
Harcourt Brace Jovanovich for a line from the poem "Little Gidding" by T.S.
Eliot.
Dylan Thomas, *The Poems of Dylan Thomas*, Copyright 1945 by the Trustees for the
Copyrights of Dylan Thomas. Reprinted by the permission of New Directions Pub-
lishing Corporation.

PRINTED IN THE UNITED STATES OF AMERICA

For all the people I've worked with in the theater and loved.
Especially Phil.

Prologue

The boy sat up slowly on the broken couch that served as his bed, testing to see whether the dizziness was gone.

For three days a cold had seemed to be squatting on his chest. There were no medicines in the apartment, and little food. At one point his mother had leaned over him and touched his forehead, making his body twist with the sensation that no longer was love but was still the desire to love; however, she merely had poured a glass of whiskey and forced him to drink it. The stupor it induced had helped him to sleep, despite the constant blare from the television, and now he thought he could manage to get out, and down to the basement, where he had hidden his treasure.

If he didn't get out, he knew, he would experience something worse than dizziness: The air in the two small rooms would seem gradually to thicken and expand, pressing against him with a breath as stale as his mother's. It was to avoid that feeling that he stayed on the streets as much as possible.

The dizziness was not fully gone, but he stood up anyway. He was tall for his age, with the wiriness of muscle already pulling at the chunkiness of childhood. He had slept, as usual, in his clothes, so there were only his shoes to put on. His mother was asleep in the corner chair, breathing heavily, her breasts like two giant scoops that pushed the air in the room toward him with each rise and fall. He moved to the door.

In the hall there were runnels of grime on the walls, which he thought of as the long, bony fingers of witches, and odors he never could transform into anything else because they made him visualize human bodies in the act of creating them. Then he realized he could smell nothing at all because of his cold, and he smiled as he went down the five flights of stairs.

The smile widened into a song he had learned from old man Vecchio. *La donna è mobile, qual piuma el vento* . . . . Old man Vecchio had been hard to persuade at first; he hadn't seen how he could use a thirteen-year-old in the store, but after a week he had let out one of those rumbling laughs that seemed to grow under the white ball of his apron, and had agreed: two dollars for coming in to tidy up the shelves once a week. The money had grown with an aching slowness, but finally there had been enough. The job had had to be kept secret; the year before, when the boy had done some work for one of his teachers, his mother had demanded all the money. She had spent it on whiskey.

He reached the bottom of the stairs and pushed open the front door. The air was as fresh as apples—he knew it was, even if he couldn't smell it today. He ran around the building, leaping over piles of debris, and down the side steps to the basement entrance.

Inside, all the lights but one were burned out. He made his way over to the wall where his treasure was hidden. In the dimness he edged aside a crate and reached up to the half-rotted shelf, for the burlap sack in which he had wrapped the catcher's mitt.

He saw a small brown body poised above it; he saw sharp teeth and a jagged hole in the sack. The air moved in to choke him. "No!" he said. "You can't have it! I earned it! It's mine!"

The rat squealed and sank its teeth into his hand.

His mind thrust aside the pain. He grabbed for the dark, mocking thing that was clamped to his hand; he clutched the metal snake of its tail, ripped its teeth from his skin, and began to swing it against the wall, shouting: "*È mio! L'ho meritato io! È mio!*"

When the squealing finally stopped, he let the body fall to the floor. He took off his shirt, wrapped it around his bleeding hand, then reached up and took down the sack.

"*How* did you earn it?" said a voice behind him. "What is it? Where'd you get it?" It was his older brother. With him was the leader of the brothers' gang.

He couldn't find breath to answer.

"I want it." His brother held out a hand. "Give it to me."

"Nobody keeps nothing for himself," the gang leader said.

The boy found breath somewhere, because the rat was peering from his brother's eyes and from the gang leader's, too, and he had to try to defeat it again. He tossed the sack aside and leaped at the two of them, one hand trailing the bleeding rag of his shirt.

He found faces and heads and chests, and pounded and smashed without feeling the blows that answered his own. Then the gritty floor rose up sharply to meet his cheek.

The two figures and voices circled around him slowly—his brother picking up the burlap sack, the gang leader taking it and saying, "We got to learn him a lesson. Can't you keep better control of him, for Chrissake? He's one of your soldiers."

"Not anymore!" the boy shouted, raising himself on one elbow. "I quit! I don't want to belong to your stupid organization!"

Over his shoulder the leader said, "We ain't gonna forget that." The two figures moved to the door, with the catcher's mitt.

The boy turned away. He saw his enemy's body on the floor. The rat's behavior he found easy to understand: It had wanted something of his and had tried to take it. But how could one explain his brother or the gang leader, or his mother, who were human beings but did the same thing?

The pain in his hand bit into his brain. No, he said to it, you can't stop me, they can't have it, it's mine, I earned it!

He got to his knees, then to the door and the basement steps, and around to the front of the building. Down the block, at the corner, he saw the gang leader, still holding the mitt, talking to his brother. His anger took command and sent his body hurtling along the sidewalk as free of pain and dizziness as a bullet, to thud against the gang leader's. Then pain and nausea took control again, turning the world into a kaleidoscope—a blue arc of sky, a brown slash of garbage piled at the curb, a blur of white metal that seemed to be a parked truck, and finally black.

His next awareness was of blue—two uniforms. Then red and pale yellow and gray, oozing along the sidewalk, soaking the mitt, welling from the gang leader's body.

"These goddamn punks," a voice was saying. "Looks like this one bashed in the other one's skull."

The boy wanted to cry out, but he thought of how great and blinding his anger had been. And how he had swung a rat against a wall until it was bloody and dead.

"But I don't remember," the boy said. "I don't remember doing it!"

"Oh yeah?" said the other cop. "You're never going to forget it as long as you live." He grabbed the boy's arm. "Come on. Let's get going."

1

The sky was a spread of darkness.

At its edge a tongue of fire licked upward. Others joined it, spreading the red-and-yellow glow of their appetite along the horizon.

A man stood on a rocklike projection. He looked as tall as the sky and spoke in a voice that seemed to come from the earth. The light touched his face, leaving his eyes in shadow but striking the sharp lines of his nose and mouth. His close-fitting dark garments revealed powerful bones and muscles beneath them; when he raised one arm, he seemed capable of tearing a hole in the sky.

He turned his head; the light touched his hair, the color of sandy soil, and found his pale blue eyes, seeking their intensity as an equal. "Prometheus will carry down the fire," he said.

The tongues of flame darted higher, seeming to lick his fingers. He spoke to the flames:

"Men's hands will learn to make your secret leap
From the kiss of stones; your gift will break the chains
Of cold that hold men's bodies close to the earth
And tie their minds to the beast."

His hand closed into a fist, pulling the flames inside its grasp; they wreathed and twined about it.

Abruptly they died from the sky, which returned to darkness and silence.

"All right," a voice called, "give us the work lights."

Stark white lights came on with a jerk. The sky reappeared as a piece of patched and faded cloth covering the back wall of a stage. Prometheus' dark garments were transformed into jeans and a black T-shirt.

The voice came again—the director, calling from the auditorium. "It looks good, Erik. That's it for today. Come down from Mount Olympus."

The actor grinned. "O! What a fall was there, my countrymen!" he cried, leaping down from the rocklike projection, a crude set of steps. As a motley crew moved out on the stage and began to clear off the steps and other scenic units, he watched them, leaning against the proscenium arch. He was no longer as tall as the sky, only taller than everyone else.

Beside him, painted on the proscenium arch, was the silhouette of a child in rags, staring up at the moon, and a legend: POETS AND PAUPERS THEATER.

A figure came racing toward him from the backstage recesses. "Hey, Erik. I mean, Mr. Dante—"

"Erik is fine." He turned to the moon-faced youngster of fourteen, whose hair, eyebrows, and scruffy jeans were coated with sawdust.

"Listen, Erik, I gotta split for a while tomorrow. That's the day the welfare check comes, and I gotta get it cashed for my mother. She don't speak good English, you know what I mean? But we got the legs all cut for the platforms, and tomorrow they'll start on the tops."

"That's good. Just remember you're not allowed to work with power tools." Erik's hand raised a cloud of sawdust from the youngster's hair. "Take off all the time you need, Frankie."

"Listen, I was watching a little bit of rehearsal. The way they got the sky to turn on fire—is that the new light board? How does it work?"

Erik sat on the steps that led from the stage down into the auditorium, his big hands shaping explanatory gestures. Frankie crouched beside him.

Erik was the leading actor and producer of the Poets and Paupers Theater, and the youngster was one of those he periodically rounded up from the decaying corners of the city and put to work in the scene shop. No one knew exactly how he found them, or from what grubby, drug-infested alternatives he coaxed them, but they appeared in a fairly steady stream, with cocksure smiles pasted over their uncertainty. Within a short time they lost their self-consciousness and were hammering or painting or hunting props as assiduously as if they were paid much more than the pocket money they got. Erik had dubbed them "Dante's Infernals," and the press had picked up the name, giving nearly as much coverage to them as to him.

It was an appealing idea: ghetto kids turning from the reality of filth and street crime to the fantasy worlds of playwrights they had never heard of. And could hardly be expected to understand, for the plays the theater was dedicated to presenting—chosen for their beauty of language and grandeur of vision—were nearly always works of the past, with speech and manners more distant from the youngsters' than was the moon. Yet when Victor Hugo's *Ruy Blas* had been in rehearsal, the Infernals had discussed the story of the sixteenth-century servant who fell in love with his queen as if it were the struggle to reach a rock star. And during performances of Lorca's *Blood Wedding* they had liked to stand in the wings, faces transformed as the stage moonlight spread its cape over the two lovers.

"Why shouldn't they like the plays?" Erik Dante had told a reporter. "Wouldn't you like something that's bigger and grander and more beautiful than your own life?"

Because of its location and size—four hundred seats—Poets and Paupers was categorized as an off-Broadway house, one of the medium-size theaters that provide a middle ground between the expensive commercial fare of Broadway and the experimentalism of off-off-Broadway. Poets and Paupers might have been an off-off-Broadway operation, like the dozens of tiny theaters that exist in cafés, basements, and garages and, instead of selling tickets, ask for donations at the door, but Erik had insisted on trying to be commercial. "We're paupers but not beggars," he put it.

For three seasons he had been building his audiences, and he was now in rehearsal for a fourth. Although some people called Poets and Paupers an anachronism, hopelessly out of tune with twentieth-century drama, its subscribers—and Erik—loved it for that very reason.

He finished explaining the light board to the young Infernal. From the dark auditorium came the sound of a pair of hands, clapping slowly. Erik shaded his eyes and looked out.

The clapping stopped. "Nice explanation," said a voice. "Of course that board is some hell of a thing. Every cue fed into a computer, one man able to run a whole show. There are Broadway theaters that don't even have computer boards yet. But you've got one."

"Is that you, Codd?" Erik called. "What are you doing here again?"

The voice came down the aisle. "I figure we should talk some more."

"I figure we said everything last week."

"That so?" Into the light spilling from the stage came Morty Codd, head of the union that represented stagehands, carpenters, electricians, and wardrobe people: the Theatrical Artisans and Technicians Union—"but everybody calls us TATU," as he liked to say. He was in his sixties, but he had the torso of a boxer in fighting trim; all signs of age had been forced upward, to crowd into his seamed face and white hair. He looked at Frankie, still hovering on the steps. "So, Dante, you going to let him run that light board? This boy who isn't even out of grade school, I bet?"

"Hey!" Frankie said indignantly. "I'm going to be in tenth grade, and I'm not a boy!"

Codd stared, and Erik laughed. "She's one of the best Infernals I've had, but she's not ready for the board yet. Give her a couple of years, though—she'll be one of that special breed of theater women. You know, the ones who never want to act, only work backstage? I find they're often better at it than the men. Just don't ask them to put on a dress."

"I know more about them than you do, Dante," Codd said.

"OK, Frankie," Erik said. "Better run along."

"Sure. Jeez, Erik, thanks a lot for explaining things to me." She darted up the steps to help the people still working onstage.

"They told me you were in here rehearsing," Codd said, "so I came in and watched that last bit. *Firestorm*, that's the name of the play?"

"Yes."

"It's about Prometheus? The god who stole the fire?"

"Yes. But in this version, after he's given it to mankind, he decides they didn't deserve it, so he tries to take it back. There's a battle over whether the fire should stay on earth. Whether it's really freed men from savagery or only made them more vicious."

"That so?" Codd said blandly. "I hear the lady who finances you is the one who wrote this *Firestorm*. It's kind of a vanity production, I guess. Since the author is paying for it."

Erik's pale blue eyes glittered. "This theater is struggling to pay its own way, Codd. Maeve Jerrold backed it, but she . . . And for the record, she's not the one who suggested that we do her play. Producing *Firestorm* was my idea, and it took me damn near two years to persuade her to agree."

"That so? You told her about our talk last week?"

"I'm the one who runs this theater, Codd." Erik glanced at the people still onstage. "And I'm not going to talk about it out here. If you've got anything new to say, you can come into the office."

In the tiny business office, off the lobby, stacks of manuscripts leaned everywhere like crooked mushrooms. Erik went to the overburdened desk, and Codd took a chair opposite. His clear green eyes moved over the posters of past productions mounted on the walls: *Salomé* by Oscar Wilde. *Don Carlos* by Friedrich von Schiller. *Edward II* by Christopher Marlowe. *Cuchulain* by William Butler Yeats. "Hardly any Shakespeare," he said.

"Everybody does Shakespeare. We concentrate on plays everybody else has forgotten."

Codd raised an eyebrow at *The Faraway Princess* by Edmond Rostand; a small legend near the bottom read, "in a new translation by Maeve Jerrold." He pointed to another poster. "Noël Coward? He didn't write poetry."

"No, but *Post-Mortem* is very poetic in spirit. A fantasy about the futility of war. It had never been produced in this country. It was our first real success."

Codd leaned back in his chair. "Glad to hear you admit you've been successful."

"I'm not trying to hide anything," Erik said. "Are you?"

"Nope. We're out to make this theater a TATU house. And we're going to do it. One way or the other."

"Is that a threat?" When Codd merely smiled, Erik went on. "Why us? I know you want to get into the off-Broadway houses, but why start with us? Is it because we don't belong to the off-Broadway producers' organization—because we're loners?"

"Could be." Codd's smile disappeared into its wrinkled surroundings. "Didn't you just tell me how good you've been doing? And haven't you been bragging in the press how you're making it without any grants from the federal and state arts councils? You know damn well this house can afford a TATU contract. My membership knows it, too. And they can get pretty riled up." The smile reappeared. "Of course, me—I'm a reasonable man."

"*That* so?" Erik leaned over the desk, the muscles in his forearms swelling. "How many electricians would you make me hire to run my new light board—which we got because one person can handle it alone?"

"For a small board like yours, I'm sure we could make some adjustment."

"That's not an answer! We put on big shows down here—lots of sets and special lighting. Hiring union crews would 'adjust' us right out of business."

Codd's green eyes were as bright as traffic signals. "You producers! Twenty years ago you hollered like stuck pigs that you couldn't afford the *actors* union, either. But they got in off-Broadway, and you're all still in business."

"Twenty years ago I was a kid in the ghetto. I'd still be there if—"

"And where was your money lady, Maeve Jerrold? In Chicago, living like a princess. I grew up out there, Dante, and I heard about her family's money all my life. And her ex-husband, for God's sake, he's the head of Jerrold Industries. She could finance this whole operation out of her clothes budget, and you have the guts to call yourselves Poets and *Paupers!*"

In the kind of voice that reaches back rows, Erik said, "This theater is not a rich woman's charity project. Mrs. Jerrold has *invested* in Poets and Paupers. It doesn't take handouts. Our goal is to make it earn its own way."

"And ours is to get in."

"No," Erik said. "I told you 'No' last week, I'm telling you now, and I'll keep telling you, until and unless my staff requests an election to vote on joining TATU. But they haven't. I find that interesting—that the request is coming from you."

Codd snorted. "It's sure as hell not going to come from those ghetto kids you got down here, working for peanuts and their pictures in the paper. Besides, it can save a lot of trouble sometimes if things are worked out at the top. And I'd hate to see any kind of trouble down here."

"Then you'd better get out."

The men glared at each other, green eyes against pale blue.

Finally Codd said, "Remember what I told you last week—I'm a reasonable man. Easy to get along with. I'm sure we could work something out."

"Under the table, you mean?"

A hard dot swelled on either side of Codd's jaw, which lifted like a fist. He moved to the door and jerked it open. "You'll be hearing from us, you sonofabitch."

Then there was empty space where his young man's shoulders and old man's face had been.

Two nights later the moon trailed its light across the city, turning the East and Hudson rivers into spreads of white metal, pushing its fingers down the tunnels between buildings.

It pressed against the tall dark windows of the Poets and Paupers Theater. Inside, the red velvet seats were gray ghosts, and the sky onstage was now blacker than the moon's own home.

A cat prowled the edges of the street. Laughter drifted from a bar around a corner.

From nowhere a rectangular object sailed toward one of the windows and then through it, printing out a many-pointed star.

Another object came, and another, filling the night with the ringing tongues of glass.

Ten minutes later the street was quiet again. The moon preened in the hundreds of shards now lying in the street, then entered the theater through the windows' gaping stars.

2

Maeve Jerrold sat in the back row of the auditorium, her thin hands clutching the ends of the seat. The sleeves of her shirt, which was heavy parchment-colored silk, seemed to reproach the shabby red velvet on which they rested.

For half an hour she had been a silent observer of the meeting Erik was holding down in front, with the theater company. Everyone was there, sitting or sprawling in the first few rows, even those who worked only part-time: actors, technical staff, front-of-the-house crew, and the Infernals, whom she thought of privately as "les gavroches." There were forty-seven people in all, a cross section of generations, dress codes, and values: retirees with graying crew cuts or coiffures, who worked as costumers, carpenters, or box-office personnel; kids just out of college, with frizzled or lanky hair and world-weary expressions belied by the intensity they brought to their work on props or lights or scenery painting; even some neatly suited ones, like the part-time retail clerk who was the sound man and the math teacher who helped shift scenery during the run of a show.

"I know how hard you all work," Erik was saying. "I know you could make more money at other jobs, or other theaters. But since you haven't asked to be represented by TATU, I figure you're satisfied with the way this theater is run. And so I don't intend to change it. No matter how many times they break the windows."

One of the carpenters said, "Do they want us to join the union? Or do they want to get rid of us and put in people who are already TATU members?" Erik told them he didn't know.

The technical director, who had dropped out of the era of protest but wouldn't surrender its trappings, pushed his hands through the huge wiry bush of his hair and said, "I hate unions." That made one of the actors call out angrily, "What the hell do you know about them?"

There was little other comment; the subject seemed too complex for a consensus, and the meeting broke up slowly, with little of the usual clowning and camaraderie.

When they had all left, Erik came up the aisle and sat beside Maeve. "I'm glad you came. Wasn't there anything you wanted to say to them?"

She smiled. "I'm the silent partner."

He stretched his long legs under the seat ahead and leaned back.

"If they had indicated they wanted to join this union," she said, "what would you have done?"

"Gone along with it. I don't happen to be in favor of forcing people to do things, whether it's joining or not joining."

She reached over to touch one of his hands, which seemed huge next to hers. He smiled without turning his head. She looked at him, reflecting, as she often did, on the alchemy that the theater seemed to work on his face. Inside this building—or any theater they attended, for that matter—his face was like a child's, in one sense, open to all emotions; either comedy or tragedy could claim it fully. Outside the theater he was more guarded, as if real life, not the stage, required a touch of the mask. She thought she knew the reason for this; still, she couldn't help feeling that her presence was the real cause. "What are you thinking about?" she said.

"The company. Wondering how much they love Poets and Paupers."

"Nobody could love it the way you do, Erik. You built it."

"With your help and money."

"You mean Arthur Jerrold's money. And my family's money, which they've been making for so long now that my father and brothers don't know how to stop. The only one who knows nothing about making money is me." Erik was silent. "But since I have it," she added carefully, "I'm quite willing to use it to cover whatever additional expenses there will be from a union contract."

He sat up sharply, the motion sending a strand of dark blond hair over his forehead, and stared at her. "You're not serious."

Her ivory skin colored slightly. "Can we talk about it at my place?"

"I don't want to leave the theater, Maeve. The last time I was with you, I came back to find broken windows."

"And what else will you find," she cried, "if you don't settle with this man Codd?"

"Come on," he said. "Let's go upstairs."

He had converted the fourth floor of the building into an apartment, knocking out two interior walls to give himself the sense of living in space. There were more bookshelves than pieces of furniture. Production photographs filled one wall.

For an hour they talked but did not quarrel. They never did that; she could not fight, by temperament, and he would not, by discipline. The conversation simply went in a circle.

Finally Erik stretched out on the battered couch that was long enough to accommodate his six-feet-five and let him thrust one hand behind him. The other covered his face.

Maeve curled in the room's one comfortable chair. She sighed and pulled on one of the small gold loops fixed in her ears, something she always did to keep herself from frowning. "If you fight this," she said, "how will you do it?"

"I don't know. Keep them from doing any more damage, first."

"But if they do . . . They could stop the opening, couldn't they? How can you jeopardize *Firestorm*? You're the one who persuaded me to take it out after all those years and make it workable."

"I want you to see it produced. I don't think good plays should lie in drawers for twenty years."

"More like thirty, Erik. I wrote it before Jonathan died, when I was—"

"I know how old you are, sweetheart. And I don't care. Remember?"

Maeve closed her eyes. Her head leaned against the back of the chair as if pulled by the chignon into which her hair, the color of heavy cream, was always shaped. Its bulk contrasted with the delicate lines of her features and the thinness of her shoulders. In her twenties, she had been widowed by a young poet who was killed in a car crash; for the past eight years she had been divorced from a Chicago industrialist. Even as an adolescent she had looked both fragile and unaware of her fragility, as if wealth made the knowledge irrelevant.

She sighed. "Ah, well," she said, "*Firestorm* was probably never meant to open."

Erik lifted his hand from his eyes and stared at the ceiling. "It will open."

"I wish I could believe all things are possible."

"I never said 'all.' Just some."

" 'All' is what you meant, though, isn't it?" He didn't answer. She shifted in her chair. "Erik, what if something terrible happens if you fight this Codd man?"

"Ah, but what if it doesn't?"

"I mean the kind of thing that went on while you were working on the docks."

"I shouldn't have told you about all that."

"But you did. How the unions were involved with the Varese mob. How people were threatened and killed. *Killed,* Erik! If anything happened to you, I would . . . I don't know what I would do."

"Nothing will happen." He sat up. "Maeve, you can stop me if you want to. You own this building—you can cancel the theater's lease and pull all your money out of the corporation. But that's the only way."

"You'd start all over, somewhere else. Without me." She shivered, crossed her arms, and tightened her hands on the sleeves of her silk shirt.

"I have to do this, Maeve. Please try to understand. There's a principle here." Erik got up and began to pace the room. "Do you know what's happened since I left the docks? The longshoremen have got themselves a guaranteed annual income of over twenty thousand dollars—even if they don't do a single day's work! My mother took hers on a smaller scale, of course, welfare checks and booze. And my—

His fist slammed into the side of a bookshelf as he passed it. "I won't let that kind of thing into Poets and Paupers. Never!"

"You're very angry."

"Yes."

"You told me once that anger could be dangerous for you."

He stopped. "That's something else I shouldn't have told you."

"I shouldn't have brought it up. It just . . . came into my mind, seeing you so angry."

He turned to face her. "It happened a long time ago. I don't think about it anymore. I lived through it at the time, and I lived with it for a long time afterward, but I've put it behind me. Why should you think about it when I don't?"

"As you say, I live in the past." She smiled. "I don't belong in this century—isn't that the way you put it?"

Erik smiled too. They were both silent, thinking of the night they had met, six years earlier, at a party given by the producer of the Broadway play in which Erik made his first professional appearance. He had seen Maeve across the room, wearing something long and silver, looking so slight that the shining wheel of her hair seemed too heavy for her neck, moving her hands in small, precise gestures that were almost Oriental. The play, in which he had the role of a savage, inarticulate killer, left the stink of prison in his nostrils for hours after the final curtain, and he had wanted simply to move closer to her and absorb her silver-and-cream delicacy. When she turned to him, he had said, "You don't look as if you belong in this room. Or this century."

She didn't, he learned. She steeped herself in the arts and culture of other times, burying herself for weeks in the libraries and museums of Europe. She spoke four languages and had even taught herself to read Ibsen, and also the Eddas, in the original—"If James Joyce can do it, why can't I?" she had laughed. Erik smiled again, at the memory: Ibsen, the Eddas, Joyce—he had known only one of those names before he met her. Before she had shown him that many worlds existed beside the prison of poverty and the narrow confines of the New York commercial theater.

"About the union," she said. "It's your decision."

"I'd like you to be happy with it."

"I don't care about being happy."

"Don't worry," he said. "And don't be afraid. I'll be all right. So will Poets and Paupers."

"You almost make me believe it." She slid out of the chair and came across the room to him. "You're an artist. A make-believe artist." She fitted her body against his.

In the beginning, he thought, he had wanted to make love to her all the time. Even the very first night, when he took her home after the producer's party and watched her moving about her apartment, it had seemed that she was like her surroundings—their beauty inciting one's touch but their cool elegance prohibiting it. He had asked a hundred questions that night, and while she was answering one of them, explaining that an ivory carving of the Virgin and Child dated back to the fourteenth century, he had put out his hand to touch the carving and found it going instead to Maeve's face. She had gone as still as if she too were carved, and then she moved away, without comment, to show him a painting.

For weeks that had been the pattern of their relationship: she showing and explaining, leading him through the centuries of painting and sculpture, and especially of literature and drama, and he growing as thirsty for her flesh as for the books he was reading—as if she were their living manifestation and he had to enter and possess both of them.

He could not remember when his thirst had begun to subside. He thought of the times before it had; he slid his hands along her sides.

"The light . . . " she whispered.

He turned it off. The moon slid through the windows. He lay beside her on the couch, seeing the skin that looked like silver in the moonlight but felt so warm to his touch, knowing what she wanted of his hands and mouth, feeling her struggle to pretend she did not want it, and finally her shuddering admission that she did.

He took her down and got her a cab over on the Bowery; she was never comfortable spending the night away from her own apartment, which surrounded her with not only her beautiful objects but also a glorious view of the East River.

He walked the three blocks back to the theater and stood looking at the windows. Boards covered them like bandages.

The night after they were broken, he had kept watch in the lobby, in the dark. The next night he had been unable to stay awake; jerked out of sleep by an unaccustomed noise, he got out into the street only in time to see dark figures disappearing and to find garbage piled on the sidewalk and in front of the lobby doors.

Perhaps, he thought, the union firebrands who had done it believed they were acting in a good cause. But their actions were no different from those of the gangsters he had seen and heard about while he was growing up. When he finally had broken out of the world bounded by his childhood, eighteen years earlier, that had been one of the greatest culture shocks: the discovery that the gangster tactics he detested and had escaped from were indistinguishable from those of people calling themselves idealists.

He thought of the kids' street gang he had been forced to join. The members had had a common goal: to grow up and join the Varese crime family. Some of them, he knew, had succeeded. He didn't know how long he had been part of the gang; it had seemed like forever. Until that lurid afternoon when he had rebelled and attacked the leader . . . He shoved the memory out of his mind; it was only Maeve's comment that had brought it back. But of course when he had been sent back home from the juvenile detention center, the gang had still been there, taunting him because he kept going to school, punishing him in whatever ways they could, even though he had grown too strong and clever for most of their schemes. Once they had managed to lock him in an empty warehouse, intending to leave him there for two days so he couldn't be in the school play. But he had fashioned a megaphone out of wood and cardboard scraps and had hollered through a crack in the door till someone heard him.

There were always two ways to fight, he thought—with mind or with muscles.

He went inside the theater and set up for his vigil in the lobby.

By dawn nothing had happened, except that his muscles ached and his mind had decided how he should fight.

3

The sun slid into the open window of a bedroom, striking sparks from the face of an alarm clock. As if in response, the alarm began to ring.

The woman in the bed slowly curled one hand, lifted it toward her ear, and said, "This is Jac Sanda."

The ringing went on. Her eyes opened. She stared at the clock, laughed, then swung into a sitting position and pressed the alarm off. At the window she felt the freshness of an August day that had not yet absorbed the odors of baking concrete and asphalt. Across the street and six stories below was the cool green enclave of Gramercy Park, a relentlessly private piece of property in a city where public and private wills clashed so often.

Such clashes had finally become her business. As she got into the shower, she considered the interview she would conduct that evening. She had not yet formulated the main questions, which would be crucial. In the years before she herself had begun working on camera, she had been frustrated by the questions reporters asked; so often they seemed to be the wrong ones, allowing interviewees, especially if they were politicians, to vault over the issues and land safely on the spongy turf of platitudes. Tonight her two guests would be discussing rent control, and as usual she would get her questions from thinking about the phenomenon itself: Why had it come into existence? Whom was it designed to help and/or protect? Whose rights were involved? As she considered, the water bombarded her face, striking the high, wide cheekbones that gave her the look of an American Indian, and ran in a soapy stream down her tall, athletic body.

When she was toweling off, the bathroom door opened, and a shining face peered in at doorknob level. "I see you, Mother, you're up!"

For a moment Jac was pinned between two emotions—one induced by the small, perfect presence and the other by the realization that since she woke up, she had been thinking of *Jac's Journal*, not of Jac's child.

"Good morning, sweet girl," she said, pulling her daughter into her arms.

The child nestled into her neck. "Mother, it's wet behind your ears."

"And we're both going to be wet all over when we go to the beach this weekend, right?"

The child laughed, a sound as high and sweet as a flute.

For a while they sat on the bed, talking about clams and oysters because Karen was intrigued by creatures that lived in shells. Every second question seemed to be "Why?"; Jac knew all children did that, but she could never shake the feeling that it was a part of her, transmitted to Karen.

If only, she thought, she could do as well with explaining other things as she was doing with mollusks. During the long talks she had had with Karen after the divorce, she had sometimes caught herself speaking as if the child could understand what had turned her parents from a one-celled, loving creature into halves that still could be friendly but were now separate. It was too easy to assume there was adult comprehension in those large brown eyes—perhaps because they were so much like her own. But then she would find that Karen had absorbed only a fraction of what was said, like a tiny but willing vessel that could be filled only to its capacity. What was that capacity, though?

She recalled vividly what her own perceptions had been at age five, when her parents, too, had undergone that cell division, but of course she would never subject Karen to an experience like her own.

She looked at the clock. "Hey, kid, time for mothers to pull themselves together," she said. She dressed quickly and then brushed her hair, which was as dark, straight, and shining as a long pour of molasses. She had breakfast with Karen and the woman who took care of her, promising to be home as soon as the show was over. Half an hour later she got out of a cab at the WXNY building, which housed one of the three independent TV channels in the city.

Armed with the morning papers, she strode through the lobby, feeling the pleasant surge of tension that always seemed to rise from its tiled floors. She got off the elevator at the fourth floor and walked past some narrow cubicles. She had started in one of them, six years earlier, as a researcher and writer; finally she had moved on camera, but then there had been three years—frustrating but necessary—in the consumer-reporter slot.

She reached the section of the news department where the hour-long early show, As It Happens, was created. The office where she prepared her five-minute segment of that show had been hers for seven months, but the paint on the door seemed as fresh to her as yesterday.

Her phone was ringing; she reached it on the third ring. It was one of the assistant housing commissioners. She dumped her purse and papers, slid behind her desk, and started making notes on a yellow pad. Tacked above her desk was a caricature drawn by a colleague: legs so long they ran off the page, a narrow waist that swelled into athletic shoulders, a face that was all eyes and mouth, the latter asking "Why?" in half a dozen languages.

She hung up but went on writing for ten minutes, the interview questions coalescing in her mind and emerging in an angular hand. The questions were aimed at finding the underlying themes in people's views and exposing either the contradictions that existed— the week before, a businessman advocating free enterprise had also argued for the continuing government regulation of his own industry—or, more rarely, the intellectual consistency.

Her phone rang repeatedly: one of the deputy mayors, a press colleague, several viewers who had ideas for the show. The tenth call altered the crisp efficiency of her manner; it was the man she had been seeing recently, a former State Department official whose knowledge of world affairs fascinated her. He pressed her to have dinner on Thursday, when he would be in New York again. The layer of intimacy coating his voice made clear that he would not be content much longer to leave their relationship as it was. She visualized him; the thought of learning what lay beneath the handsomely tailored suit he was no doubt wearing stirred little feeling in her. Perhaps, she thought, that was a reason to let him put an end to her celibacy since the divorce. She agreed to see him and hung up, feeling as indecisive as a campaign speech.

She had gotten through the last of her newspapers when the phone rang again. "This is Jac Sanda. . . . Who? . . . Oh yes, I know the name." She listened, reaching for a yellow pad. "What do the police say about the damage?" She frowned. "They actually said that?" She listened again. "I'll have to think about it, but I know this much already—if I do it, I'd want to have both you and him on the program. I'd need both protagonists, you see." She smiled faintly. "I stand corrected. One protagonist, one antagonist. Will it be clear which of you is which?" She laughed. "Let me think about it. How do I reach you?" She jotted down the numbers, hung up, and leaned back in her chair.

There was no reason, she thought, that she couldn't do the story. The divorce had removed all "conflict of interest"; she could explore whatever she liked. She called for a researcher to get her some specific information.

By three o'clock it had come; by four she had finished reading it, and sat back to make her decision.

In college, studying history, she had learned that the days of bloody labor struggle had been over, for the most part, since the thirties. Now the battleground lay in the courts and Congress, where labor lobbied ceaselessly for more and more legislative power—just as industry lobbied for protective rules and tariffs. The two seemed to her like Goliaths trying to tie each other up in red tape. Somewhere along the way the fundamental questions had been sidestepped; the rights of those who supplied jobs and those who filled them had become issues to decide, not by principle, but by reference to bureaucracies and regulations.

If she did this interview, she thought, it would be simply two individuals, face to face, arguing an issue.

She pushed back the dark weight of her hair and stretched, her soft yellow blouse falling back from tanned arms. Her arms stopped in midair; across the room was a photo of Karen on the Central Park carousel, rising high on the wooden horse, held by the camera in permanent glee. "Quite true, honey," Jac said to the grinning face. "I wasn't thinking of your father."

She brought her arms down and sighed. TATU was affiliated with the Brotherhood of American Labor. All the entertainment-industry unions, including the one she herself had had to join, were Brotherhood affiliates, along with the butchers and canners, the public-transport employees, and dozens of other groups. And Mr. Burton Sanda's prominence as a labor lawyer led him often to be involved with Brotherhood unions.

"Sorry, babe," Jac said to the photo, "but I can't run the *Journal* to please Daddy. If I'd had a career before I married him, I wouldn't have started it as Jac Sanda. Maybe I wouldn't have done a lot of things." She smiled. "But I wouldn't have you, either, so it's OK."

She reached for her phone. After a long wait her party came on the line. She identified herself, made her request, and listened. "I understand how you feel, Mr. Codd," she said sweetly, "but the *Journal* is going to do something about this situation, one way or the other. Don't you think it would be a mistake to let Erik Dante appear by himself? To have your point of view left off the show?"

4

Burton Sanda finished checking a list of items with his secretary. "I'll call you when I get a chance tomorrow," he said. "It could be either a friendly long session or a table-thumper that everybody storms out of early." He smiled. "That's why I never charge by the hour for arbitration."

When the secretary left, Sanda rubbed his eyes and smoothed his thick curly black hair. He checked his watch; he tried to catch Jac's show whenever he could, and there was time to do so now. He got up, left his office, and went down the carpeted hall to the conference room.

He opened a wall panel, switched on the TV set inside, and settled into a soft leather chair. He put his feet up on another of the chairs, something he would not have done if anyone else was in the room, and noted that Jac was just starting an interview. She was getting very tan, he thought; then his attention sharpened. Two strong ver-tical lines formed between his eyes.

". . . has been steadily declining," she was saying, "so that today less than twenty percent of America's work force belongs to labor unions. However, that is still nearly twenty million Americans." The camera moved to a close-up of a seamed, intense face as she contin-ued. "This union represents all technical workers in the Broadway theater, but its domain does not yet extend to theaters outside the Broadway area. Mr. Codd would like it to, of course." The man smiled. "Let's start by hearing from management," Jac said. The camera panned to a much younger face, with jutting bones and blue eyes that seemed to look right into the conference room. "Mr. Dante, why are you opposed to becoming a TATU theater?"

The man considered for a moment. "Suppose you're giving a big party, and you hire three people to help—a bartender, a cook, and a maid. But then someone comes in and says you can't do that. You have to hire *two* bartenders—one to open the bottles and one to pour the drinks. And at least three cooks, because whoever peels the veg-etables can't be the same person who cooks them, and neither one of them can do the washing up. And as far as a maid goes, how can somebody who takes the coats also pass around the food? That's the kind of thing that's been happening on Broadway with the unions—specialization carried to crazy lengths."

Sanda's feet pulled back from their perch and thudded on the car-pet. "Jesus, Jac," he muttered, and then listened intently as the man went on talking, citing examples: of the job of changing some lamps that took two men half an hour, but a Broadway producer had to hire three electricians for four hours' work apiece; of scenery that had to be driven to the loading doors by one union but could be unloaded only by another; of musicians who never played a note during the run of a show—who played cards in the basement instead—but who had to be hired and paid full salaries.

The man must be a lunatic, Sanda thought, to challenge publicly what any sane businessman accepted as the price of doing business. But of course Dante was not a businessman; he was an actor. Sanda stared at the man's face, and something clicked into place in his well-organized memory: Once he and Jac had gone to see a Broadway play about a prison breakout, and the hulking giant the critics raved about had been named Erik Dante. On the screen was the same quality Sanda remembered seeing on the stage: a kind of intangible force that could draw people like iron filings to a magnet. Those who had it and knew how to use it could be dangerous, he thought, for it was the simplest and most effective means of acquiring power.

He looked at the screen and groaned, for Jac was saying, "So you object to featherbedding and to certain work rules because they're inefficient and cost money. How would you—"

"Excuse me, but you have to understand that it's more than a budget matter. I don't think it's *right* for someone to come in and tell me how many people to hire and how much work they can do. And I think my staff and I should be free to operate with or without a union, as we see fit, with no coercion on either side. Or from the outside."

Sanda slammed his fist on the conference table. "Dammit, Jac! Why the hell couldn't you stay home with Karen?"

But she merely turned her head and said, "In the name of fair play, and of keeping Mr. Codd from exploding, I think it's time we heard his side."

"Better make it good, Morty." In the den of his Manhattan townhouse, V. I. Joncas, the general secretary-treasurer of the Brotherhood of American Labor, stared impassively at his TV screen, glad that his wife had called him in to watch. "Look, Vi," she had cried, "isn't that one of your people?" He had been wary as soon as he saw who it was.

Codd's face filled the screen. "Dante talks about what's not right I'll tell you what's not *right*. To grab kids from high school, the way he does with his Infernals, and college kids and retired senior citizens and let them do the work that should go to people with families to support. Dante's a throwback to the old sweatshop days, when no worker had any kind of job security at all. He's antiunion, plain and simple, that's what he is."

Cecelia Joncas lifted her wineglass to the screen. "Hear, hear!"

But Erik Dante was saying, "I'm not antiunion. Can't anybody question union practices without having that label slapped on him?"

"Are you a union member yourself?" Jac Sanda said.

"Yes. Guild of Stage Actors. If you want to act professionally, you have to join."

Codd was bristling. "I suppose you object to that, too? No, no, let me say something here." He looked into the camera. "Dante says he can't afford our union. The public should know, with all due respect, that that's a joke. He's got a real wealthy backer. Besides, I never met an employer yet who said he could afford to pay his workers more. But if you've ever noticed, they always get the money."

"From the public," Dante said. "They raise their prices."

Codd cried, "How about some sympathy for the employee, instead of moaning about producers who make millions?"

"And how about all the shows that close because their payrolls are too big? How about—"

Jac Sanda cut in. "Let's stick to your situation, gentlemen. Mr. Codd, I understand you're not planning to request an election at the Poets and Paupers Theater, at least not now. Why is that?"

"Because it could lead to pressure being put on the very people we're trying to help. And the thing could turn into a confrontational situation. We'd rather try to get what we want by using persuasion."

Dante's eyes were pale blue flames. "Persuasion—is that what happened last week, when the windows in my theater were broken?"

"Now just a minute!" Codd cried, his color rising.

"And garbage thrown on the sidewalks at night, and tires slashed on the theater's van?"

Jac Sanda prevailed over Codd's shouts. "Are you claiming the union did that?"

Watching, Joncas muttered, "Christ," then listened carefully to Dante's reply: "I'm saying that it started a couple nights after I refused Mr. Codd's second request for a contract at my theater."

"Have you told that to the police?"

"They say they don't get involved if it's a matter of union organizing."

Joncas smiled.

"Speaking generally, of course," Jac said, "labor history is filled with examples of violence. How do you feel about that, Mr. Codd?"

"You mean all the owners who have busted heads trying to keep us out? I had a brother got his arm broken during the Memorial Day massacre!"

Joncas said, "Keep your shirt on, Morty."

"Such an odd-looking shirt, too," Cecelia Joncas murmured.

"Do you think," Jac went on, "that a union is ever justified in using coercion to get what it wants?"

Two bulges swelled on Codd's jaw. "What about *economic* coercion? Paying a man too damn little for his work?"

"How is that coercion?" Dante shot back. "When the man is free to leave anytime? Coercion is breaking windows and slashing tires and—"

"Gentlemen, please!" said Jac Sanda. Both of them drew slowly back in their chairs.

Cecelia Joncas frowned. "What on earth is going on?"

"This Dante," said her husband, "is a smart bastard, that's what's going on."

"Mr. Dante," Jac said, "do you believe either labor or management is ever justified in using violence?"

"Not in starting it. Never."

"You mean it's all right in retaliation?"

He hesitated. "I'd like to see the police brought in if anybody, on either side, started using violence. And I'd just like to add here that I haven't done so and that I pledge never to do so, right here in front of your TV audience. I hope Mr. Codd will say the same."

Jac Sanda's expression wavered between amusement and admiration as she turned to Codd, whose face now seemed to match the color of her lipstick. "Do you agree?" she asked.

"You have to, Morty," Joncas growled. "So do it quick."

"Sure," Codd said finally.

"Jackass!" said a man watching from the depths of a chair in one of the twenty-four rooms of his Westchester County estate. The elderly couple who were his parents looked at him cautiously.

"Donald," said his father, "do you know that man?"

"I know a jackass when I see one."

"Oh dear," said his mother. "All this talk of violence . . . God must be—"

"Shut up! I can't hear."

There was quiet in the room. On the screen Jac Sanda was saying, "So if you two can agree on nothing else, at least you can agree that your dispute will be settled by peaceful means."

"I hope so." Dante laughed. "Leave the violence to Shakespeare." Then he added, with a curious emphasis, "Or to the mob."

The man named Donald sat up slowly in his chair.

On the screen Morty Codd said, "And you leave the sweatshops back in the nineteenth century!"

"Gentlemen," Jac said smoothly, "I'm afraid our time is up. I thank you both for coming and for giving us the two sides in this classic labor-management confrontation that's developing in the unusual setting of the theater. This has been *Jac's Journal* for Thursday, August 8, closing with our usual question to viewers: What do *you* think?"

"Lady," said the man in Westchester, "I think you better be more careful what you put on the air." He snapped off the set. His parents watched cautiously as he left the room.

5

Jac led her two guests from the controlled chaos of the newsroom into the hall. "Thanks again for coming," she said to Morty Codd.

"As I told you, I really prefer to do the interviews live, and I appreciate your cooperation."

Codd let out a breath he seemed to have been holding since they went off the air, and shook her hand. "You had to talk me into this, Miss Sanda, but now I think it was a good idea. Now we all know what we're dealing with." He looked at Erik. "You remind me of a cop we used to have in Chicago. Of a lot of things we had to put up with then."

Erik was silent. The corners of Codd's mouth tucked in like pleats. He turned on his heel, his boxer's torso growing even shorter as he moved to the elevator.

Jac watched him go; Erik stood looking at her profile. "May I tell you that I think you're good? Very good?"

"Thank you." She turned to him. "But I didn't have much to do tonight. Usually I have to drag things out of people, but you seem to have thought out your views very carefully."

He grinned. "Do I take it you've decided I'm the protagonist?"

"I don't take sides," Jac said firmly. "I only present them."

He raised one eyebrow, which was as dark a brown as his suit and tie. "You mean you chose to gather information as a career, but you have no opinions about what you gather?"

"Of course I have. But they're not supposed to affect what I say on the air. Only what I choose to put on it."

"Why did you choose to put on my story?"

She smiled. "Let's just say that certain phenomena interest me more than others."

"Such as?"

"Oh . . . power, the abuse and misuse of. Why liberals crusade against it in business but don't want to hear about it in unions. Why conservatives do just the opposite. What makes an actor take on a political battle about it. Things like that."

"I don't have any politics. I just want to be able to run my theater my way." He frowned. "What's funny about that?"

"Nothing," she said, still smiling.

"I like the way you come at things. You were the one reporter I wanted to do the story."

"You watch the *Journal*, then?"

"When I can. Have you seen any of my shows?"

"I haven't been to Poets and Paupers, but I did see you years ago, in *Behind the Walls*. Which seems as far from poetry as you can get."

"Yes."

"The clips I read said you turned down a chance to be in the movie version. Why?"

He looked into the distance. It wasn't often, Jac thought, that standing beside someone made her feel small; she had to look up at the planes of his face. "I turned down the movie because I'd already spent too much time behind walls."

"You mean you'd actually been in prison?"

"Let's say I didn't have to do much research for that role. It gave me a big break, but the play was about things I wanted to get away from in real life. So I wasn't keen to be part of them in art. Especially in a permanent form, like a movie."

"You're not interested in realism, then?"

"I didn't say that. I just don't think the dark side of life is the only one that's real."

"I see." They were looking at each other; suddenly Jac felt as if her mind were a camera, shifting from a long shot to a tight close-up; the conversation faded to some outer distance, and she saw only the face a few feet away and the eyes that told her he too had forgotten what they were saying.

"I have to get back," he said abruptly, and her perspective reverted to normal.

"And I must get home. To my daughter."

"And husband?"

"I'm divorced."

"But married to your work?" Her chin lifted, but he said, "That wasn't a criticism. Well, good night. And thanks for the show." He started down the hall.

"I hope," she said, "that you're aware of the possible consequences of what you said tonight."

He turned back. "Sometimes you want to do things regardless of the consequences." He lifted his hand in a salute and walked away. As he neared the elevator, he pulled off his tie and snapped it once against the wall before he put it in his pocket.

Jac went back to her office and her desk, to do her usual postmortem on the show, but the assistant news director burst in on her. "Jac, the switchboard's going crazy with calls about the *Journal!*"

She ran out and down to the board and was standing there watching, sometimes helping out, when she turned and saw the man with whom she had made a dinner date at the beginning of the week. "I couldn't get through to you on the phone," he said, "so I thought I'd just come by."

She was unprepared for the feeling of revulsion; it took her a moment to collect herself and explain that something had come up and she couldn't go to dinner after all.

Erik saw, when he got back to the theater, that the tech director was still working in the scene shop. He decided to join him, and went up the narrow flights of stairs to the apartment, to change.

At one end of the huge room a lacquered screen the shop had built for *Turandot* served to define his bedroom. When he pulled off his shirt, he saw traces on the collar of the makeup they had put on him for the TV show. It was less heavy than stage greasepaint, but then, he thought, television was supposed to be the medium of close-ups and truth, whereas the stage was the realm of artifice. That was the conventional wisdom, but for him the stage was the most naked place of all, and the freest.

He thought of the moment in the corridor outside the TV studio, when Jac Sanda's dark eyes had suddenly held him by more than their intelligence, and the skin visible in the open neck of her blouse had seemed to exude the smell of sweet grass. Onstage, he thought, in *Blood Wedding*, he had played a moment like that, of sudden consuming awareness of a woman; but he had done it very differently, finding ways to let the audience know what he was experiencing, instead of turning away as if nothing had happened.

The phone beside his bed rang. "You're there," said Maeve's voice, sliding upward in relief.

"Sure I'm here." He stretched out on the bed, the phone cord across his bare chest.

"I saw the show. You were marvelous."

"Thanks."

She talked for five minutes about his comments on the program. Then she said, "The Sanda woman was very good, too. Sometimes, when the two of you were talking . . ."

"Yes?" He reached over to a drawer, fishing for a T-shirt.

"She was very good. I taped the show. Will you come over and watch it with me?" He hesitated. "Not tonight," she said. "I know you don't want to leave the theater. Can't you hire some security guards?"

"That's expensive, Maeve."

"Please do it. For me. I can't stand worrying about you. I know you got that man to agree to no violence, but . . . please, Erik."

"All right. I'll look into it tomorrow."

"Then you'll be able to come and see the tape."

"Sweetheart, I . . . Yes. OK."

When he hung up, his eyes went to the small framed object on the wall by his bed. Years before, when blankets of dust lay over everything in the building, Maeve had brought him here and said he could fix it up if he really was determined on the insanity of starting a theater. That night, in a bar over on Third Avenue, he had picked up the cocktail napkin on which she'd been sketching something, and had seen a ragged child staring at the moon. "It's what you looked like while you were talking," she had explained. He had made it the theater's logo.

He sighed. To bring Poets and Paupers into existence had required two transformations—of the building and of himself. Piles of rubbish had had to be cleared out of the auditorium, the second floor knocked out to provide space for the flies and the fly loft, the third floor converted into costume rooms. And out of himself and the raw talent he possessed, he had had to hammer an instrument capable of speaking verse lines and moving with discipline. Often he had locked himself alone in the unfinished building, experimenting with his voice, learning how to control it—howling vowel sounds into the emptiness, followed by whispers; practicing articulation exercises, making his t's and d's and th's lose all memory of Brooklyn; analyzing Shakespearean passages for meaning and then trying to make his voice and body project it.

He got up abruptly, finished dressing, and went to the window. It was still dusk. After a while, he realized that a car had parked across the street but no one was getting out. He watched for a bit longer, then ran down the stairs and into the auditorium.

Through a space between the boards on one of the windows, he could see three figures in the car. One of them seemed to be using binoculars. While he hesitated, the engine started. He rushed to the lobby and out into the street.

As the car sped by him, he caught a glimpse of a face in the backseat. He froze. Ritchie, he thought. No, that wasn't it—Louie. Louie the Limp, from the old gang, who had gone to work for the Varese family.

He stood in the middle of the street, telling himself that he could just as easily have been mistaken, that the light was going. That the Varese couldn't be coming back into his life.

But they were involved with unions, he thought; on the waterfront it had been common knowledge that they ran things. There was no evidence, though, that they were involved in the theater. The one connection was very tenuous: TATU was part of the Brotherhood of American Labor, and the Brotherhood's secretary-treasurer, V. I. Joncas, had once had ties to the Varese family. But that had been years ago; since then he had turned against the Varese and cleaned them out of several unions.

After all, Erik thought, wasn't a man entitled to live down his past?

A taxi came along, honking for him to clear out of the way.

He went back to the sidewalk. If there was any chance that he was facing Varese muscle, he thought, he would have to know it, and prepare himself accordingly.

He hesitated, looking at the windows. Then he went back inside and down to the scene shop, to tell the tech director he was going out. By the time he got on the subway, it was nine o'clock.

The ride lasted forty-five minutes but seemed to take twenty years. When he got out, memories rose like steam from the subway grates.

He followed their trail, up and down streets where the women's clothes flashed invitations as bright as the neon signs.

By midnight he had been to every Varese hangout or connection he could recall, talking, listening, and asking for a man called the Swede. He had no luck, but he left messages wherever he stopped.

6

The next morning one of the papers carried the story of a fight in a bar in Queens, where the TV had been tuned to *Jac's Journal*. The crowd had split into two factions, and it had taken three cops to sort out the free-for-all that resulted.

In Brooklyn the board of directors of a large co-op apartment met to discuss the strike and picket lines that virtually had paralyzed the complex and made its grounds a shambles of bricks and garbage. The board believed it neither needed nor could afford as many maintenance and security men as the new union contract would require it to hire. The weary men could think of no new answer to their plight, but they sent a telegram of support to Erik Dante, copies to all major New York media.

In Manhattan, a managing editor decided to order an interview with Erik Dante, for more reason than the story itself. In the last newspaper strike the major issue had been featherbedding—having to hire fifteen men to run a press that ten could handle easily—but for fear of making settlement more difficult, management had voted not to publicize the issue. Afterward that vote had been seen as a mistake.

At City Hall the mayor of New York, a scrappy man known for saying what he thought, told reporters at a press conference that in the city's current negotiations with its labor unions, productivity should be the key issue. "Do you know some of the work rules and practices we have to live with?" he said, with the owlish look of incredulity that was his trademark. "We have sanitation workers who spend less than half their workday actually picking up garbage.

And how about this rule? If a bus driver calls in sick, he's got to be replaced with somebody else—even if there's been maintenance trouble and there's no bus for him to drive! New York City has been giving in on these kinds of things for years, but it's got to stop. If the unions want higher wages—why am I saying *if?*—we've got to get some productivity back, in return. We've got to have a proclivity for productivity!" Then he laughed and said, "You see? I'm a poet and pauper too."

In his office on Broadway, a producer reluctantly confirmed to a reporter who called that on his last long-running musical he had paid over $400,000 to musicians who never played a note. Expecting to hear from the head of the musicians' union when the story appeared the next day, the producer escaped to the back row of an auditorium to watch the rehearsal of his new musical, which would feature the return to Broadway of one of Hollywood's top stars.

The star, a comedian who was incredibly tall and thin, insisted on inserting into each scene some of his "shtick"—the vocal and physical mannerisms that had made him famous. If the director protested, the star would say, standing on one foot like a stork and peering down at the top of the director's bald head, "Forty years I been in show business, nobody tells *me* what doesn't work." Then he would break up the entire company by pecking at the director's head with lips pursed into a beak. The producer watched gloomily; he had been caught before in the tyrannies of talent, and there was nothing to do but live through them. Suddenly the comedian called out, in one of his famous bird voices, "Look, our producer's here! The big man with money and influence! Why don't you use some of it to lean on this off-Broadway pipsqueak, instead of talking to the press about our musician friends? If you did that, I'd like it a lot. But if you didn't . . . " Suddenly the comedian was lying on the floor, squawking, his spindly legs up in the air like a chicken's. He stayed that way for several minutes, and even though the producer knew it was an act, he couldn't help the feeling of panic induced by the thought of his two-and-a-half-million-dollar investment, all of it riding on a star who looked like a dead chicken.

Two blocks away, in another Broadway auditorium, there was a "cattle call"—more politely known as a day of open casting interviews for a new play. The Guild of Stage Actors required that such interviews be held for every show. As usual, nearly three hundred actors showed up, to sign in, receive a number, and then wait weary hours in the backstage area, perched on stairs or leaning against walls. Among them there were two topics of conversation: one, whether there were in fact some roles open or whether, as often happened, the producers had already cast the show and were just going through the motions; and two, Erik Dante, who had announced in the trade papers that he would hold interviews the following week for minor roles in *Firestorm*. Several actors who had worked for him became the focus of a group debating whether people should go to those interviews or boycott them, in light of Erik's public statements. Both sides had passionate adherents; things were growing heated when someone came out and called, "Numbers 207 through 220!" That sequence included most of the disputants, who fled inside, holding their pictures and résumés. When they saw they would be interviewed only by a stage manager, not by the producers or the director, several of them swore under their breaths. Eventually they were all told, politely, "Sorry, there's nothing for you." All of them had heard those words many times before; they were the standard rejection formula in the theater. As he left, one actor muttered, "At least Erik Dante interviews everybody himself."

V. I. Joncas looked across the large fruitwood desk in his office, to which he had just returned after five days in Washington. Morty Codd sat on the other side, looking uncomfortable even though his chair was beautifully upholstered.

"One lousy little theater," Joncas said. "Was it really worth it?"

"It could have been important to us," Codd said defensively.

"Didn't you do any checking on that actor before you went in there?"

"Why didn't he do some checking on me? Do you know that sonofabitch hinted that I wanted to be paid off? Me! Morty Codd! Who's never taken a penny under the table in his life, and everybody knows it!"

Joncas sighed. "You know how many idiot congressmen I have to have lunch and dinner with when I go to Washington? You know one of the things they're talking about now? Making the federal government responsible for any violence that occurs in labor disputes. You think I need to come home and see every paper in town talking about vandalism at this lousy little theater?"

Codd slicked back his white hair with both palms. "Labor never won a battle in this country without having to break a few things. But the membership knows I'll bust their heads if any of them get out of line again."

"Good. Because it would look damn bad for you, and for all the theater unions, if you didn't keep your word. After you gave it on TV."

Codd flushed.

Joncas sighed again and turned his head to a side wall, where fish were gliding in colored swoops inside a glass cage. Even when he was not in repose, there was in him a quality of seeing the world from some detached vantage point. His gray eyes were not hooded, but people often felt that his personality was.

He had first come to public attention as the president who had reformed the Union of Public Transport Employees and gotten them two of the best contracts they ever had. From that position he had moved into the executive councils of the Brotherhood of American Labor; he was now the second man in that federation of over three million members. Yet there was little of the workingman about him. He had a lion's head, but its coarse, dark hair was tamed and cut by an expert, and his suits and grammar both were tailored to fit the higher levels of the city's political and artistic circles. The press called him one of the new breed of labor leaders. Some of the membership put it a little differently: They said V. I. Joncas wore silk shorts but had steel balls.

No one knew his first name, at least no one who would tell it. Some said his initials stood for Vassily Ivanovich and he came from a family of Russian émigrés; others claimed he was from somewhere south of Rome and was really named Vitello Ivano. "Just say I'm stateless," he once had told a reporter. "But not powerless."

His gray eyes went back to Codd. He leaned forward so the light hit his lean, swarthy face and said, in a soft voice that was like sneakers crunching on gravel, "I've had a call from the musicians. They're upset about what you did. So are the actors. And so are the transport workers. Don't you realize the transport negotiations are going on right now? Don't you know the worst place for any kind of labor fight is on TV and in the papers, with the public looking on and everybody grandstanding? The actor understands that, too goddamn well. You let him suck you into the spotlight. You gave the mayor just the kind of act he was looking to get in on."

"The press will get tired of Dante."

"They haven't for almost a week now. Because he comes across on TV like a million dollars. And these aren't normal times, you know. People are in a strange mood, at least enough of them to turn that loudmouth actor into some kind of Boy Scout symbol of earning your keep. Sure, it's simple-minded, but whoever said the public had brains?"

"They don't understand anything about us!" Codd cried. "How the hell could they? All they hear is a lot of antiunion crap from the big corporations. Or else they read about gangsters muscling in on some union. The press likes to play that up, all right! They say . . ." He stopped suddenly and flushed.

"Say what?"

Codd looked more uncomfortable than ever.

"Morty, I know what some idiots say about me. Some people like to throw garbage, but it doesn't faze me. It just falls to the ground and stinks." Joncas glanced at the framed picture on his desk, from which two pairs of dark eyes smiled—Cecelia's and their daughter's. The expression that crossed his face was not quite a smile, more a momentary lightening of his air of detachment. His eyes found Codd's again. "I've never denied that my wife's cousins had connections to the Varese family. Why should I? Since all I ever had to do with them was getting them out of the Transport Workers?"

Codd cleared his throat. "If I didn't believe that, Mr. Joncas, you can bet I wouldn't be here. In fact, I'd be working like hell to get you out of the Brotherhood, instead of hoping you'll be the next president."

"Would you, Morty? Yes, I believe you would." Joncas leaned back in his chair. The leather sighed softly. "So what do you plan to do about this mess you started?"

"We got a picket line up at the theater yesterday. And I've asked the Labor Department to look into those damn Infernals of his. But I was kind of hoping that . . . well, that you'd lend a hand. You've got the right connections."

"The thing is to be practical, Morty. That's the only test of an action—will it get you what you want?" Codd didn't answer. Joncas went on, looking at the aquarium. "Fish are very stupid, ever notice that? Even the way they look—bug eyes and gaping mouths. And they swim to any bait you dangle in front of them."

"I thought you kept them for pets."

"I do."

Codd looked nonplussed.

"Well," Joncas said, "thanks to you, we can't let anything, shall we say, happen to his theater. I suppose we could get the fire or building inspectors to find some code violations and shut him down for a while. But that wouldn't shut him up, would it? We could work up some kind of complaint against him for the Labor Relations Review Board, but they take forever and six years to decide anything. In the meantime, he's still loudmouthing. So unless he fades out of the picture on his own, which is damn unlikely, the practical thing may be to beat him at his own game." Joncas turned back to Codd. "All right. Your job, Morty, will be to stay off TV if he's within a hundred miles of you. And to let me take care of the rest."

The club was called the Jumping Joint.

It had been designed as a place to separate men from their money, by paralyzing their capacity for thought.

First it nearly blinded them, with colored lights that cut arcs through the drifts of smoke. Then it deafened them, playing music just below the level of endurance. Finally it engulfed them in flesh, which gleamed from the blouses and slit skirts of a horde of young women, none over twenty-five, who came to the Joint in order to cling to the fringes of an illegal world and would do anything for signs of recognition from its rulers. In booths or rooms in the rear, cards and deals were parceled out, loans were made and called in, and the mouths and thighs of the young women opened, like flowers, to take in the men's resistance, and any last remnant of their capacity for thought.

The man called the Swede had come in about eleven. He was often at the Joint: Sometimes he was on a job, any odd job he could get, for some member of the Varese family, who owned the place and whose underboss worked out of a suite upstairs. More often the Swede was there because he didn't know where else to go.

Nothing about him looked Swedish, except perhaps his hair, the color of cornsilk, which he supposed must have come from his father. He was a big man, tall and beefy; when he had last done time, he had been a bodyguard for one of the Varese captains, who was in for armed robbery.

The Swede sat at the back bar, brooding over a bourbon and water. It was his birthday, and the music, the smoke, the lights, and the flesh all seemed to be calling out a chorus of "Thirty-eight." He swore at them.

"What're you saying, Swede?" asked the man next to him, a numbers runner for the Varese.

"I said they don't treat me right. What am I, some jerk? Some crud? How many years I been doing jobs for them, anyway? How long they gonna put off taking me in the organization?"

The man cupped his hands around his mouth and shouted into the Swede's ear. "You dumb ox, you fooled around with one of their women. Just be glad they didn't cut off your *coglioni*."

The Swede grimaced and turned away. The business with the woman had been years earlier; weren't they ever going to forget about it?

"Hey," the numbers runner yelled. "That guy who was looking for you. You ever go see what he wanted?"

The Swede shrugged.

"Seemed like he wanted to see you real bad."

"OK, OK!" the Swede shouted. "I heard about it. All over the street." He hollered at the red-headed waitress for another bourbon. The numbers runner wanted to keep on talking, but the Swede turned away.

He looked toward the back rooms and their closed doors. Thinking of what went on behind them made a warmth that was more than bourbon spread through him. He thought of a birthday present for himself, delivered by the hands and mouth of the young blond he'd talked to the night before. She had been friendly, especially when he told her he worked for the Varese.

He was planning his birthday gift in some detail when the growing smile suddenly was stripped from his face. He saw the young blond heading to one of the back rooms, towing a man old enough to be her grandfather. The Swede knew she was setting him up for something, probably a loan-shark swindle. Probably she was doing it for Big Tiny Varese—doing all those wonderful birthday things to somebody else.

The Swede watched the door of the room close behind her and the old man. He swore. What if he was sitting there in the same fix on his next birthday? And his fortieth? And forever? Still just a street punk for the Varese.

The music rose to a deafening howl, which seemed to come from his own throat. He began to think of the man who had left so many messages for him.

7

Maeve Jerrold curled into a gray silk chair in her living room to look at the book-review section of the Sunday paper. She was a day late in doing so, but she often put it off, feeling reluctant to look, yet oddly reassured when she finally did so.

She read two reviews—one hailing a novel about a man who had chosen to live with pigs, another praising a fictional diary in which a woman recorded all her orgasms in detail.

There were other kinds of reviews in the paper, about other kinds of books, but Maeve put it aside; she had found what she expected. There was no place for her in a world where such works could earn the attention and praise of serious critics, where talent was placed in the service of depicting ugliness and depravity. How was it possible that even Erik could exist in such a world?

But of course Erik himself was not possible. If he hadn't existed, she thought wryly, no one would have invented him.

Certainly not she. On the night they met, at the producer's party, she had been convalescing from her divorce, a detached observer who was there because people sought her as an investor, even though she had put money in only two shows, both of which failed. She had watched Erik for some time, struck by the way his physical presence dominated the room, and when he came over to her, a savage who wore a tailored suit and spoke her language, she had thought he could not be real. And when he took her arm to guide her through the rest of the evening, that contact seemed to make the whole party larger than life: Suddenly she could see and feel everything, from the unspoken bond between him and the other actors, which came from the shared intensity of doing a play, to the desperation of an elderly star who couldn't remember lines anymore because he drank and drank because he couldn't remember lines anymore.

The sense of unreality had stayed with her for weeks as she introduced Erik to some of the things that were precious to her—the miniatures of Liberale da Verona and the music of Guillaume Dufay and the flawless lines of Racine and the voice of Fritz Wunderlich—and watched his face. When she gave him some of the literature, and history, of the extravagant nineteenth-century theater, he had been like someone discovering his homeland. She still could hear him exclaiming over the battle of *Hernani*, that war waged against Classicism by Victor Hugo and his fellow Romantics: "My God, they even fought in the streets—just to get the kind of play they wanted on the stage! And it went on for a hundred days!"

With that same exuberance, he had wanted the two of them to be lovers. She had refused for weeks, knowing it was against all reason and sense to love him, giving him the obvious excuse. He would not accept it—"I don't care when you were born!"—and finally she had confessed the truth: If they were lovers, it would only hurt more deeply when he left her. At first he had laughed, disbelieving. When he realized she meant it, he said, "How do you dare do that—guarantee what I'll do in the future?" Finally, his eyes frosting over, he said, "All right, then," and started to go. She had had to stop him; and from that night, which lasted forever but could not be long enough, she had felt as if she were riding a wind. It was a heady, wonderful sensation, except that one could not trust a wind to carry one to safety.

She frowned, pulled on a gold earloop, and shifted in her chair. Just the day before, the very producer whose party had brought Erik into her life had called her, probing to find out what "that magnificent madman is going to do next," warning her that "Broadway isn't happy," and reminding her how touchy TATU members could be: "Did I ever tell you that at the first dress rehearsal of Behind the Walls, Dante moved a piece of furniture during a scene change? The chief stagehand came out in bristles, and I had to almost sit on Dante in order to avoid a situation with the union."

Maeve realized that she was still frowning. She stopped, smoothed the skin with her fingertips, and leaned back to look around the room—at the blue-glazed T'ang horse, the Raphael study her family had owned for decades, the tiny birch trees that seemed to be both lace and ice because they were sculpted inside a block of crystal. The tension began to recede.

It came back when the intercom buzzer rang. She went to it slowly, fearing that one of the reporters who had been calling her for days was trying physically to break through the barrier of her refusals.

The doorman announced Mr. Burton Sanda.

She could hardly believe it, but it was he, looking only a little older than the last time she'd seen him, eight years earlier. He had been one of the smooth-surfaced people from her ex-husband's world, the business world, who had slipped through her life and her memory like marbles.

He swore that her ex-husband had not asked him to come, although he admitted they still kept in touch. After she gave him a drink, he said, "When I learned you're involved with this theater, I couldn't help feeling concerned. Even if we're hardly old friends, I liked you." He smiled. "Of course I know you're wondering: What's in it for him? You're thinking there must be some connection with my practice."

"No," she said. "The fact is, I can't remember exactly what you do. Some kind of law?"

Sanda laughed, a genuine sound. "If I ever get the feeling that I'm somebody in this town, I'll come to you and get straightened out. The fact is, I've mediated some of New York's toughest and biggest labor negotiations and arbitrated some of the contracts. But really, Maeve, there's nothing behind this visit but goodwill. When I saw the ad today, I thought: Maybe I should go talk to that nice lady, even if she does think I'm out of line."

"What ad?"

"But . . . I just assumed you'd have seen it." He took a paper from his briefcase, folded it open, and laid it on the coffee table.

The headline read, "WHAT UNIONS HAVE DONE FOR THE AMERICAN THEATER AND ITS WORKERS." All the theatrical unions were signatories; across the bottom ran "Brotherhood of American Labor."

The copy summarized the history of early organizing days, gave examples of the exploitation that had inspired them, listed many union contributions to the well-being and security of theater workers, and concluded: "Dante's ideas are as self-contradictory as they are outdated. He claims to speak for 'earning one's way,' yet his backer, Ms. Maeve Jerrold, has never known what it is to need a job. We certainly do not protest the wealth that finances this theater, nor its nineteenth-century repertoire. Only its destructive nineteenth-century ideas."

Maeve reached for a gold earloop. "I did have a job once, you know. After my first husband died, I finished my doctorate in comparative literature. I taught freshman composition for a year. I wasn't . . . good at it."

Sanda's dark eyes were soft with sympathy. "I'm sorry about the ad," he said. "It's cruel. But Dante invited it, you know. I mean, when he gives newspaper interviews and says things like 'Featherbedding is for the birds.' Somebody's made a bumper sticker of it! And one of the tabloids runs a cartoon with Shakespeare telling a sanitation worker, 'I work for what I eat.'"

"Earn," Maeve said.

"What?"

"The quote is 'I am a true laborer; I earn that I eat.'"

"Yes, well, I hope quotes are the worst things that happen. Situations like this can get ugly, you know."

She changed the subject quickly, asking what his ex-wife thought about the widening effects of her TV interview.

"I haven't discussed it with her," he said curtly.

Maeve thought then that she understood the purpose of his visit: He wanted her to keep Erik from giving any more incendiary interviews to *Jac's Journal*. But he denied that and began asking questions about Erik: Was he as stubborn as he sounded? Could she persuade him to do business with Codd?

"I'm just the silent partner," she said.

"Silence can be dangerous, Maeve." Sanda drained his glass of Scotch, the late sun glinting on a square gold cufflink. "I'd like to help you, if I can. You didn't ask for my advice, but I do think you should get yourself out of danger. You could cancel Dante's lease on the building—any good lawyer can get you out of it. I'll be glad to recommend somebody, if you like. If Dante doesn't have a physical plant, he'll be out of business long enough for the affair to blow over."

"I can't do that."

"Why not?"

She hesitated. "I could say it's because he's doing a play I wrote."

"Are you saying that?"

"Yes." She leaned forward, wanting suddenly to make someone, anyone, understand. "No. There's more to it than the play. There's . . . *Je l'ai dans la peau*. You know the English for that? How do you deal with something that's inside your own skin? I'm forty-nine, Burt. He's thirty-four. Don't you think he sees every minute of that difference? Do you think I could bear, or would dare, to test what he feels for me by betraying him?"

She watched his embarrassment, wondering tiredly why men so often reacted that way to a woman's emotions. She let him extricate himself from the conversation and then the living room.

At the door his awkwardness melted away. Once again his eyes softened, and he said, "Please think over what I said, Maeve. It's for your own sake. And Dante's too, you know. It could save him a lot of grief." He squeezed her hand and left.

Half an hour later she heard a key in the lock. She smiled.

Erik came in, wearing light slacks, a dark blue shirt, and an air of controlled tension, and carrying a newspaper. He kissed her. "There's something I have to show you," he said. He looked at the coffee table. "But I see you've already got it." He touched her cheek. "Poor sweetheart. I'd give anything if I could keep you out of all this."

She heard herself say, "You could give it up." Quickly she added, "I'm sorry. I didn't mean that."

"Ah, God, I'm the one who should be sorry. For what I'm doing to you."

"But it's my money that makes you vulnerable," she said lightly.

He went to the coffee table. "You realize what that ad is for? To get people to come down and protest. To join the picket line. There, at the bottom—'We ask all who value our contributions to the American theater to join us and show their support.' They could get a good crowd. The ad ran in all the papers."

"How is the picket line today?"

"Noisy. But they're not trying to keep anyone from going in or out."

"I've just realized," Maeve said. "You think it's the battle of *Hernani* all over again, don't you? But that was a battle over art, not money, remember? Is money really worth fighting over? No, no, don't frown, I take it back. I didn't say it. Do you want a drink?"

He glanced at the empty glass, Sanda's, which was still on the table. "I see you're ahead of me." Maeve hesitated, unsure whether to tell him about her visitor.

"No drink for me," he said. "I came about something besides the ad. Jac Sanda called this morning. She's doing something else on the theater tonight. I thought we could watch it together."

In the bedroom the sun's fiery eye was mirrored on the TV screen. Maeve drew the curtains and sat on the bed. "Here's Channel Ten," Erik said. "The *Journal* should be on soon."

She looked at his profile. When she reached over to run her fingers through his hair, he smiled. She wondered how it would feel to have a mind like his inside one's skull, to perceive obstacles as challenges, to be an artist who was also a practical man. But no one, she thought, could ever know such things about another. The skull was the most impenetrable substance on earth, harder than diamonds or tungsten steel: It locked every human being away from all others, a stranger in a shapely cage of bone.

"I don't think I told you," she said after a moment. "I met Burton Sanda years ago, through Arthur."

"Did you?" He swung to her. "What was he like?"

"Oh, pleasant. If a bit slick."

"Intelligent? I suppose so, if Jac married him. Did you meet her, too?"

"No."

"I wonder why she kept his name after they were divorced."

"Why don't you ask her?"

He looked at her oddly and seemed about to say something, but the anchorman gave the lead-in to Jac's *Journal*. When her face filled the screen, he smiled.

Dimly Maeve was aware of Jac's two guests: a TATU stagehand and Frankie, with a moon face beaming above a blue T-shirt lettered "Dante's Infernals," talking about what she did at the theater, talking as excitedly as Erik himself often did. . . . No, Maeve thought, she could not tell Erik about Sanda's visit; he would want to know every detail, and she would have to confess her outburst. Her *tirade d'amour*, delivered simply because the man had been kind and concerned.

She heard Erik laugh, heard the disembodied voices coming from the screen, and finally the set clicking off. "How did you like that?" he said.

"Why is Jac Sanda doing all this?"

"It's a good story, I guess. Hey, let's go have dinner—clams at Scarfuto's. We can talk about the show. And you can tell me what you remember about Mr. Burton Sanda."

"I'd rather stay in, Erik."

"You haven't been anywhere for a week. Not even to the theater."

"I feel . . . better when I'm here."

He looked at his watch. "Actually, I should get back. There's a pile of invoices and checks to sign."

"All right," she said, keeping her voice light, walking to the door with him, holding his hand, making herself let it go easily.

Jac put down her pen and reread her postmortem on the evening's interview. She made a final note, stood to cross to the desk, and stopped; in the space where the closed office door should have been stood Erik Dante.

He smiled. "Beggar that I am, I am even poor in thanks."

"I suppose that's a line from some play?"

"*Hamlet*. If you're in the theater, your thoughts start coming out in other people's words, I'm afraid."

"Sounds like a dangerous habit."

"Sometimes. Once, when a friend of mine was rehearsing Falstaff, he walked into a bar on Seventh Avenue, banged on the counter, and cried, 'Give me a cup of sack, boy!' They damn near threw him out."

She laughed. "You didn't have to come and thank me. There was no need."

"Not even for making it clear tonight that I'm not violating any child-labor laws?"

"My purpose was to present a two-sided interview. You did hear the gentleman from the union talk about how precarious it is to work in the arts? Why a professional's livelihood has to be secured? How difficult the union's entrance exams are?"

"I also heard you ask how complicated the work could be if a

stagestruck teenager could pick up so much of it in a couple months."
He put his hands behind his head. The sleeves of his dark shirt were
rolled to the elbows. "Do you want me to pretend that you're not
helping me? And that I'm not grateful?"

"You raised some issues I think should be explored. That's all."

"Where do your own views lie?"

She realized she was still looking at the naked flesh of his forearms.
"Why do you care what I think?"

"I'm not sure. I only know that I do." He smiled.

Her eyes followed the upcurving of his mouth. "I hope," she said,
"that you don't see me as some kind of symbol of the media you're
trying to influence."

"I don't think so. I think I just . . . see you."

She let her eyes meet his. "Why did you come here?" she said
softly.

For a moment she knew why, knew it as clearly as if the long
muscled arms had reached out to pin her in their circle. She caught
her breath. He brought his arms down slowly. Her breath released in
the same rhythm.

Then, with jolting impersonality, he said, "I came to thank you.
And to ask you a question. Is there anything you know, professionally, about V. I. Joncas of the Brotherhood? Anything about his connections with organized crime?"

She sat down. "Do you mean the rumors that he still has ties to the
Varese family? No one's ever found a shred of proof."

"Has anyone looked very hard?"

"I believe the government has."

"Do you personally think there's anything to the rumors?"

"If you're suggesting that the Varese family is somehow involved
with Morty Codd's union, through Joncas—I think it's pretty far-
fetched."

"Why? The theater is immune to organized crime?"

"No, but . . . I think people are too eager to think in stereotypes.
To assume all unions are crooked just because a few of them are.
There are hundreds of decent unions in this country, you know.
Thousands and thousands of men who abide by the law."

"I know," he said. "I just thought that maybe, as a journalist, you could check around a little. Ask a few questions."

When she didn't answer, he stood up. "I shouldn't ask you," he said. "I shouldn't . . . "

The sentence hung between them, unfinished. He left.

8

The Brotherhood ad was posted on many backstage bulletin boards.

At one Broadway theater, a play about Cosima Liszt Wagner starred a European actress who was famous not only for her talent but also for her political activism; once she had refused a Tony award, to protest British troops in Ireland. She already had tried to enlist her cast and crew in the cause of world revolution, to which she contributed heavily from her family's fortune. In the tattered robe she always wore to make up, she stormed through the dressing rooms, waving the ad, calling on everyone to follow her "down to the robber baron Dante."

Across the street, one of the *grandes dames* of the theater was appearing in a flimsy play that only her warmth and talent kept afloat. The cast gathered in her dressing room while she told, in her gentle, rich voice, horror stories from preunion days: how, for example, a theater manager had refused to pay her for two weeks' work but had suggested she could find a position in his office—a paying one. Backstage the three electricians who had had to be hired to do work one man could handle decided to sign up for picket duty.

Two blocks away a young woman was getting ready to replace the female lead in a play that had been running for two years. She had worked for and dreamed of Broadway all her life; on her face excitement battled cool professionalism. She wanted very much to fit in smoothly with the veterans of the cast, but all around her they were talking about Erik Dante and what to do. Erik had given the young actress her first break—playing the title role in his *Salomé*. So she too went through the dressing rooms, urging her colleagues to go down to the theater—and support Erik. In her agitation she forgot to check that her props had been placed correctly; she couldn't be sure it wasn't an accident that in her big second-act scene, a hand mirror was missing, so that she had to improvise for agonizing minutes, ruining her timing and much of the scene's impact.

At a theater around the corner, an aging actor, whose imperious offstage manner infuriated most of the cast and crew of the comedy in which he was starring, sulked in his dressing room and snapped at his manager: "A nice gesture to the stagehands? To go down to some grubby theater off-Broadway? You've got to be kidding. They want to see gestures, they can watch me onstage. No, no, wait a minute. Find out who is going to go down there. What other stars, I mean."

Two days later, when the technical director of Poets and Paupers returned to the theater from the supply house, he was in a bad mood: The heavy-duty casters he'd ordered for the *Firestorm* revolving unit were mysteriously not available, a man from the Labor Department had shown up to watch the Infernals, and the heat lay as heavy in the air as sawdust.

"You like working in there?" said one of the men on the picket line. He carried a sign that read "We Don't Buy Dante's Pauper Act."

"I like it fine," the tech director said tightly. The chanting started up again around him: "Do not pat-ronize, till they u-nionize." The line had grown since the ad, and some of the newcomers looked familiar to him—not their faces but the feeling that animated them. Once he too had gone out eagerly to march for causes—different ones of course—and there was no mistaking that look of taking-on-the-establishment.

He headed to the alley and the side door to the scene shop, wondering by what screwy logic they had decided that Poets and Paupers was part of the establishment. If it was, he thought, Erik would have called the police that day three years earlier. New on the job, the tech director had gone into a hardware store on Third Avenue and lifted a couple of cheap items. He still didn't know why he had done it, except maybe as a last gesture against the world of paychecks and responsibilities. The owner caught him and was ready to hand him over to the precinct but agreed to call Erik first. Somehow Erik had talked him out of pressing charges. Walking back to the theater, Erik had said, "The way you're running the shop, you've already saved me money and man-hours. Now I've saved your hide. I believe in second chances. But not third ones, OK?"

"Hey," said an older man with a hard, red face, blocking the way to the side door. "Hey, you like working for peanuts?"

"Let me by."

"Hey, look at this guy," yelled the man.

The chanting died down. "Leave him alone," said one of the younger picketers; others shouted their agreement.

"I ain't gonna touch him. I just think he's cute, with all that hair and that pretty blue T-shirt under his coveralls."

The tech director looked at him contemptuously. "Don't tell me you types are still hung up on hair?"

"And what are you hung up on? Being exploited by imperialists?" Startled, the tech director saw that those words had come from a very famous face. He should have known, he thought, that she would show up. "The cause of world revolution supports you!" she cried. "Dante and his rich bitch are exploiting you!"

"Hey!" cried the red-faced man. "Does Maeve Jerrold let you be her shoeshine boy?"

A disapproving murmur came from part of the crowd. "Get out of my way, you bastard," the tech director said. "You and your stupid union—get out!"

The disapproving murmur rose and turned against him. He didn't know which hand moved first, his own or the red-faced man's; but he fell into a whirl of fists and faces that smashed and leered as it spun. Finally it did slow down, and he saw with absurd relief that above one of the blue uniforms that was making the world level again there was a face as black as his own.

* * *

Morty Codd looked around his kitchen with satisfaction before taking up the morning paper. He lifted his cup, smiled at his wife and her excellent coffee, patted the ancient Irish setter sleeping at his feet, and started to read.

The story was on page three: "RACIAL INCIDENT ON THEATER PICKET LINE." Codd read it carefully, especially the statement that there were conflicting reports as to who had begun the fracas. He hadn't been able to sort it out, either; the picket organizer, who should have been on top of things, had been no help. The black man had been treated for cuts and bruises; afterward he'd said, "One of the things about being black is that you can't turn black and blue," and of course that was in the story, too.

The setter growled, and Codd reached down to stroke it, thinking suddenly of Joncas and his fish, wondering why a man would have pets if he thought they were ugly and stupid.

Joncas, he knew, wouldn't like this racial-incident story. He decided it would be best to go see him and then issue a statement—get someone to help him turn out a fancy-sounding paragraph. He would be no good at it himself; he knew he was too hotheaded. Whenever there was violence—anywhere, for any reason—his mind always went back to the old days in Chicago, to the long-ago Memorial Day massacre—when the steelworkers had called a public meeting and the cops had come out with tear gas and clubs and guns. His own brother had come home with his hand broken, hanging as crooked as a puppet's, and blood pouring out of the side of his head. His brother was lucky; ten of the steelworkers had been killed.

"Morty," said his wife's soft voice, "it's too early to look like thunder."

He cleared his thoughts and his forehead. There were things she couldn't understand; she met him only after he left Chicago and came to New York, looking for something in the building trades but discovering the theater. He had liked the idea, but membership in TATU was so restricted he hadn't thought he could get in. Until he discovered that one of the officers of the local regularly took payoffs from producers. Then he had extracted a union card as the price of his silence. He'd had to wrestle his conscience to do it, but now *he* was head of the local, and anyone caught taking payoffs caught hell.

As Mrs. Codd moved to the beautiful birch cupboards he had built for her, to start his breakfast, he leafed through the rest of the paper. He stopped short at a headline on the editorial page: "PICKET LINES BREED A CLIMATE OF VIOLENCE." He read the column, color seeping into his lined face as if through a net.

"Dammit!" he said. "This bastard writes as if we want picket lines! As if it's *our* fault! Don't they understand the whole reason the line is down there is because Dante is keeping us out? Why the hell can't people understand that?"

That evening he appeared on the local news programs, reading a prepared statement: "We deplore the incident at the Poets and Paupers Theater, especially because it was racial in character. TATU is committed not only to justice for *all* workers but also to the peaceful settlement of disputes. However, when an employer embarks on a flagrant policy of antiunionism, then the primary responsibility for creating a climate of violence lies with the employer."

A reporter asked, "Do you mean you're charging the theater management with causing yesterday's fight?"

"We don't know how that particular fight started," Codd said tightly. "But the point is, the theater is determined to keep us out. If they weren't doing that, there wouldn't be any picket line or any 'climate of violence'!"

The man who was watching in his Westchester estate clicked his teeth in irritation and reached to turn off the set, but his hand stopped in midair.

"Is something wrong, Donald?" his mother asked.

"I'm thinking. Just thinking."

Erik and some of the technical crew watched the newscasts up in his apartment. The technical director was so outraged by the "climate-of-violence" charge, and so bitterly self-reproachful for the fra-

cas that caused it, that Erik took him out to dinner. It helped both of
them; to calm down the tech director, Erik had to do the same for
himself.

They wound up discussing the set and went back to the shop to
work for a couple of hours. Around ten they finished. Erik went into
the lobby, chatted with the security guard, and stepped outside to
check everything for the night. The picket line, subdued somewhat
by the "racial incident," had been gone for hours. The street was
silent without their chanting, and clouds were scudding across the
moon. He walked halfway along the block and then turned back. His
feet, in sneakers, struck no sound from the sidewalks.

"Hey, Arrigo," said a voice.

He stopped. So did his breath. A cat slid from a doorway. "Swede?"

"Yeah."

"Come out, then."

The big man came from the same doorway as the cat, and as quietly. "You were looking for me," he said. "I heard it all over."

"Then why did it take you over a week to get here?"

"I'm here now. What you want?"

"Come up to my place, and I'll tell you."

Neither of them spoke while they went into the lobby, past the
quizzical guard, and up to the apartment. The Swede stood inside the
door, surveying the place with blue-gray eyes that challenged the
furnishings. "You don't live so good," he said. "Couple blocks away,
you got winos all over the street."

"That's to remind me of the old neighborhood. Sit down."

The Swede sank heavily into the couch. He wore leather boots,
and over his green shirt was a leather vest with copper studs. "Why'd
you want to see me for?"

"Let's call it family reasons. Did the Varese take you in yet?"

"What if they did?"

"Then you might know something useful."

"You paying for it?"

"Maybe. If it's good."

"Like what?"

"Did Big Tiny send some boys over to trash my theater? And show
up on the picket line?"

The Swede leaned back into the couch. "I heard about that on TV. Why the hell would Big Tiny do it? You think he still remembers you?"

"Oh yes. And you think so, too."

"You were just a kid."

Only thirteen, Erik thought, when Tino "Big Tiny" Varese had heard about him and called him up to the family's local office—on the second floor above a bowling alley, which later had become the Jumping Joint. Tiny said he wanted to meet a kid that young who got away with murder. He had pulled out a twenty and told him to come back for more when he got older. And when Erik threw the money back at Tiny and said he wasn't a hired killer, Tiny had called him a smart-ass kid and laughed and laughed. The whole neighborhood had heard about it.

"You were a jerk," the Swede said. "Big Tiny don't give a crap about you."

"Really? Then how come I saw some men casing this theater one night and one of them was Louie the Limp?"

"You seen Louie here? You sure?"

"About ninety percent sure. And I know damn well that Louie went to work for Big Tiny."

The Swede looked thoughtful. Then he repeated, "Tiny don't give a crap about you."

Erik shrugged. "I guess you should know. You're his right arm by now, I suppose. That's where you said you were headed, the last time I saw you. You must have gotten there in ten years."

"What if I have?"

"Then you know what he's up to. Is he working with Joncas again? I know Joncas threw him out of the transport workers, but that doesn't mean they couldn't be back together. Are they?"

The Swede frowned. "I ain't telling you nothing."

Erik folded his arms and said sarcastically, "You do know who Joncas is?"

The Swede's answer was just as sarcastic. "Sure. He married one of Big Tiny's third cousins."

"Everybody knows that. Don't you know things everybody else doesn't know?" No answer. "Did Joncas get Tiny to work over my

theater?" No answer. "Has Tiny got men in this union I'm fighting?"
No answer. "You're not telling me the union is doing this alone?"

"I ain't telling you a goddamn thing."

"I'll bet I know why," Erik said softly. "I'll bet you don't *know* a
goddamn thing. I'll bet you're no closer to being Tiny's right arm
than his toenails are." He watched clots of color form on the Swede's
cheekbones. "You wanted to be one of the boys Tiny sent over here,
didn't you? Only he figured bricks and garbage and picket line
would be too big a job for you. You're still nothing, Swede, the way
you always were. Still just a street punk for the Varese."

The Swede got to his feet, squaring his shoulders like gun barrels.
"And you're still in the smart-ass business, Arrigo, like you always
were. I'll tell you this much—*somebody'd* like to take your face apart
and I hope to Christ they do. I never shoulda came here. I'm getting
the hell out of this rat hole."

Erik shrugged. "Suit yourself."

The Swede swore briefly and headed for the door. As he reached it
Erik said, "So long. Punk."

The door thudded shut. Boot heels and curses faded down the
stairs.

For a long time Erik stared at the door, his shirt damp with effort.
The hardest of all acting jobs, he thought, was to act as if one felt
nothing.

The Swede got into his car, gunning the engine as if it were a horn,
and pulled out with a screech.

He had made up his mind; he'd been thinking of it for weeks, and
now he really was going to do it. He would make an end run around
Big Tiny, to somebody who would give him the recognition he deserved. Louie the Limp had done it, and he had more to offer than
Louie did. A lot more.

He drove alternating between fury and caution. Someone had
shown him where the place was, but still he was tense each time a
parkway or street sign appeared. With several wrong turns, it took
him over two hours to get there.

Finally he turned into the driveway of the big Westchester estate. Dogs began to bark; he cursed them all the way up, until he stopped at the front entrance, now lit up like a prison yard when somebody had gone over the wall. Two men came running from the house. He tightened his arm over the familiar, steadying bulge under his jacket and said to their tight faces, "I want to see Mr. Shaw."

"He don't see nobody but people he asks to see."

"Yeah? Well, just tell him this." The Swede took a breath and delivered the speech he had rehearsed. Their faces shook down a little, and one of them went inside. The other stayed behind, leaning against the hood of the car, around which the dogs prowled as if they were hungry enough to eat the metal.

Inside the house a slight man in his forties came down the long stairs. A tuft of light brown hair stood up at a sleepy angle, and his face seemed to need glasses; it looked as naked as the pale feet showing beneath his dressing gown. "What is it?" he said. "I suppose you woke up my parents, too." His voice was so deep and authoritative that it seemed impossible for his narrow chest and thin lips to have produced it.

"Sorry, Mr. Shaw," the aide said. "Sorry. But I figured you should hear. Some guy outside says he wants to talk to you."

The man on the stairs waited, his eyes unblinking.

"He says to tell you he figures you ain't happy with a guy named Erik Dante. And that's his brother."

Another unblinking moment. "Bring him in," said the rich voice.

9

Karen Sanda looked pleadingly at her father. "Why can't I stay up till Mother gets home?"

"Because it'll be too late, darling." When Karen's lower lip swelled in protest, Sanda added, "But we can have a story."

Karen clapped her hands, settled on her narrow bed, and tucked a balding cat with blue fur beside her. "What'll it be?" Sanda said, starting the routine he had begun with her when she was three. She was allowed to pick any three objects, as different from each other as possible, and he had to weave them all into one story.

"A cookie," she dared him. "A cookie and a bear . . . and a sunburn!"

"Wow, that's a hard one. . . . Well, once upon a time a girl named Karen Sanda decided to make a gingerbread man, only she forgot to put in the ginger, so he came out all pale . . ." The story flowed easily, for Karen always liberated in him an imagination that he did not otherwise possess. With her, the pressure of client conferences and phone calls and mediation sessions seemed to fall away, leaving the man he knew to be the real Burton Sanda. The true secret of a child's appeal, he had decided, was that one felt free to be, not young again, but oneself again.

"Daddy!" Karen squealed. "How could a bear unzip his coat?"

"He just did it. Zip, zap, zoom. Because he wanted to be a bare-naked bear . . ." Sanda's mind leaped ahead to what he had to say to Jac. He hadn't planned to do it that night, but when he brought Karen home from the zoo and an early dinner, the woman who looked after her had said Jac would be quite late. And when he heard where Jac was going, he had sent the woman home and decided to wait.

"Daddy!" Karen tugged at his hand; he had stopped talking. He went on, spinning out the story until her lids grew heavy, finishing with the bear and the gingerbread man each giving her a bear hug.

He stood quietly, turned out her light, and went to the living room to wait for Jac. However long she took and whatever she was doing.

A flute began to play. A young woman stood with arms tight behind her back, staring ahead fixedly. Slowly she looked down at her feet, which seemed to be rooting her to the ground. A look of disbelief crossed her face. Her shoulders twisted, and her body began to move—slow, dancelike gyrations that lifted her head higher and higher, as if she were trying to break free of the anchor of her feet. Her body stretched like a bowstring; her mouth opened in a howl that was all the stronger because it was soundless. Then her body sagged, lifeless but still hanging on an invisible stake. The flute gave a shriek of triumph and stopped.

The director of *Firestorm* was crouched at the edge of the stage. "Too quick at the end," he said to the woman. "The rest is good—feeling the first touch of the fire, lifting yourself away, and the scream. But when unconsciousness hits, you can't let go so fast, like a sack of cement. Let's go back. Sound, cue up again."

From one of the back rows of the darkened theater, where she had been for an hour, Jac watched the actress position herself to do it again. The scene apparently was the first in a series of battles: Three victims of ignorance and hatred—put to death at the stake, by a firing squad, and in the gas ovens—were pitted against three primitive creatures who pleaded for warmth. Sitting above and behind them, on a platform, was a watching figure who moved or stretched only during the breaks; yet he dominated the action. His immobility was the most intense form of motion on the stage.

He stood up and came down from the platform. Jac saw that he wore an old pair of work pants and a blue T-shirt lettered "Dante's Infernals." He began to speak.

The director's voice interrupted him in mid-phrase. "Erik, sorry. It's eleven o'clock. If we finish the scene, we're on overtime."

The other figures onstage tensed slightly and looked at Erik.

"I haven't said a line the whole goddamn night. This speech will just take five minutes."

"It's in the rulebook," said one of the actors defensively. "Anything over eight hours goes into overtime."

For a moment Jac was sure Erik's next movement would be explosive, but he merely shrugged and said, "Let's quit."

Quietly people began to leave. As the stage lights started to go out, he called, "Leave me some work lights." When he was alone, he looked out into the dark and said, "So you did come."

"How did you know I was here?"

"Prometheus is a god. Gods can see in the dark, like cats. Why don't you come up?"

She took her shoulder bag and went up the aisle, her slim brown skirt sliding against her thighs. He put out a hand and helped her up the steps at the side of the stage. "I'm sorry I couldn't come down during the day," she said, "but it was chaos right up to airtime. And I didn't want to discuss what I have to say over the phone."

"It's all right. This way, you got to watch rehearsal."

"I think I see why the critics have been good to Poets and Paupers." She hesitated. "I have to ask you—if there wasn't any rulebook, what would you have done?"

"Asked everybody to stay for ten minutes, then stood for a round of beers."

"What if they're afraid to say no because you might lower their salaries or fire them?"

"Look," he said, "when you work a long day, you should get off early another time. But when you try to turn that principle into specific rules to cover hundreds of situations, then you get into these idiotic clock-watching tugs-of-war. And the parties start to feel they are at war."

"But suppose you ran a factory, with hundreds of workers? Where the work isn't fun but mindless and stupefying?"

"I don't know. I'm not a captain of industry. Just a poor sonofabitch trying to run his theater without a lot of interference." He smiled. "Have you been on stage before?"

"Not since high school graduation."

"Take a walk around."

She moved forward, her sandals clacking hollowly on the bare wood. "Are there trapdoors in the floor?"

"Yes. For bringing scenery up from the shop in the basement."

There was nothing on the stage but the platform on which he had sat. Light came in harsh white spills from some metal cones hanging just inside the proscenium arch. She went to the center of the stage and turned around slowly. On three sides was space bounded by bare concrete walls. Above her head was more space, a hint of rope lines in its depth, and in front of her was the dark auditorium, with a dim suggestion of headless rows. "It seems so much bigger, and yet so . . ." She stopped; her voice was too loud and hollow.

He was sitting against the arch, watching her, one leg stretched in front of him, like a man relaxing in his home. "Some people say an empty stage is full of ghosts, but I think it's empty of everything. That's why I like it. Bare space, waiting to be filled, with whatever one chooses."

"You could say that about a TV screen, too."

"But the screen shrinks everything. Brings it down to the size of your own living room and your daily life. The stage makes you sit up, and look up. Maybe the camera can't lie about things, but for me the stage can go even deeper. It can strip away all the clutter and give you the heart of an experience."

"This theater means a lot to you, doesn't it?"

"It's mine," he said softly. "I earned it."

From somewhere below a voice called, "Erik, I'm leaving. Everything's locked up, except the front."

"OK," he called back.

A door slammed. The echo rolled around them and was pulled up into the blackness overhead, leaving behind a space that seemed smaller.

"Let me tell you why I wanted to talk to you," she said. "About Joncas and the Varese—I'm afraid you're on the wrong track. I checked with several people who would know. A newspaper colleague who's covered every mob story in New York for the past ten years, and someone at the Organized Crime Strike Force. They both say there isn't anything to the rumors—just some people's desire to keep a colorful story afloat. Joncas really did throw the Varese out of several Brotherhood unions. He got the transport workers one of the best pension and welfare plans in the country, and then he extended it to the whole Brotherhood. And he—"

"You're selling very hard," Erik said.

She felt herself flushing. "I just don't want to see you waste your time and talent on this mob idea. I know how you must feel, especially after that business on the picket line, but wouldn't it be better to be realistic?"

"I guess so." He got to his feet. "Except that I learned something a couple nights ago. Someone is looking to take my face apart—I think that was the expression. And because of who my informant is, he had to be referring to someone in the underworld."

"Who was the informant?"

"Someone I know pretty well but may not be able to trust. Call him a family member."

"One of the Varese?"

"In a way. But I really meant a member of my own family."

"You don't mean you have relatives in the mob?"

"On the fringes. Where I grew up, in Brooklyn, the Varese looked to a lot of the kids like the best way out of the ghetto."

"But you took the theater instead."

"It would make a good story to say I was rescued by Shakespeare, wouldn't it? By a production of *Henry V* here in the city that some teacher took us to." He lifted his head and called out, " 'O for a muse of fire, that would ascend the brightest heaven of invention . . . And it did, with horses and armies riding out of your imagination.' He turned back to her. "But the truth is that I got out in order to earn a living. On the docks for five years, loading and unloading cargo. Of course the Varese ran the local, but I liked a lot of the men I worked with."

"Why did you leave?"

"There was a strike." He started moving around the stage. "Strongarm tactics were, shall we say, not frowned upon? Except by me. I got into a hell of a fight about it with the picket organizer. He wound up with a broken arm, which is pretty ironic, and I wound up leaving. I wanted to get away from places where I could hurt people. And cause a climate of violence," he added sourly.

"I think Morty Codd's charge, trying to blame you for *his* picket line, is ridiculous," she said. "Where did you go after the docks?"

He passed the proscenium arch, touching it with one hand. "I hung around Broadway for a while—I didn't really know there were any other kinds of theaters then—talking to some of the technicians. TATU people, a lot of them. I learned it was almost impossible to get in without some kind of clout. I also learned there was a hell of a lot of payoff going on. I decided it wasn't for me, after all."

"But what about acting?"

"At the time," he said slowly, "I didn't think that was possible. So I just . . . got out of New York. Bought a bus ticket to Indianapolis, because I liked the name. From there I moved around the country, doing odd jobs, talking to people. It's a hell of a country, you know that?" He stopped by the platform. "So that's how you get people to talk to you. You ask questions and then *listen* to the answers."

"It doesn't work if people don't want to give them."

He said nothing. His face was partly in shadow, but she could feel his eyes moving over her face. "Tell me," she said, "that logo you use for the theater—the beggar child who wants the moon—is that you?"

He leaned against the platform and put his hands behind his head. His upper arms made two triangles of smooth, hard flesh; a blue vein swelled on one of them. "Don't all children want the moon?" he said.

She smiled. "I hope so. I think my daughter does. And I think you still have that feeling—that you can reach up and pull down something you want."

He said nothing.

"Or maybe you feel that you've put something of yourself up there, to hang where everybody can see it. Including you."

He brought his arms down slowly. "I shouldn't have told you to come here. We should have talked on the phone."

"Why?"

"I feel too free when I'm on a stage."

But she did not feel free, she thought; she felt locked inside a cage of space, with him.

"You should leave," he said.

"Why?"

"Because for me, this is the place to take risks."

"I thought an actor had to have control."

"Yes, but not caution. You have to be willing to make a mistake, to try for the outer reaches of your imagination. And your desires."

"Is that how you think of me?" she said. "As a mistake and a risk?"

"I'm afraid I just . . . think of you." He held out his hand to her. "That's why I told you to come down here tonight."

She felt herself entering the channel of space that still separated them; she tried to root her feet to the floor, but her shoulders twisted, and she moved, pulled by his eyes, pulled within his grasp, her mouth opening to meet the silk of his lips in soundless acceptance.

He pulled back so his lips were barely free of hers and said, "I knew you would feel this way. The right size." She smiled, because her body felt stronger and taller than ever, yet smaller, too, dwarfed in a way it had never been. His lips closed over her smile, and his hands went deep into her hair and moved along her bare arms. In some small corner of her mind she stood watching with astonishment because the waves of sensation mounted so quickly inside her, and spread so far, and went so deep.

He broke away, and then he was on the platform, pulling off his clothes as unselfconsciously as if he were alone. He stood looking down at her, very tall and lean; she wanted to look up at him for a moment, but he reached down and pulled her up. He made her stand quietly while he slipped off her clothes, and the act of being motionless under his hands made the sensations go deeper and rise higher, thudding against the confinement of her skin. He smiled and pulled her to the carpet he had made of his clothes, and she saw that she sank down on the legend "Dante's Infernals." He moved his mouth lingeringly on each of her breasts, as if answering their cry, and then down to her stomach, leaving a bruise over the place he would enter; she twisted around, wanting her mouth on him, too, wherever he wanted it, though he had not said a word; she felt all of her body becoming a space only he could fill, and at last he did so, making her want to close around him more tightly still. She lost the capacity to distinguish between the motions of her own body and the sensation of his; there was a single driving force urging a single body on to the moment of greatest tension, which was also the moment of greatest release.

When she looked outward again, she saw the dark cavern overhead, where ropes were strung, and the bare concrete walls, and the cones of harsh light. He was sitting beside her, his lips soft and full, the dark blond hair loose over his eyes. "Jac," he said softly. "Why does a woman like you have a name like Jac?"

"It's short for Jacqueline. Which sounds too much like somebody's pet." He smiled. "Were you really born Erik Dante?" she said.

"It's close enough. But you are not." He bent down, his mouth just meeting the corner of hers but its touch running down the length of her body.

Her cab headed up Third Avenue, its motion pulling the still air through the open window and creating a warm, false wind that agitated her hair. The only other motion she felt was internal: her body still holding the aftershocks of sensation, her mind struggling for supremacy over them.

For her mother's generation, she thought, sex had been either a sin or a sacrament, unmentionable in either case. Her own generation had rebelled and divorced sex from both poles; she knew people who announced their physical desire as casually as if they were ordering from a fast-food counter: "I want to sleep with you." "Fine. How do you want it?"

She closed her eyes and leaned back. The trouble was that she had behaved tonight as if sex were fast food but had felt as if it were some kind of profound commitment.

And if it were, where would it lead? Consider the issue, she thought wryly; arrive at the fundamental questions. Her mind tried to do so, but her body responded with a faint tremor, and as the cab turned into Gramercy Park, she abandoned that thought, and all others. When she went into the building and up in the elevator, she was thinking of his hair and mouth and eyes, and when she took out her keys and pushed open the door of the apartment, she was smiling.

She saw a blur of dark clothes against the pale gold of the couch and a filigree of cigarette smoke. "Burton," she said stupidly. "What's wrong? Is it Karen?"

She saw him get up, heard the reassurance and the explanation of his presence. "All right, we can talk," she said, sinking into a chair, "but not long. I'm exhausted."

"You shouldn't work so late. It's almost one o'clock. Karen missed saying good night to you."

"You know I'm usually here for her bedtime. What do you want?"

He sat back on the couch, putting out his cigarette with three meticulous taps. She saw his square jaw lift slightly, and marveled that a single moment could summon so many ghosts. "Mary told me you were at the Poets and Paupers Theater," he said. "Which happens to be what I wanted to talk to you about." She made her hand settle slowly on the arm of the chair. He went on. "I suppose you thought it was a *coup* when you launched that story."

"Obviously you didn't."

"Hardly the first time we've disagreed." He smiled for a moment, his easy charm as strong as when she had seen it first, as a college senior who called the eminent labor lawyer's office with some questions for a term paper. "How long are you going to keep on with the story?" he said.

"As long as there are things to say. Don't forget that the days when you could influence my work are over."

"And you could hardly wait for that to happen, could you?"

"I did consumer stories for three years because of your position. Because it could have been a conflict of interest for Burton Sanda's wife to do political stories."

"Which you wanted to do a hell of a lot more than you wanted to be Burton Sanda's wife."

"Burt," she said more quietly, "let's not rehash ancient history. We might say things we'd regret."

"You mean I might, don't you?"

"Either of us," she said evenly. But she knew the night he was recalling. He had been in the midst of his first and only try for political office, for the House of Representatives, and while they were discussing their possible future, he had said, in reference to something she no longer recalled, "But in Washington you'll have time." Six innocuous words. But they had made her go rigid with disbelief: the man whose rational attitudes she had admired, who talked as if their relationship was truly one of equals, could not possibly be assuming that she automatically would give up her work for him. But he was. He had admitted finally that he expected her career to bend to his, that his took precedence. Her disbelief had turned to rage; from the corners of her mind, where she had tucked them carefully for months—perhaps for years—all the things that disturbed her had come rushing forward, to take up the flag of this treachery: something that finally was definite and provable, because he was admitting it. At the end, her rage had turned into the demand for a divorce, which no amount of his apologies and pleas could alter. Only the thought of Karen could have stopped her. Should have stopped her, perhaps. But it hadn't.

She watched him light another cigarette. " 'The past is a bucket of ashes,' " she said.

"I don't want the present to be a can of worms."

"Meaning?"

"I don't like to see my daughter's mother become a mouthpiece for an antiunion crusade."

"I'm not a mouthpiece for anybody. And what's it got to do with Karen?"

"Don't you realize you're in the public eye? There are lunatics out there. You make one of them mad, and he could take it out on Karen."

"That's pretty feeble, Burt. Can't you invent a better story? Or maybe even tell the truth. Which client is it who's upset? Which one of your union-leader buddies? The one who tried to get you elected?"

"Leave Joncas out of this. He has nothing to do with it. He's a professional associate, that's all."

Her head began to ache, as if questions were building up pressure. "Why don't you ever want to talk about Joncas?"

He shot to his feet. "That would clear your conscience, wouldn't it? To think I'm in bed with him?"

"My conscience is fine," she cried, leaping up too.

"How can it be? After all your talk about politics needing men of principle, you're the one who cost me the election. You couldn't wait till it was over—you had to get the divorce right away!"

"Because I don't believe in hypocrisy! And it wasn't the divorce that hurt you. It was your opponent."

"I know that's how you rationalize it, but the fact is that you di
me a lot of harm. And now you're doing it again—helping that dam
Boy Scout actor. I suppose you think he's *right*, is that it?"

"I think he's something much rarer—someone who stands up an
fights for what he believes is right."

"My God, you never change. Two teaspoons of morality ever
night before bed. That's supposed to make it all right, whatever yo
do to me? How do you think it looks when my ex-wife is giving air
time to this goddamn Dante? And that's not all she's giving him!" Hi
jaw was high now, his eyes bright as glass. "You're sleeping wit
him—I knew it the minute you came in the door. You think I don'
remember what that cat smile means?"

She forced her voice out, past the air frozen in her throat. "It's n
business of yours what I do."

"Do you even *know* what you're doing? You've heard abou
Dante's silent partner, Maeve Jerrold? Well, he's getting a hell of
lot more from her than capital. Ah, you didn't know that, did you
Some reporter you are. You think he's going to cut off the hand tha
feeds him? He's just using you to get stories on the air."

"Don't! Please don't!"

It took Jac a moment to realize that the words had come not fron
her but from Karen, who stood in the hallway to the bedrooms, he
face a blur of sleep and hurt. "Mother, don't be mad at Daddy
please."

Jac ran to her. It felt as if she were running backward in time, to th
child she had been herself.

10

At seven A.M. Maeve was still up. Unable to sleep, as she often wa
she had been listening all night to music while looking through he
old notebooks full of poetry.

Every so often she took them out to see whether a fresh eye woul solve the problems in certain lines that had always bothered her. Some of the poems were over thirty years old and contained lines that still were off—not in major respects but in ways so slight that they tortured her by eluding correction.

Only two people besides herself had ever seen the notebooks; Erik was one of them. She had hesitated for a long time before showing them to him, the way she had hesitated before going to bed with him, and for the same reason: It would hurt so much more when he finally did leave her.

If she had never shown him the notebooks, she thought, he never would have seen *Firestorm* and persuaded her that it was stageworthy, and the whole dreadful situation would not now exist: no ads, no picket lines, no appearances for Erik on a TV news show with an interviewer who—

The intercom buzzer sounded. When Maeve answered, she heard that two repairmen were on their way up to check the air conditioning. She put her hands to her hair, which she had not shaped into its coil, and then shrugged. When the doorbell rang, she undid the locks, ready to say, "You're at work very early," but the two men in coveralls also wore partial face masks.

They came in, shoving her backward. Then they took out guns.

She screamed: a long, high, liquid sound.

The phone woke Erik, pulling his eyes open.

The first thing they saw was the inner sight of Jac—smiling, laughing, moving to him, her presence so vivid that he nearly reached out for her.

He turned his head and saw the framed sketch of the beggar child and the moon.

He realized after a moment that nothing in the room had moved; it was only his own perspective, jolted back to reality.

He got up to shower and shave, letting the phone ring.

With a cup of coffee, he wandered around the apartment, stopping by the wall filled with production photographs. The theater, he thought, had given him the sense of experiencing things in a form more intense than reality usually provided, or than he would permit.

Now, with Jac, he had had that sense in reality. And the hunger he felt for her was even greater for having been satisfied.

It had been that way with the theater, too. When he finally found it.

He had been in Colorado, in country that rimmed his vision with mountains. By then he had been roaming for several years, stopping to work whenever he needed money: on the Minnesota grain harvest, a Kansas construction site, a Wyoming ranch. In the small Colorado town, a poster had caught his eye: A summer theater was opening that night. He had squeezed his frame into one of its rows of old church pews. When the stagecoach lamps that were the house lights went out and the faded curtains parted, he felt salt in his eyes; at the end of the first act, the tremors in his muscles told him he hadn't moved for nearly an hour.

Afterward he had gone into the street and then along a trail that led out of town, walking until the tree branches snared the cold fire of the rising sun. He had believed so strongly in one's obligation to earn a living; why had he tried to do so only by means of using his muscles—on the docks or behind a tractor or a drill? Even the attempt to find technical work on Broadway had been a compromise, he saw; what he wanted wasn't really technical work. It was to be part of the plays themselves. So why hadn't he tried?

The answer had been as chilling as the air that frosted his breath: It simply had never entered his mind that a career as an actor was possible to him. That people who wrote plays, and acted and directed in them, did so to earn a living. He laughed at his idiocy, then stopped laughing and looked deeper, realizing that on the same day he had discovered the theater—at that performance of *Henry V*—he had both fallen in love with it and accepted that it had no bearing on his own world. The true ugliness of poverty, he saw, was not its physical grip but the mentality it bred, which he had accepted: the view that reality was grim, and anything that was not grim could not be part of reality.

He still could feel the knobby texture of the rock against which he had leaned, swearing to let himself know what he wanted, always, and never again to place it outside the realm of the possible. Later that day he had gone to the theater and offered to work as an apprentice. By the middle of the summer they were paying him to do small parts; at the summer's end he had set off with two of the company members who were heading for New York.

The phone cut into his thoughts again. He ignored it, finished dressing, and went down into the lobby.

"Hi," said Ruth, who ran the box office. "Aren't the police going to close down that picket line? After what happened?"

"They're checking it more often now. Aren't you afraid to come down here, Ruthie?"

"Sure. So what?" She tossed her head, rocking the piled white frosting of her hair. "That guy from the Producers League called. He wanted to know if you got their letter—you know, the one calling you an irresponsible bastard in such nice, polite language? And Mrs. Jerrold called twice in the last ten minutes."

Erik's smile remained in place, like something applied with spirit gum. He went into the office, sat at the desk, and reached for the phone. But he couldn't lift the receiver; the weight in his mind seemed to settle in his fingers and paralyze them. He would either have to relegate Jac Sanda to the realm of the impossible or accept what he felt and tell Maeve about it.

He had never given Maeve as much of himself as she wanted, he thought. But he had never given anyone more.

The phone rang beneath his fingers, three times. There was a pause, then a buzzer signal from Ruth. He lifted the receiver.

Maeve's voice came from it like water under pressure.

"What?" he said. "When? . . . Did they hurt you? . . . What did they tell you? . . . It'll be all right, Maeve. I'll be there in five minutes and I'll take care of you. I won't let anything happen to you. I promise. Now, let me hang up, so I can get to you right away."

Her hair was hanging loose, but her eyes seemed frozen on some inner sight, which she described over and over. "They said they had to check the air conditioning. But when I opened the doors, they had masks. And guns. Two guns. Like a pair of eyes that never blinked.

They said I had to close down the theater, turn you out. Or else they would come back. And the guns would be used." She looked as if she were held together by spiderwebs.

"It's all right," Erik kept saying. "You're safe. I'm here."

"Settle with Codd! That's what they want. Give up this crazy fight!"

"I can't, Maeve. It's gone too far. Don't ask that of me, please."

"Oh, God, don't look at me when I'm this way." She ran her hands along her pale lilac robe and then brought them up to cover her face. "Maeve, Maeve, rhymes with not brave. . . . I despise the way I am!"

"You can't blame yourself for being afraid of a couple of thugs with guns."

"You wouldn't be."

"Of course I would. Anybody would."

She sank on the gray silk couch. "You wouldn't feel this way. Those men couldn't do this to you!"

"Maeve, please. You're making it a hundred times worse than it is. Somehow you're . . . you're afraid of the fact that you're afraid."

"You don't know what it does to me! Do you know what it feels like to have your nerves crawl backward and try to pull you inside with them?"

"No, I don't. But I do know that fear can't hurt you unless you let it make your decisions for you."

"That's like telling a cripple her paralyzed legs shouldn't matter."

"You're not a cripple, Maeve."

She twisted to one side, hands still covering her face. "I know what I am. The woman who had everything and did nothing. Silver spoons and private schools, a doting family that actually encouraged her to be a poet. So why wasn't she—"

"Please, darling, stop it." He sat beside her.

"Oh, God, I wish I could." She moved into the curve of his arm as if it were a tree in a storm. He could feel the shivering of her body, and her mind. "I wish I could have made myself into someone different," she said. "I wish I hadn't fallen apart when Jonathan died. Do you know it was years before I could ride in a car?"

"Don't think of that now," he said, knowing that if she did, she would relive completely the night when her first husband had been struck by a hit-and-run driver and left to die at the side of the road. "What matters is that you did finally pull yourself together."

"Oh, yes. To finish a doctorate that was about as practical as learning to make bows and arrows." He stroked her hair, his face tight with helplessness; in six years, he had never figured out how to deal with her when she was in this mood. "I couldn't even teach!" she said. "I couldn't do what thousands of people do every day. I ran back to my father and brothers. And when I married someone like them— someone practical—I couldn't even make a go of that! I did try to live his kind of life, poor man, but I couldn't. He divorced me, and I don't blame him!"

"All right, Maeve," he said. "Your whole life has been a failure. Is that what you want me to say?"

The shivering stopped. She sat up straight. "God knows I've been indulged in every material respect, so I can't complain if I have to pay the price."

"Don't talk as if you deserve some kind of punishment! As if you're the rich lady who can never get into heaven."

"No. I'm the failed poet who lives by the grace of practical men."

"Who hasn't tried to get published for years. Who's always telling me *Firestorm* won't get on."

"Will it?"

"Yes, goddammit, yes! I'm going to show you that something you want can be accomplished, if I have to walk through fire to do it!"

"Why should you? I gave up expecting success a long time ago."

"That's exactly the reason! Sometimes I wonder if you really want to succeed. Sometimes I think you like dreams only so long as they're impossible ones."

His words hung in the air, punctuated only by her small, forlorn sound. He told himself he was a bastard, saying that to her only because he couldn't say other things. "Christ," he whispered. "I'm sorry."

"I only wish I could help you. Instead of being the way I am."

"My God, look at everything you've done to help me."

"I don't mean money." She turned to him. "I mean help you the way Jac Sanda does."

He would not turn away from her gaze, but it seemed a very long moment. "You've helped me," he said, "more than anyone ever has, or will. And now you're going to be safe. Here's what we'll do. Those men threatened you because the theater is in a building you own. So you'll have to evict Poets and Paupers. Once we're out, you'll be safe. Or at least safer. I'll find someplace else to go."

"No! I won't throw you out! You can't make me!"

"Then I'll have to get whoever sent those two bastards and put a stop to it."

"You can't put yourself in danger!"

"Maeve, something has to be done to keep you safe. Why don't you leave town, then? Go to Paris or London for a while. Or out to Chicago to see your family."

"No! I'd rather die than leave you!"

"Then at least go to some hotel, where you can be incognito."

"I can't, Erik. I can't!" She slid to the floor and looked at him, hands across his knee as if it were the railing in a church. "How can you ask me to leave you? Don't ask that, don't ask me to leave you!"

He looked down at her for a long time. "You're right," he said finally. "I can't ask it."

Long after he had gone, Maeve sat by her bedroom window, staring at the orange ball of the setting sun. For a moment it seemed to hold, condensed into one blinding sensation, the year of her first marriage, when, in a haze of love and confidence and creative power, she had written *Firestorm* while Jonathan worked on his own poetry.

Threads of fire began to unravel across the sky. Some of them were red, almost like trickles of blood, running. . . . That was the terror of blood, she thought: It could still run, even when its owner couldn't any longer. For an instant, in her mind's eye, it was not Jonathan who lay at the edge of the road, but Erik.

She turned her head sharply to banish the sight. But the feeling lingered—of disaster, coming from nowhere, confirming one's expectations.

Just like the expression on Erik's face, she thought. Perhaps he hadn't realized it. Perhaps when she mentioned Jac Sanda, he had been aware only of a feeling of control and not of the guilt that had darted to its surface for a moment, like a bird smashing against a window and then jerking away.

She visualized him: naked, smiling, holding out his arms to the Sanda woman; putting a hand into her long dark hair, pulling her body to his own, which gleamed like marble; but they met in a fusion of fires.

She stared into the sun again. Gradually some words of poetry came into her mind, words Baudelaire had put into the mouth of Icarus as he tried to reach the sun on wings of wax. *Sous je ne sais quel oeil de feu, Je sens mon aile qui se casse; Et brûlé par l'amour du beau* . . . So beautifully simple, she thought, yet not so simple to render into English. "Under I know not what eye of fire, I feel that my wing is breaking; And burned up by love of beauty . . ." It would have to be "Under an unimaginable eye of fire." Or perhaps "An eye of unimaginable fire."

She thought of the solution she had found to the impasse between her and Erik, a way around the fact that he would not settle with the union and she would not evict the theater. It had come to her while he was speaking of his gratitude. Eventually he had accepted it.

Gratitude was the meanest of ties, she thought, one that could become a chain and strangle all other feelings. If in fact any of those other feelings still existed.

As she watched the sun's fire melt its way along the horizon, she began to feel calm—gliding out to meet the fire on arms that were wings, lifting her face to the touch that would be so warm at first and then would begin to scorch, feeling her wings turn brittle and frail and finally surrender their burden.

11

The Joncases made their way into a hotel ballroom where a glittering cocktail party was in full voice. A group called Friends of Broadway was staging the affair, both to publicize and to raise funds for its crusade to save a landmark Times Square theater.

Monday evening had been chosen for the affair because most of Broadway was dark on Mondays; the casts of the top shows in town could be well represented.

A musical-comedy star, feeling euphoric because she was free of the stagefright that paralyzed her every other night of the week and twice on matinee days, sailed toward Joncas, arms wide, but at the last moment she felt the barricade of his personality and decided not to embrace him. "I'm going to go on your picket line," she said. "It's a wonderful idea."

Joncas smiled.

Over the next hour many of the other performers approached him to tell him the same thing—even including the famous comedian who was on his seventh wife ("Marriage?" he often said. "I'm gonna keep doing it till I get it right.") and the staggeringly beautiful ingenue who wore satin jeans, diamonds, and little else, and had a longshoreman's vocabulary.

At the massive buffet table the mayor of New York was talking with one of the state's senators; the mayor waved the Joncases over with a hand holding an impaled shrimp. Cecelia Joncas said little, merely listening to a conversation that seemed to be about the transport negotiations.

When they moved away, Cecelia whispered, "I never can tell what the mayor's thinking. Was he criticizing you?"

"He was just telling me, in his subtle way, that he won't back off. That he's going to keep using public opinion to put the screws on the transport union—to try to make them give back what he calls 'productivity points.'"

"Good heavens. Doesn't he remember how much you did to help him get elected?"

Joncas laughed and squeezed her hand. "Don't ever change," he said.

They stayed for another half-hour, talking to the wizened, jewel-encrusted widow who was spending her husband's fortune on the opera, to the head of the country's third largest bank, and finally, to the performer who headed the Guild of Stage Actors. He told Joncas that the Guild had now decided to have official sign-up sheets for supporting the TATU picket line and would be informing the press each day which celebrities would be there.

As they were leaving, a hand with inch-long violet nails touched Joncas's sleeve, and one of the most famous voices in America drawled, "Joncas, darling, I hope you don't expect me to show up on your picket line."

Joncas raised one black eyebrow. "Kerry, I've never deluded myself into thinking that your loyalties lie with the labor movement."

"That's right. They lie here." The violet nails tapped their owner's chest. The woman laughed huskily and moved on.

On the way home in their limousine, Cecilia said, "Vi, how do you know Kerry London?"

"Oh, we met somewhere."

"What's she like? Does she really do the things they say? I mean, have temper tantrums and refuse to sing unless they put fresh orchids in her dressing room every night?"

"She behaved when I saw her," Joncas growled. The growl was deceptive; in fact the party had put him into a good mood. He took Cecelia's hand.

When they got home, she followed him into his den. "Why wasn't Morty Codd there, by the way?"

Joncas grunted and pressed several wall switches. The TV went on; so did a light above a small aquarium, where the fish glided on unperturbed, their lidless stares affected by neither dark nor light. Joncas pulled off his tie and said, "Codd wouldn't know how to swim in that kind of water."

Cecelia sat on the arm of a chair and mused, "You know, Vi, they all seemed to respect you. Well, maybe not the one who swore so much—why does a pretty girl like that have to swear all the time? doesn't she know how unladylike it is?—but the rest of them . . . When they talked to you, they seemed to be, I don't know . . ."

"Afraid of me?"

"Good heavens! I hope not. That wouldn't be very nice, would it?"

Joncas smiled. "Under that very sleek black dress, which I look forward to helping you out of after dinner, there's a naive old-country mamma, isn't there?"

"Grandmamma, pretty soon. Don't forget that Coral's in her seventh month."

"How could I forget? She's too damn young to be having a baby. Or even to be married. A husband still in school, for God's sake!"

"Now, now, Vi. They're in love. That's all that matters."

Joncas reached for a jar of fish food. When he scattered some on the water, all the fish darted to it. He looked at them affectionately; they were too stupid to know their whole world was just a glass cage in the corner of someone's den. Someone who had figured out the ultimate way of controlling the bait.

"Oh dear," Cecelia said. "That theater is on the news again."

Joncas raised his eyes to the TV screen. A reporter was saying, "Maybe you thought a theater ticket was just a ticket. But Erik Dante, much in the news lately because of a union-organizing dispute at his Poets and Paupers Theater, has a different idea."

The image shifted to a film clip of Erik holding a press conference. "We're scheduled to open at the end of September," he said, "with an original play called *Firestorm*. As of today, I'm asking the public to show whether they approve or disapprove of the position I've taken. From now on, all *Firestorm* ticket orders will be tallied as votes of support, and the figures will be released to the press each week."

The reporter's face filled the screen again. "Dante insisted that his new ticket-as-a-vote crusade is not just a promotion gimmick. It's too dangerous to be that, he said, because the public could go against him and buy so few tickets that he'd have to close down."

"Then it's a very foolish thing to do," Cecelia said. "Or is it very smart?" Her husband didn't answer.

The reporter went on. "Dante had another surprise announcement to make today."

Erik's face reappeared. "My second item pertains to the building he theater leases. Formerly it belonged to my partner, Maeve Jerold. It no longer does. I own it now."

"Why?" called half a dozen reporters' voices.

"Some people apparently thought they could intimidate Mrs. Jerold through her ownership of the building. This is to let them know hey can't, that all intimidation will have to be directed at me." He ·aised his hands to silence the calls of "Who?" and "What do you nean?" and said, "The people who did it will know what I mean. That's all I have to say."

"That sonofabitch," Joncas muttered. He pressed a switch, and the TV went off.

"I don't care what he's done," Cecelia said. "I wish you wouldn't ise that kind of language."

"I use what fits. You want to leave me alone for a while, sweetheart? I've got something to do."

"I don't like to see that look on your face."

"That's why I'm telling you to leave. OK?"

"I don't like it!" Cecelia's voice was uncharacteristically sharp. "You get that look on your face, and then you tell me to leave . . . just the way you . . . I don't like it!"

Joncas went to her, squeezing her shoulder. "Cara, don't worry. Everything's fine. I'll be up in a little while, OK?"

She hesitated, smoothed the black cap of her hair, and left him.

Joncas reached into a cabinet behind his desk for a phone he used only occasionally, and then to dial only one number. The phone was checked regularly to make sure there were no taps on it. When a resonant voice answered, Joncas said, "I just saw the news. You sonofabitch."

There was a pause. "What happened to 'hello'? I thought you were the one with the fancy manners."

"And I thought you were going to stay out of this! Did you send some boys over to twist the woman's arm?"

"So?"

"So why?"

"After you told me the actor was sleeping with her, I figured it was worth a try."

"It wasn't worth a damn thing!" Joncas said. "You got him into the building more solidly than ever. And now he's on TV hinting that somebody used muscle on her!"

"If it wasn't for you, I'd have gotten rid of him right at the beginning, and this whole business would be over already."

"Dammit, what else have you done?"

"Nothing."

"You swear?" Joncas said.

"Maybe you forgot, oaths are for Italians. I'm *telling* you I haven't done anything else. I sent some of the boys over to case his theater, the night he did that TV debate with your stupid fish-name friend, but that's all. The rest of the time I've been bowing to your superior wisdom. To your stupid P.R. campaign."

"Don't knock it. It's doing exactly what I planned—diverting attention from what the actor is actually saying and making it an issue of his being antiunion. We got a lot of coverage, you know, especially since the so-called racial incident. Some big-name stars have already gone down there to put in time for the TV cameras, and a lot more are going to go. And it's getting wider than the theater, which is good. Yesterday we had a group of NYU students."

"College kids," the man said contemptuously. "They go to school and learn how to lie down in the streets. Civil rights, Vietnam, nuclear power—it changes every couple of years, but they don't even notice."

"Don't remind me," Joncas sighed. "You know where my son-in-law was last week? Up in Connecticut, marching around some power plant. But the point is, college kids and Broadway stars get press coverage. *Good* coverage, not like what I just saw tonight."

"Well," the man said blandly, "twisting the woman's arm didn't work. But now I've got a plan. Your friend Codd gave me the idea."

"He's not my friend. He's an idiot. An old-time radical with a reputation for absolute honesty."

"Exactly. You're always saying he's a pain in the butt, so how'd you like to get rid of him? And at the same time fix it so the loudmouth actor is finished?"

"How?" Joncas said.

The man chuckled. "I heard Codd on TV, with his 'climate-of-violence' crap, trying to make the actor take the heat for what happened on the picket line. Did you feed him that?"

"I just encouraged him. It's been said by bigger people than Codd. Walter Reuther told the McClellan committee that any company that keeps operating during a strike is morally responsible for whatever happens."

"So we'll make something happen. We'll show everybody that the actor's responsible for a 'climate of violence,' all right."

"What do you mean? How?" Joncas listened for a moment. "His brother?"

"Swear to God. Showed up out of the blue. With the news, by the way, that the actor suspects you might be involved with the Varese again."

"Christ!" Joncas said. He listened again, his dark eyebrows rising. Suddenly they clenched. "No, no. I'm not going along with that."

"Yes, you are. I can't move much deeper into theater in this town with people like Codd around. He's got to go. And this is the perfect way to do it—made in heaven."

"You'll never get the brother to do it. Not if he has any brains."

"I'll think of a way. I always do."

Joncas frowned. "We agreed to avoid rough stuff whenever possible."

"Listen, my friend." The voice was as hard as a diamond. "I know you like to be seen around town in your handmade kid gloves, but they've got brass knuckles inside. That's the whole point of the deal, remember? Now, you want to let this goddamn actor spin it out to fifteen rounds? Doing God knows what to the transport talks? And keeping the whole damn town thinking about *theaters* and *unions*? And having him wonder if you're with the *mob*? What the hell's the matter with you, anyway?"

Joncas sighed. "I suppose we have to be practical."

"That's right. P.R.-actical." The man laughed. "Tonight's Monday. Set it up for Thursday afternoon, OK?"

"OK," Joncas said. "Thursday."

12

Along the Bowery, late Tuesday night, clouds of insects hung above the moons of the streetlamps. A light wind blew the litter into occasional life, but the men never stirred.

The Swede walked past them quickly, avoiding the sight of winos slumped in doorways like bags of old clothes. He had used to pretend, when he was young, that his unknown father was someone like Big Tiny Varese, but as his mother sank further into the depths of the bottle that killed her, he had come to accept that his father must have been a drunk like her. He sidestepped a pair of outstretched legs and walked the three blocks over to the theater.

There was a light upstairs, where Arrigo lived. The Swede stood across the street, looking at it, the thought of his brother automatically triggering certain feelings. Arrigo had known who *his* father was—a sailor, even if he'd never seen him. Arrigo had always had the luck, even with Big Tiny. When he threw the twenty dollars back in Tiny's face, all Tiny had done was laugh. And afterward, every time Tiny saw Arrigo on the street, he would stop his big car and ask him when he was coming to work. Even after Arrigo ran away, at sixteen, Tiny would still stop sometimes and say, "Swede, where's your smart little brother?"

The Swede smiled, thinking how good it was going to be, telling his brother which one of them was the smart one. And making sure Arrigo believed it. He checked his shirt pocket; the stuff was there, if he decided to use it.

When a shadow crossed the lighted window on the fourth floor, the Swede crossed the street. He told the lobby guard what to do with himself if he couldn't recognize a man who'd been up to the apartment before; he ran up the narrow stairs, lightly for all his size, and pounded on the door. "Surprised you, huh?" he said to the lifted eyebrows.

"You did. What do you want?"

"Let me in."

The door opened fully. Arrigo said, "I was thinking about you, in fact. Wondering whether you'd been to Sutton Place recently."

"What the hell you talking about?"

"Did you and some other goons pull guns on Mrs. Jerrold? Because if you did, I'll take you apart piece by—"

"Take your hands off me! I never been to Sutton Place in my life!"

"Somebody has. And if you know anything about it, you'd better start talking before I tear you into bits."

Suddenly two fists were locked on the Swede's vest; he put his hands on them. He could keep them from digging further but could not force them away. "How come you're asking me if I know anything?" he said softly. "I thought you said I was just a punk." The pale blue eyes so close to his own narrowed. "What could a punk know?" he said, still softly.

Arrigo released his grip and walked over to a desk. He picked up a newspaper and came back. "Did you see today's paper? What I said at my press conference about intimidation?" His finger jabbed the page.

Despite himself, the Swede felt tension in his gut. "I didn't come back to this rat hole to talk about that."

"Why did you come then?"

"I'll tell you when I'm good and ready. So you can just sit down and wait." Arrigo's face struggled and gave in. "That's better," the Swede said. He sat down too, stretching one leg in front of him and crossing the other over it. "Last week you was so busy calling me a punk, we didn't have no time to talk over the old days."

"Living through them was bad enough. Why talk about them too?"

"You want me to go? Without telling why I came for?" The Swede laughed. "That's better. But I still don't like the look on your face. That same old smart-ass look. Like when you lectured me about taking old lady Fracci's purse."

"You want to get to the point? I haven't got all night."

"It'll take all night if I say so. *Punk*. That's what we should've called you, instead of 'the Actor.' Arrigo 'the Punk' Dantino."

"You still use those idiotic names, don't you? The dog tags of crime. Michele 'the Mick' Lorenzo. Angie 'the Cleaver' Minetta. Rossano—"

The Swede sat up. "If you're listing the old gang, don't forget Carlo Belluci. After all, you're the one gave him his name—Il Morto."

He watched the memory leap into Arrigo's face: the catcher's mitt, lying in the blood and brains of the boy Arrigo had thrown to the sidewalk. "Carlo was my buddy," the Swede said. "I seen you whack him out."

"Is that why you came? To tell me that again?"

"I seen it," the Swede said softly. "I seen you knock Carlo down. Then I seen you get up and reach inside the back end of that parked truck. I seen you take out something heavy and bash in his head."

"If you saw all that, why didn't you stop me?"

"Because you went crazy—screaming and smashing that thing. And throwing it back in the truck before you passed out."

"Why couldn't the cops ever find the truck, then?"

"Because it drove away. And the cops never find nothing."

"I think you're lying," Arrigo said. "I think you're the one who did it."

"Still trying to sell yourself that bill of goods? Why would I do it for? I'm not the one who wanted to get out of the gang."

"True. You're the one who's thirty-eight and still can't get in."

"Shut up!" the Swede said. "I ain't listening to no more of that crap. Always telling me I'm lying, and saying I'm nothing."

"You are."

"Yeah? You want to know where I'm living now? On a big estate up in Westchester." He felt Arrigo's laugh slip under his skin like burs. "You can't call me a punk now, because I'm with somebody big—so big and so smart you ain't even heard of him."

"I'll bet nobody else has, either."

"That's right. He's too smart to get his name in the papers."

"Or too small-time." Arrigo laughed again.

"Small-time! Somebody who could cut out Big Tiny without even starting a war?"

"Wait a minute," Arrigo said. "Wait. What are you telling me?"

"That you don't know nothing. *Punk.*"

Arrigo's fist hit the arm of the chair. "You mean when you were 1ere last week, you weren't with the Varese anymore?"

The Swede hesitated. "I was getting ready to leave."

"Have others left too? Like Louie the Limp?"

"A few, I guess. But Louie don't mean nothing to the boss, like I do."

"What the hell would some new don want with you?"

"Listen, he was glad as hell to get me."

"Ah," said Arrigo softly. "You mean because of me?"

"No, goddammit! Because of *me!*"

Arrigo shrugged. "You never could make up a decent story. You leave too many holes. If nobody knows anything about this man, how did you know who he is and where to find him?"

"Because I got contacts!" The Swede thought of the man who once had tried to leave the organization. Big Tiny had told him to take care of it; but before he put the man out of his misery, the Swede had forced him to tell where he was going and why, and to show him the place in Westchester. Ever since then, the Swede had paid special attention to any rumors about Mr. Shaw.

"You've got contacts?" Arrigo was saying. "You should get somebody else to write your dialogue. What's the name of this mystery man—*il padrone invisibile?*"

"He's real, dammit! And he ain't Italian."

"Now I really don't believe you."

"You don't *want* to. Just like you don't *want* to believe me about how you killed Carlo. But this time I'm gonna *make* you believe me!"

Arrigo stood up. "When I was thirteen, you could get to me with your stories about what a big shot you were and how you saw me pull something out of some truck, but now I'm—"

"It was there! A white truck that said 'Plumbing and Heating.' It was there, goddammit!"

"Sure, sure. Just like you're in with some new don in Westchester."

"You bastard. I knew you'd talk like that." The Swede made a decision. "You're gonna eat what you just said, because I'm telling

the truth. Just like when we was kids. And this time I've got proo
Something I took out of the boss's own desk—you think some pun
would have the guts to do that?" He reached into his shirt pocket an
pulled out an envelope. He formed the contents into a fan and wave
it the way Arrigo had waved the newspaper at him.

"Oh, Christ," Arrigo said. "For a minute I thought you might hav
something, like letters or some records. But pictures?"

"Of him, you bastard! Because I knew I'd have to *show* you!"

"They could be pictures of anybody. What the hell has he got,
T-shirt saying 'I am the Swede's big new boss'?"

Furiously the Swede took one picture from the fan and waved i
under Arrigo's nose. "You see who he's with? You see?"

Arrigo saw. The Swede started to laugh.

He was still grinning on the way back to Westchester, with the ca
radio going full blast.

Luck had been with him all the way, he thought, replaying th
scenes that proved it: how he'd lifted the set of spare keys that after
noon, when the man who had them was in the john; how he'd made i
into the boss's office. He laughed aloud, remembering the way Arrig
had tried to keep the pictures from disappearing back into the safet
of the shirt pocket. He patted them, leaned on the horn, and pulle
out around a white Beetle. "Piece of junk!" he hollered, knowing th
driver couldn't hear him but feeling good anyway.

As he turned into the estate driveway, the problem of how t
return the pictures suddenly loomed at the end of the road. Th
sweat began to trickle down his sides, leaving his mouth hot an
dry.

Barely saying a word to the two men on front guard duty, he wen
around to the wing where a dozen or so of Mr. Shaw's men lived. H
lay on the bed in his room and smoked a joint. Soon the pressure o
the pictures in his pocket lightened, then became nonexistent. It ha
been a hell of a risk, he thought, but the look on Arrigo's face wa
worth it.

When he got up, he felt light and powerful and lucky again. H started along the halls that led to the office. Nobody was moving anywhere. He wondered whether the boss was over in the other wing with his parents. Funny, he thought, the boss having a preacher for an old man. Almost as bad as having a wino. He stifled a laugh.

The office door was locked again, but the spare key worked with a quiet snick. He felt his way to the desk, turned on a lamp, sat in the leather chair, reached down, and put the pictures back in the gray envelope where he'd found them. He shut the drawer and sat up, smiling.

All the lights burst on.

"What are you doing in here?" said the voice that could sometimes sound like God's. This was one of the times. "Why are you at my desk?"

The Swede's heart pounded on the bars of his ribs. He stood up, but Mr. Shaw said, "No, no, stay there. Since you've taken such a risk to get there." Mr. Shaw looked as he had the first night the Swede had seen him—short and thin inside a bathrobe, hair askew. Soft-looking, except for his eyes. "You stole the key from Fritz, I suppose," he said. "Have you touched anything in the desk?"

"No, sir. I just wanted to see how it felt to sit here. Honest to God."

"Last year a man came into this office without my permission. He doesn't see too well anymore. Permanent trouble with his eyes." Mr. Shaw cocked his head, as if listening for the pounding of the Swede's heart. Then he smiled, as if he had heard it. "You're in luck," he said. "I'll give you a chance to make up for this. By doing a hit."

The flood of relief was almost as painful to the Swede as the fear it displaced. "Sure, Mr. Shaw. Anything you say. I took out guys before. Two of them."

"Good. Now, we're going to take advantage of the fact that you've been to see your brother recently."

The Swede clutched the desk. "You mean . . . like last week?"

"Yes. Right before you came to me, isn't that what you said?"

"Yes, sir. Yes."

"Fine. It works in very nicely. You see, we're going to stage a hit on the picket line at your brother's theater. Day after tomorrow—

Thursday. You'll go down there with a group of the boys, and you'll all pretend to be supporting the theater. You, Swede, will start a fight with one particular union man, somebody I want to get rid of. You'll pretend to get mad, so mad that you take him out."

"Right there? On the picket line?"

"Yes. Then you'll let the cops catch you."

The Swede stared at him. "But they'll put me back inside, Mr Shaw. And with my record, how'll I ever get out? I can't do that, Mr Shaw. Honest to God, I can't."

Mr. Shaw smiled. "Oh, we'll do our best for you, Swede, don't worry. And I'm afraid your only alternative is to have a little permanent work done on your eyes. You don't want that? Fine. Then you'll tell the cops you killed this man for your brother. That means your brother will be blamed for the killing, you see."

In spite of himself, the Swede started to smile back.

13

For a long time after the Swede left the apartment, Erik did not move.

He looked down at his hands hanging loosely between his thighs. On the right hand there were marks, very faint because they had healed long ago. The cops had had him treated for rat bite when they took him to the stationhouse. They had taken the Swede, too, who cried and finally, unwillingly, told his story. The cops believed it; after all, there were pieces of the dead boy's flesh under Arrigo Dantino's nails, but none under his brother's. So he had spent a week in detention at Spofford House, where the faces of the young inmates were old with knowledge. Finally, at the Family Court hearing, the judge had ordered him released because there was no evidence; the white plumbing truck and the alleged weapon could not be found.

He clenched his right hand. Over twenty years, he thought, but the feeling induced by the rat and its teeth could still be summoned up in a moment. "Emotional memory," they called it in acting classes. He had used it once, to prepare for Othello's killing Desdemona. Was it easy to kill onstage because he once had killed in reality? He tried to produce the full memory of what had happened that afternoon, but as always he could recall only his murderous rage, then blankness. And, when the blankness faded, the image of a white truck.

To believe or not to believe the Swede—that had always been the question. And still was. But this time there was evidence: the pictures of a slight, nondescript man, photographed with V. I. Joncas. It could all fit, Erik thought. If Louie the Limp had in fact been working for some new boss. If that boss had been glad to take in the Swede because the Swede's brother was fighting one of Joncas's unions. If . . .

He stirred and saw that the newspaper still lay beside him, with the story on his press conference: "DANTE CALLS TICKETS 'VOTES,' HINTS AT INTIMIDATION.'" The Swede's eyes had darted away from the story like animals running from fire. Because he was one of the men the new boss had sent to threaten Maeve?

It could all fit. The Swede could have been telling the truth. About everything.

He stood up and went into the bathroom. He drank three glasses of water, throwing back his head after each. Then he looked at his face in the mirror, at the angles and colors that tied it to the Swede's. He wanted to smash the mirror and destroy the evidence of his blood-and-bone tie to a man he hated.

He wondered whether it had ever been different, whether he had ever reached up a small hand for the Swede's, seeking a friend and guide out of the prison of their lives. He must have done so, he thought. One couldn't hate a face in which there were pieces of one's own unless one had wanted first to love it.

The apartment seemed claustrophobic, for the first time, so he left and wandered down to the third floor, where the ranks of costumes were a silent army against the night, and down again, to the dressing rooms, which permanently held the sharp sweet odor of greasepaint, and finally into the auditorium. He touched the back of one of the red velvet seats; he had found the lot of them in an abandoned movie house in the Bronx and negotiated a price lower than his best hope.

He remembered that now he owned not only the seats and everything else in the building but also the building itself.

He sighed. The dull heaviness he felt seemed appropriate, not to ownership, but to a burden.

On Wednesday night Jac and Karen Sanda were on their stomachs on the living-room rug, a book in front of them, when they heard a knock.

"That's funny," Jac said. "I didn't hear the doorman ring us." She got up, went to the door, and opened the peephole.

"What's the matter, Mother? Did it peek back?"

Jac unbolted the door and opened it a crack. "What're you doing here?"

"I want to see you," Erik said. "I have to see you."

"You can't come in."

"You didn't answer my calls to your office. And you didn't come to my press conference on Monday. How am I supposed to see you?"

"My daughter is here."

"Is there some reason I can't meet her?"

"I won't have her involved in anything or hurt in any way."

"You can't think I would hurt her?"

"She's the most important thing in my life."

"Then I'd like to meet her. Please."

Finally Jac stepped aside to let him in. "Karen," she said sharply, shutting the door, "take the book and go to your room."

The child was already up, walking toward them. Erik got down on his haunches. "Hi, Karen Sanda. My name is Erik Dante."

"How do you do?" she said with adult formality.

"I see you were reading. Do you like stories?"

"Yes. My daddy makes them up for me. When he comes to see me."

"Karen, it's bedtime," Jac said.

"Yes, Mother. I can read the letters on his shirt. P-o-e-t-s . . ."

"Very good, sweetheart," Jac said. "That spells 'poets.' They're people who write poems."

Erik stood up. "That's a pretty nightgown, Karen."

"It's my favorite one that I own. It's like orange sherbet, all cool and smooth. And my mother's dress is like orange sherbet with stripes of white frosting."

"Your mother looks pretty, too."

"Karen," Jac said, "it's time for bed!"

The child kept looking at Erik. "Is he going to stay for a while?"

"Ten minutes," Erik said. "Please."

When Jac sighed, he said, "Thanks," and moved to a brown velvet chair, stretching out his legs.

Karen perched on the ottoman beside him. "Why do you have that word on your T-shirt?"

"Because it's part of the name of my house. The house I built for stories to live in."

"And which you've apparently bought," Jac said. "If you could find the money for a piece of New York City real estate, doesn't that weaken your position that you can't afford a union contract?"

"I don't believe there could be a house for just stories," Karen said.

Erik smiled. "Don't you? When I was your age, I believed that a terrible old troll who lived in our basement had sent all the stories way to the moon, where he locked them up behind silver bars. Silly, isn't it? But if I leaned out my window and listened hard, I thought I could hear a faint little cry—'Oh, find us, please find us, and bring us back.' And if it was a summer night, I could go up on the roof of the building and hold up my hand and almost touch the edge of the moon."

Karen looked at his outstretched hand. "Did you get them back?"

"No. They were too far away. But one summer night, when I was way out West in the mountains, I looked up at the moon, and sure enough, I could hear those voices again: 'Oh, find us, please find us, and bring us back.' So I came back here and built a house for them.

When it was done, I went up on the roof one night and sang the man in the moon to sleep. Then I threw up a ladder, and all the stories climbed down and came to live in the house I built."

Jac was still standing, watching them. "Please don't confuse her with fairy stories."

"Mother, I'm not confused. I know what a fairy story is."

Erik laughed.

"You didn't build the house by yourself," Jac said.

"That's true."

"Why don't you include that fact in your tale?"

"You're quite right. You see, Karen, I met someone who showed me there were more stories in the world than I'd ever dreamed and who gave me money to build the house for them."

"You mean like a fairy godmother?"

He touched her cheek. "I really do need to talk to your mother. Do you think you could go to bed, the way she asked, and leave us alone?"

She regarded him gravely, then climbed off the ottoman and went to her mother. "Good night," she said, kissing her. "I love you." She gave Erik another look and padded down the hall. In a moment her bedroom door opened and closed.

In the silence Jac said, "Don't look at me like that."

"Is it that obvious? The way I feel?"

"Please. I'm like Karen. I can recognize a fairy tale when I hear one."

"What does that mean?"

"That I know the truth. You've been . . . exploiting me in order to get me to help you."

"Who told you that?"

"Let's just say I've learned you're committed elsewhere. Isn't that so?"

"Yes. That's what I came to tell you."

"Oh." She blinked. "Well, you've told it. So you can go."

"Just like that?"

"What else is there to say? Do you want to hear how much I resent the way you treated me? How cheap I think it was for you not to tell me about Mark Jerrold? To come on with your best actor's manner?—which is damn convincing, I'll admit that. Don't you understand that it wasn't necessary? That my help and interest and admiration don't have to be *bought?*" She swung her head. Her hair slid along her shoulders like a brown silk shawl. Her eyes were brilliant, dark, and too dry.

He closed his. "I do understand. That's why I can't look at you and see how damn wonderful and beautiful you are while I'm telling you I can't see you again. Unless it's on news business."

Her chin lifted. "Fine. But if that's the way it is, why wasn't it that way last week at your theater?"

"Because I was . . . letting myself know what I wanted. Allowing myself to think I could have it. No, that's not true. I wasn't really thinking. I was just . . ."

"Grabbing a little fast sex on the side?"

One of his hands curled into a fist. "I'm not apologizing for any of the time we spent together. Not one moment. I meant everything I said and did. But . . . I owe Maeve Jerrold more than I can ever repay. Jac, I'd tell her how I feel about you, I'd tell her I can't feel that way and stay with her . . . if I could. But she's too vulnerable. More than I realized. Do you think I would do this if I had any choice? I haven't! She's just . . . She can't be hurt."

"But I can?"

His mouth went white.

She moved away to the small fireplace. Above the mantel was an expanse of mirror. She watched his reflection.

"Maybe," he said slowly, "I should give you the chance to think I'm doing this because I'm afraid of losing her money."

"I've thought it already. When I remembered how you called me a mistake and a risk."

"Here's something that will make it easy to believe. Something you can use against me in public if you want to. What you said earlier, about my having enough money to buy a piece of New York real estate—I didn't need any money. She gave me the theater building."

Jac turned from the mirror image of his eyes and faced their reality. "Gave it to you?"

"I paid her one hundred dollars, to make the transaction legal."

"You're crusading against the unearned," she said softly, "yet you take a gift worth hundreds of thousands of dollars."

"I knew you'd see that. I told you it could be used against me."

"Shouldn't it be?"

"She was threatened. Told to evict Poets and Paupers, or else. That's what I was hinting at in my press conference. I had to guarantee her safety. She wouldn't leave town, so I tried to get out of the building. I looked all weekend, but nobody wants a tenant with a union fight and a picket line. And there's no way I could get a mortgage to buy the building. I really am a pauper. She offered to give it to me. She wanted to do it very badly, so I accepted. I had to let her contribute the only thing she feels she has to offer. Money."

"Conscience money, you mean? Only it's your conscience that has to be cleared, so that's why you take it?"

After a moment he said, "I won't say that had nothing to do with it."

"A cynic would say she's using her money to hold you."

"I don't think that's her motive. But if it is, she's earned the right to hold me by any means she likes."

"Nobody could earn a right like that!" He said nothing. "I don't understand anything you're telling me. Deal with people on the basis of merit, that's what you say in every interview you give. But now you tell me Maeve Jerrold has some kind of absolute right to whatever she needs or wants from you."

He put his head in his hands. "I guess I am."

"You haven't said you loved her," Jac said finally. "That would make it easier to understand."

"I do love her."

"Ah."

He looked up. "But not the way I'm starting to love you." She shook her head faintly. "And there's not a damn thing I can do about it," he said. "Except tell you, and ask you to believe me. And then leave."

At the door he turned back and said, "This is only for the record, not because I expect you to do anything about it. I've now got reason to believe Joncas is involved. But not with the Varese. With some kind of new crime boss. I couldn't get his name or anything else about him, except that he lives in Westchester and he's not Italian."

"How can you know that?"

"I've seen some pictures. In a couple of them this man was with Joncas."

Her eyes widened. "Did you get this from some relative in the mob?"

"Yes. My brother."

Her eyes grew wider still. "Thanks for the news tip," she said stiffly.

"The mystery man looks to be in his forties. Very unprepossessing. In one picture he and Joncas were talking with Kerry London, in what looked like a dressing room. Part of a theater poster was showing. I made out some of the letters—B-r-i. Probably it was part of the Briarwood chain. Those big dinner theaters. I think London did a show for them last year. They go for the big Vegas-type talent. Jac? What's the matter?"

The blood seemed to be draining from her tan, leaving her face muddy. "You're positive? It was Briarwood?"

"Well, just about positive. It was—"

"I knew it," she said.

"Knew what?"

"I had my life together before I met you! And everything you do and say is tearing it apart!" She put out a hand. "Don't come near me. Just go. Please!"

"All right," he said finally.

When he left, she turned and stared down the hall at the door of Karen's bedroom.

14

On Thursday morning Erik was in the box office, helping Ruth organize the way in which the ticket-as-a-vote results would be tabulated and reported. There had been a good increase in orders but also several dozen negative calls, some of them hostile.

Ruth was telling him about one of them when the idea hit him: Kerry London had been in one of the Swede's pictures. Even if she was famous as a singer, she probably also belonged to the Guild of Stage Actors. He left Ruth in mid-sentence and went into the business office.

He called the Guild for London's home phone and address. Such information was given only to fellow members; as always, he was asked his name and social-security number in verification of his request.

When he gave them, there was a stiff silence. Then the woman said, "You said you want to know how people feel? I'd just like to tell you that my husband drives a city bus. He goes on at a quarter to five in the morning, and he works hard. You think it's easy, in this traffic and the public screaming if they have to wait five minutes? And he's never done anything harmful to anybody in his life!"

"Your husband sounds like my kind of man." There was silence. "But I'll see that your view is counted at the box office," Erik said.

"Since you're a member," the woman said coldly, "you're entitled to use Guild services."

"I pay my dues."

"I'll get you the Kerry London information."

After eight rings, the famous smoky voice answered.

"Hello," Erik said, his voice light enough to sound tenor or even contralto. He introduced himself as a salesperson from the city's most exclusive jewelers. "I'm sorry to bother you, but I hope you won't object when you hear why. I'm working with a customer who wants to send you a little gift, just a token of his appreciation of your art, and he'd like to know whether you'd prefer rubies or emeralds. I said I'd try to find out."

"Oh? Who's your customer?"

"Ms. London, the problem is that he wants this gift to be anonymous."

"I have to be careful who I take presents from. You wouldn't believe some of the creeps that hang around stage doors."

"But you know this man, I believe. He gave me your phone and address, and I'm sure they're not in the book." London said nothing. "Perhaps I could just tell you that he has a rather handsome address in Westchester. And I've heard him speak of going backstage to your dressing room at the Briarwood Theater."

"Donald?" she said. "Could it be Donald?"

"I just can't mention any names, I'm afraid."

"In his forties? Sandy hair and a face you forget while you're looking at it?"

"I think we understand each other. Now, should it be rubies or emeralds?"

London laughed. "Why don't you plant the idea that if I had both of them, they'd go with everything I own?"

By noon on Thursday the air was as hot and still as if it had just been ironed.

The union regulars, who had arrived on the picket line around eleven, shouldered their signs wearily. Soon the actors started coming for a rehearsal. "I've signed a contract," pleaded one of them, darting into the building. The others said nothing.

Shortly after one o'clock appeared a large group of newcomers, who seemed to be of college age. They lifted signs that quoted political thinkers from Marx to Marcuse. Several bore the legend "Run Anti-Unionism Off the Stage!"

Other strangers to the line arrived over the next hour, including a well-known TV actor who had been prominent in the strike that closed down TV production for three months the year before, and the dancer-actress who had achieved "overnight stardom"—after ten years of dedicated hard work—by bringing down the house with her one solo number in a new musical, in which she cartwheeled spectacularly across the stage.

Soon several TV vans pulled up, the stations having learned from the actors' union which celebrities would be there.

A car arrived just behind them, bringing Morty Codd and two other TATU officials. As a cheer went up, the picket organizer, smiling, handed each of them a signboard. The three of them walked among the line, shaking hands, slapping backs, and calling out their support, while the cameras rolled.

Impulsively, the dancer-actress ran down the street and then cartwheeled back, landing on her feet beside Codd. The well-known TV actor, assuming the stance of the lawyer he played on his series, spoke forcefully about the importance of TATU. Morty Codd beamed and said for the cameras, "I'm real pleased for people to see the kind of support we've got. And real pleased they can see how orderly it is. I just hope everybody remembers that we're not the ones who want any trouble. We're only down here because this theater is trying to keep us out." Behind him, the line cheered. Codd and the officers rejoined it.

Shortly after the last of the TV people left, a group of about a dozen men, also newcomers, came down the street and stood eye to eye with the picketers. The signs they carried had the effect of red flags; they said, "Leave Dante Free to Run His Own Show" and "Dante Tells It Like It Is" and "Featherbedding Is for the Birds."

The two groups faced one another, brandishing words and signs. The policemen and security guards moved closer.

Standing in the middle of the new arrivals, the Swede gripped the sign he had been given to carry and felt the sweat run coldly down his sides, underneath the leather jacket he had to wear because of the gun.

Mr. Shaw finally had explained how he was to identify the man he had to hit: "Here's a newspaper shot of him, but it's not too good. Just to be sure there aren't any foul-ups, I've arranged for him to be wearing a special signboard. It'll say, 'Take It from the Top—TATU Is for You.' Everything's set up with the picket organizer. So look for an older guy with white hair, check his sign, and you can't miss."

The Swede heard catcalls all around him. They seemed to blend into one word: "Arrigo." Arrigo would pay for this someday, he thought. Arrigo had made him steal the pictures, with his "I don't believe you" and the sneers on his face. Arrigo was the reason he had been caught, with no way out. The catcalls turned into Mr. Shaw's voice: *We'll try to get you out after a couple of years. But you have to tell the cops you did it for your brother. Better a few years inside, where you can see what's going on, than walking around with empty sockets* . . .

The Swede felt as if something had been done to his eyes already. He tried to look around him, but the faces were pale, featureless blurs and the signs just unintelligible marks. He had known it would be like this; but how could he explain anything to Mr. Shaw when Mr. Shaw had him by the *coglioni?* It was all Arrigo's fault, he thought.

The heat sent rivers of sweat down his thighs. He told himself he had to get going, and felt his gut lurch. There was a face near his; he shouted obscenities at it. The face spat back, "Not me, you asshole!" and he realized it belonged to one of the men he had come with, who was blond.

He spun around, one hand still clutching his own sign. He looked at the sea of faces; all of them seemed to be capped with white hair. His heart sloshed in his chest, sending sprays of nausea into his throat. A man jostled him, shouting something. He caught only one word: "Codd." He saw that the man had pale hair.

"Are you Codd?" he cried.

"Yes! Codd! Back TATU. They're for you! For the Brotherhood of American Labor! For dignity and decent pay!"

"Pay!" the Swede screamed. "He'll pay for it!" He reached into his jacket, pulled out his gun, and fired.

The two detectives looked again at the man they were interrogating in a small room at the stationhouse. His frame was much too large for the wooden chair; each time they asked a question, he shifted, pushed his hands through his white-blond hair, and wiped them on his thighs.

"Come on, Dantino," said Detective Fagan. "You better have a lawyer before you go any further. Somebody from the public defender's office can be here in half an hour." The man shook his head. "Then call somebody on your own." Another shake. "You waiting for the Varese to send one of their hotshot lawyers down here to spring you out?"

The man sighed. "No."

"Read him his rights again," said Detective Santo. "Make real sure he understands."

"I understand," the man said.

"OK, then," Santo said, "if you want to keep on talking, at least tell the truth. You might be able to help yourself. With a sheet like yours, and being known as a Varese street punk, you need all the help you can get. Where did you get that sign you were carrying? 'Dante Tells It Like It Is'—where did you get it?" The hands traveled through hair and down thighs. "Why did you go down to the picket line for your brother?"

"Yes. For my brother." The hands made another journey. "I done it all for him. Like I told you already."

"Don't give us that crap," Santo said. There was no answer. "Why did you do it for him? He asked you as a favor?" No answer. "He paid you?" No answer. "He threatened you?"

"I told you. He made me do it."

"What the hell is this, a horror movie?" Fagan said. "The devil made me do it, that's all you can say?" No answer. "When did he tell you to do it?"

"It was . . . last week."

"When last week?" No answer, only another journey of the hands.

Fagan and Santo looked at one another. Finally Santo asked, "How did you know Steve Pomerantz would be on the picket line this afternoon?"

"Who?"

"Steve Pomerantz. The deceased."

The man blinked. "Who you talking about?"

"You hit so many guys you can't remember their names? I got news for you, pal. This isn't like rubbing out some jerk for the Varese. This is bigger trouble than you ever dreamed. You think you can gun down the son-in-law of V. I. Joncas and not have anybody care?"

The man blinked rapidly. Although the detectives went on with questions, he raised his hands, put his fingertips to his eyelids, and said nothing more. When they pulled his hands down to take him back to a cell, he still did not open his eyes.

15

"Why? Dear God, why?" Coral Joncas Pomerantz, lying on the sofa in her parents' living room, said her litany to the ceiling, then turned her head and whispered it into a pillow. She did not turn her body, which was even more swollen than her face.

Her parents each had a litany, too. Cecelia, holding her hand, whispered over and over, "We're here, Coral, right here." Joncas slumped in a chair across the room, staring at the two women with eyes that seemed circled by a red crayon line, asking, "Why didn't you tell me he was going down there?"

At length Coral frowned and raised herself awkwardly on one elbow. "Daddy, what's that you keep saying?"

Joncas regarded her unseeingly. "Why didn't you tell me he was going down there?"

"But why should I? He just got some of his friends together from Columbia, on the spur of the moment. Steven doesn't do things because he wants attention. He does them because he believes in them. I mean, he *did* them. Oh, God."

"We're here," Cecelia soothed. "Right here."

"You should have told me," Joncas said.

"Why do you keep saying that? Could you have done something about it?"

"Done something," Joncas said. It was not a question.

Coral struggled to a sitting position. "Did you know there was going to be some kind of trouble down there? Daddy? *Did you?*"

"Don't upset yourself, honey," Cecelia said. "Think of the baby."

"I'm thinking of his father! Who is dead! And I want my father to answer me. Did you know something was going to happen this afternoon? Did you know and not try to stop it?"

Joncas sat up and shook his head, like a man surfacing from a dive. "No daughter of mine talks like that."

"Please, Vi," Cecelia said.

Coral hugged the bulge of her pregnancy. "Do you swear you couldn't have done something to prevent Steven's death?"

Cecelia jumped up. "What are you saying? What are you thinking about your father?"

"Oh, God, I don't know. I'm not thinking. I'm just . . . Isn't he supposed to be so powerful? The man big enough to run gangsters out of the union? If he's so powerful, why couldn't he keep guns off the picket line?"

"The man who had the gun is your father's enemy! You can't—"

"Guns! Do you know how I hate them?" Coral's gray eyes locked on her father's. "You think I don't remember, but I do. The men who came to see you when I was little—the shiny men, I called them, because they always looked as if they'd been rubbed with oil, even their suits—"

"Coral!" Cecelia cried. "You don't remember those times!"

"Oh yes, I do. How could I forget them? Some of the shiny men would wait in the kitchen sometimes, and they'd put their guns on the table. Once I was playing under the table—nobody knew I was there—and I heard them talking about how they were going to wipe somebody out. I thought it meant like with an eraser on a blackboard! I thought it was a game! Then when I got old enough to understand, all I could think was that we had had those guns on our kitchen table. Right where we ate!"

"Your mother was supposed to keep you away from all that."

Cecelia whispered, "Children can't be prisoners in their own—"

"Mother hasn't forgotten it either. I've seen her flinch even now when people come to see you at night—she remembers what it used to mean."

"That's all in the past," Joncas said. "That's what I worked to get rid of."

"Yes! Yes!" Coral shouted. "And if I ever hear people say you didn't really get rid of it, I call them liars. I say you're the man who cleaned up his own dirty house. I believe it! Because I can't stand not to believe it! And I made sure Steven believed it, too. But then, why are there guns in my life again? Why is he dead? Why? You know what I think? God is punishing this house for what you've done. Steven was killed because he believed in you. Maybe God is telling us it's wrong to believe in you!" Cecelia tried to interrupt, but Coral pushed her hand away and cried, "Steven was killed because of you. You did it! You did it!"

"Shut your mouth."

Coral hiccuped, as if the blade of Joncas's voice had nicked her throat.

"Cecelia," he said, "she's hysterical. Get the doctor back."

"She doesn't know what she—"

"She better learn."

"But she's so upset! She can't . . . Where are you going?"

"Out."

"Vi!" she cried. But he left without looking back.

He walked to the parking garage and took out one of his cars. It had been a long time since he had driven himself anywhere, and as he pulled onto the FDR Drive, the traffic seemed to be not an impersonal force but a series of obstacles aimed at him.

A car beside him swerved and cut sharply into his lane—as unexpectedly as one part of his life had veered into the other. He swore he would force his life back onto its two separate parallel tracks. He tightened his grip on the wheel and inhaled deeply; the car was new and smelled of leather and power. Not of fear, the way leather used to smell.

He pressed buttons to roll up the windows and turn on the air conditioning, feeling that he was inside a speeding metal cell, locked in with Coral's words. If only she hadn't used those words, he thought. *You did it.* Of course she didn't mean them literally. And of course she knew nothing.

You did it. He could hear the words said by a different voice, in a different language and time. When he lived in the small town on the Iron Range in northern Minnesota, with his widowed mother and the hulking fellow émigré she found to be his stepfather. Toivo Jalkanen worked on the railroads and knew as little of human relations as of the English language; he treated his young stepson as the evil necessary to obtain his wife's services. From a hook in his closet he frequently would take a heavy brown leather belt and lay it, in rows as straight as railroad ties, across the boy's back, muttering, "You did it . . . you did it . . . " But only rarely did the beatings coincide with something that young Veikko had done; the belt seemed to come from nowhere, the sight of it making beads of dampness sprout all over his skin. He dreaded the pain less than the stench of his own fear—and the feeling that since he had not *done* anything wrong, he must *be* something wrong.

It was years before he realized the beatings must have coincided with his mother's refusing the man in some way, perhaps sexually. By then the knowledge was of no use.

Summer and winter he was sent to the small lake near the Jalkanen house. He took a homemade pole and dropped a line, through a hole in the ice if necessary, after those alien creatures who lived in the dark and wet and were at the mercy of anyone dangling food in front of them. His stepfather liked especially to eat the fish heads; at dinner Veikko would feel as if his own eyes and brain were being forked into the man's mouth.

At school he learned the difference between his own life and others'. There were many other Finlanders on the Iron Range—they were known to stay to themselves and usually to speak little English—but he was a stranger even to them. He heard the references to "Finn farmboy"; he caught the pungent odor of his clothes, and his tongue felt like an oar, unable to navigate the syllables of English. In fact he learned quickly, but he was the only one to know it. He would answer the teacher's questions in his mind, aware that he could have high grades if he would speak up and would do the written work properly. But he found a perverse satisfaction in staying silent. Why should he show what he was to teachers who shook their heads at him

ind girls who wrinkled their noses? That they could think him a
silent, stupid Finn boy was proof of their own stupidity.

When his stepfather died, he expected that the odor and darkness
of his life would disappear into the grave too, that his mother would
again become the lighthearted creature he remembered dimly from
babyhood. He waited two weeks, a month; one night, as he watched
her peeling the potatoes that were the main staple of their diet, he
began to speak of the places to which they might move and start a
new existence. A potato peel hung from her knife like a white worm;
she looked at him in as much terror as if her husband were listening
in the next room, and Veikko realized that the dead man had left his
bootprints on her soul permanently.

The next day in English class he stood up suddenly, interrupting
the teacher, and recited perfectly a passage from the Longfellow
poem they were studying. Then he reeled off half a dozen geometry
theorems and a chronological list of the U.S. presidents. While the
whole room stared as if a farm animal had begun to speak, he told
them how he hated them and how stupid they all were, enunciating
perfectly but using language that turned the teacher as white as wax.
He left the classroom, the building, and finally the town, leaping on a
freight train headed for Chicago.

A horn blasted behind Joncas, and he swerved the car back into his
own lane. It was stupid to stare into the past, he thought; all that
mattered was the here and now. When she was younger, Coral had
sometimes asked about his early life, but he always changed the subject. What was he going to tell her? "At fourteen I was with a gang on
the south side of Chicago"? Or maybe "They caught us unloading
radios, and I spent a year in reform school"? Both Coral and Cecelia
knew he'd been in the army, but he never spoke of his fury at being
drafted, like a fish caught on someone else's hook. Nor did they know
of the hatred he had felt on combat duty in the Pacific—not of the
enemy but of his own fear, and of the officers who forced him to
experience it by ordering him to kill. When he was discharged, in
New York, he changed his last name to Joncas and truncated the rest
to initials; Veikko Ivari was a name for a creature who swallowed
hooks.

The G.I. Bill sent him to New York University, with vague plan for going into business or politics. Then he met Cecelia Ornato in one of his classes.

Reluctantly she talked of the union her cousin headed, the Public Transport Employees: The rumors were true that her cousin deal with some "undesirable relatives." They even came to the Ornato house sometimes. When Joncas told her he would like to help with that painful situation, Cecelia prevailed on the cousin, Paul Ornato to give him a job as a business agent.

Ornato had come to power in the transport union by driving out the Communist leadership. In the 1930's, Joncas learned, the Communist party had decided to organize a trade union of New York City trolley, bus, and subway workers, as a potent political force. But nearly dictatorial means were required to achieve their goal; and the membership, largely Irish and Italian, balked. Ornato had articulated their anticommunist views, and in a fiery and sometimes violent election they had put him and his faction in power.

Within six months Joncas learned two things: Ornato really did hate Communists, but fighting them was merely the screen by which he had delivered the membership to another kind of gang. The union legitimately collected dues and pension and welfare payments, but it also used those activities as covers for siphoning the workers' money into the pockets of Ornato and the "undesirable relatives," the Varese. Union "salaries" were paid to dozens of friends and relatives who never came near the office. Many names on the payroll had been picked from the phone book; the bookkeeper cashed the checks and gave Ornato the money. The Varese family used the pension fund to launder their illegal money and to bankroll various projects. Strikes were threatened, ostensibly to achieve better wages and conditions; sometimes they did so, but their real usefulness was as political weapons, held over certain heads at City Hall to make sure they were "friendly" to Varese interests.

Joncas was fascinated by the duality, by the union of those who worked for a living with those who stole. He had no trouble deciding which of them was stupid. For one thing, although rumors of the

Varese-union connection were common, much of the union membership was indifferent. As long as their wages went up and their working conditions showed some improvement, they didn't care; the attitude was "If Paul Ornato's a crook, at least he's on our side." To
Joncas, that was a stupid, fish-swallowing-bait attitude. One could
feel only contempt for men who spouted the historic labor view that
their enemy was the bosses, while a bunch of gangsters was stealing
them blind.

He was fascinated, too, by Paul Ornato, who spent weekends with
the Varese but was treated deferentially by most of the city's politicians. As a schoolboy, Joncas had shown his contempt for others by
refusing to act on their terms; how much better, and more subtle, he
thought, to achieve the same thing by commanding respect from the
world while violating every standard it claimed to uphold.

He went to Ornato, told him what he knew, and demanded to be
let in. Ornato sighed, then laughed, then gave him the whole picture:
The Varese were involved in other areas, such as the meat and can-
ning industries and the docks, where they could own companies as
well as union locals and thus work both sides of the labor-management street.

Making himself indispensable to Ornato, Joncas amused himself by
dropping hints that he too was Italian. Or Russian. Let no one be sure
who he really was, he decided, or what he wanted. Not even Cecelia.
When certain business dealings had to take place at the house, he
explained nothing and let her agitation break against his impassivity
and finally wash away.

It was, he thought, more painful for him than for her. He knew
people believed he had married her only to gain entrée into the
union, but in fact he loved her. The best proof was that when a man
named Shaw came to him with a proposition—after Ornato had died
and Joncas had inherited his mantle—Cecelia was initially the reason
that he listened.

Shaw, Joncas thought, taking an exit off the highway and starting
to search for a local road. Shaw. Shaw. The name boomed in his mind
like waves smashing on a shore and hissing backward on sand.

16

When the entrance to Shaw's estate loomed up, Joncas braked and swung in. There was no locked gate and no high wall; "Let the Italians live that way," Shaw always scoffed. But there were dogs at the end of the long driveway, and two men rushed to meet the car.

"I want to see him," Joncas snapped.

"Nobody can bother him right now," said one of the men.

Something hot and red crackled along Joncas's backbone and singed his vision. "I'm going to bother the hell out of him." He flung open the car door. "Out of my way, you cretin!"

"Christ, it's Joncas," the other man whispered.

"Call off the dogs and get out of my way!"

They did so. One of them leaped ahead of him to open the heavy front door. "I'm sorry," he said, "but Mr. Shaw's busy with—"

"I don't care what he's doing. Tell him I'm here."

The man stood impaled by indecision, so Joncas pushed past him, down a large foyer. From somewhere along the hallway to the left he heard voices. But when he went to the room from which they came, Shaw was not there.

Instead, an elderly couple looked up at him, their faces soft and white. "I suppose you're looking for our son," the man said.

Joncas throttled his anger. "Yes. You must be Reverend Shaw."

The man nodded. "And my wife, Florence. I'm afraid we don't know where Donald is at the moment." Mrs. Shaw smiled vaguely, more at the wall than at Joncas.

"We were just sitting here," said the Reverend, "talking about our next letter. We put out a biweekly newsletter, you see."

"I'd heard that." Shaw had told him once about their religious institute, which occupied the east wing: "Could there be a better cover?"

"The newsletter is called *Christian Comfort*," Mrs. Shaw said. "We hope that's what it brings to people."

"Yes." Joncas could think of nothing else to say. He knew he was staring at their faces, which were lined yet seemed untouched by experience, like custard with a skin of wrinkles.

Feet pounded down the hall, and Shaw appeared in the door. Joncas saw that his face resembled his parents', except for the eyes: Two bullets had been dropped into the custard. Shaw said, "Did you have to come here?"

"Yes."

Shaw sighed. Then he smiled, to match his eyes, and turned to the couple. "You met my friend? I'm sure he didn't tell you what his name is. You know why? Because he and I do a lot of business together, but the Lord wouldn't approve of it."

The senior Shaws did not move; they looked like animals pinned in a beam of light.

"I'll tell you what," Shaw went on. "You can pray for him. Just tell the Lord you want to save the soul of Mr. X."

"Shaw!" Joncas said involuntarily.

"Yes, all right. Come on." Shaw swung out of the room and headed down the hall.

Joncas caught up with him. "Why the hell do you treat them—"

"I like it that way. So shut up about it."

They crossed to the other wing, to Shaw's office. Shaw went to a couch at the far end, stretched out at full length, and slid one hand between two of the buttons on his blue shirt. "You look like hell."

"Because I don't have any answers yet."

"Neither do I. I told you everything I know, on the phone. Dante's brother screwed up. Went berserk, apparently. Fired wild. Thank God I own three guys down at Police Plaza—they told me what the jerk has been saying. More important, what he hasn't said. He hasn't mentioned Codd, so we're still safe on that—"

"Codd! How did I ever let you talk me into something so idiotic?"

"You've been moaning about him for weeks, my friend. And it would have worked if that stupid Italian—"

"Why did you use him if he's stupid?"

"Because he's Dante's brother! And because he wasn't supposed to be alive to do any talking at all—the boys were supposed to take him out right after the hit. But he went crazy, and they couldn't.'

"Why did he do it? Why did he go for my daughter's husband?"

"You think I don't want to find that out? Apparently he's not telling the police anything at all. He started out saying he did it for his brother—that's what I told him he'd have to say when he got caught. But right away he clammed up, and now he sits there like a zombie. Thank God. As soon as they arraign him—"

"What if he was double-crossing you and doing what *Dante* told him to do?"

"Why the hell would Dante want your son-in-law killed? Besides, the brother hates Dante. He wouldn't do a damn thing for him. And I'm not sure he's got the brains for a double cross, anyhow."

"Why did you do it, then?" Joncas cried. "Why did you use somebody who's stupid and goes crazy?"

"Come on, calm down, will you? To tell the truth, I'm kind of surprised. It's a hell of a shame your son-in-law got in the way, but frankly, I didn't think you were all that fond of the kid."

The heat crackled along Joncas's backbone again. "You're the one who worked out the plan—it was you!"

"Take it easy."

But it seemed to Joncas that his body was slipping out of his control; it headed to the couch, and his fingers reached down. "The thing went wrong because of you! You planned it wrong—you did it!"

Shaw didn't move. "Maybe you forgot. I don't like to be touched."

Joncas looked down and saw blue cloth in his fingers. He released it and straightened up slowly.

"That's better," Shaw said. "Sit down."

Joncas did, heavily, on a chair next to the couch. His thighs hit the edge of the seat in an uncomfortable way, but he didn't move.

"I guess I have to overlook this," Shaw said, "since you're upset. I guess that's why you're coming on like a sermon out of *Christian Comfort*. But you're forgetting something, my friend. Why was your son-in-law on that picket line at all? You knew what was going to happen. Why the hell did you let him go down there?"

"I didn't know he was going."

"Seems like you should have. Your own family."

"Don't try to blame me! You think I'd have my own daughter's husband killed?"

"Who said you did?"

"I didn't have anything to do with killing the boy!"

Shaw pursed his lips and studied Joncas. "You want somebody to blame?" he said. "Then think straight. You and I had a plan, a practical plan to get rid of a couple of problems with one stone. But why did we have those problems in the first place? We're not the ones who got Morty Codd riled up. We're not the ones trying to keep out a union. We're not the ones turning a two-bit theater into a public nuisance. Are we?"

"No," Joncas muttered.

"Would there have been a picket line if it wasn't for Dante?"

"Codd said that. Codd is an idiot."

"Sure. But even an idiot can say a true thing. If Dante wasn't pulling all this crap, would your son-in-law have been down there to get in the way of a slug? Would he?"

"No."

"Well, then? Everything goes back to Dante, right?"

Joncas shifted on the chair, to find a more comfortable position.

"So if you want to start grabbing somebody's shirt, the shirt to be—"

"Get him," Joncas said. "Get Dante."

"Take him out, you mean? Sure, I could do that. But right now I'm more worried about the brother. As a corpse, he would have framed Dante, but as a live witness, he makes me nervous. Even if he could pull it off all right, what do we want him to say? What the hell *is* the story now?" He crossed one leg neatly over the other. "They've got to arraign him soon—Saturday at the latest. And as soon as they put him on Rikers, I'll get somebody in there to get rid of him."

"No."

"Why not?"

"I'm not going to let . . . " Joncas stopped himself. "There could be another foul-up. And if there is, God knows who might start talking. About us."

"What the hell do you want, then? To leave one brother in jail, telling the cops something I haven't even figured out yet? While the other one denies it all? Of course," Shaw added thoughtfully, "if the actor wasn't around, maybe we could make something stick. Maybe you're right. Maybe Dante's the one to get rid of."

"No."

Shaw looked up in surprise. "I thought that's what you wanted."

"No. Neither one of them. No more killing. Killing leaves a stink."

"Since when did you get religion?"

"Since a stink came into my house."

"Listen, my friend—"

"I said no killing!"

Shaw swung up to a sitting position. His eyes locked on Joncas, confident of their power, but at the back of his head was a little bent flag of hair, pushed up by his lying on the couch. Joncas looked at the flag, not at his eyes.

"Maybe you forgot," Shaw said. "I don't take orders."

"Maybe you forgot how much you need me."

"What the hell does that mean?"

"It means no more killing. Or else I'll pull out of our deal."

There was a silence. "You like it too much, the way things are," Shaw said. "You'd never pull out."

"Do you really want to find out?"

Shaw sighed. "Someday you'll know you just made a mistake. But right now I guess you're still too upset." He lay back on the couch. "So what the hell do you want me to do?"

"Dante did it. Make him responsible for killing my daughter's husband. So there can't be a question in anybody's mind, anybody's, that I could have . . . You've got the brother. You said he's already told the cops he did it for Dante. So use that. Frame Dante so tight a crowbar couldn't get him out."

"And what the hell story am I supposed to use? For Dante to have Codd killed—that would have made a lot of sense. But your son-in-law? Why? He's not even in the union. And how would Dante know who he was? Or that he was going to be there? No, the best we could do is have the brother claim that Dante gave him a general kind of order—told him to pick on anybody who was down there supporting the union—and by a freak accident, he picked your son-in-law."

"Not an accident. That's not good enough. Dante had my daughter's husband killed. On purpose. That's what it has to be."

"You don't want much, do you?"

"Just do it," Joncas said. "Do it!" He sat back in the chair, letting the voices in his mind finally fade.

They had nearly gone into silence when Shaw spoke. "Oh, Jesus, have I got an idea. If I can just find a lawyer in time, I think I know how to do it."

17

The night was long, a monochrome of moon and clouds drifting past Maeve's windows in endless slow motion.

Erik had called about five in the evening to break the news, his voice under such tight control that it forbade her own to rise. "I'm still at the theater," he had said. "The cops have everybody in the auditorium. They're questioning people individually up on the stage. I don't know how long I'll be. I'll come to you when I can."

She had stood holding the phone long after he hung up. She had turned on the TV and seen the story again and again, frowning because her mind seemed unable to extract meaning from what it saw and heard, which included something about a cartwheeling woman and then later film of a crowd and police cars and a stretcher with a covered shape on it. She had watched *Jac's Journal*, oblivious of the content of the interview, trying to tell from the woman's dark brown eyes whether Erik had called her too. But it was impossible to tell.

Hours or minutes later, she didn't know which, Erik had called again, to say the detectives wanted him to go to the stationhouse "to answer a few more questions," and he would come by after he was finished with them. For some time she had busied herself around the apartment, sorting out notes on a translation, putting some record into alphabetical order, but eventually, past midnight, she lay on the bed, watching the slow motion outside the window, waiting to feel something, waiting for Erik.

When he came, there was more gray than black in the sky. He looked weary but also faintly incredulous, as if he had been staring for too long at something impossible. "What did they do to you?" she said.

"Asked me more questions, that's all." His kiss was mechanical.

"What did they want to know?"

"Among other things, why I hadn't volunteered right away that Rossano Dantino was my brother."

"Ah," she said, taking a chair by the fireplace. "Why hadn't you?"

"I told them I'd been too shocked. Which is true. We were rehearsing when it happened, you know. Ruth came running into the auditorium screaming that somebody'd been shot on the picket line. By the time I got out into the street, all I could see was something under a makeshift blanket and two cops holding somebody. When that person lifted his head and we could see each other's faces over the crowd, I couldn't take it in. You know the way I study people on the subway sometimes and analyze expressions in case I might use them in a role? That's what it was like. I remember thinking, with no feeling at all: That's hatred. After a while I thought: Oh. That's my brother."

"But you didn't tell anybody who he was?"

"I couldn't decide whether that would be smart or dumb. By the time the cops got around to talking to me, inside the theater, they'd learned his identity. I knew it as soon as they asked me whether Erik Dante was my real name. I told them I'd seen the Swede a couple of times recently, for personal reasons, and I had no idea why he was on the picket line. Or why he killed that poor kid. And I *don't* know why he did it! There has to be some way I can find out. If I could just talk to him . . ."

"I suppose the police wouldn't allow that?"

"Not under the circumstances, no."

"What else did they ask you?"

He looked past her, into the distance. "They started hinting that I should know something about it, about why the Swede had killed Steve Pomerantz. They said the Swede was claiming I was the one who . . . I kept telling them he was lying. 'My brother is lying.' After a while I almost forgot where I was. I wasn't talking about Steve Pomerantz any longer, but about a boy with his skull—" He stopped abruptly and looked at her as if realizing for the first time who she was. "I didn't mean to tell you all that. Don't worry about it. It was nothing, really, just . . ." His voice trailed away, and he raised an eyebrow at her. "You're very calm. I thought you'd be . . . upset."

"Haven't you always said that I live with the expectation of disaster? That has one great advantage, you see. When disaster finally hits, you can feel a kind of relief. The sword of Damocles isn't up there any longer. It's fallen."

He was listening to her attentively, but she saw the blue eyes widen slightly, as if they were again seeing something impossible. She said, "I don't expect you to understand the way I feel."

"That's good. Because I don't."

Quickly, she began urging him to lie down and rest, at least for a while. Finally he did stretch out on the bed briefly and closed his eyes, freeing her own to move along the length of his body and the planes of his face. But in half an hour he was up, pacing the apartment, talking about what he had to do at the theater, and muttering about the Swede.

That night, a guitar and a human voice, amplified almost beyond recognition, howled above the heads of the Friday crowd at the Jumping Joint. When the number ended, the dancers seemed not to notice; they kept moving, the mass of their bodies spilling from the confines of the dance floor like flesh escaping over a belt.

At the back bar, a man studied the tall figure who had just fought his way to a stool. "Hey," he said after a moment, "I seen you before. You was looking for the Swede."

"I guess you're right." Erik ordered a Scotch, then watched it curl around a nest of ice in a glass.

"Now I know who you are," the man said loudly. "You're the Swede's brother. It was in the papers today, your picture and everything. The Swede hit Joncas's son-in-law, down at your place. Some kind of theater."

"Yes." Erik took a swallow of the cold, smoky Scotch, pushed it aside, and decided to get to business. He had checked the periphery of the whole room when he came in, looking for an entrance to some kind of office. He had found only washrooms, storerooms, and six small rooms at the back. Couples periodically emerged from five of them; when he tried the sixth, it was locked. He turned to the man beside him and said, as casually as he could over the music, "Is Big Tiny here tonight?"

"Why you want to know?"

"We've got business. Has he come in?"

"How the hell do I know you got business with Big Tiny?"

"Because I'm telling you." Erik moved closer to the man. "And I got a piece in my pocket that says so, too."

The man stiffened. "I don't know if he's here. Honest to God. Sometimes he comes in to work upstairs." Erik increased the pressure. "All right, all right. Ask Joann. She always knows when he's here. She's got the key."

Erik said carefully, "Joann? I don't see her around."

"You blind? She's at the end of the bar, making drinks."

"So she is. Thanks." Erik left the stool and pushed his way to the woman at whom the man had gestured. Her hair was an unearthly red and her face a coat of paint over years of abuse. "Joann," he said, "I've got a meeting with Big Tiny. You want to let me up?"

"He didn't tell me about any meeting."

"Maybe he figured the Swede's brother wouldn't have the guts to show up."

She pulled back to study him. "Yeah, you look like the Swede, all right. I just hope you don't tip like him." When she led him to the one back room with the locked door, he gave her five dollars.

There was nothing in the room but an elevator, which had only one button and moved up sluggishly. In contrast, Erik's mind raced with second thoughts: Was this the way to do it, after all? To gamble everything on his memory of Big Tiny's character—flamboyant, vicious, self-centered, and a con artist, like all the old-fashioned mobsters . . . but with another element as well?

The elevator doors opened on a reception room. A man leaped to his feet, one hand going inside his jacket.

But Erik's gun was already out. "Hold it there," he said. "Just put your hands up, nice and slow. Then turn around—that's right—and walk ahead of me to the office door. Is it locked?" The man nodded no.

Erik opened the door and pushed the bodyguard in ahead of him. The room had purple-and-red carpeting, a huge red couch, and a desk. "Hello, Tiny," he said to the squat and startled figure behind the desk. "Remember me? Arrigo Dantino?"

"Oh, Jesus," said the bodyguard. "It's the Actor. The Swede's little brother."

"I figured this would be the quickest way to get in," Erik said. leveling the gun at Tiny's huge stomach. "But getting in was all I needed it for." He tossed the gun on the desk.

The bodyguard leaped for it, swung around, and held it on him.

"It won't do any good, " Erik said. "It's not loaded."

The man looked disbelieving. He checked and looked incredulous.

"We don't keep bullets at the theater. That's a gun we use as a prop."

"The smart-ass kid," Tiny said without expression. Then his stomach began to bob like a beach ball on water; he was laughing. "Kid," he said finally, "I see you still got balls."

"Maybe that's not all he's got," said the bodyguard. "Maybe he's carrying another piece—a real one." He frisked Erik, then shook his head. Tiny rested his arms on his belly, folded his hands, and narrowed his eyes to flat lines above his full cheeks. "What you want, kid?"

"To talk to you."

"So talk. If it don't interest me after three minutes, you're out."

"OK. You know what happened at my theater yesterday, with the Swede?"

"I read the papers."

"Have you seen the Swede lately?"

Tiny blew out his cheeks. "Nobody has, not for about a week. After I read the papers, I figured he went to work for you."

"Wouldn't I be dumb to use my own brother for that job? And wave a red flag at the cops?"

"You were a smart-ass kid. That don't mean you couldn't grow up dumb." The bodyguard laughed. "I got to admit," Tiny went on, "that it don't break my heart to see that sonofabitch Joncas lose part of his family tree."

"Then maybe you're the one who sent the Swede to do it."

"Don't push your luck, kid. If I wanted it done, nobody would have got caught. And dragged the Varese name into the papers."

"OK. But if neither you nor I got the Swede to do it, who did? I've got to find out why in hell it happened, who put him up to it. I need some information, and I figure you can give it to me. If there's something Big Tiny doesn't know, it hasn't happened yet."

Tiny's cheeks stretched in a smile. "What you want to know?"

"Hey, boss," said the bodyguard, "I remember this crud. He grew up in our neighborhood. You can't trust him."

"First I find out what he wants to know. Then I decide whether to tell him or to cut off those balls he's still got. Always let people talk first. You got to learn that. So talk, Dantino."

"I want to know about the man in Westchester," Erik said. "Donald." There was no reaction, just a silence as long as a pause on the stage, where every second was like a minute of real time. The trick was not to be afraid to take those pauses when they were needed—to let the audience's imagination do its work.

Finally Tiny said, "Why you want to know about him?"

Erik took a deep breath; Tiny had acknowledged the man's existence. "Let's just say you and I have the same enemy, Tiny, and I want to go after him. He squeezed you out, didn't he? He took what's yours." Erik waited, praying Tiny would acknowledge that too, and thinking it was strange to be appealing to a gangster on the basis of property rights.

"You couldn't get nowhere near him," Tiny said finally.

"I figured you'd think that. That's why I just showed you what I could do. How I could get in here with nothing but a fake gun."

There was another silence. "What you want to know about him?"

"Who he really is. Where he lives. How he's tied in with Joncas. And anything else you'll tell me. And, Tiny, I know how you love to do people favors, so they can owe you for the rest of their lives. But I don't want to be in that position, so I'll pay for the information." Erik reached for his wallet and took out a twenty. "I think this is the amount you offered me once, isn't it?"

The bodyguard stiffened. So did Tiny. Then his belly began to bob. "Tell you what, Dantino," he wheezed, "I'll think it over. Do a little checking on you. Maybe you'll hear from me, maybe not." He took the twenty. "If not, somebody'll be around to throw this in your face."

His belly jerked again, and when the bodyguard hustled Erik into the elevator and its doors closed, he was still laughing. Tiny hadn't lost his sense of humor.

When he got back to the theater and walked up to the apartment, Erik felt as if a tidal wave of exhaustion were rolling down on him.

He slumped on the bed. After a while his head lifted slightly, to the framed sketch Maeve had drawn of the beggar child. *When disaster finally hits*, she had said, *you can feel a kind of relief.* How could she understand so many things, he thought, and yet have such an alien reaction?

He lay back, feeling sleep wash over him.

The phone rang.

He let it go five times, then reached out an arm.

"It's Jac." Her voice was brisk. "I've been trying to reach you al
day."

He sat upright, staring eagerly into the dark. "I've been . . . I wa:
busy. I wanted to—"

She cut in, even more brisk. "I can't believe what's happened. I
don't know what your brother was doing, what he was up to, but I
wanted to tell you that I'm going to look into what you told me
About that picture and Briarwood, I mean."

"Jac, my God, how can I thank you—"

"This is strictly news business, Mr. Dante. But if it helps you, I'll
be . . . glad."

The line went dead.

He lay back slowly, unable to sleep.

18

The lawyer looked at his client across the wooden table in
the small room at the stationhouse. "I'm going to ask you one more
time, Dantino," he said, "and I think you'd be smart to answer. Why
did you shoot Steve Pomerantz? Why was he the man you went
after?"

The Swede stared down at the scarred tabletop and muttered, "I
guess the heat got me crazy."

"The boss really wants to know how it happened," the lawyer said.
But the Swede shook his head stubbornly.

It was too bad, the lawyer thought; there would be a nice addition
to his fee if he could get the answer to that question, but Dantino
wouldn't explain. Every time it came up, his eyes grew tight—whether with fear or mulishness or something else, the lawyer could not
tell. "All right, Dantino," he said, "I'll have to report to the boss that
you won't talk. I just hope you do a good job talking to the detectives.
Are you all set?"

"Yeah. Just give me a goddamn minute, will you?" The Swede put his arms on the table and laid his head on them.

The lawyer lit a cigarette and tried to find a more comfortable position on the hard chair; he had been in the small room with his new client for an hour. When he had arrived at the stationhouse and announced he was there to represent Rossano Dantino, the detectives had looked relieved: Dantino had been continuing to refuse a lawyer from the public defender's office, but it was nearly forty-eight hours after the shooting, and the detectives couldn't hold him much longer without arraigning him. Obviously they had been hoping to get more information out of him first. They would get it very soon, the lawyer thought.

He wondered whether they had placed him yet; his firm once had represented several members of the Varese family. That connection had gotten him the client now slumped on the table. The call had come the night before, Friday, and he had spent most of this morning closeted with two lawyers who worked for the man who was hiring him—but was referred to only as "the boss," never by name. If the money hadn't been so good, and the possibility of future work so clear, the lawyer would have been tempted to refuse. After all, it wasn't a very savory business—including the odor emanating from his client's clothes.

Dantino had started sweating right away, the moment they were alone and the lawyer explained that he had been sent by "the boss." When Dantino learned that "the boss" would let him make up for what he had done, even his relief had taken the form of perspiration. And when he heard what he had to do, and then struggled to memorize the story, his palms had left wet smears on the table. At one point he had cried out that he just couldn't do it; the lawyer said contemptuously, "You mean your brother's an actor but you can't even act to save your life?" Dantino had gritted his teeth and gone on.

The lawyer put out his cigarette. "All right, you've had enough time. I'm going to tell them you're ready to make a statement."

The Swede lifted his head from the table. "OK."

"Now, remember, don't stick with the first story very long."

"Yeah."

Within five minutes they were all ready, Detective Fagan sitting near Dantino with a tape recorder, and Santo straddling a chair by the door. From the look Santo gave him, the lawyer could tell they had discovered who he was.

Fagan turned on the tape, made some identifying comments, and said, "OK, Dantino. Why did you shoot Steve Pomerantz?"

The lawyer watched perspiration slide down the Swede's neck, but the answer he gave was the right one: "To get Arrigo in trouble."

"What do you mean?" Fagan said.

"Well, see, he don't . . . We don't get along good, since kids. And I figured . . ."

"You figured . . . ?"

"He was acting like he owned the world, with his crummy theater, and he wouldn't give me the time of day, so I . . ."

"So you did what?"

"I went down there and shot this Pomerantz kid, so it would look—"

"How did you know he would be on the picket line?"

The Swede looked around as if the walls were shrinking in on him. The lawyer tensed, wondering whether that was part of the act or whether the man really was going to collapse. He cut in. "My client is having a hard time accepting that it's in his best interest to tell the truth."

The Swede swung his head. A strand of wet, white hair hung over one ear. He looked at the lawyer, who could not possibly give him a sign but tried to tell him "Now" by sheer force of will.

Finally the Swede said, "You want the truth? The real truth is that Arrigo and me, the both of us—we done it for the family."

Santo's chair scraped. "What family?"

"Their own family, of course," the lawyer said smoothly. "The Dantinos."

"No." The Swede gulped. "That ain't what I mean."

"Are you talking about the Varese family?" Santo said.

The lawyer cut in. "You can see that my client is confused and frightened. He knows you want to hear about the Varese, and he thinks he has to tell you what you want to hear."

Fagan ignored him. "Dantino, are you saying that you and your brother were both working for the Varese?"

"All right, that's it," the lawyer said. "No more questions. I don't want you talking any further to this man."

"Well, well," Fagan said softly. "We were getting on so good, too."

"You're confusing him, that's what you're—"

A sudden bellow came from the Swede. "I don't want that lawyer in here! They sent him down here to get me to say I did it all on my own, but I ain't gonna do it! I don't want him for a lawyer! Get him out!"

"Dantino!" the lawyer cried, finding it difficult now to sound upset, because everything had gone so well. "You don't know what you're saying, Dantino, you—"

"Get him out of here!" the Swede shouted.

So the lawyer went. But not before urging the Swede to get himself another lawyer and reminding him that he couldn't be questioned without counsel present if he didn't want to be.

Within forty-five minutes the lawyer was many blocks away, joining his wife for cocktails and thinking that he had earned more money for being fired than he often did for working.

Just when the Swede thought they would leave him alone finally and he wouldn't have to tell it again, they brought in an assistant district attorney, a young man with longish hair and very bright eyes.

"OK," Fagan said. "We're going to go through it all again, Dantino. You want a Coke or something first?"

"No." What he wanted was a joint. No, he wanted to be back in the Joint, in the days before he had ever gone to see Arrigo and then driven up to Mr. Shaw's.

Santo said, "You're talking to us without an attorney present because that is your wish, right?"

"Right." It wasn't his wish, but the lawyer had said that's the only way they would believe his story—if he "fired" a Varese lawyer and then told "the truth" on his own. But it felt very naked on his own.

The ADA took over. "All right," he said. "Why did you shoot Steve Pomerantz?"

"Arrigo told me to do it. Both him and me, we work for the Varese."

"What was the plan? How did your brother know that Pomerantz would be on the picket line Thursday afternoon?"

"He didn't know that, exactly. He told me to start tailing the kid, and the first day I did it, that was Thursday. . . . Well, the kid heads down to the theater. I got in with a bunch of pickets—guys that were on Arrigo's side. I grabbed a sign." He clenched his fists. "And I shot the kid."

"Why did you do it that way, in public, where you'd be virtually certain of being caught?"

"I figured Arrigo and Big Tiny would like it that way, with the union and pickets and everything right there." He sighed. "And I figured . . . I guess I figured I could get away."

"Why did your brother and Big Tiny want to get rid of Steve Pomerantz?"

"Like I already told the cops, because he was Joncas's son-in-law. Big Tiny hates Joncas from way back. And now Joncas was getting in the way again. So Tiny and Arrigo, they figured to send Joncas a message he can't miss. To let him know he better get out of their way."

"Explain that," the ADA said. "How was Joncas getting in their way?"

The question didn't connect with any phrases the lawyer had used. The Swede drew his hands through his wet hair, as if that act could pull some answers from his brain. Nothing came. So he went back to telling it the way he had rehearsed it. "Tiny wants to get back into the unions Joncas threw him out of."

"Which unions are those?"

"Well, like the transport workers. And the . . . the bartenders. Arrigo was trying to help Tiny get back in, and get into some new unions, too. Like in the theater. So when this Codd guy came around,

Arrigo figured, why not start getting into the theater unions that way? So he tried to pay Codd off—"

"What for?"

The Swede blinked. "That's how you get in, ain't it? You buy off the head guy. But Codd wouldn't go along. He's legit all the way. Like Joncas is. The two of them together, they'd stop Arrigo's plan."

"And that plan was to bring Codd's union into the Varese fold?"

"Yeah."

"As a way of starting to get back into other unions in the Brotherhood?"

"I don't know nothing about what else they planned. I was only part of this theater thing." There was a silence, so he continued doggedly. "I just know that Tiny and Arrigo wanted to send Joncas a message he couldn't miss."

The silence went on, broken only by the sound of a child's crying somewhere beyond the door. The Swede felt like crying too, for the stinking mess his life had become and the fact that it would end soon if he didn't pull this off. He wiped the sweat from his eyes and forced himself to look at the ADA again.

"How long," said the man, "has your brother worked for the Varese?"

"I . . . I forget exactly. He went away for a long time. Then he come around again, oh, maybe a year or so ago."

"Why did he start a theater?"

"Hell, Arrigo's always liked that theater garbage. When he was a kid, we called him 'the Actor.' He always had a thing for books. Besides, when he hooked up with Big Tiny, it made a good front."

"I hear his theater is a pretty artsy operation. Funny thing to use as a front, wouldn't you say?"

The Swede didn't know what to say. He shrugged.

The ADA consulted his fingernails for a moment. "You know what, Dantino? I think this is all a lot of crapola. If your brother's really with the Varese, why the hell is he all over TV and the papers, talking against union coercion and featherbedding?"

The Swede cleared his throat; the lawyer had warned him that this would be the part they'd stick at. "Yeah, well, it's a hell of a good cover, ain't it? Besides, I think Arrigo half-believes all that stuff he says on TV. Only, what he *don't* say is that he thinks you can't be a real businessman in this country no more. Not with the government taking everything in taxes, and all those damn rules they got. Arrigo says the only real businessmen left are in the organization."

Fagan raised an eyebrow. Santo looked thoughtful. The ADA's expression did not change. Finally the ADA said, "You've been a Varese street punk for years. The police know all about you. How come they don't have anything about your brother being with the Varese?"

"How do I know why the cops don't know nothing? Jesus, Arrigo's known Big Tiny since he was a kid. Ask around the neighborhood— everybody knows about it. Go to a place like the Jumping Joint. Arrigo was there, and a lot of other places, too, just a couple weeks ago."

"If your brother's been to Varese hangouts, we'll find out."

In the silence, the child cried again. The Swede hesitated, considering the thing that no one knew, not the lawyer Mr. Shaw had sent, not even Mr. Shaw. If he told it, that would prove he was doing his best.

"You oughta check your records, too," he said. "You oughta look back about twenty years ago, and see what Arrigo done when he was only thirteen. Only just a kid."

He sat back in his chair. For the first time, he didn't hate the story he was telling.

19

At the breakfast table on Tuesday morning, Donald Shaw picked up his newspapers and smiled. The story was now out.

One headline read, "PICKET LINE DEATH MAY INVOLVE ACTOR AND CRIME FAMILY." But he preferred the headline in the tabloid: "ACTOR AND MOB LINKED TO PICKET LINE KILLING?" Most people wouldn't even notice the question mark; Shaw had read of a survey proving that fact.

The lawyer had done a good job, he thought; too bad about the man's fatal accident, which would take place in a few days. A good plan left no loose ends.

Shaw began to read the article, still smiling, thinking that the plan was one of his best because it would accomplish so many things: discredit the actor; keep Joncas happy and shine up his public image still more; and put the spotlight on the Varese, so everybody would keep connecting "Italian" with organized crime.

Fortunately, Shaw thought, the cops didn't know much these days, but they still knew about Italians and blood ties. Even the dumbest rookie knew that crime families were built on biological families; that alone would give credence to the Swede's story about his brother. And when the cops checked and found a few things, some of which would be fed to them by informants, Dante would be under heavy suspicion. With luck, he could even be indicted and tried, although Shaw's inclination was not to let it get that far.

He read on, and laughed out loud when he saw a quote from Morty Codd: "I said Dante was creating a climate of violence, didn't I? What a hell of a sad way to be proved right."

Across the breakfast table, Mrs. Shaw heard the laugh and cleared her throat. "Donald," she said, "your father and I did some figuring last night. I'm afraid it looks as if we went over our August allotment. It was the donation to the earthquake victims. We just didn't real-ize . . ."

Shaw looked up. The window behind her gave on a velvet lawn, and the sun made her white hair a halo. "It's OK," he said. "Just let me know how much."

"That's good of you, Donald. It helps to know you're capable of goodness like that."

He looked at her expressionlessly until her eyes dropped. Then he went on reading.

His parents had been astonished when he asked them to come and live with him, saying he was a lonely bachelor. They would have been more than astonished to learn the real reason.

They had raised him in a small Florida town, hoping to instill in him the fear and love of the Lord. What he absorbed instead, and never forgot, was the sour, shabby odor of their house, the eternally bland taste of his mother's food, and the endless talk of humility and love, like a soft and glutinous rain. His parents said there was dignity in hard work and poverty; they said all people were born in sin and must therefore suffer; they said pleasure came only from sacrifice and prayer, and all other forms were weapons of the devil. They forbade him to buy records or go to the movies or to read anything but religious tracts.

He had committed his first theft—a comic book—to shock and hurt them; instead they had forgiven him. As he increased the size and scope of his petty crimes, he became skilled and clever, but his real purpose was to watch their faces—to see the distress, the guilt, and the conflict over whether to report him, and then the orgy of forgiveness and prayer that washed it all away. Soon he stopped bothering to hide his contempt for them and merely spread it to the rest of the world, which, he learned, shared their ideas to a great extent. They all preached the value of "hard work" and "earning your way," yet they said the greatest good was to give up everything for others; so what was the point of working? They all lectured against sin, yet their highest virtue was forgiveness; so what was the point of not sinning? Once he stole a black suit and gave it to his father, who looked like a scarecrow in the pulpit. His mother said, "It's a sin, Donald, a terrible thing. We'll return the suit right away. But you were thinking of your father, so there must be some good in you."

They had been pleased when he decided to become a CPA; they did not know that his schooling was financed by the gang of Miami street toughs he organized to work for him. Nor did they know that he put his skills to work for the family that ran Florida, the Torinos. He found and groomed someone to work in a large brokerage house; in a few years the man was in a position on the margins desk to invent customers for the computer and to negotiate imaginary securities transfers, almost two million dollars' worth. But the heads of the family distrusted such activity and the power it gave Shaw. They were aging men, with Sicily still in their veins and outlooks; they wore white ties, put plaster Madonnas on their lawns, and took blood oaths of loyalty, while exuding machismo and garlic. When Shaw learned they were planning to get rid of him, in the usual Sicilian way, he disappeared, taking with him a dozen of the younger men and a permanent hatred of Italians.

He began to move toward his real goal, which he had known since he was a boy: Whatever else he got involved in, he wanted to control as much as he could of the entertainment industries. He was not particularly interested in the old-time rackets—numbers, prostitution, narcotics, casinos; not only were they too filled with Italians, they were also too obvious places for the law-enforcement agencies to look. He preferred such industries as films, recordings, theater, and books; they seemed more sophisticated and challenging. It did not occur to him that they were also the things he had been forbidden as a child.

He went to Los Angeles and discovered that the financial arrangements governing the making of movies and TV shows were incredibly loose; people often had only the haziest notion of what their returns should be. It was easy to train and place people in various accounting departments, where they could siphon off huge sums under the guise of paying production costs and talent fees. At one point Shaw had five different companies set up to receive the funds.

But when he invited his parents to join him, they would not come. The Reverend Shaw refused to live in a city built on the immorality of the movie business, not even for the chance to found and administer a religious institute. New York became the compromise.

In New York, Shaw heard of a man who had surfaced in one of the Varese unions, the transport workers. Shaw had no interest in that union per se, but it was affiliated with the Brotherhood of American Labor, which also included the entertainment-industry unions. Labor, Shaw felt, was getting too large a share of the entertainment pie; in any case, one could not control an industry unless one also controlled its workers.

When Shaw met Joncas, he saw a man with dress-shirt ambitions who felt trapped in a blue-collar union; he understood, almost by osmosis, Joncas's wish to be high in the city's establishment while simultaneously despising it. Shaw offered him a deal that would grant his wish. For his part, Shaw would get the Varese out of the transport union, letting Joncas take the credit for "cleaning labor's house" and thus becoming its new Hercules. Then, by financial and other means, Shaw would help Joncas climb the Brotherhood's executive ladder. Joncas, in return, would help him infiltrate other unions in the Brotherhood and gain access to its treasury, especially its pension and welfare funds.

Shaw offered the deal because there were two situations he knew he could exploit. For one, the transport-union membership had begun to change from Italian and Irish to blacks and Hispanics, so that the Varese were no longer as comfortable there as they once had been. For another, the Varese family itself was in crisis: Old man Varese had died, without direct male issue, and two cousins were fighting one another for control. One of them had the approval of the ruling council of the New York families; the other was Big Tiny.

First, with Joncas's help, Shaw got the Varese to believe there would soon be a big federal investigation of the Brotherhood, especially of the transport union. Then Shaw offered Big Tiny a trade: He would kill Tiny's rival cousin—in such a way that there would be no retaliatory war—if Tony would then pull the family out of the transport union. As a P.S., Shaw threatened to make the same offer to the rival cousin if Tiny refused to take it.

Eventually, knowing he was losing his internal power struggle, Tiny agreed. Within a week, using information from Joncas, Shaw saw to it that the rival cousin was dead—along with his wife and children and his ten closest associates. The next day the ruling council, and Big Tiny, got a tape recording made by the cousin just before he died, saying he had an incurable and horrible blood disease and was taking the others with him in a suicide pact. The tape was quite authentic; considering what had been done to the man in order to get him to make it, Shaw thought, he had sounded remarkably convincing.

Big Tiny became angry, Shaw heard, when the federal investigation of the union failed to materialize and when Joncas started taking public credit for cleaning up the union. But Shaw thought there was little danger that Tiny would try some kind of retaliation; the risk of revealing his own role in his cousin's death was too great. As to possible conflict with the ruling council, Shaw insured against it by staying away from the old-time rackets that were still the favorites of the old Sicilians on the council. And he reasoned that his peers—the younger men who had discovered the rewards of white-collar crime—were like him: more interested in balance sheets than bullets.

The deal with Joncas had not started to pay off for several years, until he stepped down from the transport-union presidency. Joncas had kept the union scrupulously clean; it was the linchpin of his reputation, which grew still more when he got the Varese out of two other union locals, by purely legitimate means. Finally he backed a Puerto Rican to succeed him as transport president, an act for which he was much admired, and then, freed of "the ethnics," as he called them, he could concentrate on the larger field of the Brotherhood—the "great reformer" who quietly began robbing the treasury.

When Shaw located and purchased the Westchester estate, his parents came at last to join him. If anyone ever did suspect that Donald Shaw was not just a wealthy recluse, he could now be classified as one of those crazy right-wing millionaires who pour their money into religion. No one needed to know the kind of pleasure he got from having his parents with him—subjecting them to a gourmet chef, an elaborate sound system, a library that included rare nineteenth-century works of pornography, and a private screening room where he sometimes made them join him in watching X-rated films. He made it almost impossible for his parents not to know what he was; he let his men wander around freely and explained that they were gardeners, even though their only "tools" were often visible in holsters. He liked to watch the senior Shaws struggle to evade the knowledge, and try to choke down their fear of him, by clutching their amulet of "goodness."

He looked across the breakfast table. "Mama!" he said sharply.

Her face was as full of intersecting lines as a hairnet; he watched fear tug at all the lines.

"Yes, Donald?" she said.

"Here's a story in the papers you might like. About an actor everybody thought was a good Christian. Only it turns out that he belongs to a crime family and sent his own brother to kill an innocent man."

When she hesitated, he shoved the paper at her.

"Yeah, I seen the paper," growled Big Tiny Varese into his bedroom phone. "I don't know what the hell to make of it yet. I just now read it." He listened for a while, pinching the silk of his pajama leg between two fingers. "The Swede is a two-bit jerk. I can't figure out what he's up to. Maybe his brother was on the level the other day. Maybe this whole thing is coming from Shaw, like he was hinting. Only, what the hell has Shaw got against the actor?" He frowned. "No, no. Why would the actor be working *with* Shaw? That don't make no sense at all. Besides I got a nose for liars, and I didn't get no stink at all from the actor. You got some of the boys keeping an eye on him? Good. Make sure the cops don't spot them, especially now, for God's sake, but find out who he sees and where he goes. I ain't doing nothing till I get some idea what the hell is going on here." He listened for a moment, then sighed. "Yeah, well, he ain't making me laugh no more."

Jac Sanda read the papers twice, first in one frantic gulp and then slowly, noting down whatever details they contained.

No one could believe it, she thought; the story was too preposterous. But she also knew the public had an almost religious belief that whatever appeared in print was true.

She sat back in the desk chair, wondering what business she had looking down on the public when her own behavior was so contradictory.

She had decided Erik Dante was weak and opportunistic after he admitted his relationship with Maeve Jerrold; yet that judgment coexisted with a blind belief in his strength and integrity.

She had wanted to help him the moment she heard about the killing on the picket line; yet she wanted to hurt him, too, to rake her nails across his face for saying *I can't see you anymore, except on news business,* and then to let her hands . . .

She had told him to get out of her life, yet she had tried to check on the Briarwood dinner theaters. But if Joncas and some mysterious new crime czar were somehow involved with those theaters, her phone calls had as yet produced no hint of such a thing. And if they did . . . She glanced across the room, at the picture of Karen on the Central Park carousel. If checking on Briarwood did lead anywhere, she thought, if her inability to put Erik Dante out of her mind and life meant that Karen would . . . She pushed the rest of the thought away.

She looked again at the newspapers. "PICKET LINE DEATH MAY IN-VOLVE ACTOR AND CRIME FAMILY." For several minutes she sat drumming her nails on the desk, her lower lip caught in her teeth. Then she swiveled to the side, consulted her card file of sources, picked up her phone, and dialed. "Good morning, Tom," she said to her contact at the city's Organized Crime Strike Force.

"I wondered whether I'd be hearing from you today."

"And I wondered what you could tell me about this Rossano Dantino and his Varese connections."

"You and every other reporter in town. But I'm not sure I should tell you anything. I'm on to you this time, Jac."

"Meaning?"

"Oh, come on. A couple weeks ago, when you called and asked me about Joncas and whether he still had any dealings with the Varese, I couldn't figure out what you were up to. But now I know. It was this theater business, wasn't it?"

"Was it?"

"Come on, Jac, be gracious in defeat. You figured the Varese were mixed up in it somehow. You had the setup wrong—Joncas wasn't *in* on it, he was the victim—but still, you'd heard something. I'd like to know what, where, and how."

"It was nothing. Just a hunch I had, but it turned out to be wrong."

"Christ!" he said. "You people always protect your sources, don't you?" When she was silent, he added tightly, "I don't know how in hell we're supposed to do a job with no cooperation from anybody and our hands tied a hundred ways."

"Tom, I swear to you I have no information. About Joncas or the Varese or what happened at the Poets and Paupers Theater. I'm not protecting anybody." Now the silence was on his part. "Besides," she said lightly, "how could I know something that one of the top organized-crime experts doesn't know?"

His laugh made no attempt to conceal its bitterness.

"What's the matter, Tom?" she said, still lightly. "Did they cut your budget again?"

He swore, then took a breath that sounded like the preface to an explosion. "Last time we talked, you were in a hell of a hurry. You wanted to know about Joncas, and I barely got the words out before you took the answer and ran."

She sighed. "I'm not running today."

"You want a real story this time? Tell your public that police intelligence about the mobs is lousy."

"I don't know what you mean."

"You're asking about this Varese punk who did the picket-line killing? The most recent information we have on him is about seven years old. You want to know about Big Tiny Varese—who he sleeps with, who his new boys might be? I can't tell you, that's who. We haven't even got a picture of him that's newer than ten years ago."

"But . . . but don't you have taps on all those people?"

Tom laughed harshly. "You never heard of the antibugging laws? Before they came in, there were hundreds of taps, legal and illegal, all over the place. We knew the color of a mobster's underwear, and when he washed it. Now most of our stuff comes from informants. But we don't get out to check half of it, so who knows how true it is? And the reason we don't get out is, guess what, our old friend manpower cuts. Everybody's had to reduce the intelligence services. Hardly anybody's out on the streets anymore keeping daily tabs on the families. And even if they do get out on the streets, it's almost impossible to do a good job because the unions are making the city enforce its labor contracts very strictly now. After an eight-hour tour, a cop has to call in and be replaced or else go on overtime. You can't tail a mobster that way. You've got to move with him—twelve, sixteen hours, maybe more. A detective used to be able to do that and then make up for it unofficially by taking off for vacation a day early or something. But no more."

"I see," Jac said.

"Do you? There's also the Freedom of Information Act. Say we build up a dossier on somebody. Under the act, he can get access to it. And then he can figure out which of his boys have been talking to the government, and he can wipe them out. It's already happened lots of times. So now we're all shy of building up dossiers."

"You think we should get rid of the bugging laws and the act, then?"

Tom sighed, his anger receding. "I'm not thinking anything, Jac. I'm just telling you the way it is."

"Are you saying," she asked slowly, "that there could be somebody new in the picture, somebody big, whom you don't know about?"

"I'll put it this way: In the past decade, have you heard any law-enforcement agency mention a new name in organized crime?"

She thought for a moment. "No. It's always the same old ones, the New York families we've been hearing about for years."

"As far as we know, they're still in control. We did hear rumors once about somebody new moving in from L.A., but there was nothing to back it up. And there hasn't been a war, so if somebody new moved in, he did it peacefully. Which is pretty damned unlikely."

"But you're not sure? And what you told me last time about Joncas, that he's just what he seems to be?"

"To the best of our knowledge, he is. Only, if our knowledge was what it should be, we'd know why in hell a Varese punk shot his son-in-law. And how the punk's brother ties into it."

"You mean the police are taking that story seriously?"

"We take everything seriously."

"But it's crazy, Tom. Erik Dante involved with the Varese?"

"You're in the news business and you can still say something is crazy? And what makes you so sure he's not involved?"

"Well, I know the man," she said lamely.

"Did you know the boy, though?"

"What does that mean?"

"Nothing. Just keep your eyes and ears open. And if you hear something funny, consider telling your friendly law-enforcement officers."

When she hung up, the receiver was damp. She could stand anything, she thought, even contradictions, but not what she was feeling: helplessness.

The phone rang. She jumped, then picked it up and forced a normal tone into her voice. "This is Jac Sanda."

It was one of the contacts she had called about Briarwood, a woman on the drama desk at one of the dailies. When she hung up, she had heard there were rumors of a disgruntled investor at Briarwood, and she had the number of someone who might know the investor's name.

20

Maeve got to the theater just after three o'clock and sat in the back of the auditorium.

She was there because Erik had asked her to come; he had called a full company meeting and wanted her to attend, he said, because no one at Poets and Paupers had seen her for weeks. She didn't mind being there; she felt as detached from all of them as if they were in a play someone else had written.

The company wasn't a full one any longer. After Erik's TV interview with Codd, two people had left, without explanation. Four more had gone in the month since then, so the group was now down to forty. Erik said they all seemed loyal, and angered by the union picketing, but he hadn't spoken to them as a group since the killing.

He held up the morning papers and told them he didn't understand the story; he knew only that he was innocent of any connection with the Pomerantz killing or with the Varese. "Someone is trying to frame me," he said. "You know what a frame is—the attempt to make you pay for something you didn't do. And I guess you all know how I feel about paying for things that weren't done."

They almost laughed at that, Maeve thought—at least some of them.

He said it was one of the greatest honors of his life that so many of them had stuck with him—"They say you can tell a man by the employees he keeps, and I couldn't be keeping a better company." He said he hoped they would give him the benefit of the doubt now, but if they couldn't, and felt they had to leave, he would understand. However, he intended to go on getting ready to open and needed to know how many would still be staying.

One of the carpenters asked whether anyone was still buying tickets. Ruth, from the box office, said, "We started off great after Erik announced that ticket-as-a-vote business, but since the shooting, I get a lot of knitting done." The silence was long. Finally Erik broke it, his voice confident, to say they would have to make sure that the public knew they were still in business. And that he categorically denied the story in the press; he had done no wrong.

Frankie, the Infernal, cried out from the second row, "Jeez, Erik, it's like in the play! Like the part where you tell how you felt when they chained you to a rock for stealing the fire."

Erik looked puzzled, and some of Frankie's fellow Infernals told her to shut up because what did she know about it. But the girl, her moon face flushed, lifted her chin and, in an adolescent singsong, recited a passage from the second act of *Firestorm*: " 'I took their punishment, but not their verdict. While I was coupled to the rock, a beak working deep in my flesh each day for decades, one thing only kept that bird from tearing out my spirit as well: the certainty that I had done no wrong.' "

If she herself weren't so calm and so removed from everything, Maeve thought, it might have been touching to hear her own words delivered that way—badly, of course, but with such conviction and such worship of Erik.

The company reacted as little as she did. When the meeting broke up, six of them, their faces either defensive or sad, looked as if they would be leaving Poets and Paupers.

Erik was too busy to take her home, but he insisted that someone go out with her and get her a cab. He had been so devoted, she thought, ever since the two men had threatened her. Devoted, concerned, thoughtful—a whole thesaurus full of words of tenderness. But none of passion.

Of course, she thought calmly as she rode up First Avenue, she had always expected that to happen someday.

Ten minutes after she got home, before she had even changed out of the gold pantsuit or loosened the coil of her hair, the detectives came to see her.

She was not upset, not even when the two earnest, slightly awkward strangers sat on the couch and pushed questions, like sticks, into the private corners of her life: Where did you meet Erik Dante? How long have you known him? You're business partners? And good friends? Are you more than good friends?

"Surely that's irrelevant," she said calmly.

"Are you aware of all Dante's business dealings?"

"I've never been good at business. He takes care of all that."

The other detective said, "You know anything about Dante's life when he was a kid?"

"Yes. It was unspeakable."

"He ever talk about his brother?"

"They had nothing in common but a surname. Erik changed even that."

"But he saw his brother recently. Did you know that?" She nodded. "Why did he want to see him?"

She came down from her distance a bit and studied their noncommittal faces. "He said it was something personal. I don't know the details."

Without moving, the two men seemed to push themselves closer to her. "Dante's been seen recently in some of the Varese hangouts. Why is that?"

"I believe," she said stiffly, "that he had to go to such places in order to contact his brother."

"Then how come he went the night after the killing? When his brother was already in custody?"

"I . . . I don't know that he did go."

"Could be there's a lot you don't know about him."

"I don't think so."

"Good. Then you probably can tell us all about when he was a kid. He ran with a gang, you know." She said nothing. "Was he ever in trouble with the law?"

Suddenly she was separated from the two detectives only by a strip of thin ice. "I really have nothing to tell you. Except that it's beyond the realm of possibility that Erik Dante would have anything to do with people who organize and perpetrate crime."

"You seem real sure of that."

"A man can lie about anything, but he can't fake his character."

"Dante's lied to you, then? What about?"

"Nothing! You can't believe this story his brother has told?"

"We check out everything. Now, Mrs. Jerrold—"

"No! No. I can't talk to you any longer. I'm sorry. I have things to do. You'll have to leave now."

Finally, unwillingly, they did.

She closed and locked the door after them. They were going to believe the story, she thought. They would find out about the boy Erik once had killed, and then they would believe his brother and arrest him.

The sense of calm and distance, which had begun to wrap around her the night Erik called her about the killing on the picket line and had protected her for the five days since, growing thicker and colder each day, like an icy glaze, cracked away fully, leaving her alone with a familiar demon who squatted in one corner of the apartment.

Her eyes swung away from it, to the birch trees that seemed to sway slightly inside their crystal home, urging her to join them and be cool and quiet. Instead she felt hot with shame. Even an adolescent girl had been unafraid to shout to everyone that Erik had done no wrong. Whereas she . . .

"You can't hide in this apartment while they ruin him," she whispered. "You have to help him."

The familiar demon had been waiting for those words. It grinned like a cat and reminded her of the memories upon which it squatted, as their guardian and historian.

It recalled her painful attempt to climb out of the black pit after Jonathan was killed: first the convalescence with her family in Chicago; then the pitiful attempts to get some of Jonathan's poems published posthumously—but how could one explain in a letter of submission that these were extraordinary works by an original mind?—so back they came, rejected; then the slow return of her own desire to write and the black notebooks in which she indulged it, letting no one see the poems because they never were good enough; then the determination to do some kind of useful work and earn her way in the practical world; and finally the day when she had not only a Ph.D. but also a teaching contract, even though it was just for freshman composition.

She still could smell the chalky, sweaty classroom in which she had first confronted them—the students who were either mindlessly cheerful or else sulky, who knew little of grammar and less of literature and whom she could not reach in any language. She learned that they called her "Ms. Twitch" behind her back, and when she tried to confront one of them because of the blatant plagiarism in his homework assignment, his sullen, mocking hostility had made her nerves start to crawl and dive down . . . and backward she had gone, to Chicago and her family.

She had wanted to please them then, more than ever, and when one of her brothers introduced her to Arthur Jerrold, who seemed as capable as her family of looking at the world and producing money from it, she had tried hard to like him. And succeeded. She kept a beautiful home for Arthur, entertaining his business associates often and, separately, her own friends from the music and art worlds. She had not realized how Arthur felt until one night when he pulled away from her after making love and said, gasping with more than sexual passion, "You never let me *in*, goddamm it! You'll open your legs but nothing else—nothing!" She had cringed at the vulgarity of his words, but a month later she was hearing worse ones, about divorce.

She hadn't wanted a penny from Arthur, but her brothers had said, "Honey, that's crazy. Be practical, for once in your life. Take the money and start an arts foundation or something." She would have laughed if she hadn't felt so numbed.

Instead she had used the money to retreat to her useless realm of art, the one place where she could contribute something, even though it was only her passive appreciation of the works of others, her ability to stand dumb with emotion before the words and sounds and visions of those who, unlike her, had been able to make the world accept them.

She had learned nothing, she thought, from her family and from Arthur. She had no skills with which to help Erik. Nothing but her money. Not even the knowledge of how to use it in the world of politics and power, where he was fighting.

She closed her eyes. She hadn't wanted to think of money—not since making him take the theater building. More than ever now, money was tainted. But to those who ran the practical world, money was everything. Wasn't it one of the great bromides of fiction that money was both the means and the end of most human struggles? So wouldn't that be true of whoever was trying to frame Erik?

If only, she thought, she could do something without feeling afraid. Fear was ugly, like soiling oneself. *Fear can't hurt you,* Erik had said, when the two men threatened her, *unless you let it make your decisions . . . .*

For a while she seriously considered contacting her ex-husband, who surely would know what she might do, how she might use her money, for once, as the rest of the world did. But Arthur would ask too many questions, she thought; he would want to take over, not to help her. . . .

She stood quite still, thinking of someone who was practical but would have no right to ask questions and no need to take charge, who had wanted to help and be kind.

"What do you think?" Fagan asked, driving downtown to the stationhouse.

"I think she's scared," Santo said.

"Sure. But is it because she knows something about his connection to the Varese?"

"Can't tell yet. It sure smells money in that apartment. Why would Dante need a mob connection if he's got her?"

"Maybe she's in it with him."

"Come on. Her family's been loaded forever."

"I suppose. Well, maybe there'll be some news when we get back. Maybe somebody got lucky checking the old records."

"He was about thirteen, according to the Swede?"

"Yeah."

"I remember when I was still up in the Bronx," Fagan said, "there was a twelve-year-old who sliced up his grandmother to get the five bucks rolled in her garter."

"Where is he now?"

"Back on the streets. Where else?"

They drove several blocks in silence.

"Maybe the Swede is lying about that old business," Fagan said.

"And about everything else?"

"Yeah."

"If he is, why is word coming off the street that Dante's involved with Big Tiny? Why did Morty Codd confirm that Dante tried to pay him off?"

"I don't know. We keep digging till we find out."

They drove on.

"Hey," said the cabdriver as he dropped the flag, "I've seen you on TV. On the Channel Ten news."

"Yes. I just got off the air."

The driver patted a newspaper on the seat beside him. "You had that actor on once, right? And now they say he had his brother shoot Joncas's son-in-law?"

"The *brother* says it, yes." Jac hesitated. "You're a union man. What do you think of the actor?"

"You see any bumper sticker on this cab that says 'Featherbedding

Is for the Birds'?" The driver swerved to avoid a pothole. "Ah, he maybe made some sense, for a small place, like he's got. But if he was behind this killing, who the hell cares what he says?" Jac sighed. "If you're tired, lady, it's a long ride to Staten Island. You could catch a nap."

"I'm not tired. You're keyed up when you get off the air."

But that was not the reason, Jac thought. By noon, she had managed to locate the disgruntled Briarwood investor. He told her stories of suspiciously lean profits and of a bookkeeper named Amy Stone who had left mysteriously and might know something; he had always intended to talk to her but never got around to it. Just before the *Journal* went on, Jac had tracked down the woman's whereabouts.

After what was indeed a long ride, the cab stopped in front of a small house. In the failing light a sprinkler was shedding diamonds of water on a newly mowed lawn. Jac told the driver to wait around the corner.

A thin young woman answered the bell. She had the pale skin of the natural redhead and lips compressed with caution. "Yes, I'm Amy Stone."

"My name is Jac Sanda, Ms. Stone, with the Channel Ten news. I'm doing some checking for a story, and I wonder whether I could ask you—"

"I've seen your show. But I'm afraid I couldn't help you."

It took Jac five minutes to get inside, and then she had to do it by asking to use the phone to call a cab back to the city. She faked the call, told Amy Stone there would be a twenty-minute wait, and finagled herself onto the couch in a living room that had little other furniture, no rugs, and no ornament except a shining cleanliness.

She began to tell Amy Stone about the story she was planning, on dinner theaters, and finally brought up the Briarwood chain. The woman acknowledged that she had kept the books for them for a while but would say nothing about either the operation or her reason for leaving it. She sat with perfect composure, legs crossed but hands folded in her lap a little too tightly. "I can't tell you anything," she said.

"Why not?"

"I'm afraid that's my business."

"I'd keep the information confidential."

"If it's going on the air, it could hardly be confidential."

Jac put down her notepad. "Why are you so loyal to your former employers?"

"I can't help you. I'm sorry."

She was pretty, Jac thought, like the old-fashioned doll with a sweet china face that Karen had gotten from her grandmother. And like the doll's, her expression never changed. What would she be like, Jac wondered, without that polite, careful mask?

She found out. A wail came from the top of the stairs, followed by a small boy holding a broken toy truck. Amy Stone was with him on the stairs in a moment, color flooding her voice and face. She coddled and kissed him, she blotted his tears, she examined the truck and explained how it could be fixed. "And if I can't do it, honey," she said, "I'm sure Daddy will fix it when you go see him this weekend." She stood up, holding the boy, who locked a fist in her hair and leaned his head into her neck. "Hadn't you better try the cab again, Ms. Sanda?"

"How old is he?" Jac said unsteadily.

"Four last week."

"My daughter is five." Then Jac heard herself add, "I didn't tell the truth, Ms. Stone. I'm not doing a story on dinner theaters. I have personal reasons for asking about Briarwood. I'm afraid that something . . . crooked has been going on there. I know that my ex-husband, my little girl's father, was involved in Briarwood in some way, but I don't know how. I hope it's not . . . My daughter would . . ."

The little boy said, "Is the lady crying about my truck?"

"No, honey." Amy Stone sighed. "All right, Ms. Sanda. I shouldn't do this, but . . . Sit down."

At ten o'clock that night, Jac rang Burt's doorbell.

He answered, still wearing a business suit but in stocking feet.

"It's not Karen," she said. "Karen's fine. I have to talk to you."

She came into the apartment, which seemed to belong not to him but to a decorator who had loved the beige family, lithographs, and monotypes. The only real touch of Sanda's own was hanging beside the fireplace: a huge picture of Karen wearing a pink sundress and hugging a red ball as if it were the world and she had just caught it.

"You could have called first," he said. "I just got home. I'm beat."

"You came to see me uninvited, not so long ago."

"A lot of good it did. You can't say I didn't try to warn you about that Erik Dante. Thank God this picket-line killing has taken him out of the picture."

"I thought you were a friend of Joncas's," she said.

"What the hell does that mean?"

"You just said thank God his son-in-law was killed."

"Dammit, Jac, why do you eternally and forever twist my words?"

"Maybe to try to shake some sense into them."

He sank onto the oatmeal-colored couch and smiled suddenly. "Ah, God, Jac, we used to be so happy. Remember? When you were just out of school and I—"

"You were different then, Burt. Not so pragmatic."

"Why do you hate that word so much?"

"Because it means tossing principles out the window."

"According to whose dictionary? What it actually means is learning to live in the real world. Recognizing that you can't do anything worthwhile until and unless you've got enough power and influence."

"How much is enough?" He said nothing. "Never mind, Burt. That isn't the question I came to ask." She pushed her hair over her shoulders and lifted her chin. "Just before the divorce, you mentioned a certain investment you'd made. I'd like to know more about it. Briarwood."

His answer was casual. "It's a chain of big dinner theaters. Top-name entertainers. Why do you want to know?"

"I've heard that some of the Briarwood investors may have been swindled out of a lot of their profits."

"I certainly haven't heard that."

"Do you have any relationship with Briarwood other than being an investor?"

He sat erect. "What do you mean by that?"

"What I said. Are you going to answer the question?"

"I don't think so," he snapped. "Not when you sound as if you're suggesting I'm doing something criminal."

Her expression didn't change. "You said it, Burt, not me. I'm just asking."

"Goddammit! How can you even think such a thing about me?"

"Only with difficulty. That's why I'm here. To ask you to explain your relationship to Briarwood."

"Explain what, for God's sake? I heard it would be a good investment, so I—"

"Did you hear it from Joncas?"

"What the hell's the difference? The point is, I checked, and it sounded good, so I went in. But if there's been anything funny going on, you can be damn sure I didn't know about it. And wouldn't be in it if I did. Where the hell do you get these ideas, anyway?"

"I'm in the business of hearing things."

"From whom? Somebody you took seriously enough to bring you running over here. Listen, Jac, if someone's spreading stories about a deal, an investment I've made, I've got a right to know who's doing it."

"Do you swear you're not involved in or aware of any kind of skimming operation at Briarwood?" He made a contemptuous sound. "Will you swear it in Karen's name?"

"What the hell kind of melodrama is this?" His eyes swung to the photograph by the fireplace and then leaped away. "Yes. I swear it. Satisfied now?" She nodded briefly. "Then satisfy me. Tell me where you heard it. You owe me that."

She hesitated. "From someone who's in a position to know. That's all I can tell you."

"You mean someone from Briarwood?"

"I don't reveal my sources. You know that."

"Sources? You're doing some kind of story?"

"If I was, I wouldn't discuss it with you."

"I should think you'd have better stories than that to work on. Like following up on the Poets and Paupers Theater. But I suppose," he added viciously, "you don't want to learn that your actor lover is a gangster."

"He's not either one. A gangster or my lover."

"Really? He threw you over? You mean Maeve Jerrold pulled the purse strings and he fell back into line?"

"What makes you jump to that conclusion? What do you know about Maeve Jerrold?"

"Nothing! I don't care why he threw you over, as long as he did. Don't you care about Karen at all? What if it turns out her mother was mixed up with a gangster?"

"It won't. But what if her father is?"

"Goddammit!" he cried. "You don't know what Karen is to me! You've never understood. She's what gets me through all the hypocrisy and stupidity I have to . . . Don't you dare suggest I don't love her!"

"That's not what I said, Burt."

"You're the one who doesn't care about her. Who leaves her at home all day with another woman. Who doesn't give a damn about her own reputation, not to mention mine. You're the one—"

"Shut up, Burt!"

He did, in amazement. Then he said, with a flash of his normal charm, "I've been working too hard. Tends to shorten the wick, you know. But when it comes to you and that actor, I can't be too sorry."

"No?" she said. "Maybe you can't be sorry enough."

Even though Sanda's nerves had been screaming for her to go, after she left, he was alone, and that wasn't good either. He made himself a drink and thought of unloading his briefcase; he went to the phone, stared at it, but veered away; he turned on the TV without seeing it.

When the phone rang, he nearly didn't answer. "Maeve!" he said.

"I certainly wasn't expecting . . ." He listened. "Sorry, I was out of the office all afternoon, and I just now got home. What can I do for you?"

His face became a map of amazement. "I'm sorry," he said, "I don't think I've got this straight. How would *I* know who's trying to frame Dante? Assuming that somebody is. . . . Well, sure, I've been around, Maeve, but I . . ." He listened again. "All right. I'll keep my ears open and let you know if I hear anything. But I really don't think I can help you."

He hung up, shook his head, and grimaced. He moved away from the phone, but it seemed to keep pulling at his thoughts and his eyes, wherever he went in the room.

21

In the heart of the city they were starting to build a mountain: not a whole mountain, but one huge crag. They were using lumber to frame out its basic shape, which would vaguely suggest a cross, then building up its dimensions and angles with Styrofoam and canvas, which later would be painted gray, brown, and black, and stippled. From the audience it would seem like one of nature's creations, but in the scene shop it was just starting to emerge in three manmade sections.

Erik was working on one of them. With Frankie as his helper, he had been at it for most of the morning, cutting one-by-threes for the frame and nailing it together. No one was quite sure why he was there: because the crew was undermanned now, or because he needed to be working with his hands. The tech director had tried to joke: "You sure you want to do this? Build your own prison?" But Erik hadn't replied.

He was just starting to cut out blocks of Styrofoam when the shop door opened. Frankie saw it; she nudged his arm and pointed.

He had been thinking of Big Tiny and the silence from him; when he looked up, he was unprepared for the sight of Jac and thus completely open to it. He forgot the reasons he shouldn't walk across the room and take her in his arms; he was halfway there before he remembered and saw the chain of his own feelings cross her face.

"You're covered with sawdust," she said.

"Unavoidable, when you work with a saw."

"I didn't know you helped out on the sets, too."

"Sometimes."

"What are you doing?"

"Building a mountain."

"I didn't know human beings could do that."

"In the theater you can."

"And then they chain you to it?"

"Ah, but I break free."

They were grinning at each other like children, Erik thought. He saw the same realization strike her. Her face sobered, and she said, "I have something to tell you, some business. May we talk somewhere?"

"Let's go outside. It's quiet now, without the picket line." He took her arm; she wore a short-sleeved dress the color of green apples, and her skin, beneath his fingers, felt sun-warm.

They stood in the alleyway outside the shop door, a little farther apart than was necessary. No, Erik thought, it was necessary.

"Karen asked about you the other day. About the house you built for the stories."

"Tell her it's shaky, but still standing. I thought you were angry with me."

"I was. I am. But they're trying to frame you."

"Yes." He couldn't help smiling again, with the relief of knowing she believed him innocent.

"Who do you think is behind it?"

"My brother told me he had gone to work for a new boss—the man in Westchester. I wasn't sure I believed him, but I do now. He can't still be with the Varese. They wouldn't be making him tell a story that implicated their own family. Besides, I've learned that the man from Westchester does exist and that his name is Donald. But I can't seem to get any further than that."

She looked away for a moment, her mouth soft and slanting. "I've learned something that could be relevant. I did do some checking on Briarwood. I found someone who believes that a lot of money was being skimmed off the top. This person—let's say it's John Doe—suspected they were underreporting the size of the houses, by something like three hundred seats every night. That would mean skimming close to fifty thousand dollars a month."

Erik felt a tingling along his spine. "Don't tell me you found out Joncas is involved?"

"My John Doe had good reason to think so."

He saw with amazement that her eyes were fighting to stay dry. "What is it, Jac? Was someone else involved?"

"Yes. John Doe found that a large payment for legal fees was paid to a certain firm every month, from a special secret account. The firm is a legal-research organization run by . . . by Burt." A clear pearl in the corner of one eye dissolved along her cheek. "Burt says he's a Briarwood investor. The investors haven't made any money back yet but he's getting over fifty thousand a year through his firm. Which doesn't provide any services to Briarwood."

"Are you sure, Jac? Are you sure he doesn't do legitimate work for them?"

"Not according to his research firm. I asked one of the people who work there, someone who knows me from . . . from before."

"I see. You do something to help me, and you face the possibility of exposing and harming your ex-husband."

"I've already taken Karen away from the father she adores. What if I take her away in a much worse sense? What if I—?" She stopped.

"Don't look guilty, Jac, please. Guilt should be like money—don't take it unless you've done something to earn it." He stopped as suddenly as she had. "I realize I'm not the one to talk about what a person takes or doesn't take." He leaned one hand against the brick wall and stared down at the grimy alley floor. "I know you don't understand why I took this building. I can't explain any further, Jac. I just can't."

"I didn't ask you to. But I don't understand how you can . . . how she can . . ." She took a deep breath. "I didn't have the smallest intention of discussing that with you," she said.

"I didn't either."

"It's just that . . ."

"Yes," he said. "It's 'just.'" He looked up from the alley floor and found her mouth and eyes directly in his line of vision. He forced his hand more deeply into the rough texture of the building wall.

"My John Doe gave me some other names besides Joncas's," she said. "I've got to try to track them down, to—"

"I'll help you."

"No. Haven't you got your hands full enough, trying to keep the theater going? While the police are investigating you? This one is mine to handle, Erik. I'll tell you whatever I learn."

"I won't let you do anything dangerous on my account. I won't permit it."

"Really? When did I give you the right to give me orders?"

"I'm sorry. I won't patronize you. I'll just worry about you. And tell you to be damn careful."

"I always am," she said. "At least when it comes to investigating."

They looked at each other.

"There's sawdust on your dress," he said.

"Unavoidable, I guess, when you deal with a man who's building a mountain."

He barely heard the words she used to say good-bye; he watched her turn and go up the alleyway, the sun free to touch her long dark hair and to slide along her arms.

Amy Stone's friends were always urging her to lift her nose from the grindstone more often, but on Friday night she was grateful for her strong sense of duty.

That afternoon she had delivered her son to his father's house for the weekend. She had been planning, when she got home, to catch up on all kinds of chores, but she realized this would be a perfect time to take her friends' advice—to read, soak in the tub, order in Chinese food, and generally pamper herself.

She compromised by doing the ironing first. Then she picked up a book and enjoyed it for several hours before tendrils of guilt crept around the edges of her pleasure; she was, after all, wasting time. She read on, ordering herself to enjoy it. Finally she went into the kitchen, thinking that there was one useful thing she could be doing while she read—giving her face a workout.

She mixed up some clay for a beauty mask, using carrot juice and fuller's earth, for she was a believer in natural ingredients, and put the gummy result into a bowl. To ready her skin for the mask, she boiled water in a saucepan, draped a towel over her head, and steamed her face over the pan for ten minutes. When she put the towel aside and stood up, her face was red and steaming and her vision blurred.

For a moment she thought she was hallucinating. But they were real: two bulky figures wearing ski masks. In this weather, she thought irrelevantly.

"Are you the little lady with the big mouth?" one of them said.

"What do you mean? What are you going to do?" she cried, thanking God her boy was with his father.

"We're going to learn you not to use that mouth so much." In a second he was behind her, fingers clamped over her lips. "Get the kid first," he said to his partner. She struggled to speak, but his hand dug more deeply.

The other one took something from the inside of his jacket and laid it on the table: a foot-long piece of steel pipe. It was the same color as the eyes she could see through the slits in his mask. Then he went upstairs; she could hear him clumping through the two bedrooms. She closed her eyes to blot out the steel pipe and tried to think of a way to get to the gun stored in the back of the hall closet. There was no way. There were the kitchen knives, but they were all inside closed drawers, as useless at the moment as her own tongue. There was only the rack by the stove, with the ladle and spatula and roasting fork.

The fingers holding her mouth slipped a fraction of an inch; her skin was still very wet from the steaming. An idea burst into her mind.

Her eyes opened. She shot a quick sidewise glance at the counter, locating the exact position of the bowl of beauty mud. Then, in one continuous and violent motion, she slithered her head free of the man's hand, plunged her own hand into the bowl, and slapped its red-brown goo in the man's eyes.

While he swore and yelled for his partner, clawing at his face, she flew to the rack by the stove and grabbed the fork with the two long sharp tines. She heard the man upstairs start to come thundering down; she ran to the back door, but they must have locked it behind them when they came in. She put the roasting fork between her teeth and grappled with the lock. The man she had blinded came crashing after her. She swung around just as he lunged; she lifted the fork high with both hands, and drove it into his face.

His howl sounded oddly like that of the seal at the zoo, where she had taken her son the weekend before. For a moment she stood motionless. Then she wrenched at the door again, felt it give, and went racing into the street, toward the nearest house with lights in its windows.

At midnight Jac was reading in bed. A new biography of Theodore Roosevelt lay untouched on the nightstand. Instead she had fished an old college poetry text out of her closet.

Her father had recited poetry to her when she was quite young, and in her schooldays she had liked studying it, but history and political science had crowded it out of her life. In any case, she had concluded that poetry represented a passive way of dealing with the world—exploring emotions, rather than thinking and acting. But, she reflected, leafing through the book, what kind of world had the men of thought and action produced?

She stopped on a poem by Dylan Thomas, the lines echoing in her memory as she looked at them:

> Now as I was young and easy under the apple boughs
> About the lilting house and happy as the grass was green
> The night above the dingle starry
> Time let me hail and climb
> Golden in the heydays of his eyes,
> And honoured among wagons I was prince of the apple towns.

One couldn't rationally explain the power of such lines, Jac thought, wondering what it would be like to deal with the world by leaping past the edges of logic.

The phone rang. She picked it up automatically, her mind elsewhere.

Then she froze into position, the book held upright by the palm of one hand as she listened to Amy Stone describe what had happened to her that evening.

Once she got to a neighbor's house, Amy said, she had watched until the two men left. Then she called the police and reported an attempted robbery, nothing more. She was now at her sister's, where she would stay, with her son, until she could find a way to move as far from Staten Island as possible, thousands of miles. But she could never tell Jac where she went; Jac couldn't be trusted. "You told someone," Amy said. "You must have. How could you do it? After I told you I was warned when I left Briarwood never to talk about my job?" She was not hysterical or even angry; her voice might have come from a blindfolded statue.

"I felt sorry for you and your little girl," she said. "I thought it couldn't hurt to tell you about your husband. But you weren't satisfied with that. You had to get those other names out of me, too. I suppose you're proud of the way you can get people to talk. I guess you're a good reporter, Ms. Sanda. But I don't think you're much of a friend."

Finally Jac managed to say, "I have contacts, Amy. I can help guarantee that you get police protection."

"No! Please. The last thing I want is to call attention to myself. You're the only one who knows the two men weren't just burglars, and I'm only telling you so you'll realize what you've done and will stop it. If you discuss what happened tonight with anyone, anyone at all . . ."

"I won't," Jac said numbly.

When she hung up, the corner of the poetry book was digging into her palm. She wanted to take her hand away but couldn't; it seemed pinned. So was her mind—by the image of Amy Stone's china-doll face and the thought of how it would look if a steel pipe smashed it.

Burt couldn't have done it, she thought. She pressed her palm on the book even harder and tried to reassure herself by recalling the days when she had loved him: the quick mind that shared her own interests, the idealism he had not seemed to view as some undergraduate folly from law-school days. But it was hard to remember loving him; the major thing she had felt since leaving him was guilt.

Why couldn't Burt have done it? said a voice that seemed to come from the pain in her hand.

Because it was just a coincidence, she thought.

The voice wouldn't stop: A coincidence that Amy Stone was attacked five nights after you implied to Burt that someone was talking about Briarwood?

But he wasn't the only one, she thought quickly. There was Erik— she had told him something, too, and he might very well have let it slip to someone else, accidentally . . . or even deliberately. . . . He was a man she really knew only slightly, an intense and unpredictable man. . . . In her mind's eye she saw his big hand reach for a pipe and smash the doll's face.

Slowly she took her hand from the book, which left an angry triangular mark on her palm, and faced the fact that, to exonerate Burt, she had been forced to cast Erik in the role of a killer. To frame him, just as his enemies were trying to do.

Why had she been so determined to give Burt the benefit of every doubt?

She felt too tired to find the answer, but suddenly her mind leaped to the edges of logic and beyond—to a place where her mother stood, reciting the sour rosary of her husband's "crimes," filling the years after they were divorced with tales of his cruelty and infidelity, pouring their acid over Jac's image of a laughing giant who smelled of bay rum and gave her rides in her wagon and called her his princess of the apple towns.

He had died before she could learn which was true: her memory or the Dorian Gray of her mother's portrait.

She got up heavily and went into the kitchen to get a glass of milk. She drank it and then leaned on the counter for a long time, the glass held against her cheek. She thought of the things she had observed in the final years of her marriage: Burt's increasing concern with "connections," his abruptness when she inquired about certain aspects of his work, the contempt with which he began to speak of those who couldn't learn to "work the system," his defensive anger at the suggestion that Joncas was trying to buy him the election to the House of Representatives. . . . Yet she had struggled to ignore such things and to cling to the belief that she was divorcing him only because he wouldn't accept her as an equal.

She had no reason to feel guilt for leaving Burt, she thought. But even though she hadn't earned it, she had felt it anyway—because there was another, and quite real, guilt involved: her wish not to know what he had become.

It was no excuse to say she had refused to look for Karen's sake. That was not protecting her child; that was making her child an accomplice in blindness.

She straightened up, as if facing what she had done to Amy Stone. She thought suddenly of another consequence of her action: She could never accuse Burt, publicly or privately, of his role in the attack, for fear of harming Amy still more.

But she could work to expose the other things Burt had done, to whatever extent he deserved.

As she walked back to the bedroom, it was nearly dawn. Her body felt heavy with the need for sleep but also strangely light; vision was lighter than blindness, she thought.

She got into bed. In moments her eyes closed, and she fell asleep with the first of the sun.

22

"Why, Burt!" said Cecelia Joncas when she answered the door on Sunday morning. "Were we supposed to be expecting you?"

"No," Sanda said. "I just happened . . . I just wanted to see Joncas. Is he here?"

"Yes, in his den. Oh, I must thank you for your generous donation. Coral was very grateful. We all were. Some people sent flowers anyway, but we think Steven would have preferred donations to the world labor conference. Sending delegates in his name is such a nice idea."

"Yes. How are you holding up, Cecelia?"

"I'm surviving. We're all survivors in this house, you know. But if I'd ever thought, years ago, that someday the Varese would try to get back at Vi this way . . . " She studied Sanda's face. "You look very anxious to see him. I'll take you down to the den."

When she left them, Joncas said, "Burt. What the hell do you want?" There was no sense of menace in the gravel of his voice; he seemed preoccupied. He wore a casual shirt open to reveal a mat of curly graying hair.

"This is what I want," Sanda said. He held out a page from the back section of one of the Sunday papers, and pointed to a small item headlined, "STATEN ISLAND WOMAN WOUNDS BURGLAR."

"What about it?" Joncas said.

"It's the bookkeeper. You said if there had been some kind of leak, she was the most likely suspect."

"That's what I said."

"And a couple nights after we talked, two men try to rob her? Is that a coincidence?"

"What does the paper say?"

"That she stabbed one of them with a kitchen fork, but they both got away, and she can't describe either one of them."

"So what's the problem?"

"Did you . . . ? Did you send . . . ? Does this have anything to do with . . . with . . . "

"You're stuttering, Burt. Spit it out."

Sanda flushed. "Were those men sent to kill that woman?"

"I wouldn't permit that."

"Thank God." Sanda sank into a chair.

"They were sent to do a job of permanent disabling."

Sanda's face grayed. "I've gone along with you so far, Joncas. I tried to get Maeve Jerrold to kick Dante out of her building. I tried to get Jac to stop doing stories on him. But I won't do this kind of thing! I won't be part of anything that involves hurting people!"

"You're part of it already."

"I goddamn well am not! When did I ever tell you I would be?"

"From the beginning."

"Oh, no." Sanda's mind shot back to the beginning, twelve years earlier, when Joncas had hired him as a special counsel in the transport negotiations. "You're not going to pass any ex post facto laws on me," he said. "We've helped each other out, as friends, but—"

"Christ! You think I cut you in on Briarwood because we were such good buddies? It had nothing to do with the way you arbitrated the last transport contract?"

Sanda said nothing.

"How did you think I was going to get you elected to the House five years ago? Just by getting out the union vote? Where do you think I got all the money I threw in your campaign chest?"

"I don't see any point in rehashing—"

"You never want anything spelled out in plain words, do you, Burt? No wonder you're a lawyer. I didn't mind going along with you, putting everything in pretty language so it wouldn't smell so bad to you, but it's too late for that now. Too late." There were red filaments in Joncas's eyes. "No more kidding yourself that you can be some kind of saint."

"I resent that, Joncas. I never pretended to be saintly."

"No? What about the big dream where one day you're going to put on robes and sit on the appellate court and be Your Honor Who Upholds the Constitution?"

Sanda looked away, regretting the day he'd told Joncas. At least, he thought, he hadn't told him the whole thing: how serving on an appeals court, where one's job was to honor and interpret the law, would cancel out the less-than-noble things he'd been forced to do on his way up. He looked at Joncas coldly. "What's wrong with wanting to sit on the bench?"

"Telling it to a man whose associate buys and sells judges."

"I don't believe that! You're . . . you're a realist, but you—"

Joncas leaned forward, squinting as if he were throwing darts. "Playing dumb won't get you off the hook. You're caught, and you'll do exactly what you're told. Otherwise my associate . . . You did figure out that I must have an associate? Or would you rather think I got where I am just because the membership loves me? Ah, you would. All right, Burt, I'll just put it this way. Do what you're told, if you want to save your reputation. And your neck." Sanda said nothing. "Now," Joncas went on, "about that call you got from Maeve Jerrold. Here's what you're going to do."

Sanda listened. He felt his stomach begin to knot. But there was no point in antagonizing Joncas by taking a high moral tone. He cleared his throat and said reasonably, "That would never work. How could I get her to believe it?"

"Fairly easily, from what you've said about her."

"But . . . but how could I persuade her to go *there*?"

"Your fine legal mind can invent a convincing story."

"No," Sanda said. "No! There's no way you can make me do this."

"There are a dozen ways, Burt. Things I could make sure the press learned. Or the bar association. And those would be the *nice* ways."

"It's very interesting," said the assistant district attorney. "But it doesn't really help the case. I told you that." He looked at Detectives Fagan and Santo and their lieutenant; they were all in the lieutenant's office at the stationhouse.

Santo frowned. "But it's right in the record! They all thought Dante did it. Even the Family Court judge."

"So what? There was no evidence, so they just sent him back home."

"Back on the streets," Fagan muttered.

"At least now we know the Swede was telling the truth," Santo said. "Doesn't that bolster his credibility? About the rest of what he said?"

"It's still got to be supported." The ADA tapped his notes. "Besides, the Swede is going to make a lousy witness. Either he's got a memory like a sieve, or else he's not all there."

The lieutenant cut in. "We placed Dante at some of the Varese hangouts, including a visit the night after the shooting."

"It's not an indictable offense to go into a club."

"No," Santo said. "But we've got an informant who says Dante was asking to see Big Tiny!"

"Even if he did see him, what's the charge? Where's the evidence they were doing business? What you've got is suggestive, but it's not a case. There's no case until and unless you can get real evidence of some deal going on between Dante and the Varese, something we can connect with the killing."

"Cheer up, Santo," Fagan said. "At least the mayor and the press have quit slobbering all over him."

The director of *Firestorm* looked around the walls of the theater business office, at the posters of past productions, several of which he had staged. Then he looked back at Erik. "For what it's worth, I don't think you had anything to do with killing Joncas's son-in-law."

Erik said nothing.

"Nobody in town expects Poets and Paupers to open, you know. And it's starting to hurt me professionally. People wonder what the hell's wrong with me."

Erik's hands were crossed loosely in his lap. He looked at them, flexed them, made them lie quietly again, and said, "It'd be better, Ken, if you didn't give me any reasons. I'd just like to remember how good you were as a director, OK?"

The man was silent. Then he pushed back his chair. "I know this doesn't leave you much time to get somebody else, but maybe—"

"I'll take over the directing myself."

"I didn't know you had experience directing."

"I don't. *Firestorm* will be my debut."

The director looked skeptical, then embarrassed. He stood up. "I really do wish you good luck," he said lamely.

When he had gone, Erik went into the theater. There was a well-known hazard for any actor who directed a play he was in—split focus. One had to try simultaneously to look at the play as a whole and to concentrate on one's own character. He decided to do some final private work on the Prometheus scenes; as of tomorrow, when the next rehearsal was scheduled, Prometheus could no longer claim his undivided attention.

The envelope was lying on the stage floor, addressed simply to "Dantino." He picked it up. Inside, on a piece of cheap paper, was a short typewritten message:

IT LOOKS LIKE YOUR ON THE LEVEL. COME GET YOUR
TWENTY BUCKS WORTH TOMORROW NIGHT. THURSDAY.
THE PIZZA PLACE ACROSS FROM YOUR OLD GRADE SCHOOL.
TEN O'CLOCK. BE ALONE OR BE SORRY.

The leap in his chest and muscles told Erik how badly he had wanted that note, how much he needed to be able to take some action. He stretched his hands up toward the flies, arched his whole body, then looked over at the figure painted on one side of the proscenium arch. "We're not finished yet, my friend," he said.

But there were twenty-four hours to wait. He went back to Prometheus.

23

"This is it, lady," said the cabdriver. "This is the place."

Maeve paid him, got out, and stood uncertainly on the sidewalk, facing the building she would have to enter. She wore a black linen pantsuit and carried a large patent-leather bag. The fitted black hat that hid her hair made her face look white as milk. She put a hand to her cheek; it felt like ice meeting fire, but she couldn't tell which was which.

Burt Sanda had warned her there would be prostitutes and criminals inside, because it was an underworld hangout. She wondered whether she would be able to tell which were the criminals and prostitutes; to her knowledge, she had never seen any such persons, except on the stage and screen. She knew Erik could have told her a good deal about what to expect, and might even know the very place she was going to enter; but of course she couldn't tell him what she was doing. Certainly not until much later, when it was over and she had succeeded in helping him. She felt a lurch of panic but forced it down and moved toward the doors, holding the patent-leather bag before her like a shield.

It contained fifty thousand dollars—the sum Burt had told her they wanted. All the bills were one hundreds, not new ones; she had spent most of the morning going to banks all over the city. And most of the time since then fighting the desire for Valium. She had won, and now, besides the money—and the clothes she had chosen to cover her as completely as possible—she also had a fragile coating of pride.

She opened the door and went in.

A wave of sound seemed to roll down on her from above. It smashed against her stomach, filled her mouth and nose and eyes, and threatened to spin her inside it. She fought for breath and balance.

Instead of receding, the wave sucked her farther into the room, into a maelstrom of smoke and arcing lights and moving bodies. Two of them swept her along like a log, bumped her into a pillar at the edge of the room, and left her there. She clung to it, steadied herself, and tried to look at the world around her, which was pulsing with alien life. If all humans were strangers to one another, these seemed to be from an entirely different species—their foreheads canted as if to hold a more primeval brain, and their eyes designed solely as sensors for their appetites. She told herself she was committing the sin of stereotyping, but she could not find a face that seemed lit by sensitivity or intelligence; the only light came from the arcs of color that streaked across their faces and painted them to look like savages.

She could feel the deep gut sounds of the music as if they were being plucked on her own viscera. She had to get away; she pushed through the crowd with a fear that she might be sick. She shoved her way to a space at the back, hoping one of the doors there would be a restroom; but they were all locked, except one. She wrenched it open. There was a bed with a naked man on it. Where his genitals should have been was a head of long blond hair. She screamed.

The head swung around; it belonged to a kneeling woman. "What're you doing?" she said furiously. "That door was supposed to be locked! This isn't a sideshow! If you're so damn anxious to get in here, you can finish the job." The woman got to her feet and rushed past Maeve, out the door.

The man on the bed raised his head, his look a sleepy blend of anger and invitation.

She slammed the door and stumbled away. She managed to find another pillar and leaned against it, feeling more naked than the man had been—feeling stripped of the protection of her clothes, her resolve, even her skin. Her nerves began to pull far down, trying to hide within her bones, abandoning the rest of her to liquid. She knew suddenly that this was the decisive battleground of her life and that she had only two choices: to remain like this always, tethered like a slave to her own terror, or to break the tie and start to function.

She braced her back against the pillar and began whispering, begging herself not to be afraid, telling the fear that she was in charge. "You don't matter," she said to it over and over. "You don't matter."

And after a while, miraculously, it ceased to be in control. She could almost smile at the way she had usurped it—until she looked at her watch and saw that it was eleven-thirty-five. She was supposed to be at the back bar at eleven-thirty.

She gripped the patent bag and fought her way to the long, crowded bar. There were no stools, but she slipped between two men, managing to smile at them. She reviewed the instructions Burt Sanda had given her; not only had he talked to some underworld figures to find out who was trying to frame Erik, he had even contacted one of the man's lieutenants and paved the way for her. He said he had taken great professional risks to help her; in a strange way, she felt obligated to do a good job for his sake.

She leaned forward, trying to catch the eye of the red-haired woman who was tending bar. She felt someone move in to stand behind her, but she ignored that. At length the redhead noticed her. "What'll it be?"

"I'm looking for Augie Vila," Maeve said.

"Yeah? What about?"

"That's my business. He's expecting me."

"Not that I heard about, lady." The woman moved away.

"Wait!" Maeve cried.

A voice behind her said, "Looking for Augie? Maybe I can help you."

She turned around. "Are you supposed to take me to Mr. Vila?"

The man smiled. He looked not only friendly but also intelligent. "Depends on why you want to see him."

"We have some business to transact."

"You wouldn't be the lady who's here to deliver a payment, would you?"

"I suppose you could put it that way," she said.

"You've got fifty grand?"

She hesitated, but the man did seem to know all about it. "In my bag."

"What's your name, then?"

"Maeve Jerrold."

"And you're here because of Erik Dante and the Joncas son-in-law killing?"

"I . . . " Her voice stuck, and she knew then that it was wrong, all wrong, even before the man took out a policeman's badge and said she would have to come with him.

She sat for a long time in a cheerless Brooklyn police station, thinking and feeling nothing, simply waiting for her lawyer.

He finally came, sighed, and advised her to tell it to the police just the way she had told it to him. Eventually a detective came in from Manhattan, one of the two who had questioned her at the apartment a week earlier.

She had not gotten far when he interrupted. "But why did you want to give the money to Augie Vila?"

She hesitated. "To get him to leave Erik alone."

The detective looked at her lawyer. "Mrs. Jerrold, do you know who Augie Vila is? Who he works for?"

"The people who are trying to frame Erik. Who are saying he's involved with the Varese crime family."

"Mrs. Jerrold, Augie Vila is *with* the Varese family."

"Oh, no," she said. "That's not right."

"Augie Vila is a Varese underboss."

"But . . . are you sure? Perhaps there's been a change? Something recent?"

The detective sighed. "Augie has been with the Varese for nearly twenty years. And the place you were at—the Jumping Joint—is a Varese hangout." She looked at her lawyer, who nodded. The detective went on. "Now, you want to tell us the truth about why you went down there?"

She clutched for something solid—the table in front of her. "I . . . wanted to do something to help Erik."

"You mean you offered to help out and he gave you this errand to run for him?"

"No, no. I did this on my own."

"And where did you get the idea that the man to see was Augie Vila?"

She put her head in her hands. Burt Sanda had made her swear never to reveal that he had helped her; she had not even told the lawyer. Should she still keep silent? Perhaps Burt himself had been given the wrong information; until she knew that, she couldn't add betrayal to the rest of her folly. She lifted her head. "I heard Mr. Vila's name somewhere, that's all."

"From Dante?"

"I'm . . . not sure. I heard talk around the theater, you know. Somehow I got the impression that that man was Erik's enemy." She sat back, marveling at her capacity not to invent the explanation but to deliver it.

The silence was coated with skepticism. "You know, Mrs. Jerrold," the detective said, "I always like to consider the easiest explanation. The most reasonable one. Now, here we have Dante suspected of working with the Varese and arranging the killing of Steven Pomerantz. But he knows we suspect him, so he has to stay away from the Varese. But what if he has to deliver something to them? Like a payoff for the killing? Well, he's got a business partner. So why couldn't he send her down to the Joint as his courier?"

"No! That's not true! Erik had nothing—"

The lawyer cut in. "You see, Fagan? It's pretty obvious what's happened. Mrs. Jerrold is not a practical person. She's an artist. She really doesn't understand any of Dante's dealings, business or otherwise. You can see from the way she's been talking how easy it would be for Dante to get her to do something like this without her even realizing it."

"That's not true," she whispered, feeling her nerves begin their inward tug.

"Now, Maeve," the lawyer said, his voice both avuncular and hard, "would you rather have us believe you knew all about a payoff for the Varese?"

She looked around the bleak room. The only thought that came into her mind was, idiotically, that she had never been in Brooklyn before.

"It seems to me," the lawyer went on, "that the worst thing Mrs. Jerrold could be charged with here is gullibility."

The word began to rattle in her brain. Yes, she thought, gullibility . . . gull, fool, idiot . . . *imbécile, niaise* . . . *La dame aux fiascos.*

The phone rang beside a bed. There was an upheaval at its center, and then Big Tiny Varese answered. "What the hell you calling me here for?" He listened, eyes straining into the dark, one leg stretching under the covers until it touched another leg. Gradually he pulled it away and levered himself up on one elbow. Finally he said, "You know something? I can think of half a dozen reasons he might send a broad down there, and not a goddamn one of them makes me laugh. If he's trying to set us up . . . " He rubbed his eyes. "OK, that's it for him. Should make you happy. Call me in the morning. Oh . . . and Augie, I really want to get to the Swede now. He's the start of this whole goddamn mess. So get on it." He hung up and lay back, muttering. The woman beside him thought she caught the word "smart-ass," but she never asked questions.

24

With her film crew, Jac ran up the steps of the Criminal Courts Building in Manhattan and into its swollen marble lobby. She noticed none of the things that usually made her stop and frown—the grime, the odors, the hostility that sat like a birthmark on so many of the faces; she checked the directory and ran with the crew into an elevator just as its doors were closing.

"God, this building stinks," said one of her cameramen.

"Jac," said the other, "did you say this would be a bail hearing?"

"Yes." She had been in the area—at City Hall, filming some on-the-job interviews with city employees, for a story on regulatory agencies and red tape—when the hurried message had come from the station, telling her and the crew to get over to Foley Square and try to pick up something.

The elevator stopped; she ran down the hall to a courtroom and peered in. "Still in session," she told the crew, and went in. The room was dark and cavernous, almost like a theater, with figures at one end forming a tableau: judge, attorneys, court officers. And the back of a dark blond head.

She moved toward the tableau, aware that the room was already well over half full and contained many press colleagues. She slipped into a seat in the fifth row and heard a woman's voice: "Your Honor, my client is a well-known actor and theatrical producer. He's a respected artist, who's very much in the public eye. There's no question of his not honoring bail."

The judge frowned. "The charge here is procuring a murder."

"Yes, your Honor, but—"

"Mr. Dante, how much bail could you put up?"

"Your Honor, my theater is called the Poets and *Paupers*."

"Does that mean you can't raise any bail?"

From the corner of her eye Jac saw someone across the aisle start to rise and then sink back. She turned and saw a slight figure that was all black from hat to shoes, except for the pale urgency of her profile and her clasped hands. When Erik said, "Your Honor, all I have is the theater itself. I can put that up—the building," the woman leaned back and closed her eyes. Her eyelids trembled. Suddenly she turned her head, as if aware of being watched. Jac saw her own identity register on the face. The eyes, and the delicate nostrils, widened for an instant. Then the woman turned away again.

Jac felt neither the anger nor the disdain she had expected. Instead there was a leaden awareness of what she had been hoping Maeve Jerrold would be like—like those women one saw shopping on Fifth Avenue, their faces sun-hardened to look like expensive leather and their eyes lit with tolerant amusement for the men who made the money they were spending.

She looked across the aisle, trying to will Maeve Jerrold into one of those women, the failure to do so tightening her jaw.

The judge's voice penetrated: "All right, bail is set at five hundred thousand dollars." She heard him tell Erik's attorney to see that her client was taken to the clerk's office; and the hearing was over.

Like a single entity, the press moved to the hall, to spread itself as a trap for Erik. Automatically Jac moved with it, her mind struggling to frame questions. The call from the station had told her very little— only that Erik had been arrested suddenly, on an Information filed by the district attorney, and that there was an incredible, though unconfirmed, story about Maeve Jerrold.

She watched Erik walk calmly into the press trap, the lawyer on one side and Maeve on the other. He was wearing jeans and a denim jacket. His eyes were as pale a blue as river ice, and his face seemed made of bones and weariness. "Mr. Dante," she called over her colleagues' voices.

He saw her and stopped. For a moment there were no cameras present, or other people. Then she felt Maeve Jerrold's eyes watching them.

She held out the microphone, her passport to dispassion. "Mr. Dante, do you still say your brother acted alone in the Pomerantz killing?"

He didn't answer. Other voices shot questions at him: Why did Ms. Jerrold go to one of the Varese hangouts last night? Why would she go there if it wasn't in your behalf? Are you going ahead with plans to open your theater?

He started to move ahead. Jac said, "Mr. Dante, how do you plan to keep running your theater while you're under indictment?"

"Like an innocent man," he said, still moving forward. "Because that's what I am."

"Then how do you explain Ms. Jerrold's action last night?"

He stopped. "I can't." She blinked, then realized he hadn't said the words; it was his eyes that had made them leap into her mind.

She swung the microphone. "Ms. Jerrold," she said, "why did you go to a Varese hangout last night?"

The woman wouldn't look at her. Instead she stared at the mike as if it were a club. "Erik," she said in a small, tight voice, "do I have to answer that question?"

"Why shouldn't she answer it?" Jac said, unable to stop herself, looking directly at Erik.

He didn't turn away. "Ms. Jerrold has been questioned by the police and released," he said. "I'm the one under indictment, not her."

He lifted his hand; for an absurd moment Jac thought he was going to touch her, but he merely pushed back his hair and then moved past her and away from all the press.

She was turning to her crew, trying to decide where and when to do a wrap on the story, when she felt a hand on her arm and saw Maeve Jerrold's face. "Ask your husband about last night. Make him tell the truth. Please!" Then she was gone, back at Erik's side, on her way down the hall.

The cab ride uptown from the courthouse was the first time Erik and Maeve had been alone together since his arrest, but they said almost nothing. He asked whether she wanted to have dinner; she shook her head. She asked whether he wanted to stop at the theater; he said no.

They got to her apartment around seven o'clock. She unlocked the door. He looked around as if he hadn't expected to be there again.

Maeve watched him, unable even to go into the bedroom and take off the black clothes. She had had no time to change earlier; by the time the police released her in Brooklyn, her lawyer told her that Erik had been arrested in Manhattan. They had rushed there, without catching him at the precinct. Then the lawyer had delivered her to the Criminal Courts Building, to wait for the arraignment and bail hearing.

Erik went to the coffee table. He took a crumpled envelope from his jacket pocket and shook its contents into an ashtray. He picked up a lighter. The fragments sent up a burst of flame before collapsing into ashes.

"What's that?" Maeve said.

"Nothing, now. It used to be a twenty-dollar bill I was gambling with. Today it was thrown in my face. Or, to be accurate, it was slipped to my lawyer somehow. She gave it to me at the courthouse."

"I don't understand."

"That's right. You don't." He moved to the terrace doors and looked out. The sun, low in the sky, outlined his figure. The silence lengthened.

"Your lawyer is very young," Maeve said.

"Yes."

"I know she's been a good legal counsel to the theater, but does she have the experience to handle this?" He didn't answer. "Let me get someone else for you, Erik. Please."

"I think you've gotten enough for me already," he said quietly. "My lawyer is fine. She got me out on bail. She also learned that the police know about my previous encounter with the law."

"Oh, God. How did they find out?"

"I gather they found it in their old records."

"But then . . ." Maeve stared at his shoulders, as if she could will them to straighten. "Then that's why they arrested you, isn't it? Because of that old murder? Oh, my darling, can you forgive me for being glad it wasn't because of me? I realize it doesn't change anything, but just to know that I . . ." She stopped; her words hung in the air like tinsel.

"That's not why I was arrested," he said impassively. "It may have helped the police psychologically, but not actually. And of course it will have a public impact, once the papers get hold of it. But it's not why I was arrested. You did that."

The silence tightened its hold again. She told herself that he would never be convicted; she would get the best and most expensive lawyers in the country, no matter how he objected. "I don't blame you for not wanting to look at me," she whispered. He said nothing. "Erik, for God's sake be angry with me!"

He turned around. "Don't you want to remind me that anger can be dangerous? That I could lose control and maybe kill someone?" But there was no anger in his voice, and his face was as guarded as metal.

"But anger is better than . . ." Her foice faded out.

"I just want to understand," he said. "I have to assume that in some crazy, misguided way you were trying to help me. Tell me why it took the form of going to the Joint and looking for the Varese underboss."

"I didn't know that's who he was. I swear I didn't. I had just . . . heard it around that he was the one trying to frame you. And I wanted to pay him to stop it."

"I don't think you just 'heard it around,' Maeve. I think somebody told you, somebody you trusted. I need to know who it was and why you were so trusting. Because whoever told you was setting you up. You do see that? How do you think a detective just happened to be at the Joint so conveniently? Somebody was setting you up."

Somehow she got to a chair and sank into its solidity. Until that moment she had not questioned the detective's presence. If Erik was right, she thought, then her stupidity had been boundless.

"So where did you get the idea?" he said.

If she told him how she had called Sanda, she thought, how she had implored him to help her—almost inviting him to set her up, she could see that now—then there finally would be some emotion on Erik's face, and it would be contempt. Deep, lasting, perhaps ineradicable. Especially when he compared her with a woman who was never stupid, whose practicality and beauty were a hundred times more

potent when one saw her in the flesh rather than on a TV
screen. . . .

Maeve gripped the arms of the chair, realizing it was herself who
had to be protected now by silence; the price of telling about Sanda
could be losing Erik, and she couldn't pay it. No matter what. She put
a hand to her cheek; feeling fire, she snatched it away, telling herself
again that he would never be convicted; she would spend every dime
she had . . . "It was all my doing, Erik," she said. "I did make some
inquiries that I won't even discuss because they were so stupid. I see
that now. So stupid I can't bear to think of them."

"You're hardly a stupid person, Maeve. What made you act like
one? What made you think you could find out who was framing me
just by asking a few questions?"

"But if I had found out, if I'd reached the right person . . ."

"Then what? It would have been OK? What makes you think that
somebody with the power to frame me could be bought off—and for
fifty thousand dollars?"

"I'd have given them more! It could have stopped them. Why
couldn't it? Money is what they all want, isn't it?"

"Oh, Jesus," he said tonelessly. "You thought you finally were
doing something practical. Is that it?"

"Yes. Yes! So how could it be anything but a fiasco? And the part
that's almost amusing is that for once I was proud of myself. Because I
was terrified but I wasn't letting it stop me. I was doing what I set out
to do, in spite of the fear."

An emotion finally did cross his face. It was worse than contempt.

"Don't look like that!" she cried. "Be angry with me—that's what I
deserve! You believe in giving people what they deserve—be angry
with me!"

"All right," he said quietly. "How many times have you told me I'd
never succeed with the theater? You believed I couldn't—so now
you've helped it come true. Can't you see that? You make your own
prophecies happen. The more you keep thinking of yourself as a failure, the less able you are to see what it actually does take to succeed,
and the more afraid you are of failing. I think you lose the capacity to

see anything clearly—whether it's yourself, your money, or what you call 'the practical world.' Finally the day comes when you can't recognize any of them for what they really are. You let your fear blind you, and then you act stupidly. Can't you see that you wound up hurting me because of what you've done to *yourself?*"

"Don't look at me that way," she whispered.

His features struggled back to neutrality, but his eyes were still merciless in their mercy.

"Oh, God," she said, "I can't even make you angry anymore. You feel sorry for me, and that's all that's left. Isn't it?"

After a long time he said, "No. I still owe you more than I can ever repay. I can't forget that."

25

"But, Mr. Dante," said a woman's voice on the phone, "it's going to be a very small affair. Just my husband and I and three or four others, people who really love the theater."

"Have you been to Poets and Paupers, then?"

"Well, no, but we want to start!" she said gaily. "We want to get to know you. And of course all your friends, too."

"I'm sorry," Erik said brusquely. "I don't go to dinner parties. I'm too busy trying to stay in business." He hung up the box-office phone and grimaced. "I don't know why they call them the beautiful people."

"I take it that wasn't an order for seats," Ruth said.

"No." Erik leaned against the ticket racks, rubbing his forehead. "I think she wanted me for my underworld ties. My gangster chic. The hell with her. I don't need that kind of support."

"You need whatever you can get," Ruth said.

"It's that bad?"

"Disaster. Opening week was nearly sold out once, remember? Look at it now. And it's been getting worse all this morning." She gestured at the racks. "And of course a lot of the people who call in to cancel have to make a little speech about changing their 'vote.'"

"What do they say?"

"Oh . . . how come you've lost so much of your staff if you're innocent? Where there's smoke there's fire. That sort of thing. This morning one man said that you only got out on bail because you're rich."

"So the big result of my ticket crusade is that you wind up listening to abuse on the phone. Christ!"

"I'm still here, aren't I? What time is rehearsal today?"

"I canceled it."

"For how long?"

"Till I decide what the hell to do. Tell me, Ruthie, do you think things could possibly get any worse?"

She shrugged.

The doorman stood in indecision, fingering the press card and squinting against the late-afternoon sun. "I don't know," he said. "She didn't tell me you were coming. And she doesn't answer her buzzer."

"Has she gone out today?" Jac said.

"Not since I came on."

"Then she's probably home. So I'll just go up."

"I don't know," the doorman repeated. "I'm just the weekend relief, you know."

"Look, you've seen the press card. You said you've seen me on TV. Do you really think I came here to do something like rob Ms. Jerrold?"

"Well, no, of course not."

"Then I'll go up." Jac took back the card and strode purposefully to the elevator. She could almost feel the man shrugging and turning back to his newspaper. It contained, she knew, a dreadful story about Erik's past.

The tenth floor was heavily carpeted. A faint hint of a Brahms symphony came from behind one of the doors; this was a place where money insulated each life against the sounds of any other. Jac rang the bell at 10D, then waited and rang again. It was five minutes by her watch before she heard the sliding of a peephole. A bodiless eye stared at her; then the latches and chains slowly gave way.

Maeve Jerrold was wearing a silk robe the color of pearls. Her hair was smoothly coiled and her face beautifully made up, but her eyes looked heavy. "You," she said. "Why did you come?"

"To find out what you meant at the courthouse on Thursday. Didn't you expect me to come?"

"Did I? I don't know."

"Will you let me in?"

Maeve hesitated, and Jac stepped past her. The room, like its own-er, made her suddenly conscious of the deep tan of her arms and the dark red of her skirt. Its colors were as muted as a cloudy sky, with tiny lakes of crystal, mosaic, and paintings. She thought of Erik in this room; and with this woman, who moved slowly to sit at one end of the gray silk couch and rested a hand on its arm. She wore a ring of gold and mother-of-pearl.

"Were you getting ready to go out?" Jac asked.

There was a pause, then a smile and a "Yes."

"I'm sorry. I won't keep you long."

"I shouldn't have let you in."

"But you did. So you must want to talk to me. To tell me some-thing."

"Do I? Perhaps I do."

The quality of her voice, Jac thought, had the dreamy clarity of someone who had drunk too much; yet there was no scent of liquor, only of some perfume. Faint, like dying roses.

"Ms. Jerrold," she said, "what did my ex-husband have to do with your trip to the Jumping Joint?"

"Did you ask him?"

"Yes. I don't think I can trust him." The answer, Jac thought, had been Burt at his most casual: "Oh, yes, Maeve did call and ask me who I thought was framing Dante. I said something about his involve-ment with the Varese, and God knows what she made of it. She's awfully neurotic, you know. Unstable as hell. Ask her ex-husband if you don't believe me." Jac looked at the woman, wondering whether Burt could be right about her.

"Don't," she was saying. "Don't trust him."

"Why do you say that, Ms. Jerrold?"

Maeve's eyes closed. She smiled. " 'Let a fool be made serviceable according to his folly.' "

"I presume that's a quotation of some kind," Jac said tightly. "Do you think you could explain things in your own words?" She knew her anger was unreasonable; but it was so like Erik, the business of quoting something; the woman had that tie to him, and so many others; and whatever they were, he would not sever them. No matter what he felt. She pushed back her hair, and her anger, and said "Have you talked to Burt about the trouble Erik Dante is in?"

Maeve's eyes opened, and for a moment they were piercingly alert, acknowledging that Erik's name finally had been said. But then she leaned her head against the back of the couch. "Yes."

"You did talk to Burt about Erik's troubles? What did he say? Did he give you some kind of advice?"

Maeve sighed. " 'But Folly's all they taught me.' "

"Please!" Jac made a tight grid of her fingers. "Ms. Jerrold, Burt is involved with some people who could be the ones trying to ruin Erik." The woman made a faint, distressed sound. "If Burt said anything to you, anything at all, that might indicate who his associates are, I've got to know. I'm trying to help Erik." She waited. Then she added, goaded by the woman's passive silence, "I thought Erik Dante meant something to you."

"Everything," the woman said simply. "And to you?"

Jac refused to look away. "Do you really want to know?"

"No. No. I don't." Maeve made another distressed sound. "Where is Erik?"

Jac hesitated. She knew he was at the theater because she had established the fact by calling the box office and pretending to be a customer; she had had to make sure he wouldn't be with the woman who was now looking at her. "I should think," she said finally, "that you would always know Erik's whereabouts."

Maeve looked into the distance, as if he were standing there. "Do you know what it's like to hurt someone you love?"

"I don't understand you, I'm afraid."

"No, not you. You're never afraid. That's the difference."

Between us? Jac thought. She wanted to say it, badly. Instead she said, "I've been afraid of looking, sometimes."

"But what if you face down the fear and it still doesn't help you?"

"Help you do what?"

Maeve closed her eyes. "I didn't want to see you. You're the last person that I . . ." Her lips moved in what might have been a smile. "But now you can tell Erik . . . that he was right. He understood why I did it. But not . . . what I feel."

"Ms. Jerrold," Jac said sharply.

Maeve's eyes opened, but the lids fell back immediately, like curtains that had risen by mistake. Her face sagged, and the years spread across it cruelly.

The skin at the back of Jac's neck tightened; why would the woman be falling asleep if she had been getting ready to go out? Unless she had meant "go out" in some other and terrible sense. Jac leaped up and leaned over the couch. "Ms. Jerrold!" she shouted. "Ms. Jerrold!"

"No," Maeve mumbled. "*Je suis . . . la dame aux fiascos . . .*" Her head slumped over her chest.

Jac ran toward the back of the apartment. Three minutes later, on the bedroom nightstand, she found what she dreaded, beside a picture of Erik.

For a moment she couldn't move, rooted by the sight of Erik's face and the thought of doing nothing, of allowing Maeve Jerrold to succeed in what she had tried.

She made a grimace that was half-disgusted, half-rueful, and then she ran.

Everything in the waiting room was limp—the magazines, the vase of daisies, the people's posture. Only the wall clock was an exception, its minute hand moving with military regularity.

Erik sat in a low chair, his legs thrust out so far that people had to step over them, his hands dangling over the armrests. Every time the clock hand moved, he looked up at it and then away. Jac's chair was at a right angle to his; a large and dreadful ceramic lamp on the end table obscured their view of one another. At first the silence between them had seemed to be imposed by the presence of others, but as the minutes marched into an hour, the silence acquired a life of its own.

After another quarter of an hour, a doctor in surgical greens appeared in the doorway. The three other people still in the room got to their feet as one unit, faces naked with anxiety, and went out after him.

The clock measured out five more minutes.

Erik stirred. "It may be quite a while. You really don't have to wait."

"I know that. I thought you might need to talk."

"I should have talked to her. I haven't, since after the bail hearing. Two days. Christ."

Three more minutes goose-stepped forward.

"Why were you at her place?" he said.

Jac hesitated. "I was being a journalist. Trying to find out why she went to the Jumping Joint."

"I could have told you that. But then you wouldn't have gone to see her. And then . . ." He put his head in his hands. "She was trying to help me, that's what she was doing. Christ, it was pathetic."

"Erik, there's a chance that . . . that my ex-husband had something to do with her going to that place."

"Say that again?"

"She hinted as much to me before she—"

"You mean he put her up to it?"

"I don't know that that's what he did. But he may be in this more deeply than I thought. And if he is, I'll . . ." She clenched both hands.

"He's got to go to the police and tell them whatever he knows!"

"He won't. If it came to that, he'd simply tell them she wasn't quite *compos mentis* and made it all up. And he'd be very convincing, believe me. If only there was some way I could make him . . ." She clenched her hands again. "But there isn't. I'm afraid there's no help in that quarter."

He looked over at her, then away again. The clock hand jerked forward. "I was mad at her," he said. "Mad enough to kill her. I needn't have worried. She took on the job herself."

"There's a good chance she failed. She wouldn't have let me in if she hadn't wanted to fail."

Erik laughed bitterly. Another minute clicked by. He looked at the clock. "Are you obliged, as a journalist, to make this public?"

"No. If it gets out, it won't be through me."

"Thank you. But why?"

"People have a right to their misery in private, sometimes." After a moment Jac added, "Why didn't you tell me? If I'd known this is what you were dealing with . . . Did you think I couldn't understand, Erik?"

He rested his elbows on his knees, tenting his hands. "And what exactly would you have understood? That she's pathetic because she can't help what she is? That she's contemptible for making me afraid she might do what she's just done? That I'm a weak bastard for not having walked out of such a situation? That I'm a saint for staying?" Jac didn't answer. He turned to her and shoved the lamp out of his line of vision. "They're all true, but they're not enough to explain it. Yes, she was rich. And lovely. And generous. Christ, more generous than a Renaissance art patron and twice as knowledgeable. But it wasn't because she gave me money. She gave me back a part of myself. A part that was wrapped up and hidden away, in a basement, for fear someone would find it and destroy it . . ." He stopped. More quietly he said, "She knew the things I would love, before I really knew it myself. I didn't know there was a drug on the market like that—having someone see inside you, right to the heart of what matters. How could I not have loved her?"

Jac said nothing.

"She made things possible for me—made them practical, to use a word that obsessed her. The irony is that I could never shake her own belief that everything she wanted was doomed. Sometimes I felt as if she wanted to pull a glass bell over the two of us, and all the beautiful things she loved, and we would stay there forever, on some museum shelf. She couldn't understand that things under glass are dead, or in the process of suffocating." He clenched his hands. "Do you want to tell me what kind of bastard would talk that way about a woman he's helped to do what she's just done?"

"How did you help her?" Jac asked quietly.

His shoulders rose and fell. "I thought she and I had a . . . fair trade. A partnership, if you like, in which we also happened to be good friends."

"And lovers."

"Yes," he said evenly. "We were lovers, for a long time. I thought we were giving each other great pleasure. But what if to her it's also a drug against pain? I take her money, and I think I'm repaying her by working out in the world for the things she loves and couldn't do on her own. But what if I'm not repaying her at all? What if I'm just making her feel that nothing is possible without me?" He looked down at his hands. "I created that dependency, Jac. I let it happen. I stood between her and the world, and sealed the bargain by taking so much from her. So how could I walk away? Could you have done it?"

"I have walked away," Jac said slowly.

"From a situation like this one?"

"No. How long have you understood it?"

"Fully? The day I met you. And the night she insisted on giving me the theater. She said she couldn't live if I left her. She had said it before. That night I believed her. And I knew how much I wanted to leave."

Two minutes clicked by.

"But you kept on taking things," Jac said. "You did take the theater."

"I told you why at the time. To let her help in the way she was begging to help." His face, in profile, looked as spare and hard as a rock. "Goddammit, I'll be honest. I didn't want to give it up! Prometheus is never defeated, and all that crap. I just wouldn't let the theater go. Well, better late than never."

"What do you mean?"

"I mean it's over. Poets and Paupers. And maybe me, too. Monday I'm going to do two things—cancel the season and transfer the building title back to Maeve."

"But that's how you raised your bail!"

"So I won't be out on bail. They can send me to Rikers Island. Then maybe I can finally talk to my goddamn brother and find out why the hell he killed Joncas's son-in-law and who's telling him to drag me into it. Except," he added bitterly, "they'd never send me to the same place they've got the Swede."

"You mean you're giving up?"

"I've lost a lot of my staff, and a lot more of my audience. I'm under indictment for procuring a murder. And just as I was on the verge of getting a lead about whoever is framing me, Maeve's little trip to the Jumping Joint killed that possibility. What else can I do?"

"You could . . . Maybe I'll get somewhere with the Briarwood names. Maybe I'll come across someone named Donald."

"And maybe you won't. Even if I did have a chance of staying in business, it's going to be canceled by the story in the tabloids this morning." He suddenly assumed the hard-hitting unctuous voice of a commercial pitchman. "'Would you buy a ticket from this man? Whom the police suspect of being a killer when he was just a kid?' Didn't you see the story?"

"Yes. But it says nothing was ever proved."

"So you think I must have been innocent?"

"I think that even if you weren't, the environment you lived in has to take most of the blame."

"You've got the advantage of a college education," he said caustically. "I don't see things that way myself. If I killed somebody, it's because I did it. Not because some rats and cockroaches, human and otherwise, drove me to do it."

She sighed. "So you did do it, then."

"If you really believed I wasn't responsible because it was all due to my environment, you wouldn't sound so disappointed."

She flushed. "Will you tell me how it happened?"

As he told her the story, her face went as still as a photograph. "But then you really don't know what happened? You blacked out?"

"That's right."

"And the police believed your brother?"

"Somebody had to have done it—the boy was dead. And his flesh was under my fingernails. I gather now, from the police report, that the two cops who found us always believed I was the one. I'm not sure I blame them."

"Isn't it much more logical that your brother was lying?"

"Not really. The story he told didn't seem like the kind of thing he'd invent. He's not exactly imaginative. Besides, he was afraid of me, you see. So why would he squeal on me if it wasn't the truth? When he knew they couldn't send me away for much more than a year and then I could come back and get him?"

"Do you really believe you did it?"

"I always wonder. Especially when I find myself getting angry enough to . . . When Morty Codd tried to get in at the theater. When Maeve . . . You know why I haven't talked to her for two days? Even knowing what a state she was in? I didn't trust myself. I was too angry."

"I don't understand how you can live without knowing for sure."

"What's my alternative? But sometimes I think there's only one thing I want from life—'the certainty that I have done no wrong.'"

She sighed. "That's from something, I suppose?"

"*Firestorm.*"

"Which is not going to open now?"

"No. Not if trying to get it on could do this to her. She never wanted me to do any of it, you know. Not to fight the union, or make a public issue of it, or anything else. I dragged her along, and she went. And look what I did to her. Look at tonight."

"What about what she was doing to *you* by taking those pills?" He looked away. "Erik, you can't talk as if her problems, her neuroses, are your fault. You said guilt was like money—take only what you've earned."

"That's plenty," he said.

"But you're not being consistent. *You* could take the blame for killing someone while you lived in ghetto filth, but *she* isn't responsible for trying to kill herself when she has every advantage in the world? Don't you hear the contradiction?"

He smiled faintly. "Don't you ever feel contradictory things?" Then he added, "I owed it to her to remember what she was, not to expect her to change."

"Then remember what you are. You can't change into someone who gives up. You owe it to yourself—"

"Please, Jac. Look, I tried to act like Prometheus, but all I got were third-degree burns. I'm tired, and I hurt. And I just don't want to go on."

There was a silence. Then Jac said, " 'We only live, only suspire, Consumed by either fire or fire.' "

He turned to her in surprise.

"Part of me remembers some poetry, Erik. And needs it. Before I met you, that part was hidden away."

She watched his eyes fill with tears and realized that it was she they embarrassed.

"Don't turn away," he said. "Look at me. Just . . . look at me. So I can look at tomorrow."

A man and woman entered the waiting room and sat on a small couch. "How long do you think we'll have to wait?" the woman asked.

"Forever," the man said.

The two of them looked over at Jac and Erik, smiled blankly, and stared at the wall clock.

Jac lifted her hair with both hands, let it fall back, and squared her shoulders. "All right, Erik. You don't want to fight anymore. I can understand that. But what about your peace of mind over this business from twenty years ago? I think you should find out the truth about it. What if your brother was lying to the police then? Just the way he's doing now, about the Pomerantz killing. What if history's just repeating itself? Don't you want to find out?"

"I've asked him many times. His story never changes."

"But you could ask him again. If you went to Rikers Island."

"I told you they'd never send me to the same place they've got him."

"I meant going as a visitor. Before you do anything that could turn you into an inmate. Before you rescind your bail, and your season, on Monday. You could go tomorrow."

"How the hell would I get into Rikers as a visitor?"

"I can't believe you haven't thought about it."

"What if I have? It's too damn risky. The police would just love to learn that I'd been trying to talk to the Swede—they'd see it as proof we were working together. Anyway, the Swede would never agree to see me."

"But it's the one thing you could still try, isn't it?"

"I could. But I'm not going to."

"All right," she said. "Then I will. Your brother is the key to everything, past and present. If I haven't heard from you by Monday, I'll go talk to him myself."

"Don't you dare! What would that accomplish? Assuming you could get in to see him, which I doubt very much, do you know what kind of a sink the Men's House on Rikers is? Or what my brother is like?"

"I'll find out."

"No, you won't!"

"Are you trying to give me an order?"

"Jac, dammit . . . I'm asking you not to try it. Begging you."

"There's only one way to stop me, Erik. Go yourself."

They were sitting in silence, profiles lifted to each other like shields, when a doctor came to the doorway and said, "Mr. Dante?"

26

After lunch on Monday the Swede asked to be locked back in his cell.

He stepped inside when the officer opened the door made of bars. It clanged behind him. He barely could hear the sound of the turning key because the whole cellblock, three tiers high, had a noise level higher than a city street. The sight of the five-by-eight cubicle made his chest fill with a sensation as heavy as the lunch he had eaten, but he knew the cell was the place he could be surest of being safe.

In the first ten days of the two weeks he had been on Rikers Island, he had moved around a good deal, enjoying his role as the "picket-line killer" who was mentioned frequently in the press. He had found out easily how to buy grass and harder stuff; he had even enjoyed winning a few fights with fellow inmates who were jealous of his clothes.

The clothes had come from the lawyer who finally showed up to take over his case—not the slick, impatient man who had coached him in the stationhouse and whom he had "fired," but a younger man, rather sour, whom the boss had sent the next morning and who brought not only clothes but also periodic reminders of the story he was to keep telling. As the days passed, the Swede had begun to think things might go all right, after all: He had done what the boss wanted, and the boss had promised to take care of him.

Then he had a visitor, a woman. They had had a thing six years earlier, when she belonged to one of Big Tiny's lieutenants. She had gotten him in trouble then, and she had done it again, by bringing him a message. "Tiny says," she had hissed across one of the tables in the visit area, "that whatever crap you been telling the cops has got to stop. He says you better start telling them he don't have nothing to do with your brother and any unions. He says if you're planning to go into court with that story, he'll see you don't get past the front steps." When he simply stared, the woman had said, "Wake up, Swede. Did you think Big Tiny would just lay back while you lied your head off to the cops?"

The truth was worse: He hadn't thought of Big Tiny at all. The confusion of the picket-line killing and the panic of its aftermath had narrowed his mind to the single concern of saving his own skin. There had been no room left for the realization that by doing what Mr. Shaw wanted, he would be infuriating Big Tiny.

Since the woman's visit, he had kept to his cell. Outside of it, he knew, it would be easy for someone to get at him. Just two days earlier, in the yard, one inmate had ground up another's face with a weapon made from parts of a ceiling fixture. There were metal and wood and wire to be extracted from hundreds of places in the building; there were hundreds of men with nothing to do but work on extractions; there were too few officers to do anything but round up a basketful of weapons every couple of weeks.

The Swede glanced up at the ceiling light fixture. He shook his head, moved a few steps, and sat on the narrow bed. He looked around—at the desk and the sink and toilet that did not work and were only mileposts for roaches—and sank back heavily.

Then he saw the folded slip of paper on the blanket. He figured it must have been thrown in while he was at lunch, but he stared as if it had crawled in on its own. He thought that it could be another warning from Big Tiny—proof that Tiny could reach inside Rikers and kill him if he kept on telling the story. Or it could be from Mr. Shaw, who might also want to prove he could reach inside and kill—if the story *wasn't* told.

The Swede picked up the note and unfolded it. He stared at the words. He began to feel as he had on the picket line—his eyes unable to focus, his gut ready to lurch.

He looked at the toilet, needing to use it. But even if it worked, he would have to sit in plain sight of anyone who came down the corridor and glanced in. Every inch of the cell could be seen through the bars of the door.

He was still slumped on the bed when an officer came by and said, "Got a visit, Dantino."

"Who is it?" he said, tensing for the announcement that Big Tiny had sent the woman with another message.

When he heard the name, he said cautiously, "Am I supposed to know who the hell that is?"

The officer explained.

The Swede got to his feet, thinking that maybe God had heard his prayers after all. "Are you sure? It can't . . . I mean, I've never even met—"

"Yes or no?" the officer said impatiently.

It wasn't impossible, the Swede thought; since the killing, he had been all over the papers and TV. "I want the visit," he said. "Just let me shave and change, OK?"

"Not unless you can do it in one minute."

The Swede rubbed his chin; not good, but passable. He wanted badly to take the note with him, to show the visitor, but he knew they would find it on him and take it away. He put it in the drawer of the desk and took two steps to the small closet. Hope began to rise in him as he took off his shirt and put on a nicer one, pale green.

His hope rose higher all the way down from the cellblock, even through the strip and search that preceded every visit. When he got back into his clothes, he felt almost light-headed with excitement. But as the officer escorted him to the visit area, he was suddenly nervous, wondering how the two of them would recognize one another.

There was no problem, after all.

He saw the shoulders, as broad as his own even though they slumped, and the hair, like his but even whiter with age; and he knew it could be no one else.

He took a seat opposite the visitor, at one of the dozens of small tables. The man's cheeks trembled. The Swede feared his voice would do the same. Could the man really be . . . "Padre?" he said softly, not realizing he used the language of his childhood. "Sei tu veramente mio padre?"

The visitor said nothing.

How had the man found him? the Swede wondered. And where had he come from? "Come mi hai trovato?" he asked. "Da dove vieni?"

"Mi conosci, Rossano?" The voice was thin and watery.

But how? the Swede thought—how could he know the father he had never met? "Come potevo conoscerti?" he asked.

"Mi conosci molto bene, Rossano."

The Swede was even more puzzled; how could he know the man "very well?" Unless . . . Maybe they had met someplace but his father hadn't wanted to say who he was. . . . The Swede stared at the pouched eyes, the raddled skin, the beard that seemed clean but moth-eaten. Slowly the features seemed to dissolve and reveal another shape within them. "No!" the Swede said. "Voglio che sia mio padre! I want it to be my father!" But the double vision remained; there was a face inside the face. "Oh, Christ," he said bitterly, accepting it at last.

"That's right," Arrigo said.

The Swede swore softly.

"I had to do it like this, Swede. I couldn't let them know it was me but it had to be somebody you would agree to see. This was the only way. I'm sorry. I didn't know you'd look like a kid expecting Christmas."

The Swede turned away. "You can go to hell," he said. "You never fooled me for a minute. I knew it was you right away."

"Would it really mean so much to you to find your father?"

"Why the hell did you make him look like that?" the Swede said thickly. "Like some old wino."

"I didn't mean anything by it. It was just the easiest way to disguise myself. I really am sorry."

There was sympathy in the voice; the Swede clung to the sound. He turned back to the sound, hope beginning to rise again. "*Aiutami, Arrigo,*" he said softly. "They're going to kill me."

"Who is?"

"I don't know! Big Tiny will kill me if I don't shut up, and the boss will kill me if I do!"

The aging face hardened. "You poor sonofabitch. Do you really expect *me* to help you? You got me arrested."

"Why'd you come to see me, then? You want me to die? Don't it mean nothing to you that I could die?"

"About as much as it meant to you when you shot Steven Pomerantz and claimed I was in it with you."

"*Non è colpa mia, Arrigo.* They're making me do it."

"Who is?"

"Jesus, I can't tell you that. They'd kill me if I told you."

"I thought they were going to kill you anyway."

"You said you were sorry, Arrigo—can't you help me, then? Get the cops to give me some kind of protection. Tell them I got to have protection!" He couldn't keep the hiccups of fear from his voice. A woman at the next table turned to him curiously. He lowered his voice. "Please, Arrigo. You could go see Big Tiny—he always liked you. You could make him leave me alone."

After a pause Arrigo said, "I wouldn't even consider helping you unless you paid for it."

"You want money?"

"Something better. The truth. Tell me who put you up to shooting Joncas's son-in-law."

"I can't do that!"

"Then I can't do anything either. Sorry." This time Arrigo did not sound as if he meant it. He pushed back his chair and started slowly to rise.

"Wait a second." The Swede thought of the note in the desk drawer in his cell; he wiped the moisture from his upper lip. "I'll tell you one thing," he said. "It . . . it was a mistake. I wasn't supposed to shoot that kid."

"I don't believe you." Arrigo was still standing. "How could you make a mistake like that?"

"Because I . . . I couldn't see good. It was hot, and I . . ." He stopped; he couldn't tell it to Arrigo. Arrigo would laugh. Anybody would laugh.

"Go on," Arrigo said. He sat back down.

The Swede looked at his face, with its pouches and sags and tiny seam lines at the mouth. He closed his eyes, holding the face in his mind, pretending it really was his father's. A father would not laugh at his own son.

"I was . . . I was supposed to get some old guy, with white hair," he said. "They showed me his picture, but it wasn't too good. They said he was like the head honcho. They said they'd make sure he was carrying a special sign like nobody else had—"

Dimly he heard a voice say, "Jesus Christ, you mean Morty Codd?" But his mind was filling with the catcalls of the picket line and the signs that had waved before his eyes, taunting him. "They told me to check the old guy's sign, to make sure," he said. "But how could I do that? All the signs . . ."

The signs had been nothing but marks, those mysterious curls and strokes that could be drawn on the thinnest sheet of paper but still had the power to make the world a foreign country. As soon as he saw the marks, anywhere, his mind and gut always started to liquefy, anticipating the laughter of those who could understand the marks; each day was a sweaty battle to keep them from discovering he was not one of them—to avoid being asked to check a map, to pretend to read the paper whenever others did, to memorize landmarks for wherever he wanted to go, to steal a driver's license because he couldn't take the written test; he had even learned laboriously to trace out and sign his name, without knowing why the marks went the way they did. . . . "Just marks," he whispered. "The signs were just marks." He felt his thighs trembling and tried to stop them with his hands.

He heard his father whisper, "Dear God."

"I got a note this morning. I can't tell who it's from! I can't tell which one is going to kill me if I don't do what they want!"

There was silence. "You poor bastard."

The Swede opened his eyes. The voice and face were Arrigo's. He tried to speak to them calmly. "You got to help me, now. I told you. I paid you."

"You haven't told me who sent you to the picket line in the first place. Your boss, I suppose? Donald?"

"You know his name? Jesus, he'll think I told you! He'll kill me just for that!"

"Then it won't matter if you tell me his last name."

"I can't do that. I can't!"

"You can't do anything, can you?" Suddenly Arrigo's eyes went wide. "Now I understand why you had to bring me *pictures*." He shook his head. "How did it happen, Swede? You got as far as the tenth grade—how could you do that?"

"They kept passing me. They didn't give a damn."

"Why didn't you ever tell me? Maybe I could have helped you."

"You'd have laughed your head off. You were such a smart-ass little bastard, always reading, reading, reading . . ."

"Maybe things could have been different, if you'd trusted me."

"Why the hell should I? You never done nothing but make trouble for me. You know how much crap I had to take from the gang because my little brother wouldn't shape up and be a good soldier? You know how many times they came to me and said if I couldn't keep you in line, they'd . . ." His voice trailed off when he saw Arrigo's eyes. "What's the matter?" he said.

"The white truck," Arrigo whispered. "You said I killed Carlo Bellucci with something I took out of a white truck."

Before the Swede's mind could follow the sudden switch, the hairs on the back of his neck warned him of danger. "You did it," he said uncertainly. "I seen you do it."

"I reached into a white truck that said 'Plumbing and Heating'?"

"Yeah."

"How did you know what it said on the truck?"

The Swede heard his ears pounding. "There was a white truck. I seen it."

"I have a vague memory of it too. That's why I've figured, all these years, that you could have been telling the truth. But it can't be the truth. Because you can't read. You bastard! You can't read!"

The Swede said nothing.

"That's why the cops could never find the white truck—they were looking for one that said 'Plumbing and Heating.' But you made those words up. You made up everything else, too. You bastard."

"There was a truck! The back end was open, and there was a bunch of tools inside! I saw the wrench, and I . . ." He froze.

"Ah," said Arrigo. "You saw the wrench. You took it out. You killed Carlo."

Against his will, the Swede remembered how it had been: Arrigo hurling himself at Carlo, knocking the gang leader down, then passing out. The two of them had lain at his feet, both helpless. The sudden power he had felt seemed to come from God, who was telling him he could get even with Carlo. Could keep Carlo from throwing him out of the gang, as he had threatened to do just that afternoon. In a kind of trance of invincibility he had gone to the white truck parked at the curb, checked that no one was watching, taken out a wrench, and smashed in Carlo's head. It had caved in like a watermelon.

He had tossed the wrench back in the truck and hidden in the alley, where he could see everything: the truck driving off, a patrol car cruising by ten minutes later and stopping, Arrigo starting to come to. The feeling of invincibility had drained away, leaving only the terror of being caught. When the cops searched the block, they had found him easily. At the stationhouse, when he heard the cops talking about flesh under Arrigo's nails, he had realized what to do: He had told the truth exactly, except that he had ascribed his own actions to Arrigo. And when the cops tried to get more information about the truck, hoping he had seen a license number or a name, he had decided to invent some detail that would strengthen his story. "Plumbing and Heating"—he had liked that, because it sounded as if he could read.

"Look at me," Arrigo was saying. "Look at me and tell me you didn't kill Carlo."

The Swede looked, and said nothing.

"Ah," Arrigo said. He said it again, as if he were sucking in air. "Do you know what you've done to me? What you've made me carry since I was thirteen? Yes, of course you know. You liked it that way. I bet it makes you laugh, to be pinning another killing on me now. Why, Swede? What did I do to make you hate me so much?"

"You were . . ." The Swede wrestled with what he felt, wanting for once to have it between them in words. But only three came out: "You just . . . were."

"And you just wanted me . . . not to be?" Arrigo leaned over the table. "You made me feel something for you today, Swede, in spite of everything. You even made me wonder . . . But now I wouldn't help you if you were bleeding to death right here on this table. I'd watch, and think you deserved it." He stood up slowly, eyes bright in their wrinkled surroundings.

"Arrigo," the Swede whispered.

He watched the figure move away, stooped and shuffling. It seemed to him as if everyone were leaving—his brother, his father, and his hope.

Back in his cell, he took out the note again.

He knew the marks were going to do what they always did: destroy him.

But he could take Arrigo with him, he thought; he could pay Arrigo back.

He took out the only other thing in his desk: a slip of paper with his lawyer's phone number on it.

27

The green Department of Corrections van made its way from the Men's House back to the central reception building. When it stopped, Erik got out, putting both feet on each step. The motion seemed incongruous; he felt like leaping.

He went into the main waiting room, still holding his body as if it were tired and much heavier, and headed toward the front entrance.

Halfway across the room he heard someone call, "Erik!" It took all his stage training to keep from swinging around.

He turned slowly and saw Jac, sitting frozen on one of the benches, a guilty hand over her mouth. He shuffled toward her. The motion felt ludicrous; he wanted to run.

He stood in front of her and said, "Don't call attention to me in here. I'm going out to wait for the bus. Come out in five minutes. Don't say a word till we're on the bus."

She nodded almost imperceptibly.

Twenty minutes later she was beside him in a narrow seat. When the half-empty bus had crossed the bridge that linked Rikers Island to Queens, he heard her laugh softly. "You look scabrous," she said.

"You don't."

"Where did you get those awful clothes? The Bowery?"

"The theater's costume racks."

"Did you do it, then?" she said. "Did you pull it off?"

"Better than I dreamed."

"Tell me."

"First tell me why you were there," he said.

"Because you didn't call to tell me you were going. And I knew you didn't have any reason not to go. I mean, the hospital told me Ms. Jerrold was all right. So why didn't you tell me you were going to do it?"

"I wanted to be sure I could pull it off first. I'd have called you as soon as I got home. I didn't know you'd be so impatient."

"I told you I was taking today off," Jac said. "I didn't want to waste any time."

"So you just walked in and said you wanted to see Rossano Dantino?"

"I thought maybe he'd recognize the name Jac Sanda when they gave it to him and be curious enough to want to see me."

"And if he had, what would you have said?"

"That I was secretly working for Joncas. That Joncas wanted the truth about his son-in-law's death and might be willing to help your brother if he told it."

Erik raised his eyebrows, feeling the weight of the added false hair. "You might have pulled it off, by God. You're a. . .remarkable lady."

"Then why was I so scared?"

The bus turned a corner and crashed into a pothole. Their bodies slid together, shoulder to thigh, and could not seem to separate. Her hair smelled of lemons and grass.

"The streets are like this in all the boroughs," she said.

"Yes."

When the bus finally righted, they pulled apart. "But why were you still in the waiting room?" he said. "Didn't they tell you the Swede already had a visitor? And that inmates are allowed only one visit per day?"

"Yes, they did. But I decided to wait for a while anyway. I hoped the visitor was you, and if not, then I would try to see whether I could recognize whoever it was." She laughed. "And I did."

"How? How did you know me right away, across the whole room?"

"I don't know. Everything was different—your looks, your walk— but I just knew."

He thought that he would have known her across a room, too, no matter how her face was disguised. And her body.

"Tell me how you got in," she said. "Didn't you have to give a name and show some ID, the way I did?"

"I have an old driver's license from Colorado, for Arrigo Dantino. I spilled something on the first name and said it was Enrico. I told them to tell the Swede his father wanted to see him."

"Is that the way your father looks? So scabrous?"

"I have no idea. I've never seen him. He was a sailor, I guess. The Swede's father was someone else, but Mother would never say who. I don't think she knew."

Jac stared as if he'd been speaking another language. "What did you learn from the Swede?"

He meant to start at the beginning, but what came out first and could not be stopped was the story of the day he had not killed the boy. As it came, he tried to name the feeling that had been possessing him since he learned the truth, which was too profound to be called relief.

When he finished, her eyes were so dark they seemed filled with black light. She touched his hand, which the makeup had aged with vein lines. "Thank God," she said. "And thank God I didn't get in to see your brother. I think I'd have wanted to kill him." She leaned an arm on the seat in front, so that a river of dark brown hair ran across one of her wide cheekbones. "Inside that beard, you look as if you feel about twelve years old."

"No," he said. "Thirteen. The way I felt right up to the day it happened—innocent. No, that's not the right word." He turned to look out the window and saw a row of drearily identical houses. When he was a child, they would have seemed like palaces. "I lived inside myself a lot when I was a kid. I always thought that core of private thoughts and feelings was . . . was good. After the boy died and I had to accept that I might have killed him, I felt I couldn't count on myself in the same way. I had to be very careful about what I did. Especially about the way I dealt with people. Maybe that's why I didn't leave the ghetto sooner. Why I went back to it after they released me from Spofford House, and stayed for three more years. Maybe that's why I did a lot of things the way I did. Why I held back . . ." He stopped. "Trusting, that's the word I want. I used to trust myself, without question. What the Swede did made me always distrust myself a little, be a little guarded."

"Except in the theater," she said. "You told me that's where you always felt free."

"Yes." He turned to her wonderingly. "It sounds as if I'm saying that the thing I can never forgive the Swede for is the very thing that turned me to the theater."

"What if it was?" she said. "No one builds his life in a vacuum. You found one place where you could be yourself, where your brother's lie couldn't affect you. Just be glad you found it."

He looked at her, wanting to say that he had found two places and she was the other. But he was stopped by a sudden question. Perhaps the Swede's lie had led to something else; perhaps he could have loved Maeve as fully as she wanted if he had been free of that guilt when he met her.

But he had not been free of it, he thought, when he met Jac.

"How did you get him to tell you the truth?" she said.

He told her the rest of it, then, starting with the Swede's terror of being killed. While he described what had happened on the picket line, she put her hands around her neck and into her hair and lifted her head toward the ceiling.

"You mean," she said, "that the original idea was to frame you for killing Morty Codd?"

"I think so."

"And when your brother killed Pomerantz by accident, they just adapted the frame to the new situation?"

"That's the way I see it."

"And 'they' is the Swede's boss in Westchester? Whose first name is Donald?"

"And who was with Joncas in the Briarwood photograph."

She brought her hands and her head down abruptly. "Are you going to tell the police what your brother said?"

"Not until and unless there's a chance they'd believe me."

"Can you make him tell the story himself?"

"I think I've just played my last card with the Swede."

"Then the only other possibility of clearing you is to find this Donald on our own and expose him. I still have those Briarwood names I got from the . . . from my source. I haven't gotten anywhere, but I'll get back on it tomorrow. I'll take a few more days off and work on it nonstop. Did you ever hear of any of the names, by the way? Crescent Enterprises? Greenwich Holding? Intercomp? And one that my source wasn't sure of getting right, because it seemed so odd—Christian Comfort?"

He shook his head. "This isn't your fight. Why are you taking it on?"

"If I help you break this frame, I'll get a smashing exclusive for myself and Channel Ten, you know."

"Yes. But you've done so much, Jac. I—"

"Are you thinking that you owe me now?" She said it without sarcasm or bitterness. "I don't think of what I've done as 'giving' or 'owing.' I don't feel that such considerations exist, with you. I'm not doing these things just to help you, Erik. I'm doing them because . . ." She lifted her chin. "You came into my life and disrupted it. You let me know how you felt. You involved me, Erik. Still, I could have pulled away. I guess there's always a point, in any relationship, at which you still can pull away. But once you go past that point . . . Do you know when it was, for me? At the hospital, when you were telling me how you felt about Maeve Jerrold." She smiled ruefully. "It hurt to hear that. But you didn't soften anything for my sake. You talked to me as if you were talking to yourself. No one else has ever done that." The bus braked sharply. She grabbed for the seat bar. "Maybe you'll decide you can't walk away from Maeve Jerrold, but I can't walk away from you." After a moment she added, "Unless you ask me to."

The bus stopped; it had reached the subway station. He let out his breath slowly. "You know I can't do that."

Around them, passengers began to stand. Jac took her shoulder bag from the floor. "Are you taking the subway back?" she said lightly.

"I don't think a man who looks this way would have cabfare."

"I do need a cab. I have to pick Karen up from school in forty minutes."

"Go ahead, then."

"I'll be in touch." She grinned. "Stay young."

He watched her run down the aisle of the bus. He got slowly to his feet.

*　　*　　*

At six-thirty, showered and back in his own clothes, he was at the hospital.

Maeve was sleeping, so he took a chair beside her bed. The curtains were drawn against the sunset.

She had not spoken to him when he finally saw her on Saturday night, or on Sunday either. She had lain with her face to the wall; either she hadn't heard what he said to her, or else it hadn't mattered.

Now her face, without makeup, framed by the long hair spread on the pillow, looked oddly girlish, yet also haggard, as if a child were wrapped within a veil of time. One hand, which had never seemed so thin, lay on the white spread like a wax carving. He felt that he looked at her across a chasm. He could explain, perhaps, the things that had made her want to take her life, but he had no inner means of understanding that wish.

Her hand moved slightly. He leaned forward to touch it, but she didn't wake. He kept his fingers on hers, willing himself to recapture the night they had sketched out the theater's logo. It seemed so far away that he had to bring it back by using the technique of emotional memory; and when he did, he realized that he had felt no sense of obligation that night, only of closeness and love; the fact that she was giving him something, and what she might be getting in return, simply had been irrelevant. He had not been thinking in such terms.

He searched through the six years of their relationship, looking for the time when the sense of owing her had begun. He could find no answer that fit the calendar; there had been only his slow awareness that they shared nearly everything in the aesthetic realm but much less in the real world.

His eyes darkened as a connection formed suddenly in words: When two people felt the same way about one another, neither thought in terms of "owing." Only when one of them began to change—to experience the differences between them as greater than the similarity—did he or she begin to feel obligated. Obligation was the residue of love, and the proof that it was no longer shared equally.

He closed his eyes, realizing what Jac had been confessing when she said that "giving" and "owing" didn't exist between the two of them.

Maeve's money, he thought, was not the issue. Nor was the fact that he had begun to love her less. The issue—the mistake—was that he had not stopped taking her gifts of love and money the moment he began to experience them as gifts. And the theater building was the worst of it, for he had taken that when he already knew he loved Jac.

"You look like Prometheus," Maeve said, "when they're hammering in the chain."

He opened his eyes and tried to smile. So did she.

"It's wonderful that you're back," he said finally.

"I wish I could think so." Her voice was very soft.

"I suppose it's natural for you to feel that way. At least for a while. Do you want to talk about it?"

"No."

"All right." He kissed her hand. The veins stood out, the way his own had when his hands were made up to look old.

"Don't say it again," she whispered.

"Say what?"

"What you said on Saturday night, and yesterday too."

"You did hear me, then."

"Yes. Don't tell me you were too hard on me after I went to that place in Brooklyn."

"But it's true."

"I can't stand to hear it. Any of it."

"All right. We won't talk about any of it till you feel better."

"Never," she said. "Never."

He wondered which she meant—talking about it, or feeling better.

She clutched his hand. "I never told you, Erik. This happened before. After Jonathan was killed in that car accident. I wanted to go with him. To be with him forever. A nurse stopped me. I hated her. Now I . . ."

"Yes?"

She sighed. "It's not Jac Sanda's fault. It's mine. I let her in."

"You must have wanted to see her."

"She's very much like you, I think." He said nothing, merely watched her eyes look into the distance. "Sometimes it hurts," she said.

He thought of the day when he would have to tell her the truth of his feelings, and wondered whether she was thinking of it too.

"To live," she said.

"What do you mean?"

"I mean that sometimes it hurts to live."

"Yes," he said lamely. "But sometimes it doesn't."

She gave the ghost of a laugh. "You always say that."

"Because it's true. Today, for instance, I learned something that makes things different for me. Better, I mean." He hesitated, wondering whether he should be talking to her about it. But no other subject seemed safe. "I talked to my brother. He finally told me the truth. I didn't kill that boy, years ago. My brother is the one who did it."

He saw both her smile and the effort it took. "That's wonderful," she said.

He leaned even closer, pushing some strands of hair from her forehead. "I don't want you carrying any unnecessary guilt, either. The things that happened last week don't matter to me anymore. Please don't let them matter so much to you." She turned her head away. "Does that sound fatuous?" he said.

"No. Just . . . irrelevant."

She did not move again, but he saw her drifting out into a sea of strangeness and then sinking, until only her pale hair was left on the surface like foam. He could not let her go, he thought, even though he knew now that he could not sacrifice his future to hers.

"Maeve," he said softly, "*Firestorm* is going to open. The world is going to see your beautiful play—even if it runs for only one performance—and you're going to see the world seeing it. This fight I took on and the mess it got me and the theater into—I'm not going to let that stop you from seeing your play open."

"How can that happen now?" she said, still turned away.

"Let's make a pact. I'll find a way to do it, if you'll find a way to face me, and face yourself, and leave this hospital and come to the theater and see the play. OK? All you have to do to make it start happening is turn your head now and look at me and say, 'All right, Erik, I want to see *Firestorm* open.'"

Her hair on the pillow looked like drowning ropes; he wanted to reach for them and pull her back, but he knew he could never again make the mistake of doing for her what she had to do for herself.

The second weighed like hours, but finally she did turn to him. "All right, Erik. I want to see *Firestorm* open."

28

Cecelia Joncas called downstairs to the den, "Vi! Dinner is almost ready. Coral and I are waiting for you."

"In ten minutes," Joncas said. "I've got to make some calls."

For several of those minutes, even though the light was almost gone, he continued staring out the window at the back patio, his lion's head sunk on his chest. When a leaf floated onto the sill, he rubbed his eyes, turned around, and reached for the desk phone.

"Burt?" he said. "How are you?" His thick eyebrows slanted into a frown. "The question was rhetorical, Burt. I already know the answer. That's what I'm calling about. People are coming out of the transport negotiations and asking what the hell's the matter with you. They say you look as jumpy as a cat on a griddle. Better pull yourself together, my friend." He listened, then cut in again, gravel crackling in his voice. "I don't want to discuss it, Burt. You did what you had to do. Lucky for you, you did it well. If it bothers you, take tranquilizers. Just keep your mind on the talks, OK? And don't forget whose side you're on."

He hung up and smiled grimly. The only tolerable part of what he had gone through, he thought, was the pleasure of making Burt Sanda share it. He dialed again, sighing; the next call would be no pleasure at all.

"Morty? I hear you've been trying to reach me. Sorry I couldn't get back to you sooner."

"It's OK, Mr. Joncas," Codd said. "I guess you've been busy. We haven't talked since that Labor Day service for your son-in-law, you know. Of course, like I told you then, I could understand if you were trying to avoid me—"

"I told you it was all right, Morty." Joncas's jaw tightened. "I've been busy, that's all. What's up?"

"Well, I'm real glad for you and your family that they charged Dante, that they're going to nail him. When it came out that he's in with the Varese—I mean, Christ! And then when they said he ordered the killing to warn you off! I'll tell you, if there's anybody left who could still listen to those old rumors about you, I'll take him apart personally."

"Thanks," Joncas said curtly.

'This is the end of Dante. He'll have to close down the theater now that he's indicted, don't you think?"

"That's what a normal man would do."

"I was wondering if you thought I should make a statement when he closes. You know, about how TATU is glad to see the mob exposed, and how ninety-nine percent of labor is clean as a whistle, including the—"

"No!" Joncas took a short, deep breath. "No public statements, Morty. Just let the courts and the media handle it."

"Well, OK. I just thought—"

"Is that it, Morty? My wife and daughter are waiting for me."

"Sure. Give them my regards, will you?"

Joncas hung up and wiped his hands along his gray slacks.

"Vi!" Cecelia called.

"All right. I'm coming."

He left the den and went up to the dining room, where the light from the brass chandelier seemed as warm as a fire.

When the soup arrived, Cecelia lifted her spoon and then put it down with a happy sigh. "Oh, Coral honey," she said, "it's so nice to have you living with us again, I can't pretend it isn't. All three of us together for dinner. I mean, all three and three-quarters of us."

"Eight-ninths, Mother. If you want to be precise."

"Oh, I hardly ever want to do that."

Laughing, Coral lifted the salt shaker and put it closer to Joncas. "Here, Daddy. I know you're going to ask for this in a minute."

"I wish I could tell you," Cecelia said, "how good it makes me feel to see you and your father at peace with each other again."

Coral put a pale hand on Joncas's swarthy one. "He knows I'm sorry for what I said when I . . . before I knew the truth. But sometimes I think he still hasn't forgiven me. Sometimes his eyes look so tight and, I don't know, kind of jumpy."

Joncas cleared his throat. "It's the transport talks," he said.

"Of course it is." Cecelia tasted her soup. "Do you know, he doesn't even have time to tend to his fish anymore? That's how busy he is. Everybody puts pressure on him. Everybody depends on him. So we just have to see that he can relax sometimes."

Both women smiled at Joncas.

He blinked several times, and then, unfolding a crisp white napkin, he smiled back.

"I didn't want to do this on the phone," the young lawyer said.

"You're cautious. I like that." Donald Shaw's smile neither reached his eyes nor sent any warmth across his desk. "So, Dantino called you in a panic, and you went to see him. What did he want?"

"He wants you to get rid of his brother."

Shaw pursed his lips. "Why?"

"Most of what he said didn't make any sense to me." The lawyer consulted his notepad. "He was furious at his brother. He kept saying, 'Arrigo can't make a fool of me no more.'" The lawyer took a breath. "Whatever it was, he wanted me to tell you that he stole something one night from your desk, there. Some pictures of you and Joncas. He wants you to know that he showed those pictures to his brother. He figures that should make you get rid of him."

The only sound was a tiny click, as the digital clock on the desk changed from 8:33 to 8:34.

The lawyer went on. "Of course I questioned him closely. He swears he never told his brother your name or anything about you. But he says he did show him the pictures before he returned them to the desk."

The clock reached 8:37 before Shaw spoke. "You think Dantino was telling the truth?"

"I can't imagine why he'd make it up."

"If it's true, I can't imagine why he'd tell it. I thought he wanted to stay alive."

"He seems convinced he's not going to do that anyway, so he wants to take the brother with him."

"Ah," Shaw said. "That, I believe." He picked up a glass paperweight; it seemed softer than his eyes. "As soon as it's a question of family—take it either way—those damn Italians let their brains leak out their ears."

The lawyer shifted uncomfortably; his maternal grandparents had come from Rome. "Is there anything you want me to do about it?"

"I'll let you know."

When the man had gone, Shaw looked around the office, which would do justice to any board chairman in the country. But now it had a mess of glass and fluid in one corner, where the paperweight had just crashed against the wall.

For the first time in the whole Dante situation, he felt something other than annoyance: the deeply personal rage of someone whose privacy has been violated.

He went to a suede-covered panel; it hid a small safe, where he kept the pictures most of the time. He opened it and took out a large gray envelope marked "Insurance and Pension Fund." It was his private joke to camouflage the pictures that way; would Dantino have looked in the envelope if he hadn't read the label? Perhaps he had actively been looking for evidence of union-fund involvement, to show his brother.

But if so, why?

Shaw took the envelope back to the desk and opened it. The contents were "insurance" in that they provided a pictorial record of a number of the men he had made deals with—politicians, producers, judges, union leaders. He had discovered early that if a man would not let his picture be taken with you, he could not be completely trusted.

In a way, the pictures were also a "pension fund"—at least the ones that proved the depth of his involvement in the entertainment industry. Those were his favorites: The shot of himself with the star of a

Broadway show he had financed, in which sexual intercourse was not merely simulated. The shot of himself with the best-selling author of soft porn, who did not know he owned part of her publisher's firm. The shot of Kerry London with her arm around him—Kerry London, whose songs were too blue for an upright Christian and who was said to snort coke through rolled-up hundred-dollar bills. And half a dozen others, all of whom would turn the senior Shaws' eyes blank with shock. The fact that he could produce the pictures anytime, if he chose—that he had such a fund—gave him a great deal of pleasure to contemplate.

Sometimes, when his parents' homilies were particularly irritating, he kept the pictures in the desk drawer for a day or two. Obviously that was how Dantino had found them. But had he really shown them to his brother?

Shaw separated out the photos in which Joncas appeared. Apart from the "insurance" shots of the two of them, taken early in their relationship, the only others were those taken in Kerry London's dressing room when she was playing Briarwood. He and Joncas had had a business meeting there, in the very private office, and afterward Joncas had wanted to meet her. There had been no harm in it: London had no idea of what Shaw really was and did. And if she had, she probably would have liked it; she had gotten her start in Vegas as a teenager and had played footsie all her life with several of the West Coast families. She was wonderful at denying all connections with them: She could look straight into the eye of a camera or a judge and swear that she "met too many people" in her busy life to "be asking what they all do to earn a living."

That night in the dressing room, someone in her ever-present entourage had been taking pictures, and Shaw had quietly commandeered the ones with himself and Joncas. He picked one up and studied it. There was a Briarwood poster clearly visible in the corner. If Erik Dante had seen that, he thought, then Dante might no longer be a thorn safely pulled from one's side. If he was nosing around, if he got a hint of the skimming going on at Briarwood, or how the skim was divided up . . . The simplest way to ensure safety, Shaw thought, would be to disband the whole Briarwood operation at once and create new corporations to absorb its traces. But that was an accountant's solution. It would provide no personal satisfaction.

He picked up one of the desk phones, as if he wished it were another paperweight. He dialed but got no answer. He dialed another number. After someone answered, there was a long wait. Finally he heard "Joncas here. Who's calling and what's the emergency?"

"It's me."

"What the hell are you doing calling me on the regular number?"

"You didn't answer the special one."

"Because I'm eating dinner."

"Get ready to lose it."

"What do you mean?"

When he had explained, Joncas said, "Christ. Oh, Christ."

"He never helps."

"Right in the middle of the goddamn transport negotiations, too. Listen, maybe the brother is just bluffing."

"Maybe. Or maybe Dante is getting ready right now to give some information to the DA. Or the press. That goddamn Sanda woman would put it on the air in a minute. Don't forget, her ex-husband told you she'd already asked him about Briarwood. What if Dante put her up to it? And that goddamn nosy bookkeeper disappeared into thin air, while one of my boys sits around with a bandage over the fork-hole in his eye." In the silence Shaw could almost hear Joncas sweating. "So," he went on, "I guess you see what the answer is."

"All right. But no mistakes this time. There can't be any more mistakes!"

29

"And then, Mother," Karen said as she and Jac got off the elevator at their floor, "we got all the dominoes set up just like the pattern we made. And *I* got to be the one who pushed the first one over. It

knocked over another one, and that knocked over another one, and
they all went over in a flash, and we could see our whole pattern! Just
laying there on the table!"

"*Lying* there," Jac said automatically, unlocking the apartment
door. Then she laughed, grabbed Karen up in her arms, and carried
her inside. "Three kisses for the domino lady," she said. They sank
into the brown chair, laughing and hugging one another.

"I love it when you come get me at school, Mother."

"That's why I gave Mary a couple days off, so we could be
together, just the two of us. And I'll bet right now she's down in
Baltimore, hugging and kissing her granddaughter. So everybody's
happy, right?"

"Yup. Except I think one of us is hungry."

"Why don't you go change into your jeans and purple shirt, and
then we'll make something. How'd you like a snake snack?"

"A *what?*"

"A snake made out of carrot and zucchini slices and cream
cheese."

Karen ran down to her room, hollering, "A snake snack, a snack
snake, a snickety snake . . ."

Jac went to the small desk by the window, where her notes were
still scattered. She had spent most of the day, and the day before, on
the phone, working on the names she had wormed out of Amy Stone.
While Amy still trusted her.

Even then, Amy had told her very little. She said only that after
she had already begun to suspect there was skimming going on at
Briarwood, she had overheard a conversation about the theater's
grosses, in which some names were mentioned that she knew weren't
those of stockholders. One of the names had been "Joncas," but the
others were corporations. Amy thought no one knew what she had
overheard, but her suspicions began to weigh on her so heavily that
she soon quit. When she left, the business manager had told her
never to discuss any aspect of the business—and then had asked
pointedly about her little boy's health.

Jac finally had established that none of the corporations were reg-
istered in the Northeast or listed by the U.S. Attorney's office as the

subject of an investigation. If the whole setup involved offshore or foreign corporations, as she was beginning to suspect, then it could be as complex and interconnected as Karen's dominoes. And finding the name that would knock the whole thing over could be virtually impossible.

The last name, Christian Comfort, was the one Amy thought she must have heard incorrectly, and Jac had begun to agree. Still, around one o'clock she had decided to try a different angle; if Christian Comfort existed, perhaps some religious group would have heard of it. In the yellow pages there were four columns of names under "Religious Organizations." She had gotten nearly to the end, and then a woman had answered her question easily; "Oh, yes. They're not affiliated with us, but I do know it's some kind of charitable organization. I have a friend who gets a newsletter from them." Jac had gotten that friend's name, called her, and finally mined two pieces of information from her garrulousness: the name Reverend Joseph Shaw, which meant nothing, and the address, a post-office box, which could mean something because it was in Westchester County. From Westchester Information she had gotten a phone listing for the Reverend Shaw, although there was none for Christian Comfort. She had been ready to dial the number when she had had to leave to get Karen.

She heard Karen still chanting to herself in the bedroom; she hesitated, then picked up the phone and dialed.

"Hello," said a soft voice that could belong to either sex. "May we be of comfort to you?"

Jac stared. "Are you . . .? Is Reverend Shaw there? Of Christian Comfort?"

"Speaking."

"Oh." She began to improvise. "This is Sandra Jackson. I'm researching a magazine article on theaters. Dinner theaters. Someone told me you were interested in the Briarwood chain, and I wondered whether I might ask you some questions."

"Theaters?" The voice was gently shocked. "No, no. I'm afraid you were misinformed. Theaters are not part of God's ministry on earth. They are one of the devil's snares."

Jac nearly dropped the phone. She gripped it more firmly. "So no one in your organization has any kind of connection with theaters? Or anyone in your family?"

There was a pause; she was certain she had startled the man.

"Oh, heavens," she said brightly. "I've been going down a list of names, and I see I've gotten mixed up. I wanted someone named *Donald*, but you're Joseph, aren't you?" She hoped he wouldn't notice the non sequiturs.

"Donald." The voice was flat, as if pressing down on some emotion. "There must be a mistake. There *must* be."

She made a decision. "I've read your newsletter," she said, trying to recall some of the garrulous woman's conversation about it. "I found your thoughts on the power of prayer quite inspiring. In fact, that's really why I called you. I need help with a personal problem. I'd like to come and talk to you."

"We don't usually see people in person," the man said regretfully.

"But I need help. I . . ." She grimaced. "I find I'm very tempted by the theater."

"Well . . . when would you want to come?"

"Tomorrow morning."

"Oh, no."

"Tomorrow afternoon? Or evening?"

"No, no."

"You tell me, then."

"It's difficult. We never know when he'll be . . . Excuse me a moment." Jac thought she heard a whispered colloquy in the background. Then the man returned. "Unless you could come now?"

"Now?" Jac looked down; Karen was hanging on to one of her skirt pockets, grinning up at her.

"We'd have to be through by seven o'clock," the man said.

Jac smiled ruefully at Karen and asked the man's address.

When she hung up, Karen said, "Have you got a hot lead, Mother? Too hot to make a snake snack?"

"I'm afraid so, darling." She knelt down and took the face that was so like her own into both hands. "Do you have any idea how much I love you for putting up with me and my work and not fussing?"

For twenty minutes she tried desperately to find someone to look after Karen; when she was about to give up, because Burt was the only possibility left and she couldn't risk his learning where she was going, she called the Poets and Paupers Theater.

As Erik moved through the scene, his mind alternating between directing it and being part of it, he would glance out occasionally at the small figure in jeans and a purple shirt. Sometimes she got up and changed her seat, but she stayed in the front row, and when she did sit down, she was quiet. The sight of her made him smile and think of her mother; and that thought made him worry.

He had been unable to go to the apartment and stay with Karen, as Jac wanted; he simply couldn't cancel two hours of rehearsal, because *Firestorm* was going to open in nine days—even if there were more people on the stage than in the audience—and he was breaking in six new cast members.

He had tried to keep Jac from going, but she wouldn't be stopped. "I have a personal stake in this," she said. "Don't forget which little girl's father is involved in Briarwood." If she was worried at all, it had been for Karen, not for herself, although Erik had assured her that everything had been quiet since his indictment; there were hardly even any more hostile calls to the box office. Privately he thought that his enemies had already written him off as finished. Like most of his audience.

At least he had made Jac go into one of the dressing rooms, put her hair into a twist, and change the shape of her eyebrows and mouth. He got her a slouch hat from costumes and a pair of fake glasses from props. When she left, she didn't look much like Jac Sanda. Karen had been astounded.

After an hour he dismissed all the actors but one. He had found and cast her only the day before; she was not as good as the woman she replaced, but she was willing to work for a man under indictment for procuring a murder. He got Karen a soda and then ran through the scene twice more. The last time, he sat in the front row and called out his lines, so he could watch the actress. He made a few changes in her blocking and then told her she could go.

Karen held out a small box of raisins. "I bet you're hungry."

"Thanks. That was hard work. What did you make of it all?"

"I guess it's for grown-ups. Mother says there are things I won't understand for a while. But I like to listen to your voice. Why did you and that lady talk about a fire?"

"Because this play is a story about what all of us do with fire."

"Me too?"

"When you grow up, yes." He stretched his legs. "You see, a long time ago there wasn't any fire in the world. So I—the character I play—stole some from his friends, who were all gods, and brought it down to the world. My friends got mad and punished me, and when I got away, I came back to earth to see whether people were worth the punishment. I went around to see the things they'd done with the fire I gave them—good things and bad things—and I was just about to decide they weren't worth it when I met that lady."

"Did you like her?"

"Yes."

"Why?"

"Oh, dear. Well, she was . . . It was as if she herself were made of fire, so she could wrap tongues of it around you and make you forget everything else."

Karen ate a raisin. "Did she burn you? Is that why you hollered at her?"

He managed not to smile. "I hollered because she could be cold and hurtful, too, like falling on the ice. And I didn't like loving somebody who could be good and bad. But most people are like that. That's what I—my character—has to accept."

"I'm bad sometimes. Then my mother says, 'Karen Joann Sanda, what am I going to do with you?'"

It was a good imitation; Erik laughed, and the empty spaces around them echoed the sound. "OK," he said, "time to get you home. Your peerless, fearless mother left me a key, in case she didn't get back before rehearsal was over."

"Couldn't I see some more things? She said you probably would show me your whole house for the stories."

"Did she? I guess you could see the prop room before we go."

When he led her up on the stage, she reached for his hand. He showed her the trapdoor and then led her down the back stairs to the basement. The scene shop was empty because the crew had gone to supper, but he showed her some flats they were painting and then took her into the prop room.

He showed her a jeweled gold goblet, made of wood and glass, from *Cuchulain* and a sequined headdress from *Turandot*; her eyes shone like fairy lights. He let her try a huge feather fan from *The Faraway Princess*; she giggled when her nose peeked through the feathers. He explained the Egyptian sarcophagus standing in one corner of the room and, in the other, the huge throne from *Ruy Blas*. She climbed up into it and sat grinning at him.

Suddenly in the midst of her chatter he cocked his head and put a finger on his lips. The silence rubbed coldly against the back of his neck. He knew the building like his own body, and upstairs, on the stage, he could feel there was someone alien. He looked around the prop room; to get to the scene shop and the back door, they would have to pass the foot of the stairs.

He leaned down to Karen. "Let's play a game," he whispered. "Let's pretend we're ancient Egyptians and we have to get into our sarcophagus without making a sound. OK?"

"OK," she said in a stage whisper.

"Not a sound now, or Anubis the jackal will get us." He led her carefully to the sarcophagus, which had a plaster-and-paint pharaoh on its lid.

In front of it were piled boxes of plastic champagne glasses. He moved them carefully, although his hands were shaking. When he started to open the sarcophagus lid, it made a furious squeak, like an angry rat. Karen squealed too, then clamped a guilty hand over her mouth. He heard footsteps at the head of the stairs.

The sarcophagus was meant to lie horizontally, not to stand upright, and what was now its bottom was only thin plywood. When he stepped on it, the case rocked alarmingly. He steadied it. He was too tall to fit into the space, but he picked Karen up, holding her against his chest, both of them facing outward, and finally twisted his head and legs into the sarcophagus, feeling like Quasimodo. "Close the lid," he whispered. "Just pull it back toward you."

She could get it only three-quarters shut. "It's OK," he whispered. "Now, be as quiet as a cat. This isn't just a game. Some people are really trying to find us."

Her body was soft against his; it smelled like a flower. For a moment he was not in the theater but in a long-ago cellar, hiding treasure from those who would take it.

She squirmed in his arms and started to say, "My leg feels—"; somehow he got his right hand up and covered her mouth. "Quiet," he breathed in her ear. "Anubis is coming now."

She went still again.

Alarmingly near, a man's voice said, "Check the back. Maybe he got out that way." Karen jerked inside Erik's grasp. He tightened it until neither of them could breathe and his contorted body started to grow numb.

"I don't see no sign of him," said another voice.

The first voice sank to a whisper. "Let's keep it down, man. Maybe he's hiding down here somewhere."

There was a long silence. When the whispers started again, they were closer.

"What the hell is that junk in there? Look at that thing—like a throne."

"Never mind the goddamn throne. Look at all the cupboards and places to hide."

There was a click, like a gun being cocked.

30

There was a huge Tudor house at the head of the long winding driveway, and an elderly man in a black suit standing by the door.

Jac stopped the rented car, checked her strange appearance in the rearview mirror, and got out. In the distance she heard dogs barking.

"Miss Jackson?" the man said. "Joseph Shaw. I guess it's all right if you leave your car there. We won't be long. And I told the . . . I said I had someone coming. Come inside, please. Please."

He looked like a paper scarecrow, agitating in some private wind, as he led her into a spacious foyer and then down a long hallway on the left.

Only when they were inside a sitting room did he seem to relax. "My wife, Florence, Miss Jackson," he said, going to the elderly woman on the love seat by the bay window. She was as frail as he, with white hair that looked like Christmas-tree angel dust.

Jac took a chair. On the end table beside it was a small Bible. There were several pictures of the Crucifixion on the walls, the kind available in every dime store. Yet on the sideboard was an amazingly good small-scale reproduction of the Pietà. "That's beautiful," she said. "I've never seen one that good. Where did you get it?"

"Our son." Mrs. Shaw sighed. "We shouldn't keep it, I know. Such a luxury. But . . . our son insisted. He's a good man." She leaned forward, frowning. "You know, you look sort of familiar, Miss Jackson. Like someone I've seen somewhere."

"Yes," Jac said easily. "People often tell me I look like Senator Foster's wife."

"Of course. That must be it."

Jac smiled. "Would you tell me something about *Christian Comfort?*"

For ten minutes they explained: They were retired from the ministry and not able to get out much or see many people. But they could still serve through their newsletter and their many charitable contributions.

"Forgive my asking," Jac said, "but how do you finance all your good works?"

They looked at one another. "Our son makes it possible," the reverend said. "He's made a good deal of money, and he wants it to be used in a good cause." He seemed on the verge of adding something, then clasped his thin hands and said, "Now you must tell us how we can help you. Are you struggling with temptation?"

At that moment Jac was tempted only to abandon the ridiculous story she had prepared. But she began anyway, explaining that while doing research on theaters, she found herself more and more drawn to the notion of becoming an actress, a profession she feared was immoral. She kept expecting the two people on the love seat to raise their pale eyebrows in disbelief, even to laugh, but they did not.

It was her own eyebrows that wanted to rise as the reverend explained that actresses had been "fallen women" throughout history and should still be regarded that way, for they were merchandisers of the sins of the flesh. As Jac listened to Mrs. Shaw read passages from the Bible, she began to feel increasingly that she was defrauding two aged children. When it became obvious that they would ask her to pray with them, she said quickly, "I have to apologize, Reverend. Feeling the way you do, you must have been shocked when I called and asked whether *Christian Comfort* was involved with a theater."

Again the two of them looked at one another. The reverend clamped his hands over the knees of his black trousers and said carefully, "We hoped you could tell us more about that. How did you come to hear it?"

"I don't really remember. I got leads from all over, you see. Perhaps your *Christian Comfort* foundation invests in various companies, and someone mistakenly thought the Briarwood theater chain was one of them." She waited, then went on. "Many charitable organizations invest their money, as I'm sure you know. Perhaps yours is invested in something with a name similar to Briarwood." Still no response. "Or does your son handle all the finances for you?"

Their faces told her he did.

"I'm sure it's just a mistake," she said easily. "I wouldn't worry about it."

But their faces told her they did.

Suddenly the reverend stiffened. "Don't say any more about it!" He sank to his knees on the faded rag rug. "Let us pray," he said urgently. His wife joined him. "Please!" she said to Jac. "Kneel down!"

There was such terror in the request that Jac could only obey it. The reverend began to pray, his words filled with the genuine sound of pleading, but not in her behalf, Jac thought.

"Hello," said a powerful voice.

Jac looked to the doorway. The man who stood there was a contradiction of the voice.

Mrs. Shaw scrambled to her feet. "You're back early," she said breathlessly.

"Yes. Aren't you going to introduce me?"

The reverend stood with dignity. "This is Miss Jackson. My son, Donald. Miss Jackson read our newsletter and has come to us for help. She has found herself tempted. We are praying with her."

Jac felt the younger man's eyes move over her like a computer scan. Her knees seemed to soften; for the first time she did pray—that she looked humble and pious and nothing like the newswoman who tried to project confidence from the TV screen five nights a week.

"How do you do, Miss Jackson," the man said. "It's a rare pleasure to have a visitor. Do you mind if I join you? I'm deeply concerned with matters of the spirit, as I'm sure my parents told you."

"Yes," they said, almost in unison.

He moved to the edge of the rag rug and knelt, bowing his head. His parents went down as if he had pulled them. Jac followed, and they all prayed with Reverend Shaw to save her from the devil's temptations, from the "painted and evil world of the stage, which sets itself up against the pulpit of God." To Jac it was like a bad farce, except that all the actors but herself seemed completely serious.

When it finally was over, the son accompanied his parents while they saw her out. Just before she got in the car, Mrs. Shaw grabbed her arm and whispered, "You see? We told you he was a good man."

Jac started the car, prepared to believe her—at least to find it hard to accept that this was the Donald who had something to do with corruption at Briarwood and with Erik's enemies.

Then, pulling out, she saw two men coming around one side of the house. They did not look as if their lives belonged to God. One of them was leading the other, whose eyes were bandaged. As they might be if someone had struck at them with a kitchen fork.

When she got back to the apartment, Karen and Erik were not there.

She called the theater and got no answer. She told herself they were on the way, so there was no point in going down there. She restored her hair and makeup to normal, made a cup of coffee, and felt panic slide down her throat along with the first sip. She drank standing by the phone, trying to decide whether to call the police.

When a key finally turned in the lock, she could only stare at the door. Then, somehow, she was with Karen, kneeling and closing her eyes to everything but the feel of the small body.

"Mother, you're crushing me!" Karen said. Jac loosened her grip, trying to laugh. "Mother, we had to hide in a sarcophagus, just like ancient Egyptians, and some men with guns came in looking for us, and we couldn't move for so long that it *hurt*. And the men were getting close to our sarcophagus, only one of them was sneezing a lot because it was dusty and he probably had . . . What did you say he probably had, Erik?"

"Hay fever."

"Yes. And then he said, 'Oh, hell, there's nobody in this place,' and the other one smashed up some things just for fun, and they left. And I'm not using that word myself, Mother, I'm just telling you what the man said."

Jac looked up at Erik for the first time. He wore derelict's clothes, as he had on Rikers Island, but his face was his own, except for the helpless look of apology that gave his mouth a new shape.

As he told her what had happened, she rose slowly. Karen clung to her right leg.

"Finally I decided it was safe to leave," he said. "But I thought I should look a little less like Erik Dante before we went out on the street. I'm afraid there's no way to disguise a child, though. I got a cab on the Bowery and . . . here we are."

"Thank God," Jac whispered.

"Karen was wonderfully brave. She didn't cry, and she did exactly what I told her she had to."

Karen pulled on Jac's arm. "I'm hungry, Mother. All I had was that box of raisins you gave me."

"I'll go now," Erik said. "You'll want to look after her."

"Yes." Jac swung her head, trying to clear it. "So they're trying to kill you?"

"Apparently. I don't know why that should happen now, when I'm . . . Well, never mind. I guess it was stupid of me not to have considered the possibility, but if I'd thought there was the remotest chance of danger to Karen—"

"Mother!" Karen cried. "Shouldn't we call Daddy and tell him?"

"Don't worry," Jac said slowly. "I'll see that he knows."

Erik held out his arms to Karen. "Good-bye, kiddo. You're a great lady in a sarcophagus." He swung her up, and she kissed him.

"And you thought I was the one walking into danger," Jac said to him.

"You mean you didn't?"

"I don't know what it was I walked into. I can't seem to think right now. It's as if it happened years ago. I'll tell you about it tomorrow."

Erik nodded and started to the door. Then he swung back. "London! Kerry London! Now that you've come up with a possible last name for Donald, the cops have got to ask London what she knows about a man named Donald Shaw." He sighed. "Only they'll never do it if I ask them to."

Jac frowned, working it out. "You're right," she said finally. "I'll do it. I'll ask my contact tomorrow."

He nodded. "I'll call you then."

"How can I ever thank you for keeping Karen safe?"

"It's not the kind of thing that needs any thanks, is it?"

When he left, she was under perfect control, feeding Karen, bathing her, putting her to bed. But the moment she closed Karen's door, her smile folded into a tight line.

She went to the living-room phone. Quite calmly, she told Burt what had happened.

"You're saying she could have been killed, Jac? *Killed.* God."

"She's fine, I promise you. She's behaving quite normally. She doesn't show any signs of brooding over it or of being terrified. You can talk to her tomorrow. She's asleep now."

"And where did you have to go that was so damned important? How could you leave her at that theater? With a man who's implicated in a murder, for Christ's sake! Who probably started killing when he was a kid! Didn't you read that story in the papers last weekend? How could you leave her with him? Are you so hot for him that you can't see anything straight anymore?"

"I don't need you to tell me what I did, Burt. But it has nothing to do with Erik Dante's character. Only with the fact that someone is trying to kill him. You wouldn't know anything about that, would you?"

"Say that again," he said tightly.

"I think it's possible that you're helping the people who tried to kill Erik today."

"That's a goddamn lie! I don't know anything about it!"

"No? You talked to Maeve Jerrold about her trip to the Jumping Joint—I don't care how much you deny it. That trip got Erik arrested, not to mention what it might have done to her. Don't you have any—"

"You'll believe anything as long as it makes me look bad, won't you?"

"To the contrary, I fought doing that for years. For Karen's sake. But now I see you pretty clearly, I think. And I want you to do the same—to look at the kind of people you're dealing with. Because I think they're the ones aiming the gun that might have hit Karen today."

"Don't you dare say that! Don't you dare!"

She hung up.

Half an hour later Sanda had his car out of the garage and was heading across town, going nowhere except away, the wheel providing him with a sense of purpose and control.

The last time he had used the car, he had been taking Karen to see his parents at the Jersey shore. She had asked dozens of questions about her new swimsuit and the shells she would collect and her grandmother's cookies.

Before he quite realized, he was at the tunnel entrance. He knew then that he wanted to take that same trip—to drive up to the big white house where the steps of his progress from law school to labor lawyer to influential arbiter and adviser were enshrined in clippings and photographs, where his father emitted gruff pride with every pull on his old briar pipe.

Briar . . . wood. Sanda shivered, telling himself that whatever he had done, it was only what he had to do, that the goals and ideals of his youth meant no less to him now; they were not tarnished, only put away for safekeeping—until the day when he would sit on the bench of an appellate court. Jac could not see those ideals any longer; but Karen could, for she was their incarnation.

He sped along the New Jersey Turnpike, the huge lit structures of industrial complexes streaking by at the edge of his vision. In the foreground was an image from his undergraduate years: the old woman who had done the cleaning at his rooming house and who had been trying for over a year to get information about her son in a military hospital somewhere in the Southwest. Sanda had gone on her behalf to local officials and had written to state and federal agencies. He had gotten nowhere. Then one of his friends said he knew someone who could fix it. He had taken Sanda to a nightclub and to an upstairs office where an older man, perhaps showing off for "the boys," had called Washington, joked with a senator, and as a "favor" gotten immediate action for the old woman.

That was the way of the world, Sanda thought, switching onto the Garden State Parkway. One could not do good unless one first had position and power. Or dealt with those who had. There was no other way.

When he took the exit for his parents' town, he felt calmer, and his fingers no longer were so rigid on the wheel. He drove a few miles, thinking that perhaps it was foolish to drop in on his parents; they could be asleep or busy or even out.

His mind was on whether to turn back, not on the road; he saw nothing before he heard the small thud against the side of the car, as if a ball had been thrown at it. He was not going to stop, but something pulled at him to do so. He looked back and saw nothing; he was on a country road with no lights but his own. He made a U-turn and drove back slowly, not wanting to look but unable not to. A hundred yards back, he saw something at the edge of the road.

He pulled over and got out. The air, chilly for late September, penetrated his lightweight turtleneck. He locked his arms over his chest and looked down. It was a small animal he could not even identify—something with grayish-brown fur and a sharp little muzzle, its head stretched out on one paw.

It had crawled in a small circle before dying, and its blood made a pattern of feathery tracks around it, like a wreath.

Sanda stared as if he too had no more power of motion. There were always dead animals by the roads, he thought. They ran into the paths of cars, and no one could be blamed for killing them. No one meant to do it.

But he gagged anyway and began to cry.

He got back to the city about ten-thirty. This time he knew exactly where he was headed.

Joncas himself answered the door. The yellow shirt he wore made his face look sallow. "These aren't my office hours," he said.

"This isn't office business."

Joncas shrugged and led Sanda into the library. They took seats on opposite sides of a small fireplace. A few logs were smoldering in the grate.

Without preamble Sanda said, "Some men with guns went after Erik Dante today at his theater. My daughter was with him. The men didn't find them, but if they had, she could have been killed."

For a moment something flared in Joncas's eyes, like a coal in the grate. "How did she happen to be there?"

"Is that all you can say?"

"I could say I'm glad she's all right, which I am, and sorry that it happened. Which is also true. Now I'd like to know why she was there."

"Jac took her."

"I see. You never could control your wife, could you?"

Sanda closed his eyes and his fists. "I went along with your setup against Dante because I thought I had to. You didn't tell me you and your 'associate' were going to have him killed. You made me an accessory to something that put my own daughter in danger!"

"I didn't take her to Dante's theater. Any more than I took my own son-in-law."

Sanda looked at him. "What's that got to do with it?"

"Dante had my son-in-law killed."

"But he's been charged with that. Let the law take care of him, for God's sake. I thought that's what you wanted."

"He might get off. Lawyers can be bought," Joncas said sourly. "Dante deserves whatever he gets."

"Even if it involves children? *Children*, Joncas. What about that bookkeeper? She has a little boy, I hear. Did she deserve what she got?"

"Jesus!" Joncas said loudly. "You know who's a little boy? You are. You want to play, but you can't stand to get hurt. Don't you know there are only two kinds of people in this world?—the idiots who swim around in schools like fish, and the ones who sit up on deck and spit into the water. If you want to be on deck, you have to do whatever it takes to stay there. That's the way it is."

Sanda stared. "I used to think I understood you. That we understood each other. I didn't know you wanted to spit at people. I thought you wanted to be . . . admired."

"Shut up," Joncas said. "Or grow up, whichever you can manage."

In the silence, one of the logs on the grate broke apart. Sparks popped and then faded to gray.

"I can't look at it the way you do," Sanda said. "I'm involved in something that . . . I'm responsible . . . Those men could have shot my daughter, Joncas!"

"It won't happen again. I'll see to it."

"That's not good enough. I want to know who the men are."

"I thought you never wanted to know anything."

Sanda got to his feet and stood over Joncas. "If you don't tell me, I'll go to the police. I'll tell them how I set Maeve Jerrold up, and I'll tell them who made me do it."

"Really? I didn't know you wanted your daughter to have to visit you in jail."

Sanda turned away. He leaned on the mantel, staring at the corpse of the fire, his eyes still burning from his earlier crying. "If you don't tell me," he said, "I'll do everything I can to screw up the transport negotiations."

"I doubt that. Because if you do, I'll make sure every union in the country hears that you're unreliable." After a moment he added, "The fact is, Burt, I don't know who the men were. I never get involved on that level."

"But you know who gives the orders—your 'associate,' I suppose. You could call him and find out."

Joncas leaned forward. "Maybe I should tell you who he is," he said viciously. "Because if he knew you knew his name, he'd put you under a microscope. You'd be dead the minute you did something he didn't like. If he bothered to wait that long. He doesn't give a crap for you or your daughter or your law career or the law or anything else. Except getting what he wants. You understand that, Burt? There'd be no more kidding yourself that someday you're going to kiss the Constitution. I'll tell you what you'd be kissing, if you stayed alive."

"I'm not asking for his name," Sanda said stiffly. "I don't need to talk to him. I just want to be sure about my daughter."

Joncas's laugh sounded like a substitute for spitting.

31

Jac's doorbell rang at nine-thirty on Thursday night.

She ran from the bedroom, tucking a pink silk shirt into dark red slacks, and tore the door open. Relief spread across her face. "You're safe," she said. "But I was expecting a bum, not Erik Dante."

"Glad to hear there's a difference." He was smiling too. He wore a blue shirt and cardigan that made his eyes look as bright as if a child's crayon had drawn them. "You look back to normal yourself."

"I'm fine. I told you that on the phone. Why no disguise to-night?"

"To tell you the truth, I forgot. We rehearsed all day, you know, and then I had to help work out the light plot. I was thinking about that on the way up here, not about whether somebody would take potshots at me."

"It's not very smart to forget that, is it?"

"No. Very dumb."

After a moment it seemed to occur to them that they were still standing in the doorway, smiling. "Come on in," Jac said. "I've got things to tell you."

"Ditto." Erik took the deep chair with the ottoman, stretched out his legs, and looked around the room. A small TV set in one corner was on, the sound very low.

"I always try to catch the Channel Ten late news," Jac said.

"Where's Karen?"

"In bed. Look at what she did today." Jac took something from the coffee table and handed it to him. It was a drawing, in a child's crude perspective, of a woman with electric-looking hair and a man whose mouth was open, issuing flames.

"Good Lord," Erik said. "Prometheus as a dragon."

"According to Karen, the story you're practicing is about a man who plays with fire and a lady who wants to burn him."

"But that's not *Firestorm*," he said gravely. "That's the story of my life."

Jac's mouth trembled, and suddenly they were both laughing, the laughter growing and feeding on its own sound, no longer tied to the child's drawing or to anything but their capacity to experience and share it.

"Dear God," Jac said finally, sinking onto the couch. "My ex-husband is involved with crooks, and people are trying to kill you, which is practically the least of your worries, so why are we laughing like fools?"

"I don't know. Because we are?" He put his arms behind his head. "I don't suppose it could be that we're happy?"

"Never," she said, smiling again. Then she sobered. "But how *do* you stand it, Erik? On top of everything else, you're supposed to be putting on a play, a complicated one, and now you have to direct it, as well. Why aren't you flying into hundreds of pieces?"

"I have," he said. "Many times. Actually, the play is my salvation, the way I work off most of the tension. And then, the final week of rehearsal is like a kind of demonic possession, you know. Or maybe you don't. It's hard to explain, but at this stage you get so deep into the play and the production that everything else moves all the way to the outer edges." He smiled at her slowly. "Except you."

After a moment she went into the kitchen, came back with a glass of wine for each of them, and stood at the fireplace sipping hers as she told him what had happened on her trip to Westchester the day before.

He listened intently, his face tightening until the cheekbones and mouth were sharp lines. "You're sure the son didn't recognize you?"

"I don't think so. I hardly recognized myself."

"Because if he did—"

"Yes. I know what it could mean. If he's the man we want and not just some born-again millionaire. I could argue it either way." She put down her glass and ticked off points on her fingers. "He fits what you said about the man in the picture, but 'nondescript' covers half the world's population, doesn't it? And if he's the man we're looking for, why would he come in and expose himself to me? Even if he didn't recognize me? Wouldn't he avoid meeting strangers? As for the man with the bandaged eyes and his companion, they could just be body-guards or workmen. And finally there are the parents. It's true they were afraid of him—so much so that I'm sure they'll never tell him I mentioned Briarwood—but I'd also swear they're the genuine religious article."

"The son could be using them as a cover," Erik said. " 'The devil can cite Scripture for his purpose,' you know. It sounds damn likely to me that you were up there praying with the Swede's boss. Jesus." His fist hit the chair arm. "Do you realize what kind of risk you could be . . . Jac, be careful, for God's sake."

"I will. I'm keeping Karen housebound. The woman who takes care of her will be back in the morning, and this weekend I think I'll take both of them out to Karen's grandparents."

"Fine, but what about you? Don't go anywhere unless you abso-lutely have to."

"Look who's talking. Anyway, I have a camera crew with me a lot of the time. Let's get to the important thing, which is that I made some inquiries today, to see if this Donald Shaw could really be our man. My contact in the Organized Crime Strike Force says they've never heard of him or of a religious organization that's used as a front. They're going to check further, but they confirmed what I've heard elsewhere: If somebody's hiding behind a screen of offshore and foreign corporations, he's virtually impregnable until and unless he makes a slip or one of his associates turns against him. And of course mobsters kill off an associate the second they have any suspicions at all. Now, I didn't bring your name into it, of course—I just talked vaguely about a source—but even if we both told them everything and they believed it, they'd need more to go on than your verbal description of a photograph and my story about a family that prays together."

"What about Kerry London?"

"She's in Madrid, on a European concert tour, and won't accept calls from the American police. 'One country's cops at a time'—that's the message she sent back. But just suppose she knows something and tells it. Just suppose there is an investigation—even if it was successful, it almost certainly would take years. So it could hardly help before your trial." After a moment she added tightly, "And if Burton Sanda knows anything that could help, he's not talking."

For fifteen minutes they went over it. Erik threw off his cardigan and began to pace the room. Jac stayed at the mantel, her eyes leaving him only to glance occasionally at the TV screen. Finally he stopped, straddled the ottoman, and said, "We're going nowhere. There's no way to get anything on Donald, Shaw or otherwise, or to prove that he and Joncas are framing me, and there's no hope the Swede will tell the truth."

"Did you tell the police about the men who came after you at the theater?"

"Yes. They came down, saw a lot of smashed props, and went away looking as if I'd staged the whole thing myself just to back up my story that I'm being framed." He finished his wine and then cradled the glass, its bowl disappearing inside his big hands. "Listen, Jac, I didn't come just to talk about all this. There's something I want to say to you. About Maeve."

"Yes?" There was a silence, except for the low TV sound. "You haven't told me how she is," Jac said softly.

He looked up at her. "She's fine. Physically. But still in the hospital. I'm . . . I haven't told you the real reason I decided to open the play. It's for her. Because of all the things I've put her through, ever since the day Morty Codd walked into Poets and Paupers and I walked into your newsroom. I've got to give her the one thing that's still in my power to give—her play. That's why it's got to open, why it takes precedence over everything. Even over trying to clear myself. But I . . . Jac? What's the matter?"

Her head had swung to the TV. Then her whole body catapulted to it, and she turned up the volume to a roar.

" . . . body was found in a corridor, after the inmates had come back from dinner. Authorities at Rikers Island suspect that the weapon which pierced his heart was a TV antenna from one of the communal dayrooms, sharpened to a lethal point. It is not yet known what effect Dantino's death will have on the trial of his brother, Erik Dante. Dante has been charged with conspiracy in the killing of Steven Pomerantz during a picket-line squabble at the Poets and Paupers Theater last month."

When a commercial began to scream at them, Jac switched the set off and stood up. Erik's face was as blank and still as the screen.

She brought out more wine. "Do you want to talk about it?" she said. "You look as if you don't feel anything at all."

"Oh, but I do. Many things. Relief that he can't reach me any longer. Rage over what he's done to me, and the people he's killed. Even pity. I'll bet the poor sonofabitch never even knew which gang had him killed." He sighed and pushed his hands through the hair that was darker and finer than the Swede's. "The underworld thinks that blood is the strongest tie of all. I guess they're right. Because you can't be indifferent to it. You have to feel *something*—love or hate, contempt or regret, rejection or acceptance. And even if you try to reject everything about it, the way I did, you're still acknowledging it by rebelling. The things I've felt the most strongly about in my life, the things that made me take on the fight with Codd—they came from the blood tie, didn't they? From the life I lived with the Swede and my mother. I don't mean the poverty itself, but the way they dealt with it. They both wanted something for nothing. She drank herself to death on public welfare, he stole. Handouts or holdups, there wasn't much difference. He had an attitude that if he wanted something, it belonged to him. Once, when he stole an old woman's purse, he told me the money was really his and she just happened to have it. God's truth, Jac—that's what he said. And my mother . . ." He smiled sadly. "I guess everybody has certain things that get to him more than others because they seem to come right from the gut. But maybe they come from the blood, from whatever it tied you to when you were young." He sighed. "The Swede was my nemesis, but in a way, he was also my creator."

Jac shivered. "You remind me of how much I'm shaping Karen's life right now. Probably I've shaped it already. I have a psychologist friend who says our basic characters are set by age five."

Erik's eyes were still far away. "I went with the gang a couple of times, when I was still so young they could force me into it, and the Swede was always liquid with fear. I used to tell him that if he put as much time and effort into a job as he did into working with the gang, he could make just as much money. And sleep a lot easier. But he wouldn't quit." He leaned forward. "He despised my job, of course, at old man Vecchio's grocery. And my interest in school, and my books, and everything else that was a value to me. Everything that was . . . actually a value." He looked at Jac. "Maybe he hated it because he was afraid he couldn't do it himself. Maybe that's what the fear was all about."

"Lots of people are afraid," she said, "but they don't take lives because of it."

He winced, and Maeve Jerrold's name hung between them as clearly as if one of them had said it.

"He framed you for two murders he committed," Jac said firmly. "And now you're going to pay for this one, too, because he can never tell the truth to the police."

They looked at one another and then away, in mutual acceptance of helplessness.

Jac's nails drummed slowly on her wineglass. "You say your broth-er hated everything you stood for, and was afraid of it, too. So he had personal reasons to frame you. But why do the others want to do it—Donald and Joncas? Is it strictly a practical matter—they wanted to get rid of both you and Morty Codd, by pinning Codd's death on you? Or are they like your brother—getting something deeper out of it?"

"I wonder. If our friend Donald is a crime czar, then maybe he's just a sophisticated version of my brother. A Swede who can do a hell of a lot more than read. But Joncas . . . He lives in the establishment world."

"I'll say. He likes being labor's white knight. And wearing white tie and tails. I remember going to some kind of banquet once, with . . ." She stopped and swung around, staring into the mirror above the mantel at the questions in her dark eyes. "Oh, God, is Burt like your brother? Does he hate . . . any real value?"

"He loves Karen, doesn't he?"

"Yes. I'm sure of that."

"Maybe he's in a trap, then."

"Is he even trying to get out?" Jac whispered. "Does he want to? Is he strong enough to?" Then she lifted her chin and turned back to Erik. "Never mind him, for now. The point is that at the banquet, Joncas was on the dais with the mayor and Senator Foster and some others, and he was basking in it. So whatever else he feels for the world of real values, he wants to be part of it, too." She sighed. "And I think he's also a man who loves his daughter. And his wife."

Erik straightened in the deep chair. "If we assume he was in on the original plan, to kill Codd on the picket line—and we are assuming it, aren't we?—that means he helped lay the trap that backfired and killed his own son-in-law."

"My God. Of course it does."

"So if the truth came out, he'd lose more than his establishment position and his union. He'd lose his family too, I'll bet. So he's got to make me take the punishment. In more than a practical sense."

"God damn them!" Jac cried. "They all want you to pay their dues! They've got to frame you with lies so they can feel safe or good or important or whatever it is they need to feel!"

Erik had gone very still. "What is it?" she said.

"A frame is always a lie. But what if I could frame them with the truth?"

"I don't understand."

His eyes were on some inner distance. "But does the king have a conscience?" he murmured. He got up and began to pace again. As he talked, the sounds of hope and excitement rose in his voice. Finally he turned to her. "And you're not to say it's dangerous. You who walk into lions' dens as if they were children's zoos."

"All right. I'll just say it would be difficult to pull off. For one thing, how will you get them all to come to the theater?"

He frowned and moved on, trying to work it out aloud.

"Come and announce it on the *Journal*," she said. "Tomorrow night. I'm going back to work in the morning."

He stopped and looked at her. "I suppose I don't dare to say thanks?"

"That's right. Erik, how about your lawyer? She's warned you not to make any public statements while you're under indictment. She won't like this at all."

"No, but I don't see how she can stop me."

"OK, then," Jac said. "If you're going to do it, let's be systematic about it." She got a pad and pencil from the desk. "I see one big problem, for openers. While you're getting ready, you've got to be able to protect yourself and everybody who works at the theater from the goons who are after you."

He was silent. Then he laughed. "I just had an idea about how to do it. I guess you'd call it fighting fire with fire."

"Oh, dear," she said when he told it to her. "If the police get wind of that . . ."

He shrugged.

After they had thrashed out most of the details, Jac put aside the pad and said, "And what if we're wrong? What if your brother was lying to you every step of the way? What if there isn't any crime czar, and Joncas isn't involved at all, and nobody was trying to frame you except the Swede himself?"

"Then he was a hell of a lot smarter than he ever seemed. And everybody who comes to the opening night of *Firestorm* will have trouble following the action."

She laughed. "At least they'll know it's about a man who likes to play with fire."

"And a lady who burns him?"

After a moment Jac said, too brightly, "Well, I guess we've covered everything."

"No. Not quite." Erik stood up, squaring his shoulders. "I told you I had to open *Firestorm* for Maeve's sake. But there's more. I've . . . I'm not going to stay with her, Jac. I can't do that to any of the three of us. As soon as she's capable of hearing it, I'll tell her. I'll help her as much as I can, and I'll give her back the theater building. Because I took it when I knew I was in love with you."

She lifted a hand slowly, reaching for her throat, but he caught it and pulled her up. He put both hands around her neck and let his thumbs lie close to her lips. "I love your courage and your brains and your laugh and the way you lift your chin and the way you walk. I want you with me all the time, for the rest of my life. And I want you now, badly, even though I know I should go." His hands slid down, over her shoulders and along her arms. "I'm thinking of your skin underneath this cloth, of how it feels, how it tastes, how hungry I've been for it since . . ."

She made a small, breathless sound. He bent down; his lips parted the silk just above the rise of her breasts, and he kissed the swelling flesh. Her head fell back, and his mouth moved up the column of her throat. He put one hand behind her head and lifted it till his lips were above hers, barely touching them.

"Stay," she whispered. "It's not safe for you to go back to your place." Her lips pulled away. "Wait." She went down the hall and into Karen's room. He stood with his hands open, as if they were still holding her. She came back and said, "Fast asleep. It's all right."

They moved down the hall, his hand in her hair. In her room, with the door closed behind them and a bedside lamp glowing, they took off their clothes slowly, touching one another only with their eyes. When they were on the bed, Jac whispered, "Don't move. That night when I watched you in rehearsal, you were motionless. And so beautiful." She leaned over him, letting her hair slide back and forth along the length of his body until he groaned. Then her lips followed the path her hair had taken.

"I can wait as long as you," he whispered, arms still stretched out at his sides but his fingers digging into the bed.

"A minute for every day we've waited already," she said. She laid her breasts against his chest, their softness now tipped with arrows, and moved her tongue over his mouth, drawing its lines until his lips fell open with the weight of his groans and the sounds made her as helpless as he, and she said, "I can't anymore," joining her body to his with a long, slow motion that drove the sounds into silence.

"I love to watch your face," he said.

"Why?"

"Because it's beautiful. And because it's like watching what I'm feeling myself."

Their eyes locked as tightly as their bodies, and the act of seeing their pleasure trace its path across their faces made the path even deeper and sweeter, and longer.

They pulled apart finally and lay still, looking at one another. She put her fingers on his mouth, and he held them there, whispering through them that he loved her. She smiled, and slowly her eyes closed.

He sat on the edge of the bed for a while, looking around the room at her possessions—her books, the pictures of Karen, her pink silk shirt and dark red slacks thrown on a chair, the brushes and bottles on her dresser. When he turned to look at her again, his eyes narrowed. She stirred, feeling his desire, and woke up to meet it. This time they were violent, as if punishing themselves for the weeks they had been apart and the languor with which those weeks had just ended. Their breaths came together in ragged gasps, which lasted long after they were finished.

They turned out the light and drifted into sleep, then woke and touched one another so gently that desire took them almost by surprise.

When the light began to change outside the window, Erik sighed and got dressed. Jac, still naked, slid into the circle of his arms. Her eyelids were heavy and her mouth full and soft. "Be careful," she said. "Please be careful."

"Don't worry. I intend to be very much alive on opening night."

"I'll see you at the station at five o'clock today."

"Yes. You be careful too." He kissed the side of her mouth.

When he walked out of the building, the sky was just turning a fresh, pale blue.

32

Joncas climbed wearily out of a cab, took his briefcase, and went up the walk to his town house, looking ahead to an evening of peace.

He knew he would not get it as soon as he saw Cecelia's face. "Thank heaven, you're in time," she said, kissing him.

"For what?"

"Oh, Vi, a letter came today, delivered by hand. It's from that Erik Dante. He says we should watch the early news tonight on Channel Ten, and he says . . ." She took the letter from her skirt pocket.

While Joncas read it, a small explosion took place on his face, which then settled into grim lines. In five minutes they were all in the den, Coral's bulk now so cumbersome that she didn't rise to kiss her father.

When a commercial came on, Coral said, to break the tension, "Daddy, is there any progress on the transport talks? Or will there be a strike?"

"The city hasn't budged an inch on their productivity demands. There'll be a strike unless the members want to give away everything I got for them when I was their president."

"Look!" Cecelia cried.

On the screen, on the *Jac's Journal* set, Erik sat with Jac, his hands resting loosely on the arms of the chair, which he seemed to dwarf. When she welcomed him back to the program, he said, "Thank you. It's a pleasure to see you again."

Jac recapitulated what had occurred since his appearance with Codd, six weeks earlier: the public response to that interview and to his subsequent statements; the racial incident on the picket line and the union charge that he had created a "climate of violence"; the killing by his brother; the charge that he himself was involved with the Varese family and had conspired in the killing; his brother's death; his insistence that he was being framed; the defection of a third of his staff, and the disastrous falling off of ticket sales since his arrest.

"In view of all this," Jac said, "most people would expect you to close your theater. Are you going to?"

"No." The camera moved in, framing his face above the broad shoulders of his gray suit jacket. "Next Saturday, September 28, we'll open as scheduled, with *Firestorm*, an original play by my partner, Maeve Jerrold. But since our ticket sales for that night have dropped to only fifty, we have three hundred and fifty seats left. I'd like to take this opportunity to offer most of them, except for press seats, to members of TATU, the Guild of Stage Actors, and any other union affiliated with the Brotherhood of American Labor." He smiled. "Including the transport workers, if they'd like to come."

"Why are you making this offer?"

"For one thing, I'd like to show I'm not antiunion, as a lot of people have tried to claim—that a person can challenge certain union attitudes and practices and still respect the existence of those unions."

"You said 'for one thing.' Is there another?"

"Yes. I also want to dedicate that performance to the memory of Steve Pomerantz, the man I'm accused of helping to kill. I'm innocent of any role in his death, and I want to show how much I regret that death."

There was a pause on the screen, and heavy silence in the den.

Jac said, "Aren't you opening yourself to charges of opportunism and exploitation?"

"Listen," he said, his eyes almost burning through the screen into the den, "all I ask is to be regarded as innocent until and unless I'm proven guilty. I ask that of all my colleagues in the theater. I ask it of Morty Codd, even though we're on opposite sides in a dispute. And I have the gall to ask it even of V. I. Joncas, the dead man's father-in-law, because Mr. Joncas has already demonstrated his high regard for our system of justice, by helping to clear elements of organized crime out of the labor movement. He may have forgotten it, but he and I are colleagues—I'm a dues-paying member of the Brotherhood of American Labor, through my membership in the Guild of Stage Actors. I mourn his son-in-law's death, deeply and personally, because it took place outside my theater and by my brother's hand. That's why I want to dedicate our performance to the victim. That's why I ask Joncas and Codd and as many other labor colleagues as we can accommodate to be my guests that night."

When the *Journal* signed off, Joncas walked to the set and punched the switch as if it were Dante's face. "Death would be too good for that sonofabitch." Coral protested faintly, but he ignored her. "Give me that letter again," he said.

When Cecelia handed it to him, his gray eyes shot to the last paragraph: "I hope you can find it in your hearts to believe I'm sincere. At the performance I hope to be able to give you some information about how and why Steve Pomerantz was killed."

Cecelia watched Joncas's face. "Oh, Vi . . ."

"I'll sue him. I'll get the cops to put him in jail, where he belongs. It's a trick, an outrage, a goddamned insult. It's a—"

"Daddy, I don't know what it is, but if it's about Steve, maybe we should go."

"Coral! The bastard *killed* him!"

"But what if there's a chance he didn't? The way he says?"

Joncas turned furiously to Cecelia, but she dropped her eyes.

After watching with his parents, Donald Shaw turned to them and said mildly, "Does that Sanda woman remind you of anybody?"

"No," said his mother, puzzled. His father nodded in agreement.

"Jesus Christ," Shaw said, waiting for their pained reactions before he left the room. He went to the other wing and sat at his desk, toying with a new paperweight, certain the phone would ring soon.

At seven o'clock it did. Joncas's first words were "Why haven't you gotten rid of that bastard yet?"

"Look who's begging for it now. Mr. P.R. himself. Mr. Kid Gloves."

Joncas told him to shut up. He talked about the TV show, and described the letter his family had received and their reactions. "It's a week from tomorrow," he said. "And they say they're going to go! What the hell are you waiting for? You want to run the whole entertainment industry, and you can't even get rid of one actor?"

Shaw slammed the paperweight on the desk. "Couple of days ago you were hollering because they almost got him with your lawyer friend's kid, remember? The orders are to get him when he's alone, so they can button him into a cement coat and nobody'll ever find him. But he's goddamn slippery. And boys who kill on orders aren't exactly Einsteins, you know. You've got to map out every damn thing for them."

"And by the way," Joncas said, still angry, "I don't think it was smart to get rid of the brother on Rikers before you hit the main target. Why didn't you check with me first?"

"Because I'm not the one who did it."

"What? You mean it was Big Tiny?"

"Could be. Or some con the brother looked at cross-eyed, who knows? Those pigs would kill each other over a new shirt. Whoever did it, he saved me the trouble."

There was silence. "Get this over with," Joncas said. "Just get it over with! Before next Saturday, because if I have to walk into that theater . . ."

Shaw frowned at the sound of near-hysteria in Joncas's voice. "Don't worry. It'll be curtains long before then."

The weekend was a marathon for the technical crew at the theater.

All scenic units had to be brought up to the stage and assembled; all sound and light cues had to be integrated with the shifting of scenery and the dialogue lines on which they occurred. Some plans had been roughed out in rehearsals with the actors, but now, without the actors, all technical aspects of the production had to be pulled together, so the final rehearsal week could be a refining of the production as a totality.

The crew worked with an undercurrent of exhilaration; those who had remained with Erik had caught from him the sense of impending vindication, even though they did not know what he was planning. Nor did they know that in the attaché case he carried with him everywhere there was a gun.

Most of them stayed in the theater Saturday night, sleeping in snatches up in Erik's apartment. Frankie, who had begged to be promoted to assistant stage manager when the ranks of the staff had thinned, refused to go home: "That guy from the Department of Labor will never find out, Erik. Please!"

By four o'clock Sunday they were done, and exhausted. Erik left with them, nodding to the guards in the lobby, whom the company referred to as "the bruisers"; he had explained that they came from a special security firm.

Later he would have to go to the hospital, to take Maeve back to her apartment; she did not really want to leave, but the doctor had said a week was enough and there was no point in her staying any longer.

But first he had another errand. He took the subway with the sound man but stayed on it all the way to Queens. He got out, walked six blocks, and stopped before a small white house. A man with hair the color of the house was on his knees, planting bulbs, the muscles of his boxer's torso swelling his faded T-shirt. "Hello," Erik said.

Codd looked up. Color seeped into his face. He tossed aside his trowel and rose. "What the hell do you want?"

"I thought I should issue my invitation in person and see whether I can get you to come."

"To your opening night? No way."

"I want to find a way. You and I are the ones who started this whole business, so I'd like to have you there."

"Listen, I can't tell you what I think of you and your grandstanding because my wife doesn't like me to use that kind of language on Sunday."

"I know we're adversaries, Codd, but can't we at least talk as men who respect each other?"

Codd's green eyes sparked. "What I feel for a man who tried to pay me off—respect ain't exactly the word."

"I didn't try to pay you off. I just said a payoff was what you were after. When I worked on Broadway a few years back, I saw a lot of men with their hands out. I thought you were one of them. I was wrong. I'm sorry."

Codd grunted. "If you'd asked around, you'd have known I've worked like hell to stop that kind of thing, ever since I took over as head of TATU."

"All right, I should have known. I didn't know a lot of things at the time. For instance, I thought it might have been mob goons who trashed my theater."

"There isn't any mob muscle in TATU! You're the one who deals with the mob! TATU is clean as hell that way, and if it wasn't, I'd be the first one to raise a stink. Goddamn crooks, giving labor a bad name all over the country."

"Interesting," Erik said. "I guess you know you just admitted it was some of your own men who vandalized my theater?" Codd said nothing. "Well, that's past history. What matters now is that it appears you're an honest man."

"Like I said, anybody in the business could have told you that."

"But that's not how I learned it. I learned it when I found out what kind of enemies you have."

"Meaning what?"

"Let's just say they're people who wouldn't want an honest man heading up a union."

"What the hell you getting at, Dante?"

Erik took a deep breath. "You're in danger, Codd. From the mob. My brother told me, before he was killed. In fact, that could be the reason he died."

Shock and disbelief battled to an impasse on Codd's face. Then he glanced away, toward the old Irish setter who came ambling around the corner of the house and began to rub against his legs. "Why the hell would the Varese be after me? Because they know how I feel about the mob?"

"I didn't say it was the Varese. But a better question would be: Why the hell am I telling you about it?"

"You're grandstanding again," Codd said uncertainly.

"If you come to my opening night, I think I can prove to you that

I'm telling the truth. That I was framed, and you are in danger." The dog moved to Erik's side and stood looking up at him. He leaned down to pet him; the dog accepted it placidly.

"Hey, Ben," Codd said.

"Here's something else. If you tell anybody what I've just said—anybody at all, except maybe Ben here—you could make things very dangerous for me. I'm putting myself in your hands, Codd. I'm trusting you. Because I believe you're an honest man who wants to know the truth."

Codd said nothing, just stared at Erik's hand on the dog's russet coat.

Erik rose. "Well, that's it. Hope to see you Saturday night." He turned and went down the walk.

"Hey, Ben," Codd called. "Come back here."

When Erik brought her back to the apartment, Maeve walked about slowly, looking long at each of her treasured objects.

After a while she realized why she was spending so long with them: to keep from having to ask Erik what she had to ask. She forced herself to turn and look at him. He sat in one of the fireplace chairs, chin propped in one hand, eyes closed.

"Erik," she said. There was no response. "Darling," she whispered. "My love." She waited.

His eyelids dragged themselves open. Suddenly he shot to his feet. "Where's my attaché case?"

"Over there, by the couch. What's wrong?"

"Nothing." He shook his head and pulled his fingers through his hair. "Nothing. Are you OK? Can I get you anything?"

"No." She put her hands to her face, then pushed them into the pockets of the navy dress Erik had brought to the hospital for her. Through the fabric she could feel her thighs. They were too thin. "Erik, will you do something for me?"

"Of course."

She looked away from the cool blue of his eyes—at the big hands curving on his crossed arms. There was scene paint under one of his nails. Red paint. "Never ask me," she said, "to talk about what I . . . what happened. Ever."

"Ever?" he said quietly. In a moment he added, "All right."

Her hands relaxed. She knew she should ask him about the play, knew he wanted to hear that she was interested. She sat down, ordering her voice to obey her. "How is the play coming?"

He told her a lot of details, followed after a pause by something about a public invitation to Morty Codd and the unions. When he looked at her expectantly, she said, "That's fine, Erik. Whatever you think is best."

She asked him to put on some music, and they sat quietly, listening to Schubert quartets. When he could no longer fight his exhaustion, he leaned back into the gray silk couch. In minutes he was asleep.

She watched him. Once he smiled, his lips curling very slowly, as if some deep inner sweetness finally had reached them. The smile faded as gradually as it had come. The smile made her cry. So did its absence.

At two o'clock he woke. She started, hands leaping to her face to make sure her cheeks were dry. He looked at her ruefully. "And I was going to see that you got a good night's sleep."

"I've been in bed for a week. The one thing I'm not is tired."

She went to sit beside him. He put his arm around her and stroked her hair. In minutes he was sleeping again. She leaned her head against his chest, letting her breath come in time with his. Gradually the night gave way to dawn.

33

The last item on the agenda at the regularly scheduled New York membership meeting of TATU had been added only two days before: what action, if any, the union should take about the memorial performance at the Poets and Paupers Theater.

Amid repeated bangs of the gavel and "out-of-order" rulings, the members wrestled with what seemed a no-win situation. Most of them felt that Dante was trying to manipulate them and that a statement to such effect should be issued. However, there was a minority dissenting view: One speaker, a grizzled stagehand, felt that not attending could embarrass the union publicly because they would seem to be declaring a man guilty of murder before the courts did.

"That hasn't got a damn thing to do with it!" said an electrician. "I don't know if he's guilty or not, but that doesn't mean I can't show what I think of the way he's talked about us. I *picketed* his damn theater—why should I go see his play?"

Eventually Morty Codd rose to speak from the podium. "Brothers and sisters," he said, "I know we're in a squeeze here, and I don't like it any better than you do. But I have to tell you that I've decided to go." He held up his hands and waited for a chorus of protest to subside. "There's a couple reasons. For one, I've got a feeling Dante might try to pull something, and I'd rather see it than read about it the next day. I mean, if there's going to be anything to protest, I want to do it on the spot." He smiled, his face a network of lines, then leaned over the podium, serious again. "For another thing, if Dante happens to be on the level about this, I don't want it to look like I wouldn't join a tribute to Joncas's son-in-law."

"Millions for defense, but not one cent for tribute!" a voice called.

When the laughter died, Codd said, "I made up my mind two nights ago, but yesterday I talked to Mr. Joncas, and I'd like you to know that he and his family are going to be there. That's right," he said to the startled faces. "I guess Joncas feels the way I do. And I think the public is going to respect him for it—a man who turns the other cheek."

The discussion started up again. It was a woman in her forties, a wardrobe attendant, who made the suggestion that took fire and finally was adopted: The Union should attend as an "honor guard" to Mr. Joncas, officially stating that they were there only out of respect for him.

"And to protect him," someone added.

"Can we get the Guild of Stage Actors to go along?"

"How about the transport workers, too?" someone added; and to laughter and a majority feeling of satisfaction, the meeting adjourned.

On Wednesday night Burton Sanda was watching the Poets and Paupers Theater from the doorway of an empty building, shivering although Indian summer had arrived and the weather was in the sixties.

Since he had gone to see Joncas, after learning that Karen might have been killed, he had had little rest and less peace.

Whenever he did finally manage to drift into sleep, he would find himself driving down the road to his parents'; something would thud against the side of the car, and when he walked back to look, he would wake with a start, sweating, because he knew that whatever lay there would not have fur and claws, or an animal's face.

During the days, he had been virtually useless. When he learned of Dante's invitation, he not only had acknowledged its cleverness but had even permitted himself to hope Dante would somehow be clever enough to stop the killers who were after him. That hope died quickly, leaving the fear that when the killers did succeed, Karen would be there. Even though Jac told him in a crisp phone call that she had taken Karen to stay with his parents, the fear would not go away. Nor would the dream.

He knew they wouldn't go until and unless he made restitution. But he couldn't make it by going to the police; that would destroy his career. The only thing he could think of, to quiet the fear and banish the dream, was to somehow locate the hit men and prevent further killing.

He reasoned that they must be staking out Dante. And because Dante was nearly always at the theater, Sanda had gone there for the past two nights, watching from doorways or alleys. Once he had even opened the lobby doors, but a tough-looking guard had asked him his business, and he had withdrawn. Often he heard faint voices and music or the sound of hammering, but as late as he stayed both nights, the lights had still been on. A police car had cruised by periodically, giving him brief respites of security.

He shifted his position and leaned against the door of the empty building. As the time dragged on, he permitted himself to think about the future: After he had been appointed to the bench, Karen would come sometimes to court to watch, beaming, and afterward he would take her to lunch. And this dreadful night would be over, along with everything it represented.

But it wasn't over yet. Around ten-thirty he crossed the street and slipped into an alley beside the theater, trying to weld himself to the bricks of the wall. From that vantage point, he thought he saw the flaring red dot of a cigarette in one of the parked cars he had been sure was empty. He was ready to step out and go over to the car when he heard voices; people were coming out of the theater, telling each other to get a good rest because it would be their last chance till after opening.

For half an hour they drifted out. Finally Sanda moved cautiously out of the mouth of the alley, and then froze again. The lobby door was opening; he heard a voice—Dante's—say, "Everybody's gone, and I'm going out, too. Take good care of the place. *Ciao.*" A man laughed and said, "That's a hell of a getup tonight."

Sanda stepped back into the darkness and watched a tall, fat cop come out and lumber up the street. He held his breath as the figure passed the parked car, but nothing happened. In spite of himself he smiled, knowing that if he hadn't heard the dialogue from the lobby, he wouldn't have recognized Dante either.

The smile faded as he patted the envelope in his jacket pocket and walked to the car. For a moment he remembered the errand on which he had sent Maeve Jerrold, with her bundle of money.

There were two men in the car, one slouched in each seat. Sanda knocked on the driver's window; it opened a crack, and a voice said, "Yeah?"

"Like to talk to you. Boss told me where to find you."

"What boss?"

Sanda cleared his throat, in which his heart seemed to have lodged. "The one who sent you here to get Dante."

After an eon the man in the backseat sat up and unlocked the door. Sanda got in. The air smelled of pot. There was so little light that the men were only dark presences. "No luck yet?" he said heartily.

"You bring a message or something?" The man in the backseat spoke with a West Indian lilt. "We seen you hanging around. Why'd you wait so long to come over?"

"I . . . I didn't want to get in the way if anything was . . . was happening. You expect Dante to come out soon?"

"Who knows? They're all night in that damn theater, some of them. We're supposed to get him alone, but he always comes out with a crowd. And we're supposed to get it done by Saturday night, or else."

"Leon," said the driver, "you talk too much."

"Dammit, this was supposed to be easy, and it ain't. He's got muscle on guard in the lobby all night and prowling around the block, too. And now there's cops, too. You see that big one come out? Hey, man, I asked you a question."

"Yes," Sanda said.

"I never seen him go in," the driver said. "Did you?"

Sanda clenched his hands, aware that Dante's life was in them. "I saw the cop go in, yes."

"Yeah? When?"

"Just before you drove up."

"We seen *you* come up," the driver said. "We got here before you."

Sanda's heart caught again. "I went away for a while. To eat."

"So what you want?" the driver said sharply. "You said you come from the boss?"

"Well, he didn't actually *send* me. I came because I want to help him. You know any of his lawyers?"

"No."

"I'm one of them. And I'm afraid he's going to be in big legal trouble if this hit comes off. It could even finish him. So I . . . that is, we, a couple of the other lawyers and I . . . decided we had to step in." He took a breath. "We'll make it worth your while to see that this job doesn't come off."

There was a silence as heavy as the smell of pot.

"You haven't got him so far," Sanda said, "so keep it that way. Tell the boss you couldn't do it. Simple."

The driver snorted.

"What's the money?" Leon said.

"Ten thousand now." Sanda hesitated. "And let's say forty more on Sunday if nothing's happened to Dante."

The two men began talking in a French patois. Leon's voice slid into a whine; the driver's rode over it several times.

Finally the driver said, "No dice, lawyer-man. Maybe you want to help the boss, maybe you don't. That's your problem. But it ain't gonna be my problem that I couldn't do this hit. No way."

"But look,—"

"No way. Hey, Leon," he added brightly, "you think we should tell the boss what his lawyer friend here wanted us to do?"

Sanda froze. Leon chuckled.

"Tell you what," the driver said. "Just to make real sure we don't tell him, you hand over that ten grand you talked about."

"No way," Sanda said.

"Yeah? How about if we just start the car and drive you up to Westchester so you can explain it to the boss yourself? You want us to do that?"

Sanda closed his eyes. "No. No. Don't do that."

The driver laughed. "OK, let's have it, then."

"How do I know you won't tell him anyway?"

"We don't want to make no fuss. We just want to make a profit."

Sanda threw the money into the front seat. The two of them were laughing as he slid out of the car.

The sound of that laughter was still with him two nights later, when he walked into the WXNY Building.

The lobby guard remembered him from the old days, when he had often come to meet Jac after work, and let him go up. The news was on the air. He found Jac's office, the office he had never wanted her to have; it was empty. He sat at her desk to wait. The room held a hint of her crisp, clean perfume; the desk, full but organized, was a freeze-frame picture of her energy and efficiency. He looked at the photo of Karen on the wall and remembered a time when it was not only his daughter who had loved and trusted him.

Then Jac herself was in the doorway, the expression on her face belying his memory. She folded her arms across her ivory blouse and brown velvet blazer. "What is it, Burt?"

All the preliminary small talk he had prepared fled his mind. "Are you going to be at the theater tomorrow night?"

"Of course."

"Alone?"

"I'll have a crew with me," she said tightly. "To cover this union protest or demonstration or whatever it's going to be."

The words that had been in Sanda's mind for days forced their way out. "You're not taking Karen with you?"

Jac's wide cheekbones became ridges of color. "You know perfectly well where Karen is. And why."

"Promise me you won't take her to the theater with you."

"What's wrong with you? Are you sick or something? You're acting—"

"Promise me!"

"Of course I won't take her there. I—"

"Don't go yourself, Jac. Please don't go."

"Why not?" She moved across the room. "Do you expect something to happen?" She leaned over the desk. "Do you?"

"I . . . I've done everything I could. But the men have orders to get Dante by tomorrow night. If it hasn't happened by performance time and you're there, if you take Karen . . ."

She said his name loudly, like a slap across the face. "How do you know what the orders are? Did Joncas tell you?"

"No. He . . . I found the men. I talked to them, tried to get them to stop. It didn't work. They're still going to do it. There's no way to stop it. I tried, Jac, please believe that I tried! But I can't do a thing against them." He put his head in his hands.

When he looked up, she said calmly, "It means something that you tried, Burt. But it's not enough. You'll have to do more."

"What?"

"Tell me who's behind it all."

Sanda looked away. "I've never met him. I've never had any contact with him at all. I don't even know his name. Everything was through Joncas."

"Then here's another thing you could do—go to the police and tell them everything you know about. Including Maeve Jerrold's trip to the Jumping Joint."

"I don't know anything, Jac, I've told you that! Why do you keep asking me?"

"Because I don't think you've told the truth."

"Jac!" Sanda tried to look into her eyes, but his gaze fell to her hands, still flat on the desk. They were deeply tanned; there wasn't even a circle of white on the third finger of her left hand. But of course there wouldn't be, after two years. He said, "You don't think I'm a . . . good person, do you?" He waited for an answer without looking up. Finally he added, "You used to think I was."

"Yes," she said. After a moment she straightened up. "I'd like my desk back. I have some work to do before I leave."

At the door Sanda said, "Can't you make Dante cancel the performance? Doesn't the thought of danger mean anything to him?"

"Why, yes. I think it frightens him. The way it frightens me."

"Then why . . ." Sanda stopped, and the question burst out in its true form. "Why do you care about him, Jac?"

He watched her face, expecting the cat smile of sensuality that had betrayed her once before, weeks earlier. But only her eyes softened. "He never makes me feel that I'm a threat to him," she said. "Now, please get out of here, Burt."

34

The four hours of final touch-up rehearsal finished by four o'clock Saturday afternoon.

The actors, whose call was for six, went out to eat—a light snack for most of them, and some wouldn't be able to touch food at all. The house manager and ushers converged on the auditorium to collect paper cups and cigarette butts. The tech director roamed the stage nervously, eyes raw with the need for sleep, which he was usually the last one to get. Patterns of light moved over him; in the booth, the man who operated the light board was checking some cues. The flute music that opened the show came in disconnected breaths over the speakers, as the sound man re-cued it again and again.

Standing in the wings, Erik felt the change that always took place about this time on opening night: the shift from the inner world of the play to the knowledge that the world would see it soon, and the sudden tightening of every nerve end in the body.

That much was normal; the rest was not. He knew it would be even worse if Jac had not called the night before to tell him what she had learned from her ex-husband's visit: Joncas was definitely involved. The news had been a relief that even her other information could not dilute; if they were determined to get him by performance time, he would just have to make doubly sure they didn't. She had started to wish him good luck, but when he told her one never said that to an actor for opening night, she had said simply, "Stay alive. I love you."

He hadn't told her that on Tuesday night, when one of the "bruisers" was checking the alley and the street, he had nearly caught someone, who finally managed to get away. Nor had he told her that on Thursday night, when he finally got to bed, someone had tried to mount the fire escape outside his apartment. He had sprung the trap that was laid there: A huge bucket of glass shards, pebbles, and sawdust had rained down.

He pushed away the memory, looked at the stage one last time, took a deep breath to remind the tension who held its reins, and went into the dressing rooms to put his personal notes of thanks on each of the actors' makeup kits. Just as he finished, Frankie came in, her face a moon full of nervous life.

"Hi, Frankovich," he said lightly. "There's something for you up in the light booth."

She looked around before speaking. "Erik, listen, could we go over it one more time? I mean—"

"We can if you like. But you don't need to." He put his hand on her shoulder. "I know I can count on you, more than anybody else. That's why I asked you to help me."

The moon turned red. "Jeez, I don't even know what to say to you for tonight. I know I'm supposed to say, 'Break a leg,' like everybody else does, but I don't want to. I mean, when I think what you're going to do, and what I have to do, I don't want to talk about no broken legs."

He laughed. "I'm ordering you and everybody else to go eat. Right now." He took the attaché case that still went everywhere with him and gathered up the technical director and the rest of the crew. They went out in a group, leaving only the box-office people and two burly guards in the lobby.

He went into the restaurant with them, but in five minutes he left, through a window in the men's room. Twenty minutes later he was ringing the bell at Maeve's apartment, which he reached by one of his routes that involved rooftops and service entrances. He hadn't dared to use the front door since the night he brought her home from the hospital; he had also paid the doorman to check on her frequently and to tell anyone who asked for her that she was in Paris for the month.

She was wearing the sherry-colored caftan he had always liked, and she was carefully made up, but he saw at once that he need not worry she would change her mind and come to the performance. When she greeted him and asked how things were going, her words were heavy with effort and her eyes as distant as another century. If the drugs were in fact helping her, and he had tried to make sure she took them, he could not imagine what her state would be without them.

He felt sure he had made the right decision about that night: He simply had explained that the performance would be more like a special preview than a real opening because of the invitation to the unions, and she should plan to come the next night, when the audience would be a normal one. She had accepted it without comment.

She made no comment now, either, as he gave her a final report on the show, especially on the scene he had had to shorten while she was in the hospital because one of the new actors couldn't handle it properly. She merely listened with the forced attention that made him feel so helpless. Then, abruptly, she said, "I have something for you, for opening. I'd like you to have it now, instead of tomorrow."

It was a small piece of amber, mounted on a brass base and carved into a dozen intricate tongues of fire.

After a moment he heard her say, "Don't you like it?"

He managed to say, "Of course I do," and to hold back the desire to tell her not to let it happen—not to permit the woman who once had written *Firestorm* to become like the flames in his hand, all their life and motion frozen, in however lovely a prison.

"It's very beautiful," he said. "How on earth did you find it?"

"I sketched the design months ago, before rehearsals started. Finally I found the amber and someone who could carve it."

"Do you know why I love it most? Because it proves you always expected there would be an opening night."

She frowned, then tugged on a gold earloop. He took her hand away, kissed the palm, and then her lips. They felt cool and dry. "I'll put it on my dressing table tonight," he said, "so you'll be there, too. Now, will you try to get a good rest so tomorrow night you can be there in person?"

"Yes. I will."

"I love the woman who wrote *Firestorm*. I always will."

Erik went out the service entrance. A truck that said "Plumbing and Heating" was just pulling out; he smiled wryly and got the driver to give him a lift to Second Avenue, where he caught a cab.

He told the driver to stop at a deli on the way while he got coffee to go and some chocolate bars. He was heading back to the cab when suddenly there were two men beside him and a small, hard circle of pressure at his ribs. One man grabbed the coffee and the attaché case, and the other guided him expertly down the block to the open door of a car and then inside. In a minute he was pinned and blindfolded, and the car started up.

* * *

The Joncases got ready for the theater in silence.

Cecelia stopped frequently to look at her husband, who sat on the bed in his trousers and undershirt, staring into space. Finally she said, "Vi, I'm almost ready."

"There's plenty of time yet. I'm waiting for . . . I could be getting an important call."

"About what?" He said nothing. "Vi, don't be like this. I've hardly ever put my foot down about a thing in our marriage, and God knows there were times when I could have. And probably should have. But this is the first time, and it hurts to have you act this way. Yes, Vi, it hurts."

"You're blackmailing me, you and Coral, that's what you're doing."

"Vi, I just don't understand you. If there's the tiniest chance we could learn something about Steve's death, don't we have to take it?"

"But it's all a goddamn trick!"

"Then you'll be right there to say so, won't you? And everybody in the city will hear about it, and it won't do that man Dante a bit of good. So where's the harm in going?"

After a moment Joncas said dully, "I'm not going."

"Well, don't, then," she snapped. "Coral and I told you all along we'd go by ourselves."

"I won't let you do that! How can I? Let you go down and sit there by yourselves, while—"

"I don't mind. But you did let the unions think you'd be there, so they'd probably mind."

Joncas slammed a fist into the bed.

She stood in front of him and turned around. "Zip my dress, please?"

He yanked at the zipper with such force that it broke.

Members of TATU and the Guild of Stage Actors had begun to gather outside the theater around six-forty.

They made an unusual-looking group of pickets; they wore good suits and dresses, and at a Guild member's suggestion, most of their left arms bore a black band. From their hands sprouted a collection of homemade signs, with such legends as "TATU STANDS BEHIND THE JON-CAS FAMILY" and "SOLIDARITY AND SYMPATHY." One sign that was much admired and quickly copied by several people read, "THIS PERFORM-ANCE BETTER BE A SHOW OF RESPECT!"

Jac moved among them with her film crew, recording a mood she defined as rebellion thinly veiled with decorum. When Morty Codd and his wife arrived, she went to him and asked for an interview, but he smiled tightly and declined: "I'm here to watch, not to perform."

There were uniformed police at the edges of the crowd, watching impassively. In a car down the street were two men in plainclothes—Detectives Fagan and Santo. They had tried to buy tickets anonymously, but when the box office told them no more were being sold to the general public, they had had to produce their badges. Even so, they could get only standing-room places. They sat in the car grumbling at the thought of spending several hours or more on their feet, but they had to know what Dante was up to. The case against him had been weakened by his brother's death, but they had hopes of new developments: They had established, over the past week, that the security guards inside his theater looked a lot like mob muscle.

At five of seven Jac went into the lobby and to the box office, as Erik had arranged for her to do. "Ruth," she said to the woman behind the grille, "you can tell Erik that the crowd is orderly but high-strung and that the Codds have arrived, but not the Joncases." The woman's look was so stricken that even before she heard the words, Jac knew: Erik was not there, and no one knew where he was.

All Erik knew was that the car kept moving but the gun stayed locked on his ribs.

At first he had struggled, trying to use his long legs like weapons, but a voice that meant business had said, "Either sit still, man, or you're dead. Take it or leave it."

So he took it and tried to concentrate on the way they were traveling. But the blindfold eclipsed the world, and he had only the vague notion that they were going north.

"How did you find me?" he said bitterly. "What did I do wrong?"

There was a laugh. "You put it out that the Jerrold broad is over in France. But it don't figure she's going to be gone with her play all set to open."

"How would you know anything about the way a playwright thinks?"

"Because, crud, we work for somebody who can figure anything out. And sure enough, you go out of your damn theater for the first time in three days, and we get the word from our lookout up at Jerrold's place that you're coming out the basement entrance."

Erik struggled to force the self-reproach out of his mind and make it function. He knew there were three things to try with such men: to threaten, bribe, or bluff them. The first two were not possible. After a few minutes he said, "Well, I give it about ten minutes." He heard a grunt. "Yes, about ten minutes before they catch up with us." No response. "If you read the papers, you know I'm with Big Tiny Varese. You think Tiny hasn't got some of his boys tailing me wherever I go?"

"Shut up, actor-man," said the voice next to him. "A whole damn week I been waiting for you. You make me sick."

The gun pressed harder, but the man's words made an idea slide into Erik's mind.

He waited awhile, for what felt like several miles, then leaned his head against the back of the seat. "Sit up," the voice snapped. In a moment it added, "When I tell you to sit up, that's what I want to see."

Erik made a low sound. His lips parted and stayed open.

"I'm gonna count to three, and if you ain't sat up by then . . ."

"Oh, Jesus," Erik groaned.

"What's the matter with him?" said a voice from the front seat.

"Nothing!"

Erik groaned again. Then he transferred the sound from deep in his chest to a point in his throat, halfway between hiccup and whimper.

"You don't fool me," the voice said. "You ain't sick."

Erik was silent for a mile or so. Then he gave a breathy grunt, followed by retching noises.

"Goddammit!" said the voice next to him.

"I can't help it," he whispered. "Cars always make me . . . I'm going to be . . ." The retching noises came faster and higher. He slumped to one side and let a thread of saliva run from his mouth.

"Jesus, he's gonna toss his cookies all over me!"

"Open the window and stick his goddamn head out."

"And get barf all over me?"

"My hands," Erik groaned. "Let me use my hands . . ." He felt the man fumble at them, and when they were free, he cupped them over his mouth, leaned forward, and made sounds so explicit that the man beside him swore. Now the problem was that he couldn't feel the gun in his side, but he had to move now anyway, while the man was still swearing. He flung himself violently at the sound of the voice. The collision rang inside his own skull, and he barely heard the man gasp with pain. He groped blindly for the man's hand and found it. But it was empty. His fingers clawed along the seat and finally closed on the butt of a gun. With his other hand he forced the blindfold low enough so he could see. The man beside him was dazedly shaking his head. The driver was screaming to know what was happening.

With a quick glance Erik gathered they were somewhere on an expressway. He ordered the driver to pull over. With the gun still trained on the backseat, he leaned into the front, pulled the man's gun out of his shoulder holster, and stuffed it into his jacket pocket. Then he reached awkwardly behind himself to unlock and open the door. He backed out and kicked the door shut. Before the car could start up, he shot out both tires on the right.

As he was running along the shoulder of the road, he heard someone honking loudly. He turned and saw a cab slowing down beside him. When he realized who it was, he began to laugh.

He got in and said, "Don't tell me you chase after all your fares like this?"

"No. But I recognized you," said the driver; it was the man who had taken him from Maeve's and then been left waiting outside the deli. The driver pointed to his identification card, on the dash, and said, "Maybe you forgot, but we belong to the transport union, and I was damned if I was going to let Erik Dante stiff me. Only, it started to look like you weren't really stiffing me—like you were in some kind of trouble, so I figured what the hell, I'd see what was up."

"Brother," Erik said, "am I glad you did."

At seven-twenty, when the Joncas limousine pulled up at the theater, Cecelia said, "Oh, look! Coral, Vi, look at the signs—'WE'RE HONORING THE JONCAS FAMILY' . . . 'SOLIDARITY AND SYMPATHY.' Look how they feel about you, Vi, and about Steven."

Coral sighed so deeply that Cecelia turned to her in consternation. "What is it, darling—the baby?"

"No, no, I'm fine. It's just . . . very touching." She turned to her father. "You see, Daddy, it was right for us to come. Whatever else happens here tonight, this makes it worthwhile."

In the pale skin beneath Joncas's gray eyes, a blue vein-line appeared. He and the driver helped Coral. The family stood against the car as if the crowd's applause were pinning them to it.

Joncas smiled and waved, although the muscles that lifted his mouth and hands had to be forced to do so. When he saw a tall man loom at the edge of the crowd, he thought he was hallucinating. But then he saw Jac Sanda, grinning like a child, speaking to the man before he slipped into the alley beside the building; and he knew it was real, all of it.

"After the Joncases!" someone called, and the crowd took up the shout, clearing a path to the lobby doors, along which Joncas was pulled by Cecelia's hand.

Behind them, all those who had tickets thronged into the lobby. Members of the reviewing press, who usually arrived at the last minute, were lost in the crush. The house manager frantically tore tickets and passes in half, and the ushers sped up and down the aisles.

By seven-forty the crowd was seated and the back of the house filled with standees.

Backstage, the men's dressing room was jammed with cast and crew members, the panic in their eyes replaced by euphoria. The actor whose duties had included understudying the role of Prometheus kept saying he could have done it but thank God he didn't have to. "Come on, everybody," the stage manager called. "Give Erik a chance. Let him get ready."

Finally Erik stood up and reached for a red cloak. "OK," he said.

"Places!" the stage manager called. "Places, everybody!" It was seven-forty-nine.

At that moment a cab stopped outside the theater and two men leaped out. One ran in to the box office and demanded a ticket.

"Nothing left but standing room."

"OK, OK, gimme that." He threw some money down, grabbed the ticket, shoved it at the house manager, and made his way in. He wedged himself into the crowd of standees, his ears still burning with the venom of Mr. Shaw's voice when they had called from a parkway phone to report failure and his forehead creasing with fury at the way the actor had outsmarted them once again. He confirmed the steel presence inside his jacket; his forehead smoothed, and his eyes narrowed with pleasure at the thought of using Dante's own gun, which had been in the attaché case he left behind.

The house lights dimmed.

Down the block, his partner tried to figure out how he might get in backstage.

35

A spotlight printed a huge circle on the red curtains, and Erik stepped out into it.

There was scattered applause from the general public; the union members did not join in.

When the quiet returned, Erik said, "I'm sorry we're late. It's my fault. I'm afraid that someone wanted to stop this performance by stopping me. Permanently. I owe the fact that I'm not a lot later than this to a fellow member of the Brotherhood of American Labor."

The crowd rustled and shifted in their seats.

"Thank you for coming," Erik went on, "all of you—those who have been at most of our other opening nights, whether as critics or supporters, and those who are here only because I invited you and then put you in a position that made it difficult to refuse."

From the back a voice called, "This better be a show of respect!" A murmur that was blended of laughter, embarrassment, and anger swelled through the house.

When it died, Erik said, "A month ago, to the day, there was a picket line outside this theater, protesting my refusal to sign a contract with the Theatrical Artisans and Technicians Union. I imagine some of you here tonight were on that picket line. If so, you saw the group of people who seemed to be supporting me, you heard the shot one of them fired, and later you learned that my brother had pulled the trigger." He paused, then looked down into the fifth row, where the Joncases and the Codds were sitting. "Steve Pomerantz's death was a tragedy. And all the more so because it was never meant to happen. This performance is dedicated to his memory and to the hope that the truth of how he died will soon come out."

In the split second before the spotlight went out and the flute music cut through the rustling of the crowd, he saw Joncas's face, rigid and staring.

A hand guided him back through the curtains and to the rocklike projection upstage; a flashlight shone on the steps by which he had to mount. When he reached the top, he gathered the cloak around him and blotted out everything except Prometheus's thoughts and bearing; he braced one foot on the crag and heard the heavy sigh of the parting curtain.

They would be starting very soon, Maeve thought, looking at the tiny clock on her bedside table.

She closed her eyes and saw the stage—the sky that was a spread of darkness, the tongues of fire that would begin to lick upward and spread the red-and-yellow glow of their appetite along the horizon. Gradually their light would climb the pillar of Erik's body to find his face, striking the sharp lines of his nose and mouth, finally meeting the intensity of his eyes. And then he would begin to speak. . . .

I love the woman who wrote Firestorm. *I always will.*

She started to cry. Since that long night in the hospital, when rude hands and painful instruments had made her body obey them, she had seemed to have no responses left but tears. Only with Erik did she hold them back, afraid of drowning hope. Because hope still did exist; there still were tenderness and gratitude in his eyes. And pity, too; but now she would take even that and be content to live on it. Since they had made her live.

I love the woman who wrote Firestorm. But that woman, she knew, wouldn't have needed his pity or his protection. She had been made of more elements than tears—of earth and air, as well, and fire. When she tried to help him, she wouldn't have only made things worse. And above all, she would have been with him on the night her play was born to the world, however unfriendly that world might be. But that woman had been so young. . . .

She sat up slowly, then went to the mirror above the dresser. She put her fingertips around her eyes and pulled the skin tight and smooth.

In the box office Ruth was counting the huge pile of passes. She looked up when someone approached the grille—a woman in a long silver gown. When she saw the pale gold hair pulled into a heavy chignon, she said, "Mrs. Jerrold! I didn't recognize you. But Erik said you wouldn't be coming till tomorrow night."

"I know. It's a surprise."

"But there aren't any seats! Even the standing room is like sardines. I don't—"

"It's all right. I'll go around to the side door and watch from the wings."

"Let me give you a key, then. The doors are locked from the outside. If only I'd known you were coming! But Erik said . . . I hope this means you're feeling better?"

"A little. Thanks, Ruth."

As Maeve walked away, Ruth shook her head, thinking that she looked about as substantial as the silk of her dress, with a face now so thin that the years had no place left to hide. It occurred to her for the first time that Mrs. Jerrold must be close to fifty.

Maeve walked down the alley, lifting her skirt above the grime. The dress was the one she had worn when she first met Erik, at the producer's party years before, and it hung on her too loosely now.

She found the side door. The key turned loudly, and when she stepped inside, Frankie came tiptoeing over, frowning until she saw who it was. "Jeez, Ms. Jerrold," she whispered. "I thought it was . . . What are you doing back here?"

Maeve smiled. "I came to watch my play. What are you doing?"

Frankie leaned closer. "I'm in charge of some stuff. Especially the gunshots, you know. It's going good, real good, and the audience is keeping pretty quiet. You want to watch from over on stage left? So you'll be out of the way for most of the scene shifts?"

Maeve nodded and made her way to the left, to a spot beside an unused backing. Nearby, two other Infernals were watching, their faces intent in a spill of blue light. In the heightened stillness that always gripped the backstage area during a performance, the voices from the stage fell with surreal clarity.

Erik's was not among them. The scene, Maeve realized at once, was the confrontation, late in the first act, between the primitive creatures who begged for fire and those who had become its victims; and Prometheus, sitting high above them in his red cloak, had no lines until the end.

She listened to the speech of the young woman charged with heresy, but she did not watch the actress; she closed her eyes and saw the words as she had put them down on a page so many years before:

I could not keep my mind within the church's

Walls; it shed my kneeling body every
Sunday like a thing discovering wings
And nectar. All it hoped to suck was truth:
Why should we believe we're born in sin?
Why is suffering good and pleasure evil?
My questions brought me only questioners
In robes of black and caps that clamped above
Their eyes like vises; Listen to our words,
They said, and call thy spirit back to grace.
But none could catch my mind beneath his cap.
They built a classroom, then, of branches, where
I had to stand at strict attention as
I heard the lesson's crackling start and felt
Its wisdom propagate beneath my feet,
Searing their doubts to bone, and climb along
The curling path of my own smoke to reach
The stubborn mind that stays alive too long,
Oh Lord, how long . . .

The actress's voice died away. Someone in the audience coughed. Maeve's eyes flew open; she waited anxiously for the speech that would follow—one of Erik's favorites—in which a man described the way his enemies had made the fire reverse its normal action. "First the powder dead as ashes, then the metal burst of flame . . ." She was braced for the gunshot, but it rang so loudly, coming from the wings directly opposite her, that it deafened her to the next few lines.

When she could hear again, she was puzzled; instead of the flute music she expected, which signaled the dance-pantomime of the fire's victims, someone was still talking about gunpowder. Two men, in fact; and she did not recognize the lines. They spoke of harnessing the fire to force from people things that would not be granted freely. . . . No! Maeve cried silently; that idea was the point of the scene, but she had worked hard to keep it understated, not to make it explicit, as she was hearing it now. Someone had changed the lines—and Erik, Prometheus, was just sitting there above it all, doing nothing to stop it.

Eyes wide, she watched the stage and finally began to think that she understood what was happening and why Erik had wanted to protect her.

The hit man did not understand any of it. He simply continued his slow progress down the left aisle, heading for the spot near the sixth row where the red letters of the exit door glowed.

The two actors onstage began to plan how to use the gunpowder, their speech sliding from the discipline of iambic pentameter, becoming more ragged and contemporary.

As someone in the row behind Jac murmured, "Nice touch—from verse to gangster slang," she slid from her seat on the right aisle, to stand against the wall, and signaled her cameramen to follow. Her glance swung over the audience, which was intent.

On the stage, one of the two men gave the other a gun and told him to hide himself among a crowd, so it would look as if he fired the gun in their name and for their cause.

Prometheus was still immobile on the crag, wrapped in his red cloak. Only his eyes moved, following the action like two blades of blue light.

They moved as two groups of people appeared from opposite sides of the stage. The man with the gun slipped among them. They all wore robes, like an ancient Greek chorus, and they chanted unintelligible sounds; but they carried signs that could be read throughout the house.

Someone in the audience said, puzzled, "It's our signs—like we had that day."

Morty Codd sat erect and expressionless, but Joncas was shifting in his seat, gripping the arms as if they were anchors. His wife's mouth was slightly open; his daughter's was closed with one hand.

Another, louder voice came from the audience: "What the hell is going on? Is this a play or what?"

"Is this going to be respectful?"

Suddenly much of the audience was murmuring, "A show of respect, a show of respect," the words starting to drown out the chanting onstage.

It seemed impossible that Erik could quiet the audience. But he did, by the simplest means: He rose to his feet in one motion, the cloak flowing with him like an uprush of blood, and then stood there, his eyes commanding silence.

When they had been obeyed, his gaze returned to the scene below him.

A flute began to play, breathy and agitated. The two groups started moving toward each other again, swaying gently. Their mouths moved as if they were still chanting, but now all was done in silence, as a dumb show. With no voice but the flute, the figures seemed devoid of humanity as well; they were a single mindless creature with dozens of contorted faces.

In their midst the man with the gun raised it. It glinted in the light before disappearing again beneath his robe.

Prometheus gazed down at the man as if he were reading his thoughts. Then he began to move slightly, reflecting each of the man's movements, and to speak in a whisper, so that his voice seemed to be the man's voice and his body the instrument recording the man's growing panic: "I must kill. . . . I have been sent to kill. . . . But how am I to know my victim? They told me I must read the signs, they said his sign alone would carry certain words . . . but how am I to read them?" The voice broke into a sob. Suddenly Prometheus's eyes acquired the sightless stare of the blind; as the man ran more frantically among the crowd, the voice went on, almost keening: "I cannot read, I cannot read the signs. . . . Are you the man that I must kill? Are you? Are you? Or you? Oh, God, I'm blind because I never learned to read. Are you the man? Are you? Are you?"

A figure in the crowd reared up before the man, who pulled out his gun; the sound of a shot filled the stage; the flute gave a shriek and stopped. The noiseless crowd pulled back to reveal a body and then froze into a tableau.

The audience was motionless too, except for Joncas, whose lion head swung from his wife to his daughter; he half-rose in his seat. "Get that," Jac hissed to her cameraman.

Prometheus pointed to the body lying below him and said, "Steven Pomerantz was never meant to be that victim."

Someone in the audience sobbed.

"You bastard!" Joncas cried. "See what you're doing to my daughter!"

"I don't like doing it this way. But you leave me no choice."

"Don't let him do this!" Joncas cried to the audience. "Can't you see it's a trick?"

People in the rows around him looked disbelieving, not so much of his words as of his face, which no longer seemed like his own, without its impassivity.

"It's a trick!" Joncas cried again. "Shut him up!"

The hit man, crouching by the exit door, felt for his gun.

Erik's glance swept the audience. "My brother was sent to kill a certain man and say that I had given the order. But that man was not Steven Pomerantz. He was the man I had a quarrel with, the man who heads—"

Again there was the single, loud crack of a gunshot.

On the crag, Erik jerked backward, flung against a gray outcrop.

Below him, the actors gaped, their postures so awkward they could only be real.

Erik was awkward, too, opening Prometheus's robe in a kind of grotesque slow motion, pressing his hands to his side, on the cloth of his white T-shirt. One hand came away as red as the robe. He stared at it in disbelief.

The actress who had played the heretic screamed as if the fire had reached her. Jac felt as if the scream had come from her own throat.

Members of the shifting crew, dressed completely in black, ran out from the wings and froze into stick figures when they saw Erik.

He was on his knees on the crag, hanging on to the outcrop. But its tip was flimsy, made only of Styrofoam; it broke under the pressure of his grip. He sank lower.

Out in the auditorium the camera that had been trained on Joncas was still on him, recording lips pulled open triumphantly around clenched teeth.

From the standing-room section, Detectives Fagan and Santo were shouting for everyone to remain seated. Their voices seemed to confirm that what had happened was real; a chorus of screams erupted.

Maeve was not screaming. The sound was locked inside her.

She saw that Erik could not believe what had happened; but she could. It was so hauntingly familiar—the blood that had spilled across her life once before and left her with nothing, except the certainty that someday, in some form, its horror would return.

They had never wanted Erik to exist, she thought. She did not know who "they" were; she had never known. "They" were simply the world.

The scream increased its pressure inside her head.

One of the actors broke his paralysis and moved toward the entry stairs at the back of the crag.

Erik forced himself up on one knee. "Wait," he whispered; and when no one heard, he lurched to his feet, his motion a cruel parody of the one with which he had quieted the whole house earlier. This time the noise and the screams faded slowly, leaving only a voice on the stairs behind him: "Don't move, Erik, don't try to move. We'll get help. Will somebody please close the goddamn curtain?"

"No," Erik said. "Listen, all of you . . ." The curtain jerked, and he yelled, "No!" in a voice that was raw but still strong enough to make the curtain stop. "Listen, whatever happens to me now, you have to understand that this . . ." He looked down at the hand that was still holding his side but did not hold back the blood. "They did this because I've been telling you the truth . . . showing it to you, just the way my brother confessed it to me before he died. . . . They used my brother to frame me. They're the ones with ties to the mob, not me. And it's not the Varese mob. It's someone new. The whole Varese business was a smoke screen . . ."

He looked into the fifth row. "Joncas, your mob partner set up the killing . . . and you let him do it because my brother was supposed to kill Morty Codd. . . . You wanted Codd out of the way. Maybe he was too honest for you . . ." His voice began to die. "Ask Morty Codd, all of you, ask him whether he didn't carry a special sign that day . . . but my brother couldn't read the signs . . ."

Cecelia and Coral were trying to pull Joncas back into his seat, but he shook off their hands and kept shouting, "Stop that sonofabitch! Shut him up!"

Suddenly it seemed that a gold-and-silver bird flew out from the wings and lit at the edge of the stage. "You want to kill everything," it cried. "Everything that's beautiful—you hate it, you want to destroy it. You made me betray him—and now you've killed him for telling the truth!"

Jac, frozen against the wall, put both hands to her mouth, her eyes huge with shock and darkening with pity.

"You want me to live without him!" Maeve shouted at the audience, as if she finally were facing her enemy. "You want to kill everything that's true and good and beautiful!"

She was the only one in the theater who didn't hear Erik call her name or see him crouch on the crag and then vault four feet down to the stage floor, clearly unhurt by the leap—or by anything else.

She heard neither the collective gasp from the audience nor Frankie's offstage cry: "He's all right, Ms. Jerrold! The shot was just a blank—I fired it, so I know he's all right!"

The hit man was still crouched by the exit door, his mind spinning in confusion. He thought that his partner had managed to get in backstage and do it; but clearly nobody had done it. He lifted his gun and aimed it at the stage, where the figure in a red cloak was running toward the gold-and-silver bird, calling her name.

She seemed suddenly to hear it; she turned, saw the cloak, and flew toward it.

The hit man fired, and crashed out the exit door.

Jac screamed.

So did Joncas. "Idiot! Idiot! Not her—him! Get *Dante!*"

Beside him, his wife and daughter looked as if the gravel of his voice had hit their faces.

Morty Codd was on his feet, holding Joncas with a grip as tight as his eyes.

The two detectives were pushing their way through the milling crowd, heading for Joncas's row.

Erik saw nothing but the crumpled heap on the stage floor, where a red flower was blooming on a silver field. He knelt. "Get an ambulance!" he cried. Someone started to close the curtains. "Joncas," Erik shouted, "damn your soul to hell, you and everybody else who makes other people pay for your sins!"

The curtains rushed together.

Jac was still staring at them when the two detectives got to Joncas.

The cameraman who had been filming him all along finally put down his equipment. He touched Jac's arm. "Jesus. Did you know this was going to happen?"

"Of course not," she said heavily. "Not all of it. Not . . . she wasn't supposed to be here tonight."

"So she figured he'd really been shot? Not that I blame her. So did I."

"I almost believed it myself," Jac said, "and I knew better. But I didn't realize he would look . . . that way."

"The whole damn cast was convincing."

"Because they didn't know. He wanted to make sure they'd have natural reactions and wouldn't give it away."

"Jesus." The man shook his head. "I never liked what he said about unions, but he's a hell of an actor."

36

"I ain't gonna waste no tears on him," said the Varese underboss to Big Tiny. They were in the office at the Jumping Joint. A newspaper on the desk between them announced the arraignment of V.I. Joncas for the recent events at the Poets and Paupers Theater.

"Me neither," said Big Tiny. "Still, I don't think his wife and daughter done right. Family should stick by you. Those two—they moved out on him the next day, I hear."

"Yeah, it's a funny goddamn world," said the underboss. "I mean, look how we got rid of one brother to shut him up, and then we wound up helping the other one."

"You still complaining about what I did?" Big Tiny said.

"No, no. You're the boss."

"That's right." Tiny folded his hands over the top hemisphere of his stomach. "Augie, you ain't got a nose for people, like I got. Sure, for a while it looked like Dantino was setting us up for something, with that crazy broad coming down here with money and asking for you. But when he had the guts to come back and see me after that, after they arrested him . . . And it was a good deal. What did it cost us to have some of the boys stand guard at his theater for a week or so while he got ready to spring his trap on Joncas? Nothing. And he did just like he promised—he told the whole goddamn world that the Varese family ain't involved in any way."

Tiny laughed, his hands and stomach bobbing together. "Can you beat it? One of our boys catching the killer when he bolted into the alley, and handing him over to the cops? Jesus, I like that—one of the Varese getting one of Shaw's. And being smart enough to get himself out of the way real fast." Tiny sighed. "I wish we had more like him. We need more boys that got something upstairs, you know? Like Dantino. I wish we had him."

Two weeks after the shooting, Erik walked down from his apartment and came into the lobby. It was noon; he had just gotten up.

"Good morning," Ruth said pointedly from the box office. "How are you doing?"

"OK."

"Would you believe we've got three-quarters of a house for tonight? And the weekend looks like it could sell out. Thank God there wasn't a transit strike, after all."

Erik said nothing. He had closed *Firestorm* for two nights after the shooting and then reopened it. Some people thought he was being callous and opportunistic; some admired him for upholding the tradition that "the show must go on." He didn't know which of them were right.

He went to the lobby display boards, where the blown-up reviews had been mounted. Not all the critics had liked the play itself, but even those who didn't had been gentle with their objections.

If Maeve were here, he thought, and could know that her play was a success, if not a smash, she probably would say that critics were merely being respectful of the dead and audiences were coming only because of the sensationalism of her death. That was one of the hardest things to accept: that he never could know whether the play's reception would have helped her.

He heard Ruth say, from the box office, "I don't think you're doing yourself any good, wandering around this place like a ghost."

"I thought I was working—seven performances a week." In fact they were what kept him going. For two hours and forty minutes he would throw himself into Prometheus's world, where Maeve was still alive, and then somehow exist until the next performance. In between, he slept a great deal, but it never seemed to be enough.

Ruth said, not unkindly, "Prometheus doesn't run this place. You're the one who has to do that, remember?"

He checked his watch. "I can't right now. I have to go out."

He heard Ruth click her tongue. He swung around and said, "I'm going to see Jac Sanda. You kept telling me I should take her calls, remember? So yesterday I did. I promised I'd meet her. So that means I have to do it, right?"

Ruth nodded, her face brightening.

"And don't look that way," he said, knowing he had said it too harshly. He pulled the lobby door open and went out.

Jac sat by the window in the coffee shop, waiting to see him come walking up Third Avenue.

Since the shooting she had spoken to him only twice: an awkward call when the charges against him had been dropped, and then nothing until the day before, when he had agreed to meet her. It had taken her an hour to decide what to wear; at last she had chosen a plain white blouse and black slacks, as if the absence of color would help her be as impersonal as he had sounded and would make her stick to the business at hand.

If only, she thought, there had been some progress in finding evidence against "Donald." But her friend Tom at the Organized Crime Strike Force had said just the day before, "Unless Joncas starts talking about his mob partner, which looks bloody unlikely, or unless we come up with a witness of some kind, we're stymied."

She put her head in her hands, staring into her coffeecup. She thought of the ex-bookkeeper from Briarwood and of the reason that Amy Stone would never come forward and that she herself could never volunteer either Amy's name or her information.

"Hello." It was Erik's voice.

She felt her hands go wet with hope. She looked up slowly, seeing first the jeans, then the dark pullover, almost afraid of what would be on his face. It was worse than she had feared: There was no expression at all. "How are you?" she said, too brightly.

He sat down. His shoulders seemed to fill the booth. "I'm OK. I just don't feel a lot like talking about how I feel."

"Of course," she said, "sure." They looked at one another across the vast distance of the tabletop. She went on. "What I said I had to talk to you about, Erik, is this. I don't think you're safe."

"Oh?" he said quietly. "From whom?"

"From Donald, of course. If he's really Donald Shaw, the police still can't prove it. My contact tells me that *Christian Comfort* is all in order with the tax people and there's nothing at all against the son, the man I saw, except that he's very wealthy and lives like a hermit. Of course the police will keep on investigating, but until and unless they come up with something . . . Erik, you're probably still in danger. After those charges you made in public, about Joncas's having a mob partner, Donald could be even more anxious to get rid of you. He could just be waiting till things die down a little before he does it." There was no response. "The police think so, too," she said. "My contact told me that if he had to bet they're still after you, he'd make book on it."

Erik looked away. "If it's true, I don't know what to do about it."

"And you don't care?"

"I didn't say that."

"No, but . . ." Somehow she had to reach him, without using her hands. "Erik, you're blaming yourself, aren't you? For not telling her about your plan?"

He made a fist and carefully pressed it against the table. "Ah, yes, my famous plan. To make my accusations while I pretended to be dying, because everybody knows a dying man tells only truth, right? And if Joncas saw and heard it, his reaction might give him away, right? Might even make him reveal something about his mob partner, right?"

"Most of the plan did work," she said doggedly. "Wasn't Morty Codd convinced? Didn't he tell the police that Joncas had practically forced him to go down to the picket line on the afternoon of the killing? And didn't the picket organizer corroborate that Joncas ordered him to make sure Codd got one particular sign?"

An expression no stronger than the memory of a smile crossed Erik's face. "Codd came to see me. To say he still thinks I'm a bastard but now he knows I'm an honest one."

"That's all?"

"No, he also told me he's spearheading a Brotherhood investigation of how Joncas ran their pension and welfare funds. And he said that Poets and Paupers probably was the wrong place to start getting in off-Broadway, but he's going to do it someday. 'You producers can fight like hell,' he said, 'but someday you'll have to give in.' To which I replied, 'Or else you'll ruin our buildings?' He started to turn purple, but we decided to shake hands instead."

Jac smiled. "You sound exactly like him." But Erik was expressionless again. She clenched her hands under the table. "The film I got of Joncas that night is devastating. He can claim innocence, he can try to cling to his cover as a labor reformer, he can even pressure his political buddies to go into court as character witnesses for him, but none of it will work. Not with the film, and all the people who saw and heard it live that night, and Codd's testimony about the picket-line killing. So it did work, Erik. You've got to focus on that."

He leaned over the table, but his eyes and voice took him farther away, not closer. "I'll tell you what I focus on—the gun. The cops were sore as hell at me, you know, because I carried a gun while I was under indictment, and that's forbidden. And how did they know I'd been carrying it?"

"I don't know," she whispered. "How?"

"The killer had it. And that proved I'd been threatened and abducted, because there was no other way the killer could have gotten it. That's why they dropped the charges against me so quickly—the killer had my gun. The *killer*, Jac. Maeve was shot with my own gun."

She saw in his eyes what he really meant: "I did it, Jac, when I decided I wanted you."

But he wouldn't say that directly, so she couldn't answer it. She could only look at him, her glance clinging to the planes of his face, her mind numb with the realization that the price of having become part of Erik Dante was to now be part of the self he was castigating.

He stood abruptly. "I can't stay. I should get back down to the theater."

"Of course," she said. "Sure."

He ran his hands through his dark blond hair. "I'll be going, then."

"Will you let me know how you're doing?"

"Of course," he said. "Sure." He moved away.

Then he turned back, gave her a look that made her throat ache, lifted his big hands in a helpless gesture, and went.

She felt as helpless as the gesture; there was nothing more to do. Through the window she watched his tall figure receding. She told herself that she would see it again, that time would be the remedy, that the condition was not incurable.

She leaned her forehead against the window glass, wishing there were some action to take, something to do besides hurt.

* * *

"Sanda," said Donald Shaw, looking at the man sitting across his desk. "I guess that's an Italian name?"

"Yes."

"Well, I'll tell you, Sanda, I'm not too fond of Italians. So why should I want an Italian lawyer to come and work for me?" There was no answer. "Tell me two things," Shaw said. "First, how you knew who and where I am."

"Joncas told me." When Shaw raised a skeptical eyebrow, Sanda added belligerently, "It's true." Perspiration was beading his palms and scalp.

"Well, maybe it is. God knows Joncas made a lot of mistakes recently. Do you think he's going to talk, by the way? If you want to come to work for me directly, aren't you afraid he's going to spill everything about his deals with me?"

"If he talked about them," Sanda said slowly, "he'd be admitting his own part in them. I don't think he can do that."

"That's just how I read it," Shaw said approvingly. "He never could stand to take any blame. Now, tell me the second thing—why you care whether that actor lives or dies."

Sanda looked away, hoping the question would somehow be forgotten.

Jac had delivered the ultimatum, in a manner as brittle as dead leaves. She had told him that it looked as if he was safe—his connection with Joncas and company might very well not come to light, and whatever he had done to Maeve Jerrold, she was not alive to tell about it. "So I'm asking you for the last time, Burt: Are you going to go to the police and tell them what you know? About Joncas and Briarwood and whatever else you've been involved in?"

He had tried to make her understand that he couldn't sign a death warrant on his own career; but her face hadn't softened once.

"I wish I had the evidence to turn you in myself," she had said. "But I don't. So I have to treat you as what you are. When you protect yourself, Burt, you're also protecting men who live by violence.

You can't have it both ways—if you're not against them, you're with them. So *act* as if you're with them. Go to the man in charge and fix it so Erik Dante is safe—so the order to kill him is canceled, permanently. If you don't do it, Burt, I'll make it as hard as I can for you to see Karen. And I'll see that she learns everything I know or suspect about you. *Everything.*"

And when he told Jac he couldn't do it because he knew nothing about the man except that he was somewhere in Westchester, she had smiled bitterly and astounded him by producing a name and the address of the estate where he now was, and refusing to explain how she knew them.

"Well?" Shaw said impatiently. "Why do you care about that actor?"

Sanda closed his eyes. It was for Karen, he thought, so she could keep on seeing him, keep wanting to see him, and love him. Besides, he thought, after a while he would be able to cut away from Shaw somehow and start planning in earnest for the future he had always intended: for the time when he would serve the law with the best that was in him, that had always been in him, if others hadn't prevented it from—

"Well?" Shaw said impatiently.

He opened his eyes. "What do my reasons matter?" he said. "There are plenty of ways I could be useful to you, after all."

"Let's hear a few."

Sanda shrugged. "I work a lot for the city. For instance, I'm the official arbiter for all disputes under the new transport contract. Joncas and I had it set up so that if the city did win productivity increases, I'd rule they couldn't implement most of them."

Shaw laughed. "Didn't Joncas tell you I stay out of the transport union? There is a way you could be useful, though. There's going to be an opening in one of the appeals courts. Somebody owes me a favor, and I like a judge I can count on."

"No," Sanda whispered.

"Come again?"

"I can't do that. Anything but that."

"Why not?"

"The bench is where I . . . My daughter . . ." The words ground to a halt.

"You work for me, I call the shots. That's the way it is."

Sanda cleared his throat. "We can't do business, then, I guess. I'm sorry."

"I think you'll be a little worse than sorry." Shaw moved a paperweight on the desk. "As a lawyer, would you advise me to let someone like you just walk out of here? Someone who knows where I live, who has seen me, and who knows I was out to kill that actor?" After a moment Shaw said, "Stick to the original idea, Sanda. I cancel the contract on the actor, and you—you work for me, you put on those black robes and do what I tell you, and everything will work out. I'll be in touch soon."

When the man had gone, Shaw smiled. Mr. Burton Sanda would have looked even sicker if he'd known that he had sold himself for nothing.

The decision not to keep after the actor had been made weeks before, right after the fiasco at the theater. If anything else had happened to the man after that, the police would have seen it as further proof of his public charges. The practical thing was just to cut one's losses and lie even lower than usual for a while.

Only two things still made Shaw a bit nervous. One was Sanda's ex-wife. But after all, what could she say except that she'd seen a family praying? And now that he had Sanda, he could make the man feed her red herrings if she got nosy again.

The other reason to be nervous was Kerry London. She had called Shaw when she got back from Eruope to say the police had asked her about him. She had played dumb, she said, but only because she was momentarily expecting the gift he was sending—rubies and emeralds, she hoped. That was worrisome—not because it had wound up costing him thirty grand in "gifts" but because somebody had used his name in talking to her, and he didn't know whether it had been the actor or somebody else.

Still, Shaw thought, at the slightest hint of trouble, he would relocate to London or the Bahamas. And if anyone ever did manage to cut through all his lawyers and untangle the web of dummy corporations behind which his empire operated, he still had a trump card. Because nowhere—certainly not on anything involving his milking of the Brotherhood of American Labor—did his name appear. The only names to be found, if anyone ever did get that far, were Joseph and Florence Shaw.

He smiled, glad that he wasn't like the stupid Italians, who let their family feelings run their lives, and went in to have dinner with his mother and father.

37

A December wind was rattling the city's bare tree branches like snare-drum sticks.

When Erik got back to the theater, Ruth said to him, "You look like a wild man. Who did it—Mother Nature or the Guild of Stage Actors?"

"Both." He combed his hair with his fingers. "I had to sit there and listen to a lecture. They wouldn't believe that the only reason they didn't get our last check for pension and welfare contributions on time was that I just didn't get around to signing it." Ruth was silent. "I know, I know," he said. His cheeks burned as if the wind were still at them. "I should have done it."

"You should have done a lot of things. Like deciding whether to rehearse a new show or not. And while we're on the subject of what you've been ignoring, what about Frankie?"

"What about her?"

"Lord, don't you see anything anymore? She's been moping around in corners for weeks, and the crew tells me she hardly talks to anybody."

"I'll look into it."

"Right now would be a good time. She should be in school, but she's sitting in the auditorium all by herself."

"Why?"

"I don't know. Ask her."

His old grin reappeared for a moment. "All right. Anything's better than listening to you."

He went into the theater, pulling off his jacket. The only light came from one of the big windows, where the curtain was drawn, so it took him a while to spot her, sitting way down in front, on the steps that led up to the stage. Something in her posture made him acutely aware that he hadn't really talked to her since opening night.

"Hey, Frankovich," he called. "If this is a school holiday, nobody told me about it."

Her head was on her knees, her arms locked around her legs. "I didn't feel like going. They don't teach you nothing at that school."

"Not good English, that's for sure." When she only gave a heavy sigh, he sat on the steps below her. "Listen, Frankie, if the Labor Department finds you're here when you should be in school . . ."

"If I don't want to be found, nobody can find me."

In the silence, he looked above her head at the proscenium arch, where the ragged child was gazing at the moon. "How's everything at home?"

"Same as always."

"You still cash the welfare checks for your mother?"

"Yeah."

"Any of those brothers and sisters of yours going to want to be Infernals when they grow up?"

She lifted her head. "You mean you're going to keep on with the theater? Start rehearsing the new show?"

"I'm . . . not sure yet, Frankie. I've got a lot of things to sort out. Money, for one."

She looked away. "I heard Ms. Jerrold left you a lot of money."

"She did," he said evenly. "But I'm not taking it. I have this building—that's enough. If Poets and Paupers keeps running, it will have to run on its own steam. And I haven't figured out whether I can do that."

She turned to him, eyes wide. "What do you mean? You can do anything you set out to do." Then she sighed. "But I guess I can understand why you maybe don't want to go on with the theater."

"Do you? Tell me."

She shook her head and put her chin back on her knees.

"Hey," he said, "you never told me how you like what I gave you opening night—the volume of Shakespeare's plays." She didn't answer. "Come on," he said lightly, "don't tell me you don't like the Bard? The greatest poet of them all?" Only when he leaned closer to her did he realize she was crying.

He moved up to sit with her and put an arm around her. "Frankie, hey, what's the matter? You can tell me, can't you? Don't you know you're special to me, because you grew up in the same kind of place I did, and you fell in love with the theater, just like me—"

She gave a howl and quickly muffled it against his shoulder.

"Frankie, you're scaring me. What's the matter?"

"I know how you hate me," she wailed. "And I don't blame you."

Astonishment paralyzed him for a moment. Then he lifted her face with one hand. "Why in the name of heaven would I hate you?"

"Because . . ." She swallowed, as if trying to keep the words down, but they poured out. "The guy who shot Ms. Jerrold, he's in jail. So is that Joncas creep. So how come I'm not? Because I saw Ms. Jerrold when she came in backstage that night, and I could have told her it was only a blank I was going to fire, only I didn't tell her because I figured she knew. But she didn't know, so she thought you were dying, and that's how come she got killed. It's my fault she got killed!"

"Oh, Jesus," he said, feeling as cold as if he were back in the wind.

Finally he got her to stop crying. "You had nothing to do with what happened, Frankie. Who wrote that special scene and made everybody rehearse it? I did. Who asked you to fire the blank that nobody else knew about? I did. And I'm the one who didn't tell Ms. Jerrold about the plan, because she was going to stay home that night and I didn't want to upset her, because she'd been so sick."

Frankie looked at him doubtfully. "What was wrong with her?"

"Lord, how can I explain it to you? She was . . . the kind of person who never expected to be happy or to have things go well in her life. She thought she was a failure. She believed it so strongly that it became a kind of self-fulfilling prophecy. And that made her . . . sick."

"But, Erik, jeez, her play isn't no failure. I mean, there's whole parts of it that give me goose bumps all over, and not just on my arms."

"Me too, Frankie. But it was hard for her to see things the way you and I do. She was . . . She lived with a lot of fear."

"You think she was scared that night? When she was hollering at the audience? She didn't look scared to me at all."

"How did she look to you?"

"I don't know. Kind of like one of those Greek ladies, you know? With wings and snakes in their hair? She was, I don't know . . . kind of like, wonderful. And if she was trying to keep anybody from hurting you . . . well, jeez, she did it. Didn't she?"

He realized after a while that he had been staring into space. "I'm sorry. What did you just say?"

"I said . . . " Her voice was tearful again. "If you don't blame me for what happened to Ms. Jerrold, then how come you hardly talked to me since that night?"

He pulled her into his arms, so she wouldn't see what he was feeling. "I guess I've been too busy blaming myself. When you're doing that, you don't realize what you're doing to other people."

He sat rocking her gently for a long time, not sure which of them was being comforted. Finally he said, "Come on, Frankie. If you're not going to school today, you can help me start running this theater again."

* * *

When the phone rang, Karen raced to it. "I'll do it, Mother. Let me do it!"

She picked up the receiver. "This is Karen Sanda."

There was a moment's pause, then a laugh.

"Who is this?" she said. "This is Karen Sanda!"

"And this is Erik Dante. Remember me?"

"Well, sure I do. I asked my mother about you a lot of times."

"Oh? And what did she say?"

"She said you went away to do something, but I forget what it was. Wait, I know. She said you had to play with your dues and maybe we wouldn't ever see you again. But I guess you came back for Christmas." After a moment she said, "Say, is there anybody on this telephone?"

"I think so," he said in an odd voice. "May I speak to your mother?"

When Jac took the phone, he said nothing but her name, three times.

She sat down. "Erik. Are you . . . all right?"

"Yes. Now I am. Are you?"

She smiled. "Yes. Now I am."

"I'm sorry it's been so long. I was . . ."

"I think I know what you've been going through, Erik."

"I think you always know. And what have I made you go through?"

"It doesn't matter, Erik. Really it doesn't. It's over, isn't it?"

"Yes." There was a pause. "Will you come and see me tonight? Onstage, I mean."

"Why not?" Then she gave a mock sigh and said, "But will there be a play going on?"

He started to laugh. So did she.

Across the room, Karen grinned at the sound.